23 MAR 2011

23 APR 2023

1 4 MAY 2011

71 JAN 2011

PETERBOROUGH LIBRARIES

24 Hour renewal line 08458 505606

This book is to be returned on or before the latest date shown above, but may be renewed up to three times if the book is not in demand. Ask at your local library for details.

Please note that charges are made on overdue books

By Paul Magrs

The Bride That Time Forgot

PAUL MAGRS

headline
review

First published in 2010
by HEADLINE REVIEW
An imprint of HEADLINE PUBLISHING GROUP

First published in paperback in 2011 by
HEADLINE REVIEW

1

Cataloguing in Publication Data is available from the British Library

ISBN 978 0 7553 5945 5

Typeset in Garamond by Avon DataSet Ltd,
Bidford-on-Avon, Warwickshire

Printed and bound in Great Britain by
Clays Ltd, St Ives plc

Headline's policy is to use papers that are natural, renewable and
recyclable products and made from wood grown in sustainable forests. The
logging and manufacturing processes are expected to conform to the
environmental regulations of the country of origin.

HEADLINE PUBLISHING GROUP
An Hachette UK Company
338 Euston Road
London NW1 3BH

www.headline.co.uk
www.hachette.co.uk

For Deborah Moody

Whitby

North Sea

West Pier

East Pier

East Cliffs

Western Cliffs

St Mary's Church & Graveyard

Whitby Abbey

1. Brenda's B & B
2. Effie's Antiques Emporium
3. Hotel Miramar
4. The Christmas Hotel
5. Cod Almighty
6. The Walrus & The Carpenter
7. St Mary's Church & Graveyard
8. Whitby Abbey
9. Bridge over Harbour
10. Woolies
11. The Spooky Finger
12. Casa Diodati
13. The Demeter

Brenda's Christmas

Hello there!

Winter in Whitby and here I am. Up to my eyeballs in hard work and intrigue. I'm out chopping logs in my back garden and I find it quite therapeutic. Thunk, thunk, thunk, making all this noise. Bits of mouldy bark flying about all over the place, and my breath puffing out in white clouds. Of course, then I notice that I've gone and cracked a couple of the paving stones I laid for my path just last spring. I don't know my own strength.

As I'm taking a breather, and sipping a mug of hot spicy tea, I catch a glimpse of Effie in a top window of her tall house next door. She's looking down at me. Funny look on her face. Watching me and thinking I wouldn't notice her up there. I go, 'Yoo-hoo, Effie!' Waving my axe around.

Effie doesn't wave back. Doesn't even crack a smile. She backs away into the dark upper room till I can't see her any more. Not very friendly at all. But Effie's not been the same for a few weeks now. People have remarked on it. Sometimes it's like she's a completely different person. And only I know the real reason for that, don't I? Only I know what's really turned her head.

But enough of that for now. We're all pretending nothing has changed. We're all carrying on as normal. Behaving as if nothing queer has come over the owner of the shabby antiques emporium next door to me.

I think I've been able to put Effie's moodiness out of my mind because I've been run off my feet. For some reason this winter season my little guest house is besieged by bookings, right through the approaching festive period as well. This is good news because for the past year or so I'm afraid I let things get a bit slack and slapdash. Oh, the place was always immaculate and tidy, of course, and I never gave my guests anything less than fantastic value and a superlative sojourn, but it was like my heart wasn't quite in it. Days and weeks started slipping by with my B&B only half full. Sometimes it was even empty. I think I had too many distractions, if I'm honest.

Now, however, I believe I'm back on track. Brenda's B&B is open for business and filled up for fifty-two weeks of the year. Six double rooms furnished in olde-worlde splendour. Tasty, nourishing home cooking and good company. A chintzy oasis at the very heart of this small, antiquated fishing town on the breathtaking coast of north-east England.

Now I'm sounding like my own adverts. I've made up a little brochure that I send out, blowing my own trumpet. My young friend Robert helped me with all the technical gubbins on his laptop and we had hundreds of the things printed up. I now also have a website, which is my little window on the world, Robert says. Or rather, it's the window through which the whole world might peer and decide on a sudden whim to book themselves in for a visit.

Robert came round with his new digital camera and we took some lovely snaps of my house, front and back, and all the rooms done up their nicest. He even tried to persuade me to have my own piccy on the website. 'Give it the personal touch, Brenda,' he urged, but I demurred at that one. Essentially I'm a very reserved person.

Anyhow, I reckon I'm being proactive enough. The publicity certainly seems to be paying off, what with all the new bookings I've been getting. Soon I'll be able to offer guests what I hope will be the best room in the house. Shortly I'll be putting finishing touches to the Red Room, which is sumptuous and glamorous, and I'm half tempted to take it for myself.

I'd certainly say my B&B was on the up-and-up. Perhaps it won't be long before I'm able to afford a little help around the place. I could get someone in to lend a hand with the cleaning and the breakfasts some days. Give myself a little break. Robert warns me against overdoing things. Apparently I'm not getting any younger.

I had to smile at that. For so many years it felt that the very opposite was true – that I wasn't getting any *older*. I've been just the same for donkey's years. However, the rigours of recent times have worn me out and I've even started to feel my age. Really! Well, *some* of it, anyway.

I'll not dwell for too long on the exhausting depredations of recent years that I have just alluded to. I would rather press on and tell you about more recent happenings. All I'll say here is that it's not just the general hard work of running my own business that has me frazzled. Nor is it the demands of a very active social life among the bright lights of Whitby. I've also had a hectic time of it with my love life, as it happens. (Me! Me who was convinced all that malarkey was well behind her.) I had a little dalliance a while ago with an eminent Professor Cleavis, who was here on business of a fairly mysterious kind and happened to renew his acquaintance with me. It turned out he was a very old flame of mine, though you know what my memory is like – which is a good reason for me keeping a proper diary like this.

Professor Cleavis whizzed off and left me in the lurch, just as he did the first time we met, decades ago. I felt quite gutted, as a matter of fact, and came to the conclusion that he was just here for the monsters.

Oh, yes. The monsters.

Something we're famous for, here in Whitby. Sometimes you'd think the town was swarming with them. Ghosts, goblins, ghoulies, witches, mummies, anything you can think of. Real ones, fake ones, madly deluded ones. And even ones from different dimensional planes. They all seem to make their ghastly way here. Just lately we've been having a spate of what I call the Walkers. That's supposedly dead bodies that get up and simply walk away from the morgue. But I'll not elaborate on that ghastly topic just yet . . .

There are several very good reasons for our town's various infestations, which I shall go into presently. For now, I'll just say that we are a kind of Mecca for the monstrous. It is my – and that snooty mare Effie's – job to guard this little town, this bijou bastion, against supernatural terrors of all kinds.

That keeps us pretty busy, as well as everything else that we get up to.

Oh, I should say, I had another disappointment in love just recently. Just over a month ago, in fact. I'd had a rapprochement with my ex-fiancé after many years apart. I wasn't keen on us joining forces again, but he was pretty persistent, as is his wont. Anyway, I caved in and for almost a year we were happy again, being a couple. It seemed to be working out for us, believe it or not.

The reason he's not here now wasn't the fault of either of us. Fate intervened. Terrible, wicked fate. I haven't seen my Frank since this Hallowe'en just gone. If you'll forgive me, I won't go into the whys and wherefores of it all now. Suffice to say I'm on my tod again and I've probably got good reason to fling myself headlong into work and general busyness. I don't relish dwelling on heartache and disaster, that was never my thing. I need to look forward – to Christmas. Fun, prosperity and the company of a few good friends. And beyond that, the New Year and everything it might bring. I want to be looking lively and feeling optimistic.

I just wish that Effie was more like her old self. She seems so distant somehow. Not unfriendly, nor depressed. I've seen her like that. Many, many times. This is quite different.

I am burning with the secret about Effie I have kept since Hallowe'en. I hate being the only one who knows for sure what's awry with her.

The thing is, I'm frightened. I'm in denial about what's become of Effie Jacobs. I'm starting to doubt my own senses. I'm hoping that I'm wrong, but at the same time I know I'm not.

Enough. Enough teasing. I need to do something about these suspicions of mine. I need to get my act in gear.

Well, it's late and I've worn myself out writing all this. I've not written so much in months. Quite nice, sitting up here in my cosy attic space with my bacon sandwiches and a tot or two of sherry. Nina Simone pounding away on the stereo. Putting all of my thoughts in order.

It was Robert who said I should start keeping a diary again. Well, here I am, as instructed! Though I don't know who this is even for. I certainly don't want to go showing all my secrets to anybody any time soon.

So here I am, anyway, whoever you are! Welcome back to my world!

The next day.

I had a bit of an afternoon off today. I saw off one load of guests and I had the place cleaned up in a flash. I don't muck about. The new ones weren't turning up until later, and so when Robert called in and said did I fancy a coffee in town, I said yes, that'd be lovely.

Now, Robert's about thirty and quite handsome, I think, but then I'm prejudiced. Him and me, we've been pals since my first year in Whitby. Back then he was an elf at the Christmas Hotel on the West Cliff. Like all the elvish staff there, in their figure-hugging felt outfits, he was in thrall to Mrs Claus, the hideous owner of that gaudy establishment. Well, I seem to recall that I've told the tale elsewhere, but Effie and I were investigating that horrifying hotel together. It was one of the first mysteries we tackled as a team.

Now I think back, we made something of a hash of it, but that doesn't matter. What's important is that while old Effie and I were cementing our friendship and forming our bond over the solving of supernatural mysteries, another friendship was blossoming: between this lovely young gay man and

7

yours truly. We've been good pals ever since – through Robert's leaving the Christmas Hotel and his assuming responsibility for the Hotel Miramar, a rather downmarket (though profitable) joint further out of town.

Robert was thrust into a management role with alacrity, following the disappearance of the Miramar's owner, Sheila Manchu. (Actually, we all know what happened to Sheila Manchu. We just don't like to talk about it.) Any road up, he's enjoyed being in charge this past year, and as far as I can make out, he's acquitted himself splendidly.

Even all that weird business this Hallowe'en, with the cursed and haunted film crew staying at the Miramar, hardly put a dent in his confidence. In fact, he even seems to have profited by the publicity generated by the whole *Get Thee Inside Me, Satan* debacle. I've done pretty well out of the attendant hoo-ha myself, if I'm honest.

It seems that the more macabre the mysteries, and the spookier the shenanigans, the more Whitby seems to draw ever-increasing numbers of curious visitors. I'm torn between enjoying the booming business and lamenting the loss of my quieter life, with fewer untoward goings-on. But there you go – life's never perfect, is it?

Today Robert is all muffled up against the wintry winds that come buffeting up from the harbour. He insists that I wrap up properly with my pashmina (Effie, last Christmas, elegant), woolly hat (self-knitted, hideous, to tell the truth):

8

the whole shebang. He frets over me like I'm some infirm old biddy, but it hardly ever annoys me.

'I've left Penny in charge at the front desk,' he tells me, as I lock up and we exit at the cobbled side passage of my B&B. He's right about the cold. The keen wind slices through me as we totter on to the steep main street. 'Did I tell you? Penny's staying right through Christmas, working at the Miramar. She's not going home to her family.'

'Oh, that's good,' I tell him. 'I imagine you'll need the help.'

He nods enthusiastically. 'She says that she's found herself a new family here in Whitby, with us.'

I smile at him. 'We are, really, aren't we? That's what we are.' Then I get a stab of guilt. Not a stab – a twinge, maybe. That's because, right at that moment, we're passing by the dusty front windows of Effie's Antiques Emporium. Or junk shop, as I always call it, just to wind her up. It's not been open for custom for days, as far as I can make out.

'Give her a knock,' Robert urges. 'You know you want to.' It's good of him to suggest it, because although he and Effie get along better than they did at the start, he'd much rather it was just me and him going for coffee this afternoon. These days, on the rare occasions that she does venture out, Effie is wont to cast something of a pall.

Anyway, it makes no odds either way. I give her front door knocker a good banging, but there's no joy. She's not deigning to answer. I sigh heavily and Robert looks concerned.

'Is she still in a funny mood with everyone?'

'Seems to be,' I say, not wanting to go into it now. I turn to lead the way down the hill towards the harbour. The chill wind is really quite savage now, I'm glad I heeded Robert's sartorial tip.

Sotto voce he asks me: 'Has Effie still got *him* in there with her? You-know-who?'

I pull a face. 'I suppose so. But you know what he's like. Coming and going under cover of darkness. We're none the wiser whether he's there or not.'

'She's under his spell again.' Robert shudders.

Well, I don't want to go into it this afternoon, quite frankly. Effie has made her coffin and she can lie in it – or do anything else she fancies in it. If I've warned her once about him, I've warned her a million times. She's had at least one previous narrow escape from the leeching beggar and now she's took up with him again. I don't think he's much of a catch. Skinny little old fella. Smells of fried black pudding. Still, she seems to see something in him.

I hurry along into the mid-afternoon melee, bustling over the bridge across the harbour. Robert can tell I don't feel like endlessly dissecting the doings of Effie, so he changes the subject. Such a sensitive, caring boy!

By the time we arrive at my favourite café in the old town

– The Walrus and the Carpenter on Church Street – Robert is telling me all the latest news on the Limbosine.

'There's been another one,' he mouths, as we take our places at mine and Effie's usual table, right in the bow window. 'A middle-aged fella from Staithes, picked up in the Limbosine on Sunday night. Subsequently given the most horrifying ride of his life. Later found dumped by the roadside, not a stitch on, gibbering like a fool. He was out in the countryside, by the Hole of Horcum, four miles out of town.'

All I can offer is a lot of tutting and shaking of my head. At least he was alive, that bloke. Worse things have happened to people round here. Recently, too. What about the Walkers, eh? The waitress bobs up at my side and takes an order for coffee and walnut cake as I mull over Robert's report. I'd already read about the latest case in last night's edition of the local rag, *The Willing Spirit*. But I've noticed that Robert quite enjoys imparting these little nuggets of info to me in person. It's as if he's playing the role of my investigative assistant. Perhaps he thinks this is the part that Effie takes in happier times, when she is less preoccupied and pleased to be involved in my kind of cases. As it happens, though, she isn't as helpful an assistant as all that. I usually know more about what's going on, quicker than she does. Effie most often sits there munching on cake and slurping tea, with her beady eyes on all the other denizens of our favourite café. It's rare, really, that her mind stays for very long on our latest case.

'Brenda?' Robert prompts, and I'm ashamed then because I realise I've been distracted as well, from the spooky matter at hand.

'So, erm, who was it dubbed this mysterious vehicle "The Limbosine" anyway?' I ask him. 'Was it the press?'

He shakes his head. 'One of the first victims, remember? When they came back to their senses, days later. They said that the creepy chauffeur himself described his car in those terms.'

I frown and wish our order would arrive. My tummy's rumbling like crazy this afternoon because I skipped lunch. I was so carried away with scrubbing out my en suites with Vim.

Right now I'm picturing someone driving one of those ludicrous and extravagantly long limos around and about the narrow winding lanes of Whitby and its environs. It's a strange thing to do, in and of itself, let alone the rest of the funny abducting business. The Limbosine seems to single out lone victims and pull up beside them, very quietly. The window rolls down and a chauffeur in shades and a smart cap invites you to step inside his luxury interior. This is your night for a de luxe surprise. The night ride of your lifetime!

'Who'd be so stupid as to clamber aboard?' I ask Robert. 'I'd run a mile!' Then I'm wondering whether this business could be in any way involved with the Walkers. Could that be possible?

He shrugs. 'People like to think they've won something. They want to think that good fortune or the hand of fate is giving them something fab for nothing, just for once. People like to imagine that they can be treated like celebrities . . .'

'Indeed,' I say. 'Then they get whistled off to who knows where. And experimented on, I shouldn't wonder.'

Robert looks alarmed. 'Experimented on?'

'Ssh.' Here came our waitress with cups and pots and plates of cake. 'Perfect,' I simper, and suddenly I really do miss Effie sitting there, going over the finer points of this or any other case.

There are carols playing over the speakers. The decorations are rather more tasteful than those the Christmas Hotel boasts all year round. The other café-goers seem to have lots of parcels and bags of Christmas shopping with them – evidently stocking up on the souvenirs and historical bric-a-brac to be found in this part of town. I let out a terrible sigh and inwardly curse Effie's fancy man for taking her out of circulation just as the party season approaches.

Whoever said you had to make a choice between having a fella and having a life? Whoever said you had to stop being bothered about your friends, or having a healthy interest in what went on in the outside world? I feel like Effie is letting the side down, the sex-mad old moo.

'These people are being driven off to who knows where,' I say, as Robert organises our crockery and studies the swirling grounds inside the cafetière. 'Then, when they turn up, they're almost complete basket cases. Doesn't it sound a bit like accounts of alien abduction to you?'

He stares at me. 'Are you saying there could be aliens?'

I frown. 'I'm not saying anything yet. We need to poke our noses a bit more fully into the activities of this so-called Limbosine. It could, of course, be some great big fake and nasty scam, perpetrated by a weirdo or a pervert.'

'That's the most likely thing,' says Robert, plunging the plunger on the coffee. Like Effie, he tends to nip in before I can do it. I plunge too heartily and there have been some messy incidents.

'Let's keep an open mind, eh?' I encourage him. 'Now, the thing to do is to provide some kind of bait. Look at the places this Limbosine thing is cruising around and wait there at night, within the hours that these abductions are reported as having occurred.'

'And get *ourselves* kidnapped?'

'Of course!' I laugh. 'That's the easiest way of learning more about it, surely?'

'I suppose so.' He looks a bit worried, though.

For the rest of our coffee hour we discuss the last farrago we were embroiled in. It took the middle two weeks of November to untangle. Effie hadn't been of any help at all during the affair of Hans Macabre and his Green Gothic Ice Cream Van. *That* was a case I still don't feel we satisfactorily finished off. I don't suppose I will do until the noxious foodstuff is taken off the market. People wouldn't be so keen to gobble it up if they knew what had been going into it. Robert and I knew, of course. We broke into the frozen warehouse, one nightmarishly frigid night in November, and uncovered the awful evidence for ourselves.

It makes me sad, in a way, to rove over these recent escapades in Robert's company, and to realise that they lacked something because of Effie's absence. She is such a snitty and grumpy old bag, and yet somehow she makes the whole thing that bit much more fun.

I'd never tell Robert that, of course, in case I hurt his feelings. But I believe he can tell what I'm thinking, as his excited recounting of our pursuit of Hans Macabre and his Ice Cream Van tails off. He can see that I'm faking my enthusiasm a bit.

Without Effie constantly at my side, it seems that spooky things ain't what they used to be.

We finish up and pay and amble back through town. Robert says something about needing to be back in good time, to relieve Penny so she can have her night off. So he's not in a position to go Limbosine-baiting and getting abducted (and possibly experimented upon) this evening. He's got a busy night on at the Miramar.

'No problem.' I smile blandly and think, What am I saying? I *hate* people who say 'No problem!' like that. I'm of an age when I can't stick all that passive aggression, preferring by far some good old-fashioned bolshiness and outright crossness.

'Where's Penny off to tonight?' I ask him.

'Didn't I say?' He smirks. 'Turns out she's joined some kind of book group. They meet once a week. Penny is completely addicted. She says she can't possibly miss a single meeting!'

It hardly seems possible, but Penny has gone even more Gothy since Hallowe'en and the terrifying events of the last Goth weekend. When she comes to visit me on Thursday, she's clumping up my side stairs in these black rubber platform boots and she's jingling with chains and whatnots all the way. It's a shame, I think. I'm sure she'd look very nice underneath all that theatrical make-up and her peculiar hair extensions. It's something about being in her twenties, I think. Robert tells me that when he was that young (not that long ago, he hastens to add), he still felt like he could become anyone, and turn himself into anything he wanted. He thinks Penny is still at that stage in making up a persona for herself.

Anyway, she's come to the right town for galumphing about in spooky black outfits. Really, she hardly stands out at all here.

Thursday lunchtime and she's round mine, gabbling about

her book group, which had their weekly meeting the night before.

'Two hours!' I laugh. 'What on earth do you find to talk about for two hours?'

'You'd be surprised.' She smiles. 'It's a funny, mismatched bunch of women who take part. They come out with all sorts of stuff. Not all of it relevant to the book in hand.'

'And where is it held again? The Pointy Finger . . . ?'

'The Spooky Finger,' she says. 'It's a new shop – used and new paperbacks – on Silver Street. Mystery, horror, fantasy. It's a marvellous shop. Haven't you been in?'

'There hasn't been much time for reading of late,' I say glumly. And as I say it, I realise it's true. I've not been making time in the evening for myself and an appointment with a novel. How did that slip out of my schedule? I feel almost ashamed telling Penny this. Penny who's never without at least two books in her black leather knapsack. One being her current read, the second being for when she finishes the first.

'You should pop in. It's very interesting.'

'Why's it called The Spooky Finger? I don't think it's a very nice name, I must say.'

Penny pours our tea for us. For a second I'm surprised. Someone else playing mother round my kitchen table! I must look even more tired than I thought. 'It's the title of a Fox Soames novel from the forties,' she tells me.

'Oh no,' I groan. Fox Soames. The very name makes me

shudder. He was the wretched old man whose novel, *Get Thee Inside Me, Satan* was the root cause of our last really big adventure. Whenever he or one of his books is mentioned, trouble seems bound to follow. 'Whoever chose a name like that? It's like asking to be cursed.'

'The woman who runs the shop is quite a character,' Penny says. 'Marjorie Staynes. She leads the book group, too. She's a retired lady. Now she's indulging her passion for spooky literature, she says. And making new friends in her new town.'

'Hmmm.' I can't help thinking back to my own early weeks here in Whitby, when there was nothing I wanted more than a new career and a quiet life. When I wanted to immerse myself in the simple tasks of my B&B-owning duties. Things soon became rather more complicated than that. I even feel a little envious of this Marjorie Staynes, assuming that she'll find it easier to settle into a life of comfy obscurity than I ever did.

Penny's looking at me expectantly. 'You should join.'

'Oh, I don't think so. It sounds like a big-time commitment. And what if I don't like the books? I can't stick with things I don't like.'

Penny pulls her heavy-looking black bag on to her lap and fishes around. She produces a worn paperback with a lurid cover and presents it to me.

'Goodness!'

'This is what we're doing next time,' she tells me. 'It's Marjorie's choice. She's laid in a stock of second-hand copies, especially for the ladies in her group. It's quite hard to come by otherwise.'

The cover shows a number of nearly nude and well-muscled men, oiled up and cowering at the feet of some kind of dominatrix lady in shiny armour. A prehistoric land of erupting volcanoes and apocalyptic skies swirls around her arrogantly tilted head. The book is called *Warrior Queen of Qab* and it was written, apparently, by a lady called Beatrice Mapp.

And just at that instant, it feels like something starts trickling and fizzing at the back of my brain. My senses scramble for a second and my vision grows dark. Now, Brenda! Seize control! You don't want to be having a funny turn just now! I steady myself against the kitchen table and take a hefty swig of tea.

'Are you all right?' Penny touches my hand.

'Yes, dear,' I reassure her, and pick up the book again. Maybe the musty yellow smell of the book made me nauseous for a second. I don't know. Beatrice Mapp. No . . . I *do* know that name. Something about . . . something . . .

'Well?' Penny says. 'Will you join the group? I took the liberty of mentioning to Marjorie that you might be coming next time.'

I feel a flash of irritation and know that Penny sees it in my eyes. I hate anyone volunteering me for anything, or assuming I'll just fall in with what they want. I make my own decisions. Do my own thing, just as I always have. But Penny doesn't mean any harm, I'm sure.

'Are you sure this is my kind of thing?' I ask her, tapping the cover of the book.

'Marjorie says that the US publisher made Beatrice Mapp's books look very tawdry and tacky, but that actually they are very serious and philosophical . . .'

'Really?' I'm afraid I can't summon much enthusiasm. 'But they're about warrior queens and monsters and alien planets?'

'Um, yeah.' Penny smiles. 'What do you think? Might be a laugh.'

I sigh. Wednesday nights I'm not doing much, as it happens. Once upon a time that would be cabaret night at the Christmas Hotel, but not any more. 'Go on then,' I tell Penny, surprised by how pleased she suddenly looks. 'Can I borrow your copy, when you've read—'

She interrupts, 'You can have this one. I bought two. I knew I'd persuade you!'

We have our tea and chat about other, unrelated topics, and all the while my eye keeps being drawn back to that vivid paperback on the corner of my kitchen table. It is as if the book is exerting some strange kind of influence over me. Its pages look so tactile, and the print comfortably large for my fading eyesight. It's like the thing is calling out to me, like a siren song, eager to be heard . . .

When Penny goes, her lunch hour from the Miramar over, I snatch up the book and toss it in my tea towel drawer. I hope it's not covered in germs. Old paper can carry some nasty things. I slam the drawer shut. Never mind. I'll look at it later.

This afternoon I've got other things to concentrate on. I've a hair appointment at Rini's salon, for one. Get something done to this wig, for tonight I'm out to dinner. It's a last-minute invite, but one I don't want to miss.

The embossed card was shoved through my door by hand this morning, shortly before the postman came. Effie and Kristoff, requesting the pleasure of my company next door. Dinner this evening. It was his handwriting on the card, I noticed. Rusty brown ink. Nice touch, Alucard. Beautiful hand he's got, of course. Well, I'll go. I'll make the effort. I'll even get all dressed up.

What's this? Amongst the junk mail and everyday post that I haven't had a chance to go through yet, I notice one particular, very small envelope. Very bad handwriting indeed, but the postmark of a university town in the south that I recognise. The crest of a rather august college in the other corner. A short note slipped inside:

Remiss of me, to neglect you for so long. Returning to Whitby for festive season. Hope to see you, old thing.

21

Is there room for Henry Cleavis at the inn? Hoping so. Much affection, Henry.

I set down the card just as a huge rush of . . . *something* goes through me. Delight? Dread? Excitement? Panic? All of these things. It's delicious though, the feeling. I'm tingling. My mind is racing. Do I even have room for him? Can I put him up? There's no question in my mind but that I have to.

Henry's coming back! He's coming back to see me at last! But I mustn't be the giddy goat. I mustn't get my hopes up. I have to remind myself: I'm a married woman these days, aren't I?

Oh, but Christmas with Henry. The very thought of it.

I make sure I am looking my best when I pop round Effie's tonight. I find that if my hair and outfit and make-up are just so, then it's like wearing armour and nothing can really touch me.

When she lets me in, kisses me on both cheeks and leads me upstairs, to the living quarters above her emporium, I'm glad I've made the effort. Effie is looking marvellous. I don't get a good look at her until we're all in the drawing room and her man friend is dishing out the sherry and the nibbles, but I see then that Effie's had a colour – warm chestnut – put in her hair and it's looking lustrous and styled beautifully. She notices me noticing.

'I've stopped going to Rini's,' she tells me. 'Rini just does those old lady hairdo's. This is a new place, rather chic. Tint Natural.'

I've heard of it. It's supposed to be very dear. Actually, looking at her new outfit, Effie's been a bit flash. Her skin's glowing too and there's a glimmer in her eyes I haven't seen in a while.

Alucard's lighting candles and the whole place is looking like Christmas has come early.

'Brenda, welcome,' he purrs unctuously. I restrain my natural impulse to shiver at his touch as he clasps my hand in his cold grip. He bends to kiss me, and I feel his sharp teeth scrape against my skin. I almost yank my paw back from him, but it wouldn't do to make a scene. I'm on best behaviour, and must try to forget that the last time I was in his company I punched him in the face. I had very good reason to, as it happens.

'Something smells good,' I tell them, shrugging off my beaded shawl and flomping down on one of Effie's high-backed chairs by the fire. I have to admit, the place hasn't been as welcoming for a good long while. Effie on her own doesn't take much pride in her home.

Effie explains that Kristoff has cooked tonight's meal. It's all quite exotic-sounding. Things in tagines, cooked with wonderful spices and dates and pomegranates. 'Of course, Kristoff has travelled the world extensively,' Effie tells me. 'So he's quite au fait with the cuisines of many lands and cultures.'

'Really?' I smile. What she means is that the dandified cadaver has spent centuries hopping and flitting about the place, gorging himself on the blood of his luckless victims, being hounded out of city after city when he was discovered. She makes him sound like some kind of gentleman explorer, when we both know that he's in actual fact a serial murderer. Oh yes, I'm not one to mince my words where Alucard's concerned. But this evening I'm holding my tongue, for Effie's sake.

At least she's handy with the Merlot tonight, and after a couple of hefty glasses I feel less uptight, less inhibited. Some strange kind of folk music is playing over the stereo, and the smells from the kitchen, where Kristoff is busy, are heavenly. Nutmeg, coriander, paprika and cloves. No garlic, naturally.

'That's a funny-looking thing,' I tell Effie. 'What happened to your old gramophone?' I know that what I'm pointing to is an MP3 player, sitting snugly in its dock. I'm not that out of date. Robert has one. I prefer my old vinyl LPs, of course. I'm just feigning ignorance to keep Effie talking.

'I thought I'd modernise myself,' she tells me. 'Isn't it dinky?'

'Dinky' isn't a very Effie word. I sigh, hold out my glass hopefully for a refill, and muse on the last time Effie was in the throes of a romantic liaison with that fiend in the kitchen. Couple of years ago, when he first turned up back in Whitby. I feel like reminding her, right here and now, what a disaster that turned out to be and how he had just been using her.

That's the thing about women like Effie. They're doomed to go round and round, repeating their mistakes. Never learning anything and never moving on. Poor old Effie's just grateful for the company.

Pretty soon we're in our places round the table, and with all the panache and ludicrous flourishing of a born show-off, Alucard serves up and whips the chimney lids off the tagines. It's pretty good, as it happens. I like the pink onion, coriander and pomegranate salsa best of all.

I eat happily, and when I look up, I notice that Alucard and Effie are holding hands across the table and looking as if they're about to announce something to me.

'We're thinking of going away,' Alucard tells me.

'Away? Where?'

'For good,' Effie says, not quite catching my eye.

I'm shocked. 'You can't!'

'And why not?' Effie's got that frosty tone she often puts on. Haughty-sounding.

'You know why,' I mumble. 'We've got a job here, me and you. We were entrusted to do it.'

She picks up her damask napkin, and as she talks, she

wrings it like she's got a chicken by the neck. 'Oh, you mean how we're supposed to keep a watchful eye over the gateway into hell under the abbey. Our role as the guardians of the Bitch's Maw.'

'That's right,' I say. 'You know that as well as I do. And you know the kind of . . . dangerous personalities that the Maw attracts.' I can't help casting a glance at Alucard as I say this. 'Unscrupulous, devilish beings who want to harness those fundamental magical forces for themselves and play merry hell with them. We can't just leave, Effie! We've got to be here.'

'Pah!' Effie scowls. 'I've been here all my life, Brenda. Trapped in this house, with all my old aunties glowering down at me out of their portraits. I've seen nothing of the world.'

'And so?' I ask, too much sarcasm in my voice. 'Alucard's promising to take you away from all this, is he?'

Alucard himself leans forward to fix me with his horrible, implacable stare. Even I can't look into the glossy depths of his eyes for too long. 'Brenda, you must realise what an aversion I have to being so close to the Bitch's Maw. I was in hell for quite some time, you know. Trapped down there. Unable to return to my beloved. I had to move heaven and hell to get back to her. I had to devise the most outlandish of schemes to liberate myself . . .'

I frown at him. 'Yes. I know you did. And I did everything

I could to foil those schemes. Look at the misery and upset you caused!'

'Let's not go into that now,' he sighs. 'All we're saying is that Whitby hasn't been a very good place for us in recent times. Effryggia and I have decided that it might be for the best if we moved away.'

I stare at them both. I study Effie's face. 'For good?' I demand. 'You'll sell up? You'll get rid of this house and the legacy of all your aunties?'

For a second she hesitates. And I can see that she isn't certain about any of this. Alucard has hoodwinked her. He has bamboozled her again. 'He says we can go anywhere, Brenda. He's taking me to Paris and Venice . . . all the places he has lived. He wants to show them to me . . .'

I stand up abruptly. 'You've let him brainwash you.'

Her eyebrows rise. A look of despair shoots across her face. 'No! That's not true.'

'Oh, I think it is, lady,' I snap back. 'He's got you right where he wants you.' I move away from the table and go hunting around for my shawl and my bag. 'I'm off now. I've had a bellyful, frankly. Effie, I'll talk to you by yourself, in the daytime. Not with this awful man hanging about. I'm going to make you see sense. You see if I don't.'

She sits tight and blazes with indignation. 'I know what I'm doing, Brenda. And I'm leaving. As soon as I can. My time here is finished.'

* * *

Friday is always an extra busy day at Brenda's B&B, what with all the preparations for a whole new set of visitors. I go about my accustomed tasks on automatic pilot. I'm scrubbing and whooshing and traipsing round with the old vaccuum cleaner. I'm straightening and dusting and casting a critical, expert eye over everything in my tiny kingdom. And eventually, it's all perfect.

There's hardly a moment for a sit-down with a pot of spicy tea and a ginger snap before the doorbell's ringing. It's the Kendalls from Chester. They were here a year ago, and I remember them well. They say they couldn't wait to return to my house and they greet me like an old friend, like a beloved auntie. They are falling over themselves in my front lobby with relief at the end of their long journey. I'm smiling and welcoming, but I can feel myself being slightly distant with them. I think this might even disappoint the Kendall family, who remember me being much warmer and more familiar. I'm disappointing myself, as it happens, being so caught up in my thoughts.

Effie can't go. It's ridiculous. She belongs in this town more than anyone. She has proper roots here.

After the Kendalls, a young couple called the Mayhews arrive, and I go through the routine again, smiling and nodding and trying to be convivial.

What if the town won't let her leave? The thought pops

into my mind round about teatime. To mollify my guests and to make up for my air of perplexity, I produce a Victoria sponge and invite them into the dining room for a spot of high tea. I'm just sifting on the icing sugar when I start wondering: will Whitby itself and the destiny it has in mind for Effie even let her set off on this jaunt around the world? She's making these plans, and giving herself up to Alucard's designs for her – but she's making assumptions about how far she will get.

I think the forces here will have something to say about Effie turning herself into a globetrotter and gadabout. I hope so, anyway.

I have a quiet evening, catching up with my diary and attending to my scrapbooks. This is a new thing for me, and it was all Effie's idea, as it happens. It's my database of spooky and unusual articles from the local and national press. Now I can keep tabs on what's going on, and look for patterns and clues. It's how I first cottoned on to the activities of this bizarre Limbosine.

Speaking of which, it's because of the Limbosine that Robert comes round at seven, when he's off his shift at the Miramar and the sea mist comes creeping up the little lanes from the harbour. Town is pitch black, starless and I can't help tingling with frosty nerves as the two of us totter out of my guest house and into the shrouded streets, off on our investigations.

Can Robert really replace Effie on these do's? These dangerous quests of ours? And do I really want him to? He seems ever so eager to step into the old dame's sensible shoes.

We've decided that the best thing is a short bus ride out of town, and to get ourselves dropped off in one of the outlying clusters of houses stuck in the wilds and miles of twisty, hilly roads out towards the Hole of Horcum. It's not that far, but the landscape is wild, wuthering and unwelcoming. It's a perfect place for coming across unwary hitchhikers. And tonight that's what the two of us are going to pretend to be.

I suddenly feel very reluctant, dinging the bell and getting the bus to stop in the middle of nowhere. But Robert is looking extremely determined, so I take a grip on myself and clamber down the gangway. The driver seems mystified as to why anyone would want to get out here.

'I think it's going to snow,' Robert says. 'You know that sort of dusty smell? And the muffled sound of the air?'

Now we're standing alone on the road, watching the spearmint blue of the bus windows streaking away up the zigzagging road. Dark fields stretch out in every direction. We're tucked away in a cleft in the hills and can't even see the lights of Whitby from here. I do up the rest of the buttons on my good winter coat.

'This is the last place that the Limbosine is supposed to have been seen, about a week ago,' Robert says. I already know all of this – from my scrapbooks, and keeping an ear open for the news on Whitby FM. Robert is trying to teach his granny to suck eggs. He's acting like this kind of thing isn't something I've been doing since well before he was born.

'So, we're live bait tonight,' I say, stamping on the road to keep the blood chugging around my antiquated system. How long can we manage out here? And how the devil do we get back? 'Shouldn't we split up? Would that be more of a temptation to this strange chauffeur?'

Robert nods, but is looking less keen now, at the thought of standing alone on one of these lonely roads. I wouldn't mind a bit of peace, actually. The thing about Robert is that he tends to fill up the silence with a lot of chatter. Something you couldn't accuse Effie of. Me and her, we can be quite companionably quiet when we want to be.

So Robert and I go our separate ways for a while. We've both got our mobile phones (a recent acquisition, in my case, and I'm not at all sure about it. I leave it switched off most of the time, as it happens), and off I plod, into the darkness. I've a tiny pen torch I ply into the darkness, just to make sure I don't teeter off the road on a sudden bend and plunge into the undergrowth.

As I walk on, miles and miles under the charcoal grey of the skies, I decide that Robert might be right. I can smell snow too. And the silence out here is marvellous. A great big muffled quiet that I find very soothing. I'm in a sort of contented trance as I wander along the country road, further and further out of town.

The landscape around me becomes more and more featureless. No houses. Scrubby grass. Distant hills and the gleaming silver sash of the sea. It's like a lunar landscape, and its blankness feels immensely satisfying. This is the furthest out of Whitby I've been for a few weeks. I stand there and survey the lie of the land.

What if I suddenly decided one day that I'd like to pick up and leave? Would I be allowed to? Somehow, I think not. I imagine an invisible force shield around the town. A bell jar with its impregnable walls somewhere out here, on the frozen earth.

But I'm glad to feel at home here. Even to feel as if I'm trapped here for ever. I wish Effie felt the same.

I turn back. I've come far enough tonight. I wonder about giving Robert a ring. I wonder if he's been luckier than I have, drawing the attention of our spectral kidnapper. Probably not. It was a silly plan, really. All I've done tonight is frozen my bum off.

I keep walking and walking and walking. And eventually I'm back where we hopped off the bus. No Robert. Maybe he's in the Limbosine?

I yank out my phone and squint at the tiny buttons under a street lamp. Whoops. I didn't have it switched on after all.

Fiddly thing. Eventually I get it working and the welcoming musical jingle sounds impossibly loud out here.

There's a message from Robert, which he left about twenty minutes ago.

'Brenda? Brenda, it's me.' He's hissing down the line. He sounds rattled. 'I've found something. You'd better . . . Can you . . . Ermm . . . I'm not sure what to do. Oh, answer your phone, woman!'

There's a crackling pause then. What's he on about? I wonder testily. But my intuition is right on cue. This isn't Limbosine business. This is much more serious. The word pops into my head at just that instant: *Walkers*. The Walkers are out tonight. Then Robert's voice is going on again.

'I'm by that garage at the very end of Clifftop Terrace. I was heading back into town because I'd run out of ciggies.'

Oh, get on with it, I think furiously.

'And I've found something terrible, Brenda. I don't know what to do. The police or . . .' Another pause. 'It's a body, Brenda! It's a young bloke lying here, next to the play park on the gravel. I don't know if he's alive or what. Oh, look, I'm gonna get an ambulance. But I thought you should know . . . it's his *throat*.'

I know what he's going to say before he next opens his mouth.

'His throat's been bitten, Brenda. He's been *vamped*!'

* * *

33

It's late before the police let Robert and me go home. They know the body's nothing to do with us. We're just the innocent discoverers, but the look that DCI Aickmann gives me is filthy. He knows I'm always mixed up in the creepy and crazy stuff.

'The lad's dead,' he tells us. 'Drained almost completely dry.'

Robert's beside me, sick with dread.

'It's been a while since we had an *infestation* in Whitby,' Aickmann goes on. He looks at me very severely, 'If you know more than you're letting on, Brenda, then you'd better start talking.'

I pretend to come over scandalised. 'Me?'

Robert is shooting me a glance. And it makes me wonder: why would I even think about protecting Alucard? Why don't I just dob him in it and tell the police he's back in town, that he's staying with my neighbour? But I don't say anything.

The police get caught up in identifying the victim and tracing his relatives. After our statements are taken, Robert and I are eventually free to go home. Aickmann would still like to know what we were doing, traipsing the quiet back streets after dark. But we tell him nothing about our investigations. They have nothing to do with him.

The next day we learn that the victim was a Walker. No sooner was he put away in cold storage in the town morgue, than he was back on his feet. Hard for the relatives, those cases, I always think. Especially when they trudge in to confirm identity and the body's done a bunk.

'A Walker,' Aickmann repeated the word heavily down the phone. 'I don't have to tell you what that means, do I?'

'No, indeed,' I muse, twiddling the phone cord round my finger. 'Someone is recruiting, obviously.'

That conversation was all to come on Saturday morning, however. On Friday – when we still thought the body we'd found was a goner – Robert and I traipsed back through town towards our respective homes. We were feeling, it has to be said, a tad glum.

Just before we separated – Robert peeling off to the Miramar – we passed the darkened store fronts of Silver Street. I paused before a particular gaudily painted shop window. It was rigged with eerie lilac lights, which fell upon the serried spines of hardbacks and the lurid covers of artfully strewn vintage paperbacks. I surveyed the newly minted shop sign, creaking in the wind above our heads.

'It's The Spooky Finger,' I tell Robert. 'This is the place Penny was going on about.'

'I'm not much of a reader, to be honest,' he says.

'She's asked me to join this book group of hers,' I say. 'But I'm not sure. Has she asked you?'

'It's women only.' He shrugs at me. 'You should go. You might like it. It might be consciousness-raising.'

I frown, not quite sure what he means by that. 'I don't need my consciousness raising.'

Robert smiles. 'Penny always gets herself involved in way-out stuff. She's a good kid, though.'

I like the way he calls her kid. She's only a couple of years younger than he is.

Seeing the shop front of The Spooky Finger (and its sign in the shape of a gesticulating digit, naturally), I'm reminded of the novel Penny gave me and how it's still in my tea towel drawer. The thought of *Warrior Queen of Qab* buzzes in my head and lingers as I kiss Robert good night and turn to hurry down the hill, the short distance to my B&B. Suddenly it feels incredibly cold. We've been standing around for hours in the dark. My feet and fingers are numbed by the cloying mist.

My guest house is quiet, with no lights burning. Everyone's abed early tonight. Passing Effie's house, I squint at the attic windows, mellow with an amber glow. Is she up there with him? Is she sitting up alone, waiting for him as he flits around the town, feasting on the blood of the unwary? How can she kiss the man? How can she let him touch her?

Oh, Effie. You daft old mare.

For the first time I'm starting to think that maybe it'll be for the best if the two of them really do leave town. Then the old fiend can get up to his sordid nastiness elsewhere.

I need to talk with her alone. I need to see her and convince her that she's being a fool, getting tied up with that creature. He will consume her body and soul. There'll be precious little Effie left.

I'm relieved to be home. Once I'm indoors, I get this mammoth wave of fatigue trampling over me and it takes a huge effort to creep soundlessly up the side steps. It's like I'm having to haul myself up the banister.

But when I'm in my attic rooms, locked up against the night in my private quarters, I find that my mind is still fully alert. I'm over-stimulated by all that's been going on. Mysterious cars and kidnappings and corpses in the night. Foolish Effie and all her shenanigans. It's all whirling round and round in my head as I go through my elaborate bedtime preparations.

My sumptuous bed in my luxurious boudoir awaits. No chance of sleep just yet. I stumble heavily to the kitchen and grab Penny's book from my tea towel drawer. I might as well have a little read. Perhaps it'll soothe me and put me to sleep. I prop myself up on my silky, tasselled cushions and open the novel by Beatrice Mapp.

The book is so old its spine cracks sharply, and I brace myself for all the pages falling out. But they're okay. A stale waft of old paper reaches my nostrils. Smoky and woody and oddly delicious. I don't think this is my kind of thing at all. It's all swords and sorcery and fighting and fantasy . . . people with funny names. I like books with real people in them, and something I can believe in.

Yet I read for longer than I expected to. I fall asleep over the book, and later, I'm not certain whether I've dreamed the story or if I've been reading it. That night the book comes seeping into my dreams. That's what it feels like. And I wake up on Saturday with the strangest of feelings.

Saturday.

Dear Henry,

Just a quick note from me. Hello, dear, how are you? Keeping well?

It's been so long, it seems an age since you were last here. It was all that business of the dark secret of the beer garden of Sheila Manchu, up at the Miramar. What a terrible affair that was. We all almost karked it that time. But we lived to fight another day, didn't we? I'm sure you won't be surprised to hear that your old friend Brenda has been involved in a number of adventures since then. And I'm sure you haven't been idle either, if I know anything about Henry Cleavis, eh?

Well, my dear, this is just to say that of course you are welcome to stay here throughout the Christmas season. I have a particular room in mind; for you I'll do a special offer! Half price! And Christmas dinner thrown in! How about that?

Let me know when you'd like to arrive. The room is

free when you want it. It's my newly refurbished Red Room – the jewel in my little crown – and you'll be the first visitor ensconced there.

Oh, what fun we'll have over the Yuletide period! I can't wait to see you again!

All best wishes (and love),

Brenda

I seal the envelope, stick on the stamp and, as I write out the address of his fancy college in his decrepit old town, I wonder. Maybe I'm sounding too eager.

Funny as well that I don't mention anything about having been recently married. Since the last time Henry was here, a whole lot has gone on in my life, and I don't even allude to it.

Scribbled on Saturday night, a bit tipsy.

Robert, Penny and I are sitting in the bar at the front bay windows of the Christmas Hotel. It's Saturday night and the snow is starting to tumble down. I've just been telling Penny that I wasn't sure I was enjoying that book of hers at all. Was 'enjoy' even the right word for it?

'Oh, I loved it,' she tells me. 'It was a proper rollicking good read. All that fighting and blood and thunder. And strong female characters, as well! What's not to like?'

I don't know what to say to her.

Robert, meanwhile, is looking about at the newly done-up

bar and I can see he's comparing it with how it used to be, back when he worked as one of Mrs Claus's elves. 'This used to be where we served teas,' he sighs at one point. 'It even used to be a little bit elegant.' He's talking as if it was decades ago. But in a way, I know what he means. When I first came to Whitby I had tea here with Effie on many occasions and he's right, it was like something from a more gentle age. We had scones and cream and those fiddly little sandwiches. Silver service and hostess trollies. Now there's a quiz machine and home-made posters saying that drinks after 8 p.m. on weekend nights are two pounds a throw. I check my watch. It's ten to.

Robert keeps on lamenting about Mrs Claus letting the old hotel go a bit tacky.

It's right at the point when I'm about to tell him to stop sighing that I clap eyes on Effie. Squinting between the pillars, I've just about got a clear view of the main entrance and reception. There she is, togged up against the inclement weather, stamping her good leather boots and shaking the snow from her cloak. She looks rather svelte and dashing, I realise. She's got that snooty look about her, staring around the place, as if she can sense me watching as I lean out of my chair.

Then she sees me. Our eyes lock over the expanse of monogrammed carpet. I notice that her first reaction isn't surprised pleasure. She's not at all happy to see me here at the

Christmas Hotel. Then she smiles and gives me an elegant little wave.

'At least she's alone,' says Robert, seeing who I'm waving back at.

Penny is slow to catch on, and when she does, her face falls. I think she rather wishes that Effie was accompanied by her man friend. Penny would love to meet the nasty old devil properly, though I've told her he's nothing to write home about. She should save her hero-worship for someone more worthwhile.

I know that part of Penny is still sceptical about things we take for granted in this town. Even after what she has already witnessed here in our midst, there is still something in Penny that cries out: 'You've got to be joking, surely? You can't really mean that Effie's fancy man is really, actually the most renowned bloodsucker the world has ever known?'

I've no patience with her amazement, the daft kid. People have to live somewhere, don't they? Even the most famous. And this town is where Alucard first landed, back in the 1890s.

He's the town's most celebrated illegal immigrant. The most famous import, after haddock.

'Good evening, everyone.' Effie smiles, looking nervous. She's hovering at our bar table as if she doesn't quite believe we'll ask her to join us. How have we come to this? And it's her, surely, who's alienated herself.

'Effie, sit yourself down, woman,' I urge her warmly, as fondly as I can. 'You look frozen right through.'

'The snow's coming down like mad,' she says. 'I was trotting down Hudson Street, and it was horizontal.' She still seems reluctant to actually join us and sit.

'How did you know we were here?' Robert asks.

'I didn't.' Immediately she looks awkward. Even more awkward than before. 'I'm here to see . . . somebody else.'

'Your fella?' says Penny, shoving her nose in excitedly.

Effie shakes her head quickly. 'He's out on business this evening.'

Business! I raise both eyebrows at her. What kind of business does he have but funny business? He'll be off sating his unnatural blood lust again, I suppose.

Anyhow, I don't say anything.

'May I join you?' Effie asks. 'Just for a little while?'

We all budge up and everyone acts surprised that she even has to ask.

Penny gasps, now that she's getting a good close-up look at old Effie. 'You look amazing! Your skin! Everything. You look like you've had a month's holiday! What have you been doing to yourself, Effie?'

My friend and neighbour gives a sickly sort of smile. 'I've just been looking after myself, Penny. There's no secret. I've been living well, that's all it is.'

Robert grins at her. 'It must be the love of a good man, eh?'

PAUL MAGRS

I can't tell quite how sardonic he's being with that, but I can see that Effie assumes it's meant to be cutting. She simply purses her lips and waits for someone to fetch her a drink.

'I'll go,' I tell them. 'I think Happy Hour's just about to begin.'

Next day.

Sunday is often the day that Effie and I take a little wander about the shops in town. Being slightly quieter than most other days, it rather suits us to dawdle and take our time, gawking and gossiping as we will.

There's no answer at Effie's front door when I give her a try this morning. It's hard not to feel a bit glum as I head off by myself. The street decorations and the tinselled trees in each shop window seem taunting, somehow. It's as if Mrs Claus's tawdry tastes have overtaken the whole town.

Finding myself on LeFanu Close, I happen past the new bookshop and can't help peering in again by daylight. I might as well have a little look. What did Penny say they specialised in? Mystery? Fantasy? Hmmm. But I feel like I should support a new business in town, especially if I'm thinking of attending their Wednesday-night group.

The door's stiff and gives a macabre little tinkle when I totter over the threshold. At first I think it's a bit gloomy within, but then as I shuffle forward on the polished boards I find that the place has a delightful atmosphere. Straight away

43

I feel steeped in a gorgeous, honeylike warmth and glow. I don't know what it is that causes this. The strange, spicy incense that laces the air? The soft glow of the coloured, shaded lamps? The almost labyrinthine layout of the shop, which has ceiling-high bookcases arranged in such a cunning way that I soon lose track of where I am?

The place seems to go on and on, further and further back. And the books! They appear unusual somehow. Some are brand spanking new, slick and colourful. Others are hand-stitched hardbacks, soft and fraying with use. Lurid paperbacks and penny dreadfuls mingle promiscuously with volumes that are clearly worth a few bob. But the variousness and apparent chaos of it all isn't what makes the books in The Spooky Finger strange. The obscurity and the weirdness of the books themselves are what give me pause for thought. Only a very few titles I recognise. The rest are things I've never heard of in my life. They're like books from a different world.

After a little while I realise that there's queer, gentle music playing. Tinkly music that seems to enter into my head, pacifying me, before I even notice it's there. And something else: sound effects. I can hear whooshing waves and the distant cries of some kind of exotic beasts.

And I haven't seen a sales assistant or any sign of the owner. It feels like I have wandered alone into some kind of forest of books.

Then I round the corner and there's a short, dumpy, smiling woman sitting on a stool by the ancient cash register. She's knitting something in lilac wool and is quite oblivious to my presence. I give a little cough, to let her know she has a customer.

Her counter is wreathed in a lingering mist from a variety of fountains and miniature waterfalls that decorate this end of the shop. She's got more water features than a garden centre back here. Also, there are some stunning bonsai trees dotted about on the smaller bookcases and cabinets. They make her look rather like a giant, sitting there, pursing her lips as she plies the soft, spangly wool.

'Penny says you're going to join our little gang,' she warbles at last. Her voice is very high-pitched, girlish and breathy.

'Pardon?' I frown at her. I don't like people being familiar straight away like that. I date that back to my years on the run. I feel highly suspicious of people you don't know using your name.

'The book group,' says Marjorie Staynes, biting into her wool to snap it. Her teeth are tiny and worn down. 'My little Wednesday-night group. Penny told me that you were the friend she'd like to introduce.'

'Yes, well,' I say, sounding gruff, especially next to this dainty, feminine little person, 'I've made no promises. I may come down, if there are no other demands on my time.'

'Ha!' chortles Marjorie Staynes. 'You'll be here.'

'What?' I raise both eyebrows at her. 'How can you be so sure? I might have any number of other things to do.'

'You won't. You'll want to be here. Where it's all happening!' She casts on again, magenta wool this time, yanked from her knitting bag on the counter. 'You won't be able to keep yourself away!' Then, staring straight at me, she asks: 'How are you getting on with *Warrior Queen of Qab*?'

I purse my lips in what feels like a very Effie-like way. 'I think it's rotten, to be honest.'

'Oh dear!'

'Yes, it's not my kind of thing at all. What do you call it? Sword and sorcery? Sci-fi?'

Marjorie Staynes gives a happy little shrug. 'Some people might call it that. Vulgar people might look at it on that surface level, yes indeed. But I . . . I prefer to look deeper.'

I draw myself up to my full height, clutching my handbag to myself. 'Oh, you do, do you?'

'I see it as an allegory, myself. An allegory about women and what they might achieve. If they work together. If they bond together and work towards their goals and desires.'

I roll my eyes. 'An allegory! And not just some cheapie pulp adventure novel about a land where women enslave men and seem to do just what they blummin' well like?'

Marjorie Staynes gives that infuriating shrug again. 'Like I say, you have to look past the surface, Brenda. Things are often in disguise, you see. Things that look simplistic or obvious or ugly or crass. Why, they might be hiding all kinds of complexities and strange depths within.'

Well, that's decided me. There's no way I'm attending any kind of group run by this lumpy old madam. I'm not sitting here being patronised by the likes of her.

'Beatrice Mapp was a clever old stick,' Marjorie sighs happily. 'She hid all kinds of interesting things inside her books. Especially her books about the world of Qab. All kinds of signs and clues. Oh yes. She knew what she was doing, old Beatrice Mapp.'

The incense and the dry ice from the water features are making me feel giddy and nauseous. Suddenly I want to be away from here. I rock backwards a little on my feet and have to take a tight grip on myself.

Beatrice Mapp? Why does that name make me feel so strange? Especially the way Marjorie is saying it? Enunciating each syllable like that. Almost tauntingly, the way she's saying the name to me . . .

'Old Beatrice Mapp,' she goes on. 'All those years ago. Back in Bloomsbury, eh? Back at the start of the twentieth century. Oh, she knew what it was all about. Old Beatrice.'

'Stop saying that name!' I burst out.

Marjorie looks honestly surprised at this. 'What's the matter? Brenda?' She struggles off her stool and ambles over to me. 'Have I said something to upset you?' She starts patting me.

I actually snarl at the woman. 'Get away from me! Get your hands off me!' I shrug her off and back away, turning to get myself out of that awful shop. On the way I stumble into her sales assistant: a pale young man who's standing in my way, clutching a pile of hardbacks. I only just manage to avoid knocking him over, and he hisses as I go past. With alarm or dismay, I can't tell. I brush past him and the flesh of his bare arm feels chilly to me.

I'm glad to get out of there. The Spooky Finger indeed. Creepy place. Nasty old woman. She was getting at something. I don't even know what. But I know it's best if I keep right away.

I hurry home, and though it's an awful thing to do to a book, I toss *Warrior Queen of Qab* into my wheelie bin as I shuffle up the side passage. It's something I feel compelled to do.

Though I've got a website these days, I don't have the internet at home. I have to draw the line somewhere, in letting the world of the future encroach into my cosy nook. Anyway, I know that the Miramar Hotel boasts something called broadband and wi-fi, and those are what I suppose I need now, this evening, so I go yomping up the hill on Sunday as the darkness settles over town.

I pause for a bit to glance back at the strings of lights across the bay, and the silkily darkening skies behind the abbey. It never fails to send a shudder through me, this view. Quick breather, and then I'm hurrying on again.

'Beatrice Mapp, Beatrice Mapp,' I keep repeating under my breath, as if I'm in danger of forgetting the name. Curse this memory of mine. It's like carrying jelly about in a string bag for decade after decade.

Maybe I shouldn't be too hard on myself. I've been through a bumpy life so far. Of course bits of my past have dropped out of my ken.

Not too long ago, when my father came back on the scene – albeit briefly – I was hoodwinked into believing that he could somehow renew me. I fondly imagined that he could bring his magical surgical skills to bear on my ancient and ailing form. Of course I got let down again. My fault for raising my own hopes. We have to struggle along with what we're given in the first place, don't we? We've got to make the best of what we've got!

My old dad's in hell now, of course. Along with his fancy woman, and possibly my estranged husband. (It sounds melodramatic, to say they've been sent to hell, but it's literally true, and not as far away as you might think.)

Anyway – I'm wandering. Sunday evening I'm full of purpose, and directing my feet towards the Miramar Hotel. It's Sixties Night, I discover, as soon as I arrive. It's very noisy and I have to shout at Penny across the reception desk. 'Paper Sun' by the Small Faces is playing, and there is something different about Penny – it takes me a second or two to realise that she's shed her usual Goth look for a minidress in Bridget Riley patterns. Her lipstick is pale pink rather than her usual unflattering black.

'You can use our business suite,' she tells me, coming round the desk. 'It's a new initiative of Robert's.'

There's a kind of office hidden away behind the main dining room. Penny sits me at a sleek computer and fires it up for me.

'What is it you're wanting to do?'

'I want to look for a name. A person.'

She gets me up a page on to which I have to type the name 'Beatrice Mapp', and about ten thousand different options suddenly display themselves.

'Beatrice Mapp?' Penny frowns. 'But that's the writer of . . . the book group book! Have you read it?'

Ah, awkward. How can I tell her I binned the thing? I should fetch it out, really, given that it was a gift from Penny. Oh help, Monday morning the bin men come. I'll have to remember. It's probably already covered in eggshells and clarts and tea leaves.

'Er, yes, it piqued my interest,' I tell her. 'So I thought I'd do a little further exploration, before the meeting on Wednesday, is it?'

Penny looks delighted. 'Oh, brilliant! So you're coming along, are you?'

I hadn't intended to. But now I've gone and committed myself. Never mind. I've a feeling that further investigation is required. 'Where do I start with this lot?' I shrug, gazing at the results my search has come up with.

Penny – like most young people – is completely unfazed by all the computer stuff. She homes in and chooses a page. Some kind of encyclopedia thing. She says it's written by just ordinary people, all pooling their knowledge about stuff. About everything in the world, which sounds a bit rum to me. Whatever happened to experts? Did they fall out of favour or something?

'Here she is,' Penny says. 'Beatrice Mapp. Quite a short entry, actually. Quite surprising. I meant to look her up myself, before the book group met. I was intrigued . . .'

There's a pageful of bland information, telling me little more than the back of the paperback did. That Beatrice Mapp (1878–1969) lived for many years in Bloomsbury. Tavistock Square. 'Goodness, but she wrote a lot of books!' I gasp, as Penny scrolls down the list of titles.

'Twenty-eight of them were in the Qab series,' Penny muses. 'The other fifteen were stand-alone spooky thrillers. All of those are forgotten now. It's the Qab books she's remembered for. Hmm. Let's see if we can find a piccy of her.'

I want to tell Penny to stop. I want to knock her hand off

the mouse and prevent her from clicking. I've no idea why. For some reason I feel like nipping this line of enquiry – this whole investigation – in the bud right now. I have a premonition that we are getting ourselves into something that we're going to regret. Or this might be down to the stuffiness of this business suite. It's got no windows and it's a bit dusty in here.

And up comes a photo of Beatrice Mapp. She's a proper sepia-tinted Edwardian lady, in a high-necked blouse and her hair all swirled up like a French loaf. Her expression is one of shrewdness and vital intelligence. The way she's done up makes her seem older than she was . . . She must have been thirty-one just then? Her eyes seem to glare out at us from 1909 as if she can see right into us, here in 2009, up on the north-east coast, hidden away in the depths of a tacky hotel.

'She looks quite a severe character,' Penny says.

'She was,' I tell her. Then I blink.

Penny looks at me. 'What?'

'Yes?'

'You said "she was". Like you knew her.'

I sigh. 'Could you print some pages off for me, pet? And have a look at these . . . erm, linky things – is that they're called? – at the bottom of the page. There might be more info there. Look, the Qab fan website. Can we gather as much information as we can? I think we're going to need it.'

'Robert charges ten pence a page for printing.'

'Does he indeed!' I smile.

'But I'm sure he'd do this for free.'

I grin at her and hoist myself up, feeling my knees crack. This desk is too low. 'I'm hobbling off to my B and B. Could you bring all the pages to my place this evening, Penny? I'll cook some supper for you and Robert, if you can both get away. Then we can go over these documents together.'

She's looking at me quizzically. I'm running away from her questions just now. I hold up both hands. 'I'll explain all later, I hope. My memories are surfacing. I have to be very careful that I don't try too hard to recapture them and ruin everything. I'm going to take a walk in the snow along the sea front and have a bit of a cogitate. I'll see you later. All right?'

Penny nods readily. 'Yes, of course. And Robert and I are both free tonight.'

'Very good. Seven o'clock. I think I'll give Effie a ring. This could be big. I've a funny feeling that this could be very big indeed. She won't want leaving out.'

Something warming, I think. That's what we need. I chop onions, carrots, celery in a blur of frantic activity. I get the huge oven in my attic kitchen fired up and set the oil fizzing in the heavy-bottomed casserole dish to brown and seal the meat. When I've put that aside, I stir all the vegetables in with stock and herbs and a large pinch of flour for thickening, and give the concoction a good braising, then the whole lot goes in the dish. Then I realise I need to pop down to Leena and Raf's shop for some Guinness.

Luckily, my downstairs neighbours are open for long hours, even on Sunday night. Once I'm down there, I notice a dozen other things I'm needing: spicy tea bags, an Arctic Roll from their ancient freezer, custard powder, etc., etc. All the while I know that Leena is watching me like a hawk. She's got one eye on the black and white telly on the counter, and the other moving from the local paper's Sunday supplement ('The Flesh is Weak') to me, going up and down her aisles.

When I'm close by, she pipes up, 'So what's the story with Effie and this fancy man of hers?'

I shrug, like I don't know very much about it. That's the best way with Leena. Show any sign of weakness, and she'll have the whole story out of you.

'I hear she's thinking of moving away,' she adds, as she starts ringing my purchases through. 'That's what someone was saying. I can't imagine this place without Effie! Someone mentioned that her family has been here for loads of generations, all living in that same house. That's what someone was telling me. It'd be a real shame to see her go. Anyway, I caught a glimpse of her bloke the other night. He came in by himself, very late on. He was buying vodka and some funny kind of cheese that's been here ages, one we thought we'd never shift. And some dental floss. Handsome kind of a chap, I thought. I can see what she sees in him.'

'Hm,' I say, tightly. Sometimes Leena winds me right up. Then she claps eyes on the novel in my shopping basket as I pack my stuff away. I've just hoiked it out of the wheelie bin as I came down the side passage and yes, it's a little the worse for wear, with a bit of nasty bean juice and fried egg slime on the cover. When she sees it, Leena gives a strangled cry.

'Oh, I'm reading that as well! Are you going to The Spooky Finger, Brenda? Have you joined the club too?'

I scowl. I might have known Leena would be straight in there. She's so susceptible to anything new and novel in town. If I remember rightly, it was her who let me know all about that awful phone-in talk show *The Night Owls*, when it was all the rage.

'I'm not sure I'll be going,' I lie. 'The book's not really my kind of thing. And that woman in the bookshop – I went by there today – Marjorie Staynes, I'm not sure about her at all.'

'Oh? That'll be nineteen seventy-four, by the way.' She eyes the four-pack of Guinness cans as I bag them up, and it's as if she's thinking I'm going to sit slurping them alone all evening. Them and the two bottles of Merlot I'm putting in my bag after them. She says, 'I think she's really amazing, myself. I love being in the book group, even though we've only had a couple of meetings. Marjorie Staynes says such interesting stuff.'

'Really?' I think about that old woman with her knitting

and can't imagine it. To me she just seemed a bit rude and presumptuous.

'And I love this week's book.' Leena laughs. 'I love the very idea of Qab! A world where the women rule! And everyone obeys the Warrior Queen! And all the silly men are just slaves! Fantastic! How brilliant is that?'

I daren't say that I found the whole thing vulgar and unbelievable. Because Leena looks so excited about it. There's a funny look in her eye as she talks about this made-up place.

Then Raf, her burly Glaswegian husband, comes out of the back, rubbing storeroom dust off his white coat. 'Oh, hey, doll, are you on about that book again?' He smiles ruefully and nods a greeting at me. 'It's all I've heard about this week. The world where the women are in charge, and no mercy gets shown to the men. I feel like telling the old woman at that bookshop: you're having a funny effect on my wife.'

'Whissht,' smiles Leena, waving him away. 'Just because I've a new interest you can't understand.' She shrugs at me. 'I've never seen this one sit down with a book, the whole time we've been together. He doesn't know what it's like to have something, just a small object like that, tucked away in your handbag. Something that means you can just hide yourself away in another world at any given time in the day . . .'

She's off on a reverie and her husband is looking apologetic as he starts filling up the sweetie trays on the front counter. Leena gives me my change and fixes me with a significant look. 'So I'll be seeing you on Wednesday, then, in our little group? At The Spooky Finger?'

I nod quickly, alarmed by her fervour.

Outside, skidding a little on the now thick-lying snow, I bump – almost literally – into Effie. She's in a snood, of all things.

'I'm making beef in Guinness,' I tell her. 'You've got to come round. Robert and Penny are coming at seven. And we're talking about . . . important stuff.'

Her lips twitch in a moue of pleasure. She can't help herself. 'Just me? Not Kristoff?'

I shake my head. 'If you don't mind.'

Effie shrugs lightly. 'I think he's off to Scarborough tonight anyway. Some kind of business to attend to.' She glances up at the snow-packed sky, which seems very low over the town. 'I hope he remembered to wrap up.'

Why does she persist in pretending like he's just any old man? When she knows he's probably turned himself into a bat or a wolf or a trail of evil-looking mist for the evening? She's fretting that he's forgotten his mittens and his vest.

I manage to suppress a barbed comment and say something nice about how becoming her snood is on her. Then I add: 'I'll see you in an hour or so, Effie. There's a lot for us to talk about.'

* * *

Penny comes in with a large folder, crammed with pages she's printed off the computer at the Miramar. She's back in Goth mode, which is a shame, I think. That sixties style must just have been for work, but it suited her, I think.

She seems startled to see Effie standing there in the corner of my living room with a sweet sherry. Effie narrows her eyes briefly at the girl, as if thinking she has more right to be here than Penny, Effie being my oldest friend in Whitby.

Robert grins at her. 'Well, it's almost like business as usual, isn't it?' He's in an open-necked shirt – looking cooler and less bundled up than the two women. That's him all over, really – less guarded, less complicated. I suppose that's one of the reasons I like him so much. There are fewer layers to our Robert; fewer self-protective wrappings than there are to most people.

But as I get on with the finishing touches to dinner, I detect a slight atmosphere. I know that Robert is keen to talk about the ongoing case of the Limbosine. And there's the little matter of the vampire infestation too. I shoot a warning glance or two his way as he helps me carry through my serving dishes. I get him to push my hostess trolley and have a word sotto voce. No going on about vampires with Effie sitting there. She might take it the wrong way.

Also – and it pains me to say this – it isn't a good idea to disclose too much about it all in front of her. What with her going home to Alucard this very evening. We don't want him to know we're potentially on his case.

I try to push all of these things out of my mind and concentrate on the fluffiness of my creamed potatoes, the heady aroma of my thick beef stew. Perfect for the inclement weather. The wind is skirling round the frozen rooftops tonight. It makes me feel shivery and complacent inside. Cosy in my attic rooms.

'Oh, I do like these little shallots in the gravy, Brenda,' says Robert.

Penny keeps trying to go on about her research. She dips into the pages she's printed off for me. She has the file on her knee as she eats.

While it's fascinating, I'm not sure it fits the bill as general suppertime chit-chat.

'There seems to be a thriving Beatrice Mapp fandom out there in cyberspace,' Penny is saying, heaping her plate with mash. 'I wouldn't have thought her readership was so large or widespread, but she seems to strike a chord. With some quite funny people, as it happens. Needy, lonely people, I think. Just looking at some of the discussions and forums out there, people get very het up about the whole Qab thing. Taking it very seriously . . .'

I glance across the table and realise that Effie looks like she is feeling left out. Her plate is still empty. I ask her to pass it and give her a huge helping of fragrant stew. 'Do you know about this Qab business, Effie?'

She frowns and purses her lips. 'Far too much food for me, ducky. No, I don't know what any of you are talking about. Would you care to elucidate?'

And so we do, with Penny doing most of the talking. In the process she gives a pretty good precis of the novel I've been trying to read and an account of the details to do with Beatrice Mapp and the book club based at The Spooky Finger. The real-world stuff is much more intriguing than what goes on in the book, I think.

Effie taps her beaky nose thoughtfully with her fork. 'Beatrice Mapp . . . that rings a bell, you know. My aunts left me with a wonderful library. All these forgotten treasures. They liked a nice spooky adventure story . . .'

Penny glances at me. 'Brenda thinks she remembers something about Beatrice Mapp too. You had a funny turn in the business suite at the Miramar, didn't you?'

I roll my eyes. 'Not quite a funny turn, Penny dear. What are you all waiting for? Eat!'

Robert is giving me a serious look. Concern on his face. 'Have you got memories surfacing?'

He knows me pretty well.

'I'm not sure,' I tell him, honestly. 'But I'll have a look through the stuff Penny's brought. If there's anything pertinent in this addled old noggin of mine, I'm sure it'll come back . . .'

We start to eat then, and I realise that I'm suddenly banking on Henry Cleavis. Of course, I'm looking forward to seeing him here as a friend and companion. But he's also a hypnotist, isn't he? Once before he proved expert at working with my shattered memories. Maybe this time he might be of use once more.

The evening passes pleasantly, in a jolly, uncomplicated way, which is a surprise. Effie is back to her old, mildly acerbic self. There are no awkward scenes. No one says a word about her fancy man and she doesn't go on the turn about anything. We play some records and Robert helps me load up the dishwasher. There's a reasonably exciting game of Monopoly (the Whitby version, new out this Christmas), and sooner than usual the young people are claiming tiredness and it's time to go home to their beds. No stamina! Effie and I are just starting on our nightcaps when Robert and Penny decide to leave.

Soon we two old adventurers are left alone in my attic.

'Top-up?'

'Please.' She holds out her schooner for more sloe gin. Its mellow tang makes me feel Christmassy, I realise, and I decide to lay in a stock for the season of goodwill.

'Brenda, I'm glad it's just us,' Effie says. 'Those kids are nice, but . . .'

'But you want a quiet word?'

I've never seen her looking so in need of a quiet word. She's got something on her chest.

'I don't want to go, Brenda.'

'What?'

'I mean, I don't want to leave Whitby.'

'But you said – you and Kristoff – it was your plan. You wanted to get out into the world . . .'

'He does. Of course he does. He was never very happy here. And he's not comfortable in my house. How could he be, with the ghosts of my ancestresses loitering about in the ether? Staring down at him from their portraits? They make him feel supremely uncomfortable – on purpose, I believe! Well, they never wanted a man living there, in their house. Men were forbidden. They're very cross with me, for inviting one over the threshold.'

'I see . . .'

'And it's even worse because of the kind of man Kristoff is. I lie awake at night and I can hear my Aunt Maud stomping about in the attic, absolutely livid with me and what I've done.'

'Oh, Effie,' I say. 'I knew something wasn't right. I knew you weren't as happy as you were pretending, these past few weeks.'

'Well, now you know. Alucard wants to leave. He wants us both to up sticks and leave this place for ever. And I . . . I don't want to, Brenda! I've said I do – just to please him! What he wants becomes what I want. Like he's . . . he's taking over my volition! But he swears he isn't using his powers on me. He says he'd never do that to get what he wants. But still I find myself giving in to him . . . and going along with his . . . his desires! But this moving away . . . it isn't what I want! Not at all! How could it be? I belong here! This is my home!'

I give her a hug. 'You'll have to tell him, lovey. You'll have to stand up to him.'

She shudders in my arms. 'I can't! I just can't!'

I go cold at the sound of her voice. She's scared of him, isn't she? Her own boyfriend. Effie's terrified of him, I realise.

I sit up that night much later than I'm intending, leafing through the folder Penny left with me. See what I'm like? With the scent of a mystery wafting up my nostrils? Not the most elegant description, I know, but never mind.

Fandom. Discussion forums. Message boards. All of this stuff is new to me. But Penny seems quite au fait with the things that go on in cyberspace.

What seems clear – I think, as I polish off the sloe gin, reading at the dining table – is that Qab is a cult. The way people talk and tussle and get hot under the collar, arguing very abstruse points indeed about the books. I can't quite tell whether they are simply fans getting carried away, or whether they really believe in Qab as a real place with its own culture and landscape and religion.

I glance through some strange and poorly written reviews and synopses of the Qab books, and some very bizarre examples of what is called fan fiction to do with Qab. I dip in here and there and find that some of them are quite shocking and rude. There are also some sketchy, cribbed details about the life of the 'divine creator', as she is sometimes referred to. There is even a faded snapshot of the front of Beatrice Mapp's one-time home in Tavistock Square, London, W1.

I stare at this for a few moments. It looks like the photo was taken back in the day, right back a hundred years ago, in Miss Mapp's own era. There is a carriage of some kind waiting outside, perhaps ready to take the grand authoress somewhere. I study the smudgy upstairs windows. Is that a pale face staring out at the square outside? Staring back at the photographer? The photo is poor quality; it's hard to tell.

More reading through screeds of this mad stuff. People on the internet take their passions very seriously, it seems.

Though thinking about it, perhaps a place like Qab is worth taking seriously.

A whole new world. Primordial and fresh. Ready to be shaped by the hand of man. Or rather, woman. It's the world where women rule, isn't it? Where women get to make the world anew.

The websites aren't just the work of female fans, I realise. The message board on the most popular and biggest site devoted to Qab appears to be teeming with the fevered and fannish communications of both women and men. The men are eager to become slaves, it seems, in this new Qab world order. They would be happy to be subservient in the women's reordering of things.

On this forum – the only interactive one, as opposed to merely informative – there is some kinky stuff about being servants and sex slaves and what-have-you. You know the kind of thing. Silly men. They can get all worked up and excited over just about anything, can't they?

I'm a bit embarrassed, really, that Penny has downloaded and printed off all this stuff for me. What must she think I want to be reading?

Still, it's fascinating.

Most fascinating of all is the talk of the meetings and gatherings around the country.

Qab chapters, it seems, exist in most major towns. Groups meet once a month to discuss and dress up and – seemingly – enact some of the pageantry, rituals and scenes described in the books.

There are even a couple of blurry snaps of rather ordinary-looking people done up in glittering finery. Helmets, breastplates, swords and – what do you call them? Pelmets? Anyway, they're trying to look like figures off the cover illustrations of the books, but with very mixed results. Still, whatever turns them on. I'm not judgemental.

There's some funny stuff about a certain chapter of Qab in

Kendal, in Cumbria. Until March last year there was a lot of talk about the activities of this particular group. They got up to all sorts of interesting stuff. They even had a float in the Kendal Mardi Gras last year, showing their finery off to the natives and the day-trippers.

Members of the Kendal branch became mini-celebrities on the Qab message board. It's clear that there was some cachet to the group. They were the most prestigious, the flashiest and – the word is repeated again and again in the archive of discussions – the most 'advanced'. I wonder in what sense they were 'advanced'. What could they mean by that?

And then – suddenly, in June this year – all discussion of the Kendal branch was declared forbidden on the Qab message board.

The chief moderator of the site posted an abrupt message to say that she would take no questions on this matter, nor complaints. Any single reference to the Qab group based in Kendal in Cumbria in the UK, or any of the members thereof, would result in complete, irrevocable dismissal from the Qab message board.

Everyone was to carry on as if the Kendal chapter of Qab had never existed.

A stunned silence rang through the boards for some time after that. People – Qab fans – all over the world were too frightened and shocked to put their feelings into words. And they knew they would have to be very careful about doing so, once they found the words. No one wanted casting out, and from the forum owner's declaration, it was obvious that she would be making no exceptions. This owner of the message board seemed to wield a vast amount of power in the subculture of Qab. She was like their very own Queen of Qab.

A few hardy souls made a few obscure, allusive comments and mused aloud about this strange embargo.

What did the people in Kendal do that was so bad? Why were they scotched from the official record? What went wrong? And why can't the rest of them even refer to it or them ever again?

Ripples of fright ran through Qab-space. I can feel it still tonight, shimmering off the pages Penny printed for me.

Someone asked: Was it something to do with the Kendal Qab people being so advanced? Had they somehow got too far?

That very day that same person was banned for ever from the Qab site.

Discussion passed on to more pleasant, everyday, mundane concerns in the world of Qab fandom. Kendal was never mentioned again.

I set down the pages. I have scoured them all, without even meaning to. It is after two in the morning, and my head is thumping with sloe gin and intrigue.

* * *

Next thing, it's the last week before Christmas. I think it's one of my favourite weeks in the year, though as you know, I'm not at all religious. I like the anticipation and the slow-creeping magic, as everyone in town bustles round the shops and winding ways, making last-minute preparations for their week of feasting and self-indulgence.

I've got an extra lot on my plate with all my guests, of course. I'm shovelling breakfasts into them and whipping their bed sheets and pillowcases away for the steamy laundry. I'm dashing round with my Ewbank, collecting the dust from their travelling shoes and the crumbs they've dropped having midnight feasts. And the weather, of course – these endlessly falling snows – brings its own work with it. I'm out each morning scraping the snow from my side passage and all my paths out front. I'm laying down sea salt to burn away the frost and ice. Out there I meet Raf and Leena as they open up their shop and scrape the icicles off their awning.

Leena can't stop talking about Qab. 'I've been buying the other books in the series,' she tells me breathlessly. 'I can't keep away from The Spooky Finger! I have to read the full set! I've become a proper fan!'

Me, I'm still struggling through that first book, the one I got covered in bacon grease and egg. I found it much easier reading about the books online than I do reading the actual thing. It's composed in that very stiff and proper Edwardian English. Even the scenes of swordplay and bloodletting, and the saucy scenes of flagellation (really!) are all delivered in this very elegantly poised prose. And I'm finding it hard going, I must say.

So, the days pass and I get on with making sure that I'll have everything I need for feeding the five thousand over Christmas. I pop into the butcher's and the baker's and leave my orders with them. I dawdle around the busy shops of Silver Street and Church Street, picking up trinkets and gee-gaws for my friends, and spend a pleasant Monday evening wrapping them in hand-printed wrapping paper. That night I even put on the James Last Christmas album, just to get me in the mood.

The Red Room is finished. The crowning glory of my B&B. It's all set for its first guest, Henry Cleavis, who is due to arrive on Wednesday. I've bought a new satin coverlet for the four-poster bed. The mirrors are antique ones I found in Effie's emporium and cleaned up myself with wire wool and Brasso.

Speaking of Effie, she's opening up a little more to me, since we had our heart-to-heart on Sunday night. It's like she's back to her old self, in a way, now that she's confiding.

Tuesday afternoon we have one of our trips out, dawdling around the streets of Whitby and admiring the lights and council tinsel displays and the tree in the old marketplace, which towers above the shambolic roofs.

Effie's got her snood on again. Her face looks pink and

fresh and enlivened, somehow. Though her mood is sombre, there is a vitality in her face and a liveliness to her step.

'Are you still in a muddle over going away?' I ask her. We're hauling ourselves up the hundred and ninety-nine steps. Effie wants to stand at the top of the town, while the weather is clear and it's not too windy. She wants to look at the whole vista from the abbey. It's slippery going with the encrusted snow on the steps and across the graveyard. I haven't worn the right shoes. Effie seems to glide along effortlessly, elegantly.

'In a muddle,' she sighs. 'You could say that.' She turns to me with a woebegone expression. 'I'm no further on. Kristoff's assuming I'm happy to go. He wants to leave as soon after the New Year celebrations as we can manage. Leave and never turn back. Paris first.' She shakes her head.

That soon! I hold my breath. Kristoff is mad keen to be away. He really must be very disturbed by the ghostly presence of Effie's aunts. Perhaps, also, he's feeling the heat here in Whitby. These younger vamps, these transformed young men – these Walkers – perhaps they will lead the police to come knocking on Effie's door one day soon. Can that be what Alucard fears?

Soon we're standing amid the tall ruined walls of the abbey itself. The half-demolished arches are smoothed and softened by the snow. The place looks less ruinous with the edges soothed by the drifts.

'My aunts used to come up here at night.' Effie smiles.

70

'Did I ever tell you? During the war. They'd do their rituals here, for warding off the Nazis.'

'Really?' I chuckle. 'I suppose they danced around naked as the planes flew over?'

'Oh yes.' She nods, very seriously. 'They had a proper job to do. My aunts were the witches of Whitby and were responsible for its safety. Once or twice they brought me here with them, to sit here – on this wall – and watch them go about their vital, magical work. I thought they were magnificent. And they were! They really were!'

I picture the scene. Effie as a child, during the war. Such a long time ago.

'As the war went on, they decided that they had to send me away from Whitby. I found it very hard. I didn't want to leave them, of course. My whole life was here. My aunts were my entire world.'

'Of course.' My heart twinges for the young Effryggia, the orphan in the house of witches. 'Where did they send you?'

'Oh, to some witchy friends of theirs. Women who ran a shop in a little town in the middle of Yorkshire. Haworth. Do you know it?'

I muse on the name. 'I'm not sure.'

Effie shrugs. 'Well, that's a whole other story. What I found in Haworth, in the old graveyard. Or rather, what and who found me. Another story for another day. But the point is, Brenda, my aunts were true heroes. The way they defended this place and used their magic – those incredible powers of theirs – for good!'

I touch her arm. 'But so do you! You're here defending this place against disaster. We both do. We're doing the same job as your aunts used to do!'

She flinches at my touch. For a second my feelings are hurt. 'But I'm abandoning it all, aren't I? I'm running out on it all. For the sake of this fella of mine.'

'You can change your mind,' I gabble. 'You don't have to go if you really don't want to. Just tell him. Stand up to him!'

'The decision is already taken,' she says softly. And I think I know, without asking, what she means. She feels too caught up in Alucard's plans already. She can't turn back now. Oh, Effie . . . how far have you gone? I wonder, and I hold my breath.

'There is so much here,' I tell her at last. 'So much you'll be leaving behind. Your aunts and your house. All your stuff. Your antiques. Your books. Your heritage. Your friends.'

'I know. I know what I'll be giving up.' She takes a deep, shuddering breath. 'And something else, Brenda. Something even you don't know about just yet.'

I blink. It's starting to snow again. The wind is picking up around us. It's time to turn back and walk down into the town again. But I want to know, I've got to know what she's on about. 'I don't understand. What . . . ?'

'I've had a shock recently. A big revelation.'

'Oh yes?'

'In a way, it's yet another reason to stick around. To stay here. It's . . .'

She looks on the verge of tears. 'Tell me, Effie!' She's in pain. She's struggling with something she's kept locked inside.

'I've got a living relative here in Whitby,' she says at last. 'Someone I never even knew about. A very close relation.'

'What?'

'I know. It's a shocker. I've always believed myself to be quite alone. But . . . that's not the case.'

I wait for her to go on. But she doesn't.

'Will you tell me?'

'Not now. Not yet. I . . . I'm still learning to deal with the knowledge myself.'

I didn't get any more sense out of Effie, I'm afraid. But then, my mind's been on other things since then. Not just Christmas plans. I've had Robert popping in, still full of talk about the Limbosine, and how there's been a sighting of that long, luxurious vehicle cruising about the Western Cliff. It was parked outside the Christmas Hotel, so the gossip has it – and that's enough for me to link the enigma with my old enemy, Mrs Claus. Robert's not so sure.

Also, Penny has been round, checking up on whether I've finished reading the book club book and to see what I made of the Qab papers she gave me. 'I've been doing a bit more research,' she tells me. 'Digging around.'

'Oh yes?' I'm up to my elbows in flour.

I get the feeling that she's becoming just a bit carried away, is Penny. For now, I brush her concerns away.

Wednesday brings Henry Cleavis back into my life.

A couple of years have gone by and he hasn't changed much. There's more white in his beard, making him look a little like Santa Claus in his red velvet jacket. He's portlier than when he was last here, I think. He's moon-faced and his eyes have a keenness that can be disconcerting. To me, he's the very image of a college professor, all bluster and smelling of musty paper and stale tobacco.

He comes striding towards me with his battered old suitcases, down the railway platform. He grasps me up in this huge bear hug and I just about topple over. Silly old fool. I have to say, though, my heart melts at the way he greets me.

'How could I stay away so long? How long's it been? I was such a fool, to go running out last time, without a by-your-leave!' He fires all of these questions and statements at me as I help him with his atrociously heavy baggage.

I won't let him waste money on a taxi. It's just a short, swift uphill yomp to my guest house. The exercise won't kill us. We gabble away to each other in short breathy gasps as we struggle on the snow-encrusted pavement.

'And Effie, she's well, is she?'

'Oh, better than ever,' I pant, deliberately evasive.

'And young Robert? Still helping you to fight the good fight?'

'Indeed.' Then I remember. 'Oh! He says we're both invited to a Christmas shindig he's holding tomorrow night at the Hotel Miramar . . .'

I watch Henry's face darken, and it isn't just through exertion. 'That dreadful place. We almost came a cropper in that hotel, didn't we?' I can see he's remembering our deadly battle in the beer garden of Sheila Manchu.

But all that's over now. We expelled the spirit of Goomba the Bamboo God for ever. There's nothing to fear at the Miramar these days. 'Besides,' I add, 'since he took over the place, Robert's developed a knack for throwing fantastic parties. We should have a good evening.'

'You've got it all planned out then?' Henry grins at me rakishly. 'We've got a packed Christmas programme, have we?'

I shrug nonchalantly. 'Oh, there's a few things I've got lined up. But I thought we'd take it easy and see how things pan out. It's good not to be too tied down . . .'

He nods. 'Oh yes. One never knows, does one? What kind of thing might take one by surprise.'

He's talking about adventures, of course. I know he is. He looks at me sideways, almost slyly, as we round the bend into mine and Effie's street. There's a hopeful gleam in his clever old eyes. 'There's strange business going on again, isn't there?'

'Hmm?' I notice Leena peering out of her shop front window between the posted notices, all agog at the sight of me and my gentleman friend. I ignore her and gaze at the Christmas lights criss-crossing our street. It looks a proper picture.

'I say,' adds Henry, 'I can sense it in the air. There are weird things a-stirring here in Whitby, this festive season . . .'

'Oh yes.' I smile, fumbling for my keys. 'Of course there are! Your instincts are impeccable, as ever, lovey!'

He seems very pleased indeed with the Red Room. And so he should be, after all my efforts to get it just right. I've even put extra thought into the contents of the dinky bookcase beside his bed, should my guest wake in the night and require suitable reading matter. I've bunged in a few monster guide books from the olden days and a tawdry pulp novel or two, all filched from Effie's bargain bin. They should keep the old Satanist-hunter happily diverted.

'This is grand, Brenda.' He gazes round, at the velvet swags and polished mirrors. 'I'm not used to grandeur like this. My old rooms in college, they're so dusty and dilapidated. You really wouldn't believe how shabby a life I live.'

'It'll be a pleasure keeping you in comfort,' I tell him. Then we pause and look each other up and down. We're caught in an awkward stillness and moment of quiet.

We both look like we're going to say something. Just burst out with it. I've no idea what he wants to say to me. I want to ask him why he ran out on me last time. I want to ask him . . . Oh, it's not worth it now. I steel myself and issue a stiff warning: don't go galumphing in. Don't ruin this friendship. It's only a matter of weeks since Frank left. You're still bruised and confused, Brenda.

Henry turns and starts opening his suitcases.

'I'll pop upstairs and make us some tea,' I tell him gently. 'I'll leave you to get settled.' He'll want some peace for a bit. He's had a long journey north, I realise. He's an old gent. He'll need to catch his breath.

'Oh, yes! Good! Thank you!' He nods, struggling with the buckles and straps of his largest case. 'I'll come up to your attic, shall I? I can tell you about some of the horrifying adventures I've been caught up in, this past couple of years. And you can bring me up to date with yours, too, dear.'

'Ah,' I sigh. 'Not a great deal's been happening here. Not compared, I'm sure, with the excitements in your life.' And whatever has managed to turn his facial hair snow white, I muse.

Then I see what he's unpacking from that case of his. Hefty wooden stakes, sharpened to vicious points. They clunk hollowly against each other like cricket stumps as he bundles them into the new wardrobe. He's got a tartan flask filled, no doubt, with chilled holy water. There's a reek of garlic, a glint of multiple crucifixes.

I cough sharply. 'Is that why you're here?'

'I'm here to see you, Brenda. To spend Christmas with you.'

'And the rest,' I tut. 'You've heard on the grapevine, haven't you? Word has filtered down to you, about what's going on here.'

'Has it?' he says, stepping closer. 'Word about what?'

'That we've got an infestation here. A new one. Recent, the police are starting to find bodies, sucked dry. Then some of them are getting up and walking away. We've got *Walkers*. And I don't mean countryside ramblers, either. I mean fanged cadavers tramping and swooping about and biting folk.'

He nods grimly. 'I have heard something of the sort. What are you doing about it?'

'I . . . I . . .' I'm flummoxed by his abrupt question. Truth is, I haven't done much at all. I've left the vamps to flourish, haven't I? Henry's accusing stare transfixes me for a moment.

'I heard something else, as well,' he says. 'That an old friend of ours was back in town.'

'Oh,' I say. 'Who would that be?'

Henry Cleavis shakes his head at me. He's disappointed. 'Don't play games, Brenda.'

As I lumber away into the hall, leaving him to freshen up,

hastening to make some tea, I'm wondering once again: why would I protect Alucard? Why shouldn't I just tell Cleavis that his old adversary resides next door? There he is: he's sleeping with my best friend again. What stays my hand? What shuts me up?

Effie, of course. Concern for Effie, that daft old bat.

Poor Henry has to fend for himself during his first night under my roof because it's book club. Penny comes by to pick me up, since I'm nervous about my first visit. I'm laying out the breakfast things in the large dining room when she knocks.

She's back in full Goth mode: black lipstick, weird hair extensions, the lot. She's very interested in getting a look at Henry. I haven't told her much about him, but she goes quiet as he bustles about the place, quite at home already. I ask him if he'll be all right and he says he's quite happy catching up with some reading.

Ploughing uphill through town in the snow, Penny is wearing a troubled look. 'So, is he related to Henry Cleavis, the writer?'

'Hmm?' It's almost seven o'clock and the shops are still open. Christmas music comes tinkling out of every doorway. Each window is trimmed and lit warmly. Not for the first time I suppress a shiver: it's as if the influence of Mrs Claus has spread all over town.

'Henry Cleavis, the children's writer from the forties. Was that his dad?'

Ah, now I've got to present Penny with one of those impossible facts that she pretends to take in her stride. 'Erm, it's the same man, Penny love. Henry took a nip of some kind of potion in a lost city in Africa, some time in the fifties. I think that was the story. Or he bathed in the flame of eternal youth. I forget the details now, anyway. But the upshot was – well, he's the same now as when I knew him back then.'

'Oh!'

'Shocked?'

She shakes her head quickly. 'So it's him! The man who wrote those books . . .'

'He hasn't written for years. He's been too busy hunting for monsters.'

Penny gasps suddenly. 'I wonder if he knew Beatrice Mapp, then? If he was around all that time ago?'

The thought hadn't struck me. Sometimes Penny is rather good and useful at drawing out the connections between things. I'm afraid I tend to focus on things that are right in front of me.

Anyway, at this point there's no more time for talk of Henry. (Poor Henry! No sooner has he arrived than I'm pushing him out of my thoughts!) For we have arrived on Silver Street, which is looking very olde worlde and quaint under its freight of snow. And next thing, we are outside The

Spooky Finger, ringing the bell to be allowed access to the shop, which has shut early especially for book group. I take a deep breath. Something inside is sending shooting stars of alarm right through me.

'Yoo hoo! Hang on! Brenda, wait!'

I turn, shocked, to see Effie trudging heavily towards us. She's got her trainers on and she's evidently been hurrying after us all the way here. When she catches up, she's breathless with laughter, but not really tired. Her eyes are shining. 'I thought I'd join you! I haven't finished the book, though. Will that matter, Penny?'

'Of course not.' Penny smiles, seemingly glad to add another recruit to her list. Hmmm. Recruit. I mull over what I've read about the cult of Qab.

I ask Effie where on earth she found her own copy of the book.

'I told you, my aunts were big fans of the occult and fantastic mysteries. They've quite a collection, tucked away inside their roomful of arcane texts.' Now she's looking with great interest at the interior of The Spooky Finger as we are ushered in by Marjorie Staynes's single employee. It's that creepy boy with the very pale, almost translucent skin. He looks a bit greenish, but that must be the lighting in this shop. I dread to think that he might be a Walker. I study him briefly. His eyes are rimmed with pink and his pale hair is flattened to his skull. But I can't get a good look at his teeth.

I remember the touch of his skin, and how chilly it was.

Inside, it is warm and fragrant with incense. There's all that noise of chuckling water, and the distant hooting of birds. There is also a gentle susurration of female gossip, deep within the stacks and shelves.

In the centre of the shop there are twelve seats laid out in a ring. Marjorie is clearly holding court, sitting with a folder on her lap and a pile of books by her feet. Her pouchy old face creases in a welcoming smile as we are shown to the last remaining empty chairs by the boy, whom she calls Gila.

Effie is looking about with great interest. I have to admit, she looks wonderful, does Effie. I don't know if she's doing right or wrong, but she's looking good on it.

As we sit, the other book group members are watching our every move. I feel like I'm auditioning to be a member. I wouldn't care, but I was never that keen on coming here in the first place. It was Penny pushing me. I nod at Leena, who is keen to acknowledge me. I recognise a few other faces from seeing them out and about in town, down the shops, or at the Christmas Hotel. Only a couple are completely unknown to me. All of us are ladies of a certain age, bar Penny.

After introductions are made, we begin. Marjorie Staynes talks in this sugary, too-nice way. She's all gushing sincerity and you can see she's fake as anything. She bangs on about the importance of new blood in her group, and how she's delighted that the club is going from strength to strength.

Penny and Effie are alert throughout the entire meeting. I find it all pretty dull, I have to admit. I drift off, making calculations and memos in my head as the floor is thrown open for anyone to pitch in with their thoughts on Qab. I'm too busy going over my menus and shopping lists and then – I'm not ashamed to admit it – dwelling on Henry Cleavis. I imagine him settling into my sumptuous Red Room. I wonder what he's doing right now . . .

And that's when – of course – I realise that everyone in the book group is looking at me.

'Your thoughts, Brenda?' Marjorie Staynes simpers. I glare at her and realise for the first time that she's wearing a mohair jumper with a horse's head appliquéd on the front. No, it's a unicorn. She's looking at me like a crazy woman and I have no idea what she wants from me. I believe I gawp in response.

'What did you make of this first book of Qab by Beatrice Mapp? Were you as intrigued as everyone else here? Were you hooked?'

I shake my head. 'Not at all. I thought it was horrible, to be honest. Not my kind of thing at all.'

Marjorie looks at me pityingly. 'Oh dear. I'm sorry that your first week in the club has been blighted.'

I shrug. 'I mean, it was interesting and all. And I was fascinated by this lady, this grand Bloomsbury lady, and how she came to write about such strange things . . .' I realise I'm trying to make up for lack of enthusiasm. Typical me. I hate disappointing people. 'In fact, I'd rather have read about Beatrice Mapp, and found out more about what made her tick.'

There is a general muttering of agreement from the rest of the club. Effie asks if there was ever a biography or many articles about the old lady.

Marjorie swiftly shakes her head. 'She was very mysterious. I doubt we will ever know what put Qab into her mind. No one was ever close enough to Beatrice Mapp to know much about her.'

Even as Marjorie says this in her sugary tones, looking at each of her club members in turn, I know that she is completely wrong. I don't know how I know it, but I just do.

I'm going to have to dig deeper. And Henry is the man to help me.

'You were very quiet towards the end, Penny,' I say.

We're walking home, the crusty snow crumbling like the hardest meringue beneath our feet. The moon is bright on us as we amble along.

Effie is quiet, musing about Qab, she says. I expected her to be a bit more sarcastic about the whole do, really.

'You know when I went to the loo?' says Penny suddenly. 'You were all busy yakking away, trying to untangle the plot of the book. Well, I nipped into the customers' loo on the first-floor landing. There are lots of old prints and paintings in there and it was quite interesting, I spent some time looking at them all. Anyway, while I was . . . using the facilities, I put my bag and my book on this little shelf at the side.'

'You haven't got your bag!' Effie points out.

'Exactly. I'm telling you what happened.'

'Oh, it was such a pretty, beaded jet thing, wasn't it?' I ask.

'So I was sitting there, minding my business. I can still hear all your raised voices in the main shop. And I'm staring at this painting above the shelf where I've put my stuff. It's not a very good watercolour. Mountains and a lake. Looks like the Lake District to me. Quite nice, though, and as I'm looking at it, the colours are seeming that bit more vivid. The lake itself even seems to ripple in the sun . . .'

Effie gasps. 'The painting was coming to life!'

Penny nods grimly. 'Of course, I leap up to examine the thing.'

'Good girl.'

'And it's only a five-by-eight print in a cheap frame. But there is something weird about it. I try to touch the glass . . . but it isn't glass. It's something soft and sticky . . . like cooling toffee. When I press my fingertips to the painting, the glass yields to them. My fingers start sliding into the picture. I can feel this awful sucking on them, as if it's drawing me in . . .'

'Good heavens!' goes Effie.

'So what did you do?' I ask.

'I yanked my hand back, quick as I could. I knew it was

nothing good, whatever was going on. But I pulled back too violently. I knocked my stuff off the shelf. My little black clutch bag and my novel went flying the other way. Right *into* the picture. Into the watercolour lake itself, with a little *plop*. I cried out and the picture gave a little . . . shudder kind of thing. And then it was back to normal.'

'Well!' I gasp. 'What an experience! No wonder you were a bit subdued when you came back through.'

We walk on a bit more quietly, downhill, till it comes to the corner where Penny has to peel off in order to return to the Miramar.

'What was it, though?' she says urgently. 'What could it be?'

Effie and I exchange a glance. 'Don't worry. We'll find out.'

'I wish I hadn't lost my book,' she says glumly, and so before she goes off, I give her mine.

Effie and I walk in silence back to our street. Before she nips into her house, Effie says, 'I wonder if it was what I'm thinking, hmm?' But she doesn't tell me what that is. Old bat's gone inscrutable again.

When I get home, I find that Henry's hanging about, wanting a word. He looks proper settled in now, and I'm glad. He's the picture of rumpled suavity in his dressing gown and frayed silk ascot. I lead him up to my attic sitting room and out comes the cream sherry.

He sits in the bobbly armchair and scratches his beard, and I can see he's perturbed about something.

'Your friend Robert called by this evening.'

'But he knew I was at Penny's book group!'

Henry shakes his head. 'Came to see me, as it happens. Brought me a bottle of whisky. Very kind of him. Welcoming me back to Whitby and all that.'

'He's very thoughtful.' Of course, I'd forgotten. Henry and Robert met and went through rather a lot together during that terrible affair to do with Goomba the bamboo creature at the Hotel Miramar.

'Told me something a mite disturbing, though, did Robert,' adds Henry Cleavis gruffly.

'Oh yes?'

'I don't know if it just slipped out, or whether he was meaning to warn me, or to fill me in on what had been going on while I was away. Anyhow. Out it came.'

'What?' The sherry glass is suspended halfway to my mouth as I perch on the end of my paisley two-seater settee. I know what he's going to say.

'Why didn't you tell me yourself, Brenda?'

'Tell you what?'

'That you were married.'

Ah.

'This Frank person. Robert told me all about how he turned up out of the blue. You knew him years ago, didn't you? And he came after you, out of the past, and dogged your heels, causing an almighty fuss until he won you over.'

I sigh deeply. Henry doesn't know the half of it. Or does he? Maybe he's feigning this innocence now. Last time we met, he knew bits of my past that I'd forgotten. I wonder what he really knows about Frank. Perhaps he's testing me out. But how can Henry ever really understand about Frank and me, and about what Frank did?

Frank did more than dog my heels. I was just about blackmailed into getting married to him. It's far too complicated and shaming a story to go into right now. And anyway, who does Henry Cleavis think he is, demanding explanations from me like this? I feel myself flush with anger and I swallow down my sherry in one go.

Then I tell him: 'I thought I felt something for him again. I did. I mean, the wedding – that was a mistake. A horrible . . . blackmail kind of situation. We were in hell at the time. No, I mean it, literally, in hell. And the only way I could save my friends was by getting wed to this . . . terrible man-monster who'd been after me for donkey's years.'

'Oh, Brenda!' Henry's face is tender with concern. I can hardly look at him. Who's he to look so bothered now? Where was he when I most needed his help? 'So where is he now, this brute? Left you in the lurch, did he?'

I shake my head sadly. 'It wasn't like that. Poor Frank. We went through so much together. And we even found that we really got on, in the end. We complemented each other. Pretty soon I was even glad that he had found me again. We made a go of it . . . for about a year.'

'A year!' Henry Cleavis cries out. He looks like someone who can't imagine spending a whole year with another person so intimately woven into his life. He's an old perpetual bachelor. That's what Henry Cleavis is.

'And then he was taken from me. Suddenly. Just a couple of months ago.'

'Taken? He was . . . killed?'

'As good as.'

'Oh, Brenda. I'm sorry. No wonder you were quiet about it all. No wonder you never mentioned it.'

I shrug. Pour us some more sherry.

'How did . . . how did it happen?'

'I don't want to talk about it now, thanks. Just rest assured that Frank's out of the way.'

Henry's nose twitches at the mention of my husband's name. Like it always does when the subject of monsters comes up. He can't help himself. He's a monster-slaying machine. It's been his job for almost a hundred years. He can't be all that cut up about my Frank's demise. If Frank was still about, Henry would be the one trying to kill him, I suppose. And not out of love for me – oh no. Just because that's what Henry is most passionate about. He has devoted his long life to the killing of the creatures of the night.

And if Frank was anything, he was certainly that.

'I'll leave you now,' Henry says tactfully. 'Bit worn out after all my travels, to be honest.'

I show him to the door. He pauses on the top landing before going to his Red Room. 'How was your literary evening?'

'It was hardly that. Bunch of old women gossiping and talking about Beatrice Mapp.'

I'm not sure if I imagine it, but a dark cloud passes over his face at the mention of the Edwardian lady novelist's name.

'However, we did find something in the shop. Something weird . . .'

'Oh yes?'

But I tease him. I won't tell him yet about what Penny found in the lav at The Spooky Finger.

Thursday.

Tonight it's been Robert's shindig at the Hotel Miramar. I could sense that Henry was tense the whole time, owing to the fact that the last time he was there, he was fighting for his life. But there was nothing like that tonight.

It was a rather boozy evening. Everyone was there, though I found myself having to explain to Henry what had become of Sheila Manchu, the proprietress of the Hotel Miramar, whom he knew, and who came a cropper on one of our adventures.

'You've faced more mystery and danger than even I have in recent years,' Henry tells me. He's having to shout a bit because we're at a booth near the dance floor. I shush him quickly and laugh him off.

I notice Effie's up on the floor, sprightlier than ever in a vintage frock trimmed with feathers. Her arms are bare and they look plumper and firmer than usual as she waggles her hands about. No bingo wings on Effie tonight.

Only I know why. I just hope Henry doesn't clock her apparent rejuvenation. If I were her, I'd try drawing less attention to it.

Something makes me feel nervous tonight, so I'm hitting the sweet sherry rather harder than is sensible for a woman with my responsibilities. But there is a tension in the Yellow Peril, this gaudy niterie beneath the Miramar, and I don't know where it's coming from.

There are glances passing between clientele. There's a whisper of menace in the air. A palpable threat hanging in the dry ice itself. I catch glimpses of faces contorted in savage, predatory expressions as the strobe lights flicker. Even though everyone's in party hats and Slade and Wizzard are playing their usual festive hits, I note the dead black eyes and rictus grins of the enemy. The enemy within . . .

Or maybe the sherry is just making me bibulous and paranoid?

Except . . . when Henry gets me up to dance, holding

91

me close during Elvis's 'Blue Christmas', I can feel the shape of his biggest crucifix beneath the bristly tweed of his jacket.

He sees my look of alarm and leans in. 'They're all around us, Brenda. There's more than I thought. We've got our work cut out.'

I give him a sickly smile. I don't want to spend all of Christmas on a stake-out, thank you very much.

Then he surprises me by saying out of the blue: 'Why didn't you tell me?'

Help! I think. What am I guilty of not telling him about now? I feel itchy and cross, clutching this scratchy old man to my bosom. What right does he have to go cross-questioning me on the dance floor? 'What about? Are you on about my Frank again?'

Henry shakes his head tersely. 'Not this time, no. I'm on about Effie and her fancy fella. You never said.'

'Oh. Ah.'

'Exactly. Didn't you think maybe I'd be interested? Given that I'm here with all my slaying paraphernalia? To know that she's got the Prince of the Undead staying with her? Shacked up with her?'

'Who told you?' I say. Sounding shifty, I know. Like I've been protecting that bloody old cadaver.

'Robert let something slip when he was round last night. About Alucard living next door to you. For about as long as the vampire infestation has been going on. Funny, that, isn't it?'

I roll my eyes. 'Robert was a proper blabbermouth last night, wasn't he?'

Henry Cleavis stares up at me and frowns. The disco lights gleam on his shining pate and suddenly I feel like slapping him for being so earnest. He says, 'I'm glad he was a blabbermouth. Obviously, you don't see fit to keep me informed about what's going on.'

'See fit to keep you informed . . . !'

'You know what I am. You know what my duties are. There are certain things I need to know about. And I can see that I am going to have to take, erm, appropriate action.'

Right. I've had it with him. That's quite enough. I put him down at once, yelling: 'You can stuff it, you arrogant old sod.' I don't care if it's the sherry talking. 'I don't have to tell you absolutely everything, do I?'

'Brenda, wait!'

'What did you think I was going to do? Drop my best friend right in it? All right, so she's shacked up with Alucard. Prince of the Bloody Undead. All right? So now you know. Happy now?'

I stomp away, seething. I catch Effie's eye as I stalk across the corner of the lit-up dance floor, and she looks alarmed at my obviously furious demeanour.

In the ladies' lavs I splash some water on my face, careful

not to ruin my make-up. I touch it up delicately and sigh as I stare into my own face. Why did I lose my temper so badly? When usually it takes so long to wind me up.

Henry was just doing his job. Quizzing and cross-questioning and getting to the heart of the mystery. Ooh, but he made me mad. Criticising me! Like he has the right!

Outside the lavs there's a dark, calm little vestibule, featuring a console table with a spray of lilies, a rather lovely watercolour of Sheila Manchu in her prime, and a comfy chair. I'm sitting there, catching my breath back and steeling myself to apologise to Henry, when I notice Robert flitting about.

I'm about to yell out and give him a piece of my mind about blabbing all my news and sensitive information to Henry. But then I see that Robert has got company. He's holding some other fella by the hand. He's drawing him into a dimly lit corner round the back of the bar.

Now I'm trapped here, and it's as if I'm spying on them. I give a discreet cough, to let them know I'm here, but it's too late now. They carry on as if they're alone, these two smitten lads. They're having a bit of a kiss and a cuddle in a corner where they think no one will see.

Robert's really going for it with this young man. You'd think he'd not been near a fella in months.

If one of them looked up right now, they'd see me sitting here with my handbag on my lap and all my mascara repair work melting and my wig in tatters, like some peeping-tom madwoman golem.

I try to look away. But then realise that I can't. I am transfixed by the sight of these two kissing boys. And why?

Because Robert's companion has a curious look about him. His flesh seems strangely pale, almost greenish in this weird nightclub lighting. And I recognise this young man who's suddenly so fond of Robert.

It's the boy from The Spooky Finger. Gila. The assistant of Marjorie Staynes. And Robert's hands are all over him.

Oh dear. Robert. You and me and Effie as well.

We all get into things a bit too deep. Especially with the wrong type of fellas. Isn't that the truth?

I don't find it too hard to forgive Henry for his probing and his crossness. It is Christmas, after all. And he in turn forgives me for my outburst on the dance floor at the Miramar. When we walk woozily home that night through the streets of Whitby, we talk it over.

'No wonder you're touchy,' he says. 'After all you've been through while I've been away.'

I nod and smile. I try to put out of my mind the fact that I saw Robert snogging that strange boy. Or that my best friend Effie's throwing herself away on a fiendish bloodsucker. Right now I want to be enjoying the season and the company of this wonderful man.

I do think he's a wonderful man, after all. I thought perhaps I'd exaggerated his charms during his absence. Perhaps I had romanticised him. But you know what? Henry Cleavis makes me feel safe. It's a long time since any man's managed to do that for me. We link arms as we cross town and descend the sharp sloping streets. He's a fair bit shorter than me, which makes linking tricky, but the thought is there.

'So,' he says, 'what are we going to do this Christmas? Who are we going to see? What are we going to eat and drink?'

I laugh at his eagerness and start to unveil my plans. Nothing very spectacular: a goose and a ham and some old movies and silly hats. I don't want much excitement. Just restfulness and fun. As for who we shall see, there'll be the usual round of friends that I've made these past couple of years in Whitby.

'And Effie?' he says. 'Do you think she'll join us?'

'Who knows?' I shrug. 'Hard to tell with that one these days. But I hope she will.'

'And Alucard,' he says, in a low voice. 'I wonder if we'll see him at all . . .'

'I shouldn't think so,' I muse. 'I don't think he makes much of Christmas, as a rule.'

Henry looks at me with a sudden gleam in his eye. 'We should invite them. Round yours, perhaps . . . or out for dinner, maybe? What do you think, Brenda? I hate to think of you and Effie having this distance between you. It isn't right.'

I'm surprised to hear his suggestion. I'm pleased, too. 'It's a nice idea . . .'

'Just because her fella is who he is doesn't mean that there has to be any tension round the table. People shouldn't tiptoe round and avoid seeing each other, just because she's hooked up with a . . . erm, you know . . . a dodgy undead manfriend.'

I nod firmly. 'You're right! You're quite right, Henry.'

'So we should organise that. A little dinner. A foursome.'

'Yes, you're right. Let's do that.'

Now we're at the top of our street. There's a pale glow from the snow, almost lilac under that winter sky. The shadows are velvety, like dark chocolate. Christmas is coming now, and I've got someone here beside me to make my plans with. Lovely plans.

It's such a relief – for once – not to be on my own.

Effie's Christmas

23 December

Dear Kristoff,

I've never written a letter to you before. Not one I've sent. I've got a heap of them from your last absence. I put them away in a box somewhere. I'd never show you them. When you're here, there's always so much going on. We barely stop to draw breath, do we? Such excitement. What larks.

My life was so stultifyingly dull. It was in a rut. I was going nowhere. But with you by my side it's different. You make me feel like I could go anywhere, do anything.

I've seen my so-called friends giving me sideways glances. They've been eyeing me up and down. Suspicion on their faces. Bemusement. Puzzlement. Perplexity. What's going on with her? How can she look so good? She's over seventy and yet she's glowing. Her skin's so pink, so fresh. Her wrinkles have dropped off her. It's like someone's plumped her up. Got her circulation going once more.

It's all down to you, my dear. I've not felt as good as this in decades. I feel fizzy and light like Prosecco. Zesty as a tarte au citron.

And somehow now the rest of my life seems ill-fitting and strange to me. The petty concerns that used to weigh so heavily. The trifling miseries that beset me so. My friends and the way they chunter on. My erstwhile friends. They irritate me now, truth be told. Brenda won't shut up. She goes on and on even though she must see me rolling my eyes and looking impatient.

'Effie's not in the Christmas mood,' Robert said the other day, trying to be funny. Who does he think he is? Little upstart. Who's he to judge? What's he got to do with anything?

He's muscling in on Brenda's investigations. He's far too keen on helping out. We must watch him, my dear. He's been helping Brenda find the bodies. It was he who discovered one of your Walkers. That little nancy boy was straight down the cop shop. We should have put him out of the way before now.

Ah, but you don't care any more, do you, my love? You're way past caring. See? How talking to you, I forget? It slips my mind, what they've done.

And I remind myself and am overwhelmed with bitterness once again.

Look what they have done to us, my dear. Those finks and nancies and that dreadful woman's boyfriend. They have torn us apart again. We have no one on our side. No one cares about us. They don't believe in our love. Won't credit it. They would never leave us alone. We weren't destined for a peaceful life.

As soon as Henry Cleavis appeared in town, I knew our cosy life was ruined. The likes of him, he'd never believe us. We could protest that we were doing nothing wrong. We could tell him that the Walkers come to us and not the other way around. We could tell him that no one got bitten who didn't ask for it. But the likes of him never listen. Not him with his Van Helsing fixation and his bag of chilling toys.

Brenda, the foolish woman. She allowed that killer into her house. She can't see through Cleavis and how he uses her. He thinks nothing of her. She's just another monster to him. He'd slay her in a flash if he thought she'd lost her usefulness to him. As it is, she's a magnet. She's like a portal through which the monsters are delivered to him. And she can't see it. All she sees is that there's a fella bothering about her. Smarming round her. Taking her out in the evening to the Miramar or that

Christmas do in Mrs Claus's ballroom.

But I don't know why I'm thinking about Brenda. Forget her. I want nothing more to do with the woman. She's burnt her boats now. There's no going back. Silly old cow. How could she think I'd ever forgive her? What was she thinking of? To trick me like that. Her friend. Her partner in crime. We've been through so much.

Was she really so envious of my happiness? Is that it? And so, when Cleavis suggested the idea – the wicked idea – Brenda leapt at the chance. Yes, oh yes. Let's do it, Henry. That's a marvellous plan. And Effie will thank us in the end, won't she? She'll see the sense in it. She needs saving from herself, she does.

Ach. I can see the giant, cretinous woman nodding and grinning as Cleavis outlined his horrible plan. Oh yes. How clever. Two birds with one stone. No more Walkers. No more fuss for Effie. Effie can go back to being a quiet old spinster. No more fun for Effie. No more love in her life. Love only disrupts. Shakes up the old order. Let's put her back in her place. Let's pretend we're doing this for the good of everyone, Henry Cleavis.

So they were drawing up their plans against us, my dear. Scheming against us. Smiling and scheming at the same time.

I call myself an intelligent woman. I'm a fool. I

should have known they were up to something when they started talking to me at the Christmas Hotel that night. My mind was elsewhere. I'd been to see Angela Claus for a long talk in her boudoir. My thoughts were buzzing elsewhere. Brenda and Cleavis barrelled into me when I returned to the dance floor. What about dinner? What about a posh dinner out the next night? Casa Diodati's the fanciest place in town. What about making up a foursome and going there, eh?

A foursome? They meant you, my love. I nodded. Like I say, I was distracted. And they looked so pleased. Brenda – damn her, now I think about it – she took me aside in the ballroom and told me how much she feared we were drifting apart. How pleased she was that we'd be having dinner together like this. With our fellas. Our men friends.

'The old gang seems to be breaking up,' she said sadly. Well, I can't stick sentimentality. And it's hardly an old gang, is it? She was getting all soppy about our plans for leaving Whitby, my love. I had made a mistake in letting her see me wobble, a few nights previously. I had expressed a few doubts I was having about leaving this town. But I was wrong in my thinking, and I was wrong to voice my fears to Brenda. She had taken them much too seriously, those silly things I had said. Now she wanted me to think she was concerned about me.

But she was just thinking of herself. She was selfishly sorry and furious about our coming trip to the continent. Well, she'd certainly seen a clear way to putting paid to that, hadn't she? Scheming old besom that she is.

She meant Robert, too. He'd slipped out of her controlling grasp. Just then he was off with his new boyfriend. The lizardy-looking boy from The Spooky Finger. There's something strange about that lad from the shop. I can't quite place it. But Robert was certainly carried away with him and it quite turned my stomach, to be blunt.

And they dare to dub *your* vices unnatural, my dear!

All the while at the Christmas do, I was aware of the shrewd eyes of Cleavis on me. During the hokey-cokey, when he grabbed my left arm and Brenda my right, and we put our right legs in, and our right legs out, etc., etc. He was pinching my firm flesh between his fingers. He was examining the amazing freshness of my complexion. He knew I had been rejuvenated. I have been enlivened by the blood of the young. Of course I have. It's plain to see.

As I felt his pinprick eyes upon me, I was glad that our escape route was clear. Our plans were made. We'd be away from this town quite soon.

But that wasn't to be, was it, my love?

24 December

Dear Kristoff,

Now they all want to do Christmas together. Well, they can go to hell. I've got no interest. How can I sit round with that lot, in party hats, pretending like nothing has happened?

Brenda's a big fat hypocrite anyway. She doesn't believe in God or anything to do with it. What did she say when we first met? 'Your god and my god aren't the same thing, Effie.' That sanctimonious tone of hers. Going on all mysterious. And it turns out she doesn't have a soul, and well, we all know why, don't we?

So, no thanks. They can shove what invites they want through my front door, but I won't be joining them at the Miramar or round Brenda's to take part in the festivities. How can I? Why would I? How can they think I'd ever talk to any of them again?

After what they have done.

I'm a lonely old woman. It's like Mrs Claus said to me, just today. I went over to the Christmas Hotel again this afternoon. Pulled my snood right up around my face and the fur collar of my coat, just in case anyone clapped eyes on me. I was taking her a little present round. Nothing much. Small brooch, a pewter frog, wrapped in tissue paper. I thought it was unusual, that she'd like it. And she did. She seemed surprised and touched that I was there, in her private sitting room, giving her a gift. She even started blubbing.

Anyway, when I told her a little of what had been going on, she couldn't believe it. Her eyes flashed. She came over all defensive towards me.

'I'll never get over this,' I told her, and I realised with a shock she's the first person I've talked about my feelings with.

'I've no wonder!' Angela Claus burst out, dewlaps quivering with sympathetic rage. 'How could they do this to you? Brenda's meant to be your friend! Your best friend!'

'Not any more,' I sighed, and downed the sweet sherry I'd been given. Angela Claus's fire was raging in the hearth. Too merrily, too hot. I wondered what I was doing there, deep in the heart of the Christmas Hotel. This woman used to be my enemy. Life has become so switched about recently. So complicated.

The huge old woman looked me in the eye and reached for one of my hands with one of her podgy claws. I recoiled only briefly before holding hands with her. It still feels so strange. I'm not sure how I really feel about this new connection between us. I question it every day . . . but I know with every fibre of my raddled being that it is true. We have a very real bond, this dreadful woman and I.

Then she said to me, 'You have every right to be bitter, Effie. Just you remember that.'

'Oh!' I gasped, because it's not the kind of thing that people say. It was like receiving permission to feel bad. Almost, to revel in it. I thanked her. Angela Claus knew just what to say to me. I sat there a bit longer in her festively trimmed parlour, as she chatted of this and that and her Christmas preparations, which were, truth be told, no different from those for the other fifty-one Christmases she puts on every year.

I sat there letting my feelings of bitterness overwhelm me. And it felt quite healthy, my love. It really did.

When I left the Christmas Hotel to stomp home through the fresh-falling snow, I felt cleansed by my bitterness. I was refreshed by my ire. My fury was scorching through my veins, making me feel light-headed. I was tripping along, sure of purpose.

I was ravenous as well, I realised.

The streets were quiet.

You taught me well. Our few short weeks hunting together. You said I learned quickly. I had a natural instinct for it. This was a skill I was destined to become expert at, you said. A fine practitioner. A huntress in the night.

Fancy that! Me!

That evening, leaving Angela Claus sitting by her fire, I took the rage and gall in my heart into the dark streets and sought out my prey.

I have a particular yen for young men. You noticed that. You were amused by my choices. Young men in their twenties. You watched me lure them with old-lady wiles into dark alleys and shady doorways. You watched me set myself up as a harmless old biddy needing help, directions, a hand with her keys. Or pretending to be an apt victim for a mugging. That was a good way of reeling them in too, as I lurked in quiet streets in the night.

Now, of course, replenished and rejuvenated as I am – and it's impossible to ignore the fact of my wonderful transformation – I can lure them in other ways. Who'd have believed it? Sexy Effryggia! I'm no dolly bird, of course, but I'm finding that for the first time in my life . . . I'm actually turning heads.

Well, that night I slaked my unnatural thirst and made no bones about it. Didn't feel guilty, didn't feel much of anything at all. It was all about expedience. Like an oven-ready meal, rather than a feast. Young fellow down by the arcades, lingering late where he oughtn't. Obviously up to no good. His blood was hot and savoury.

I'm an addict, of course. You warned me, my love, didn't you?

I felt woozy. The young man had been drinking and there was something funny in his system. Marijuana or something. He'd been having a naughty smoke. It sent me a little strange as I nipped into the Demeter for a gin and tonic with the boys before home.

Ah, the Demeter. Our merry little local. Brenda and I would steer well clear of the place, thinking it rough and not being, on the whole, very fond of real ale and folk music. But since you took me there and it became our regular haunt, I've developed a fondness for the place.

It's where the Walkers congregate and do their nightly drinking. They always seem pleased to see me, as they did you. They hold no grudges. I believe they're all pleased by their altered state. Confused at first, and wondering what it's all about, but once they've joined the gang at the Demeter, the Walkers soon learn to live with their new condition, and even to relish it.

They worship you, of course. They revere you. And whatever I say, they don't believe – they can't believe – that you are gone for good, my love.

I am the merry widow. Propping up the bar after midnight, in the roughest bar in town, with all these men around me. Paying tribute to me and admiring my new looks. I've got the hot spicy blood of a young stoner swirling about my veins and giving me a becoming glow.

In the Demeter, the boys in the back room are telling me that Brenda and her man friend – the hated Cleavis – have been in.

I don't know how they dare. After what they've done.

And the boys here. The Walkers. How could they let Brenda and Cleavis continue to live? Why didn't they exact revenge?

'He was tooled up,' Eric the barman tells me. 'Cleavis was protected. And so was his woman. Your friend. They had holy water. Crucifixes. The works. We couldn't get near them.'

Brenda with a crucifix on? I hope it burns her stinking old flesh. I hope it gives her proper gyp. She's as ungodly as any of us. 'What were they after?'

The portly barman looks me dead in the eye. 'They were asking about you, Effryggia. They wanted to know all about you.'

Oh, why can't they just leave me alone?

Christmas Bloody Day

Dear Kristoff,

I'm here by myself. I don't want to see anyone or think about Christmas or anything.

All I can think about is you, my dear. And what they did to you.

Here is what actually happened. Just a few nights ago. I'll set it down here for posterity. Just in case . . . just in case you ever return and want to know.

You will want to know what they did, those two. My so-called friends.

They thought of it as a good night's work, I know – and that's the most hurtful thing of all. They just can't see any wrong in what they did.

Why was I such a fool to accept their invite to the Casa Diodati that night? Making up a foursome. Going somewhere fancy-schmancy. Pretending that we were letting bygones be bygones.

'You haven't been yourself for weeks,' Brenda told me, as we took our places in the elegant restaurant, out of earshot of the men.

'Oh, Brenda, I have. I'm just the same as ever.' I was distracted by the view from the upper bay window, across Church Street and the harbour rooftops. The private dining room was soft with gentle candlelight – very flattering.

Brenda went, 'Hmmm,' sceptically studying my expression, which I tried to keep neutral. She said, 'This place is a bit lah-di-dah, isn't it? I never even knew it was here.'

'It's nice to go somewhere a bit different,' said I, sounding ever so stiff with her.

'I'm a creature of habit,' she said.

'I know.'

'There's nothing wrong with Cod Almighty.'

'Indeed.'

'But,' she went on, 'I think Henry wanted to take us somewhere a bit classier tonight. It's important.'

I nodded, yanking my napkin out of my glass and giving it a sharp flick.

'We aren't having a falling-out, are we, Effie?'

I was wondering where those men were. Smoking outside on the cobbled lane. What on earth would they have to talk about? Plenty, I was sure, and none of it good.

Brenda was looking at me expectantly. I sighed. 'Well, ever since Kristoff came back into my life, I think you're the one who's been a tad recalcitrant.'

'Me!' she gasped.

And then you were by our side, Kristoff, my dear. Silent and debonair. Grinning at me.

'Here I am, ladies.'

Henry Cleavis was puffing up the stairs behind him. Stumpy, unkempt little man. I'd never thought much of him. His eyes were darting about and he reeked of cigar smoke.

We took our places and I thanked Cleavis for treating us all to this smart dinner.

'What is money but for spending?' he stammered. I saw at once that he hadn't intended to pay for us all, but he couldn't very well say that now. It served him right. He went on, 'Brenda deserves treating. As do you, dear Effie.'

Brenda looked flushed. She was on her second glass of Pinot Noir. She burst out, sounding rather coarse, 'Mind, it's your Christmas box, lovey! Hahaha!'

Warily we all set about our repast. We gulped down thick tomato soup. I ordered a huge rare steak, which I ate with gusto. I could feel Brenda and Cleavis's suspicious eyes upon me the whole time. I disdained a green salad. My love, you were picking at your dinner, I noticed. Bean shoots and noodles, very unlike you.

I glugged back the red wine, I'm afraid. I was feeling nervous. Under pressure. I was wishing we had never come out. The conversation was stilted and dull. None of us were free to talk about the things we really wanted to.

It was Brenda who blurted out a question about Angela Claus at the Christmas Hotel. Hadn't I been seeing a lot of her lately? What did I think I was doing, hobnobbing with the woman who – when all was said and done – was actually one of our greatest enemies?

This, over the crème brûlée. Brenda was in her cups.

'Oh,' I said, 'Angela Claus is a poor, lonely old thing. Not half so bad as she's made out to be.'

'We had a lovely time at the pie and peas dinner dance last week.'

Everyone looked startled at you, my love, piping up just then. We all stared at you. You grinned. Those teeth of yours glinted in the candlelight.

I said, chattily, 'They had that cabaret knife-throwing and exorcism act on again. Denise and Wheatley. If we'd have thought on, we should have asked you, Brenda.'

'Hmmm.'

Dessert wines and more awkward conversation. But then, all unannounced, you became loquacious, my dear. You took my hand across the immaculate tablecloth (immaculate but for the few spatters of blood from my steak. I'm not normally a messy eater).

Then you were telling them: 'I went to hell and back for this wonderful woman. I hope you understand how much I feel for her.'

Brenda coughed in a vulgar fashion and glared at us both. 'You didn't go to hell and back, Alucard. You were *sent* down into hell. We chucked you down there, if you remember.'

Impasse. Henry Cleavis suppressed a snort of

amusement. I could have got up and cracked their heads together. Smug pair that they are.

Brenda declined cheese and biscuits and coffee. Cheese and coffee were things that would keep her up all night these days if she had them too late, she said. She'd been having terrible dreams recently.

I told her, 'You're always bad with nightmares.'

She took on a martyred air. 'I am.'

'It must be your past memories. Lurking about under the surface of your mind. Coming back in the night to plague you.'

She raised both eyebrows. I could tell she thought I was being very uncaring. But I felt a bit uncaring, to be honest. She does bang on about those nightmares of hers, and how hard it is being her. It was getting on my nerves.

'Really, you could have been or done anything, in all those past lives of yours,' I went on blithely, siding up the dishes carefully. 'You'll never really know, will you?'

Brenda bridled. 'Henry can help me recover pieces of my past. Through hypnosis and so on.'

'Oh really?'

Cleavis nodded modestly.

'Very interesting. I'm sure you'll dig out some fascinating revelations about the past lives of our Brenda.'

Brenda was looking very piqued indeed by now. Her face was all squinched up at me.

Relief, then, that it was time to finish up and go home. I'd had enough. I watched Cleavis fiddling with his wallet and his many credit cards. He was lingering, I could tell, and giving us an opportunity to leap in and offer to pay our half. No flaming way.

You, my darling Kristoff, slid elegantly up from the table and offered to fetch our outdoor things from the cloakroom.

You said to Brenda and Cleavis – rather gallantly, 'Thank you for this evening, my dears. I realise that we have an antagonistic history. But I hope you can learn to accept me and tolerate me, Brenda. I hope you don't feel prejudiced at all against the undead.'

Brenda gave you a sickly smile and nodded graciously. You turned on your elegant heel and slipped off to the cloakroom. Once you were gone, Brenda said, 'I suppose he really means that he wants to use the lavatory. What a silly ruse! Mind, I don't think about Alucard using the toilet. I don't really want to. But I suppose he must do, same as anyone else, eh, Effie?'

I looked at her beadily. She was talking nonsense.

I made a concession. I thanked them both. Said I was glad we had thawed the recent chill between us.

I was startled by the sloppy, beaming smile on

Brenda's face all of a sudden. She said, 'Ooh, Effie. It means so much to me that we're getting on again. You're so important to me. You're my best friend. I want you to be happy. And safe.'

'Excuse me,' said Cleavis, waving the bill and his credit card about, and he slipped from the room as well.

Brenda distracted me for a few moments with some inconsequential chat about Robert. About how he'd helped her put up her Christmas tree earlier that evening. And then some guff about this Limbosine business that they were apparently investigating together. Well, I had no interest in that. Let them go looking into whatever macabre nonsense they wanted. I was finished with all of that stuff.

I realise now that she was deliberately holding me back. She kept me there, standing by the bay window in the private dining room of Casa Diodati for a few moments. A few crucial moments.

I could strangle her. I really could.

I thought she looked a bit shifty and sweaty. I thought that was just all the drink.

It was as we were leaving the room and following after the men down the narrow, twisting staircase that the immortal words came ringing out:

'*Die, you fiend!*'

Brenda grabbed my arm. I thought it was shock. I

thought she was after support. But again, she was keeping me back. She was clamping hold of my wrist. Both my wrists. Preventing me from bustling past her.

I was filled with confusion. All this noise coming up from the cloakroom. Pounding and thumping . . . and Cleavis yelling out, again and again, '*Die! Die! You monstrous fiend!*'

And all of a sudden I knew what was happening.

I used all my strength to push Brenda out of the way. She shrieked as she toppled down the staircase, sliding heavily along the smooth walls, bringing down a set of sailing prints with her.

I came hurtling down just in time to see her wicked fancy man, Henry Cleavis, standing triumphantly with his bloody mallet raised above his head.

My love, you were supine at his feet. There was a sharpened stake in your chest.

But there was precious little left of you.

Cleavis gave one more inarticulate grunt and brought his hammer down a final time.

Clunk. Thud.

POUFFF.

I caught a glimpse of your grey, contorted face before you vanished in a puff of smoke and ancient dust. Your hands were grasping and scrabbling the air above you. And then you were gone.

Like a dandelion clock, my love.

I heard Brenda cry, as she heaved herself up on her hefty knees, 'You did it, Henry! You actually did it!'

She had dusty fragments of you stuck in her beehive, I noticed.

I was frozen on the spot. I couldn't even breathe. Your ashes tickled my nose and lined my throat. If I'd given vent to the screams welling up inside me, I'd have choked, I think.

Henry Cleavis swung his dusty mallet about in a very self-satisfied way. 'Hmm. Last we'll see, I should think. Of that, erm, abomination.'

I'm ashamed to say, my dear, that at this point I fainted.

They took me home. I woke up in our bed.

They left me there without you. I don't even know what happened to your remains.

Happy bloody Christmas to us.

Boxing Day

Dear Kristoff,

Brenda has gone way beyond the pale, and we are friends no more. Which is a shame, given that it was just a few days before Christmas – especially since the two of us had, as usual, made such elaborate and involved plans for the Yuletide season. But that's how things go sometimes – especially when your best friend facilitates the staking of your man friend through his heart.

I woke up the next morning with my head spinning. At first I couldn't take in what had gone on the night before.

I got ready for the day and drank a single, bitter cup of tea. Today I wouldn't open the shop downstairs. I was in mourning. I looked around my home – its many floors and rooms, all stuffed with antiques and books and gewgaws, more things than I would ever need – and it seemed like some terrible mausoleum.

Just recently it had been filled with light and laughter. You, Kristoff Alucard, had made me feel young again, and silly and loved and reckless.

27 December

Dear Kristoff,

Since you went, my aunts have wasted no time in telling me how glad they are.

They're relieved. They come clambering out of their portraits and the swags in the old curtains and their hiding places in the dark shadows of the attic. They come drifting and sweeping about the upper rooms of my home.

Aunt Maud is cock-a-hoop that you've been snatched out of my life. That grand old lady is aware that I'm upset and that I'm not going to get over this any time soon. She stands over me as I sit there despairing. When I sob and shake, she thunders and proclaims, 'You're best without a fiend like that, Effryggia.'

I won't listen. I hate listening. I'm sick of these old harpies. All my life I've had generations of these witches louring over me. Telling me what's best for me. Right now I don't want to hear any of it.

'How could you bring him in here? How could you invite him over our threshold, a creature like that? You have sullied our home. It will take many years to rid this place of the carrion stench of that man.'

My heart flares up with anger. 'And me? What about me? If he stank of carrion and blood, if he was evil, then what about me? He taught me to hunt . . . he . . . he bit me . . .'

At first Aunt Maud and the others have no reply to this. They hang their heads and stay silent. They vanish for a while, whistling back off into the ether.

'Where are you? Where have you gone? Aunts . . . !'
They are ashamed of me.

They can't even talk about the fact that I allowed

myself to be bitten by him. That I let him inculcate me, and change me for ever.

Sometimes I am frightened of what I have done. I can hardly credit it. I go to the mirror to splash cold water on my face and expect to see the same pinch-faced old lady looking back at me.

But she's not there any more. Not on the surface, at least. You can't see that acidic old hag in the sparkling green eyes or in the pink cheeks and the unlined brow. I know she's there, though. She's there, under all the blooming health and youth. Still old and haggard and bitter as hell.

Oh, dear. What have I let myself in for?

I've given myself up to evil.

I *am* evil. I have killed. Or rather, rendered undead. But that's just splitting hairs. What have I done to myself? No wonder Brenda looks at me askance. And Cleavis. He's ruthless. Does he know what I am? I belong to a race he has sworn to vanquish and stamp out. I will be next on his list for staking, no doubt about it.

And what will Brenda do then? Will she stand happily by and watch him? Will she help him? Hold the stake straight in my chest as he readies his mallet? Will she chop off my head and stuff my neck with garlic, like she was preparing a Sunday roast?

I see at once that I have to move away from here.

Even without you, my dear, taking me elsewhere and showing me the wider world, I must leave this place, my home. I must start alone elsewhere. My days here are numbered, either way.

Fine Christmas this is turning out to be.

The days inch and slither by. It's the indeterminate period before New Year, when all the days merge into one long twilight. My sense of time is going peculiar too, as an effect, probably, of my solitariness.

I go out as little as I can. I'm stewing in my own dark, despairing thoughts. I can hear the folk out on the street meeting each other and calling their greetings and asking how their Christmases have been. I venture out for a few sundry things. Supplies.

My one source of happiness comes when I lure a young man or two into an alleyway. I can't help myself.

I don't drain anyone. I give them a little nibble. These youngsters seem startled. Some enjoy it. Some of them become Walkers. I try not to kill.

When I hurry home, with my veins all lit up inside me like the town-centre Christmas tree, I start to feel a bit of remorse. Not much. I'm a survivor. I have to do what I need to, to survive.

Everything has changed so much. My senses are heightened. Ironic, that: now that I'm spending so many days in solitude, locked indoors, my appreciation of the sounds and smells of everyday life has improved a hundredfold. Now more than ever my body seethes with energy and a desire to be out and about. Smelling and tasting and being close to the throb and pulse of real life.

Sometimes I pop on a fancy turban and sunglasses and nip out in the daytime.

I slink past Brenda's B&B and hope that she doesn't notice me. I don't want to confront her. I don't trust myself. What would I say or do? What is there to say? But no. She's not bothered about looking out for me anyway. She never notices me slipping by her front door. She's taken up with her fancy man Cleavis and this idyllic Christmas she's intent on having. Days on end I reckon they've had of their Christmas idyll.

She's a fool. He simply tolerates her for as long as she can be of use to him. He'll betray her in the end. You mark my words.

Some days I head over to the Christmas Hotel. Angela Claus is upset that I am so deeply unhappy and the toll it takes on my inner life. But she marvels at my outside: my glowing skin, my lustrous hair.

'I hardly got to know you when you were normal. But now we're talking at last, and you've had *this* done to yourself.' She shakes her massive head and sheds a tear.

I can't comfort her. I don't know how. My emotions feel frozen. There's a pane of glass between me and this woman. Angela Claus looks at me and says: 'My estranged daughter's come back to me at last. But you're neither dead nor alive, are you, dearie?'

Her face empurples and she smashes her fist on the arm of her motorised bath chair. 'That Alucard! That damned Alucard! He's to blame for this! He always is! Always! Thank God he's gone now! Thank God he's gone for ever!'

This startled me. 'What. . .? What are you saying?'

'I hate him. I've always hated him. I know him of old. He was no good for you.'

I gasped. 'But. . . you were all sympathetic before!'

'For your sake,' she snapped. 'Not his. I'm glad that he was blown to smithereens.'

I wasn't best chuffed by her reaction. That visit ended quite frostily, for both of us. I was a bit tearful on the way home, as well as piqued. For comfort, it seemed, I couldn't turn to Angela Claus after all.

With my aunties and Brenda out of the question, I've found myself drifting towards that bookshop and the new friend I've made there.

Marjorie Staynes at The Spooky Finger is proving to be a good listener.

She makes coffee and we sit in her back room amid

the bonsai trees and the rare editions and I . . . I open my heart to her.

Isn't that something? Effryggia Jacobs. Opening up her heart. Letting all the canker and gall spill out. To a complete stranger.

Like I say, I'm changing. Beyond all recognition.

Marjorie Staynes knits with glittering wool and listens very carefully. She's fascinated by the tale of my life and misfortunes. She wants to hear it all.

All around us, Christmas is going on in Whitby. But we're oblivious to that.

I tell Marjorie about my awful life and luck. And she starts telling me more about Qab.

Not just the books and the book group and all of that. No. Marjorie Staynes starts to tell me about the real stuff. The real Qab.

The details that only the initiated hear about.

The chosen ones.

28 December

Dear Kristoff,

There's glitter all over my welcome mat. I haven't bothered to hoover it up. Robert and that Penny. Brenda, of course. Shoving letters and cards through my box, they were, right up until the last minute on Christmas

Eve. Begging me, beseeching me. Come and spend Christmas Day with us. Please don't stay by yourself. Come to your friends.

Friends? I've got no friends.

I've sat alone in my home, reading further books by Beatrice Mapp. I bought them from The Spooky Finger, under Marjorie's direction. I looked for the secret clues and the codes that underlie all the silly action adventure business.

Yes, yes . . . there's more to these books than anyone knew . . . there's a pattern here . . .

I hunted through the untidy shelves and overflowing boxes of paperbacks in my attics and spare rooms. Lots of stuff here I've never even seen. For years I've thought about having a good sort-out and getting rid of some of this junk. Something has always stayed my hand when it comes to the books. Perhaps the revenants of my aunts themselves.

It has snowed and snowed and snowed. Coddling us coldly in our tall, ancient houses.

I've been reading until my eyeballs ached and I can think about nothing but the sweltering jungles of Qab. The shining palaces and the underground fortresses. The world of Qab became more solid to me than my own four walls.

I've been eating hardly anything. My cupboards are

bare. I slide out now and then under cover of night and slake my avid thirst. I went for a lock-in at the Demeter a couple of times, where the old boys and the newly formed Walkers still gaze at me in admiration.

I could get used to this, I thought, those nights. Being looked at like this. I've never elicited that kind of attention before.

Another reason I couldn't change my mind and rush to be with my so-called friends at Brenda's house. Not just that I could never forgive them for dispatching you, Kristoff. Also, I was looking younger than ever.

They'd take one look at me and smell a rat.

During the quiet nights of Christmas week, I would stare at my reflection in the searing light of my bathroom. The harshly unforgiving northern light poured through the pebbled window.

There was no hiding it. I looked as if I hadn't even hit thirty.

If I'd gone round Brenda's for a festive tot of sherry and a mince pie, she'd have been on my case. In the Demeter the men talked about Cleavis stepping up his campaign against the Walkers. Striding about town at night with his carpet bag of weapons. Not much luck yet, but people were rattled.

So I couldn't go near Brenda, her fella, or any of my former friends.

With my heightened senses I could hear them carousing in her attic next door. The silly records, the hissing of the turkey roasting in her range. The tooting of kazoos and even the rustling of paper streamers.

I am becoming more sensitive by the day. Quiveringly alert.

When I went to visit Marjorie Staynes, on one of these in-between days, to discuss the hidden story of the books of Qab (I've read a further six of them during the days of Christmas), I could hear the boys upstairs.

The young assistant Gila had taken Robert up to his room above the bookshop. I heard their stifled undressing and their rolling around and doing all of their disgusting business, where they thought no one could hear. But I could. I heard them whispering afterwards. I knew they were spying on me, and Marjorie. They were perplexed that I was visiting The Spooky Finger but not my friends.

I wonder if Robert knows the truth of what Marjorie told me, just that day. The truth about his new boyfriend.

That Gila comes from Qab itself.

She had brought him to our world from a world a very great distance away. The true world of Qab. That's why he's greenish round the gills. The reason he looks like a reptile is because that's what he is, partly. He's an alien being.

How I relished the thought of dropping that bombshell on Robert. You've got yourself another weirdo fella, sorry, ducky. A lizard this time. From another world.

That might simmer down his ardour.

But these are all petty concerns.

'It really is possible, then?' I asked Marjorie. My voice had gone dry and scratchy. 'To go from . . . this world to that one? And vice versa?'

'Of course.' She looked like an old Buddha sitting there by her cash desk. An old Buddha with a perm and a huge pile of knitting. Infinitely wise.

Why do I feel this new friend of mine has all the answers? I just know she has, somehow. Something powerful about her. Strange. I'm not one to give in so easily to another person's willpower or personality . . .

'Of course,' she went on. 'Most people aren't *advanced* enough, by any means. You have to progress along a certain path. Not many do. Only then can you . . . *break through*.'

I was gawping at her in the semi-dark of her bookshop. That weird incense and mist all around us.

A thrill went through me. I knew in a trice that given half a chance I'd go there. I'd go to Qab. No worries. I'd have to see it for myself.

'Many fail,' said Marjorie. 'Many just can't make it.

Many – even when they are told the truth about Qab – refuse to believe it. If even one soul in a reading group comes to believe and tries her hardest to break through, then I consider mine a job well done.'

I drew in my breath sharply. 'You mean that's what the book group's for? Like a cult? To bring in new members?'

She nodded, glancing up from her knitting. 'And you're my most promising member, Effie. You're the most promising initiate I've seen since the group I led until last year in Kendal. Of course, that lot went to the bad, in the end. But they were advanced. Oh, indeed. They were almost through. We almost made it. But . . . petty jealousies. People turning back at the very last moment. Losing their nerve. It was sad. Very sad. What a waste. So . . . I've had to start again. Right here. Here in Whitby and The Spooky Finger. And you, my dear.'

Following this speech, she returned her full attention to her knitting. Clack, clack, clack as my senses reeled.

A cult! A cult! She was saying that she is forming a cult!

And I like it. Bereft, alone, it's all I have. And I am in love with the idea of it.

'We need you, Effie,' said Marjorie Staynes. 'You're just the kind of person the cult of Qab needs. And Qab itself needs you desperately.'

'I . . . I could go there? Really?'

'Oh yes,' smiled Marjorie. 'With a little work. With a little initiation and so on. But first we must advance our cause. Bring in other members. Before we can send you there, we must observe the rituals . . .'

Send me there!

Oh, Kristoff . . . what am I getting myself into?

Something wonderful, I can tell.

I long to tell you all about it. I know you'd be amazed by all this, just as I am.

But I have no one. Not even my aunts. They're keeping away from me. They stay in the shadows and the portraits and ignore me, for the first time in my life.

I am alone.

And dreaming of Qab.

When I left Marjorie's shop the other day, with further books and a head buzzing with new ideas, I turned to see Robert gazing out of Gila's window after me. I flashed him a dangerous look. Who was he to keep tabs on my comings and goings? Who was he to judge me? He vanished back inside that darkened room.

29 December

Dear Kristoff,

I needed to get out for a while.

131

All this dwelling on my sadness. All this dreaming of elsewhere.

It was last night. Days and days after Christmas. I felt I've been hiding away enough.

I slipped up the hill to the Miramar. I sat at the bar with a gin and tonic. Foolish, really. As if I wanted to be discovered by my erstwhile friends.

And sure enough, there was Robert, suddenly at my elbow. Looking concerned, he was.

'Brenda's in bits.'

'Now there's a novelty.'

He sighed. 'You know what I mean. She's cut up about you. Worried, Effie. You've not said a word. You've kept out of everyone's way.'

'Oh yes?' I eyed him beadily.

I could see he was shocked by my appearance. Even bleary-eyed and a bit tipsy, I knew I looked magnificent. I'd popped on one of my vintage frocks. A 1920s number belonging, no doubt, to one of my aunties. It was black and glittering with sequins and beads. I had a little turban thing on too, exquisite with feathers.

'We're all very worried about you,' he said sternly. I only look about his age. Young Robert. I began to wonder what his blood might taste like, just for a fleeting moment.

I was distracted then, watching the other revellers at

his bar. They had set up an impromptu singalong. A ghastly bunch of raddled pensioners. Their flesh revolted me. Their whining voices were like nails scraping down my back. I frowned and waved to the barmaid for another gin.

'How many have you had?'

I shrugged. 'Does it matter?'

'I've never seen you like this.'

'I've never *been* like this.' I thrust out one supple arm suddenly, to take in the rowdy set intent on murdering 'White Christmas'. 'Look at this lot. They're all so blindly happy.'

'So? It's still just about Christmas time. There's nothing wrong with that.'

'I mean all these people. Everyone. Everyone in town. Celebrating. How dare they celebrate? Why should they be happy? When death and disaster are all around. Just waiting to claim them. How dare they be happy when my lovely man has gone?'

He didn't know what to say to that, did he? He looked flummoxed. 'Brenda told me about it. About that night, and what Cleavis did. I'm sure she never knew, Effie. I bet she couldn't have known what Henry was planning.'

'Pah!' I crunched an ice cube between my teeth. 'Oh, she knew all right.'

Robert tried another tack. 'Perhaps he's not dead? Look at how he's survived in the past. He's been staked before, hasn't he? He's been sent to hell again and again.'

I narrowed my eyes. 'And hell is just a few hundred metres below our feet. It's trying to drag us down – all of us – all the time. As we well know, eh, ducky?' I laughed bitterly. I was getting to enjoy giving vent to my bitterness. I did the laugh really well. 'So what's the point, eh? If that's where we're going anyway. And if it's not so different to here.'

'All we can do in the circumstances is get on with it, Effie.'

'Get on with it, he says!'

'Look, life hasn't been a breeze for me either, you know. Since being here in Whitby, I've lost my Auntie Jessie.'

'*Her!*' I scoffed.

Now Robert was starting to look depressed. Well, good. I'd dragged him out of that silly high-spirited festive mood. He went on glumly, 'I lost both my parents when I was a kid. I know what loss is like.'

Typical. He was making it all about him. Well, he wasn't alone in the misery stakes. I trumped him at once. 'I never even *knew* my parents. They buggered off. Left me with my aunts. They just put up with me.

But I never really fitted in. I've never really had anyone – ever! – who was there for just me . . .'

Robert stared at me. Still discomfited by my renewed youth and beauty. He said quietly, 'Have another drink, Effie.'

I was inconsolable, though. 'Alucard. He was there for me.' The gin was having a profound effect. Oh, Kristoff! Why didn't you warn me that alcohol is worse for vamps?

'Brenda was there for you more than he ever was.'

'Don't say *her* name to me!'

And then that receptionist arrived. Penny. That tactless girl who wears all the black. She looked approvingly at my vintage outfit and then alarmed when she got a closer look at how drunk I was. How wonderfully young-looking I was, too.

'Hiya, Effie.'

Robert told her, 'We're getting drunk.' I thought it was sweet of him to include himself. Make me look less of a drunken freak.

But why would I care what this gormless girl thought? That's one of the problems with Whitby. Small pond. Big fish. I need to be away. Elsewhere.

You were going to take me, my love, weren't you? Away from all of this. Those gorgeous old haunts of yours, where you still kept apartments. Cobwebby and forgotten. Sealed away from prying eyes. Your home in Venice, deep below water level. Your home in the Marais in Paris.

I should still go. I should leave as soon as I can.

I felt a new resolve grip me. I should go. Go go go.

I caught a jungle scent then. A whiff of wild creatures and virgin forest. I could smell a new world opening up for me. Far from here. Incalculably far. Its sultry breath was in my nostrils, all of a sudden. My cool flesh went all goosebumpy. How I longed for some warmth. Some sun on my milky skin.

'You young people don't understand about anything.'

Penny said, 'I don't pretend to know everything. Especially in this weird town. I'm right out of my depth here.'

I found myself nodding at her approvingly. There was something sensible about her after all. Only the wise can admit to knowing hardly anything.

She went on, 'But I do understand that this fellow of Brenda's, this bloke she's got staying with her, old Professor Cleavis . . . he's somehow done away with your boyfriend.'

'Kristoff Alucard. Say his name, girl.'

She looked superstitious and shy.

'Saying his name aloud won't summon him up,' I told her. 'God knows, I wish it would.'

'Cleavis m-murdered your lover. In a restaurant. In public. And the body turned to dust. And Cleavis got away with it.'

I sneered. 'Exactly. That's what he does. He's a demon-hunter. Did Robert tell you, he once shot me in the head? When he was trying to get a clear shot at Robert's Aunt Jessie?'

Robert nodded. 'It's true. Cleavis is remorseless.'

Penny was looking aghast by now. Evidently no one had told her the full story. Typical!

Briefly Robert tried to explain who Henry Cleavis actually was, and some of the circumstances of his own first meeting with the wicked man. I scowled all the while and then I broke in.

'He's just another fancy man of Brenda's. She's got them coming out of the woodwork all the time, that one. He's someone she knew back in the 1940s, apparently. Though why he's never aged is beyond me. Something about an elixir of life he once found in Africa. Probably something dodgy.'

Penny was looking at us both rather oddly. 'But how can he be a . . . killer? He's the same Henry Cleavis who wrote the books about Hyspero. Brenda told me. The fantasy books for kids. . .'

'That's the one,' Robert said. 'He was at Cambridge. He was part of that group of scholars who all wrote

137

books set on other planets and in fantasy lands. The Smudgelings. Reginald Tyler was another one. He wrote *The True History of the Planets*.'

Penny slurped a pint of snakebite the barmaid had brought her. 'The Seven Books of Hyspero! I was obsessed with those books as a kid. I read them again and again. I was convinced it was real, that land. I used to look for ways to get there all the time, just like the kids in the books did. Through secret doorways and windows. But it never worked for me.'

'I never read them,' Robert said. 'I remember there being a cartoon on one Christmas.'

'His writing days seem to be behind him,' I sighed drunkenly. 'He's just a killer now. A slayer of monsters.' Then I realised that I didn't want to be talking about Henry bloody Cleavis any more. 'Look, why are you asking me all about this? Ask Brenda! And in the meantime, I want another gin!'

I finished my drink noisily, waving for another. Robert looked disapproving again.

He went on with his explanations, 'The thing is, Penny, you see – the Smudgelings were a kind of book group, as we know. They got together to share their new chapters and read to each other in Cleavis's rooms in his college. But they were also something else. Something undercover. They were a secret vampire- and demon-hunting squad. They went after covens of witches and black magicians. They scoured the country investigating evil deeds and supernatural mysteries.'

Penny's eyes lit up. 'I wish I'd known this earlier. There's so much I'd like to ask him about.'

'He tends to vanish into the night when his work is done.'

I burped. 'I hope he's gone already. Brenda can do better than him.'

'It really gave Brenda the hump last time, the way he nicked off,' said Robert. 'She thought there might be something . . . you know, between them. But off he went.'

'She's a fool to herself. And an accomplice to murder. I hope all her spare parts rot and drop off. Look, is there any chance of another drink, or shall I just expire of thirst?'

'No more for you, lady. You've had quite enough.'

I gasped at him. 'What? How dare you?'

He ignored my protests and went on, 'Mind you, Brenda said earlier today that Henry's sticking around for a while. Definitely. His work here isn't finished. So she's glad about that.'

Penny's eyes were wide. 'What else is he after? Is he going to stake someone else?'

Both the young people turned to stare at me. I pulled

my scarf up more snugly around my neck. Bloody bite marks. Were they on show? I'd been too slack. Way too slack. I'd put myself in danger. Just being out here. Out in public.

'I don't know,' said Robert. 'He plays his cards close to his chest. Maybe it's to do with the Limbosine. Or Hans Macabre. Or any of the other monsters still lurking about, at large in town. Someone said Mr Danby was up to his old tricks.'

'Who?' said Penny. 'Mr *Danby*?'

'Just another old enemy. But the truth is, we don't really know what Henry Cleavis is up to.' Robert was looking at me steadily. Giving me a special message, I suddenly realised. Warning me. Telling me I'd best lie low. Or maybe even get right out of town. That would be the best thing. Surely.

'He'd better watch himself,' I found myself saying, slurring for the first time that night. Oof. I felt gyppy all of a sudden. 'It's him who'd better watch out. For me.'

'Brenda said something about hypnotism. He's working with her. Prying into her memories.'

'No good will come of that,' I said, hoisting myself awkwardly off my bar stool. 'The silly old cow should know better. She doesn't want him poking about in her head. He'll bring out something she won't want to know. You mark my words!' Then I swayed on the spot

140

before them. I had a raging thirst. But not for gin. 'I'll bid you young people good night.'

And before they could say anything else, I was off. All that rubbishy Christmassy music and the tawdry decorations were making me feel most peculiar.

I slammed through the doors of the Miramar bar and trotted through the beer garden, making unsteady progress back to the street and the sharp decline to the snow-shrouded harbour.

I had business to attend to.

It was a number of quiet streets later that I saw the young couple arguing. Oblivious to everyone, they were tearing at each other – verbally – in the middle of the road.

I paused in the doorway of a charity shop. Smirking at their fight. Probably about something very silly. It certainly sounded trivial.

I watched the woman getting the last word and stomping off. Leaving the tall young man in stung silence. He was exasperated. As she disappeared round the corner, he swore loudly. Just one word. An explosive shout. He ran his fingers through his long dark hair and let out an inarticulate moan.

I waited till I was quite sure there was no chance that his young woman would return. He was on his own. Possibly with nowhere to stay for the night.

Oh dear. He looked like a stranger in town. Abandoned at Christmas. A lonely puppy.

I eased out of the charity shop doorway. I slunk under the Christmas lights. I stepped across the snow towards him.

'Yoo hoo?'

He looked up suddenly, hopeful at first, then suspicious.

And then something else. Intrigued, I think.

I gave him a warm, welcoming smile.

30 December

Dear Kristoff,

Last night there was another book club meeting. Marjorie Staynes says she wants to keep the momentum up. She's done this kind of thing before, and she says if you have too much of a break, people forget and they wander away. The New Year could start and her members might lose their enthusiasm for coming to The Spooky Finger.

It turned out to be a much-depleted meeting. A mere handful of us, compared with the previous week. But that was fine. It felt more intimate, more serious. This was the hard core. The lights were lower, the attitude more focused.

It hardly seems any time at all since I first attended and first heard about Qab. But thanks to the books supplied to me by Marjorie, and those I have discovered in my own attics, I now feel myself something of an expert on the laws and legends of Qab.

Marjorie served Madeira and seed cake. There wasn't a scrap of Christmassy tat there in the back room of The Spooky Finger. Christmas isn't something our book club leader is content to waste time on. Good for her. She sat with a politely disdainful grimace as the other women discussed their Christmases and how busy they'd been.

There we were: the inner circle of the book group. The ones not put off by another book by Beatrice Mapp.

Penny was there. Her eyes lit up at the sight of me. I was feeling a bit hung-over still – very unlike me – after my evening at the Miramar, and I brushed off her feeble attempts at communication. I noticed her, upon arrival at The Spooky Finger, scanning the shelves for Henry Cleavis's children's books.

A few other women, no one I know by name. Apart from Leena, from the shop beneath Brenda's guest house. Funny, fervid look in her eye. As well as being an awful gossip, Leena is very faddy. She's obviously got herself carried away with the idea of Qab. But then, haven't we all?

Marjorie Staynes led us into a quiet discussion. This time there was no hilarity and no embarrassment. We were talking as if this book – *The Sisterhood of Qab* – was a ground-breaking work of genius. A significant text in the history of mankind.

At one level I can hardly believe I'm going along with such a preposterous thing. In the end, these books are just escapist nonsense. The very first one I read, for example, was a story in which a bunch of not very appealing characters squabble and battle their way across a prehistoric sort of planet. There are dinosaur things and quicksand and exploding tortoises. Oh yes, really. And eventually they come to a city where they are forced to undergo a series of awful challenges in order to be allowed to live freely in the world of Qab.

Most of the books have the same rudimentary plot, I've found. There are some very rude bits in them too. I suppose that's why it's a cult thing. Everyone's reading for the kinky bits. But still. Maybe I do them a disservice. There's some philosophy there as well. And some politics and feminism. And some magic, I happen to believe. Something deeply spiritual.

At least it's about women getting the better of men. All the most interesting characters are women, which is unusual for this kind of book, I understand, from my fellow-book club members. The men are just . . . I suppose you could call them sex toys. It's a bit like reading Tolkien rewritten by Jackie Collins. Not my kind of thing at all, I thought at first. Though I finished it to the end. And then scoured The Spooky Finger, Whitby library, and my own book-lined attic for other novels by Beatrice Mapp.

I wish I could ask you about this, Kristoff. I know you believed in other worlds, tangential to this one. Of course you knew about other planes of existence. You took them in your stride. We've even been in one together. But this . . . primitive jungle world, with its multifarious carnivorous life forms and its race of servile lizard men . . . its warrior women all wanting to be queen, and the terrible queen who rules over them all . . . What would you say about that?

Penny went on a bit about being a kid and loving the kind of books that effortlessly transported the reader to another world. She even brought up Henry Cleavis and his books at this point. She dropped in a bit of gossip for the others. Did they know that Henry Cleavis was the man currently stepping out with Brenda?

Brenda wasn't at book club, of course. Better things to do, evidently. I felt vaguely disappointed not to see her. I got a twinge of sadness as I thought about sitting in her attic, not so long ago, and the supper she cooked for her young friends and myself. But I mustn't let myself get fond and nostalgic. There has been a breach. Those days have gone for ever. After what she and Cleavis did.

Yawn. Blah blah. Penny was going on. I could see that Marjorie Staynes's polite smile was becoming fixed and strained. After some effort she got Penny to put a sock in it, and then it was Leena's turn. She went on about how she'd never really been a fan of 'this kind of book'. Fantasy, I suppose she meant. But then she said how she had been dreaming every night for almost two weeks about becoming a warrior queen in the world of Qab. She laughed.

'Ridiculous, isn't it? My Rafiq thinks it's hilarious. I tell him, watch out, buster. If we lived there, in Qab . . . Do we say "in" or "on" Qab, by the way, Marjorie? I suppose it's the difference between it being a planet and a . . . land. A dimension of, like, alternate existence. Oh! Listen to me! With all the lingo! Anyway, so I say to Rafiq, if we were there, you'd be my servant! You'd have to do everything I said! It's, like, a feminist Utopia or summat!'

We all chuckled at this. Mrs Brick, the chunky cook from the Christmas Hotel, gave a nasty gurgle of appreciation. From what I hear, she's already quite used to having slaves to do her bidding.

'Anyway, Rafiq thinks it's all ridiculous,' Leena went

on. 'He's dismissive. Just like he was when I went off to do watercolour painting, and creative writing. And when I joined a women's group and had my consciousness raised. That were years ago, mind. I think my consciousness has slipped down again a bit by now.'

Leena finished this speech and looked around for approval.

Then Marjorie spent the rest of the meeting unfolding a particular idea of hers.

We listened avidly. This was special. We felt intrigued and privileged. She told us that she had run this kind of affair before. A book group. And they're fine, in as far as they go. But she is particularly interested in women who are interested in Qab.

What if . . . what if we did here what she had done in other towns, at different times, hm?

Marjorie squinched up her face with pleasure. She giggled, relishing the moment.

We all felt that she was on the brink of letting us into a wonderful secret. We all crept forward on our wooden chairs.

That pale-greenish boy, Gila, was going round collecting up plates and cake forks. Marjorie told us to pay him no heed. Gila knows all the secrets. We were to think of him as just a servant. A piece of the furniture.

'What I was thinking,' Marjorie Staynes purred, 'is

that we set up a separate weekly group. One dedicated to the study of Qab. What do you think? We can let the book group discuss what it wants. Other books. Dead and buried, musty old books. Things that the other women want to read. But then, secretly, on a different night, we will be a sisterhood of Qab. Meeting to talk about these still living works of Beatrice Mapp. Well, ladies? What do you think?'

The six of us raised a cheer at this. We loved the idea immediately.

'Tuesdays,' said Marjorie Staynes, as she prepared to break up the meeting. 'And maybe I can dig out some of the Qab costumes that my previous sisterhood made. They ran up some lovely garments. Nobody quite got the wear out of them . . .'

Garments? Costumes? In the past, this might have put me off.

We issued into the snowy night. All the inner circle of the Qab sisterhood and myself.

I took off swiftly, hoping that Penny wouldn't catch up with me as I shuffled on the perilously impacted slush of Silver Street and LeFanu Close. No such luck.

'I went to the toilet again,' she told me, when she drew level.

'Oh yes?' For a moment I couldn't imagine why she was telling me this.

148

'I had another look at that painting. The one of the lake. The one my handbag fell in. I tried to push my fingers through the glass again.'

I looked at her sharply. Why does everyone think they've a right to go investigating? 'And?'

'Nothing this time. It was just a normal picture. I think. But there's something weird, don't you think? About that whole set-up? Marjorie Staynes and this Qab business?'

'I thought you believed in it!'

'I'm infiltrating,' Penny told me. 'I guess you are too, eh, Effie?'

'No,' I said curtly. 'I'm fascinated by the whole thing. I want to see what truth there is in it. And I need something, don't I? Something to fill up my lonely nights. I need something I can believe in, don't I?' I sounded devilishly sarcastic. Penny looked like she didn't know how to take me.

'Robert's getting pretty serious with that lad Gila,' Penny added, just before she turned off, up the hill, towards the Miramar. 'Funny tonight, seeing Gila being such a slave to Marjorie Staynes. I guess that's just his job. Robert says he's not felt like this about a bloke in ages. They've got something special, he says.'

I pursed my lips. 'I'm sure I don't want to hear

anything about it. Anyway, that young man is green. His skin looks a bit scaly to me.'

'I've said something similar, but Robert won't have it. Says the poor lad's got a skin condition. But Gila's telling him funny things. Things that Robert doesn't know whether to believe or not . . .'

I frowned at her. How indiscreet was this young madam? Why was she telling me all this business? Isn't Robert supposed to be her friend?

Penny went on, 'Gila keeps telling him that he comes from a different world. He has come to Whitby and this world from an immense distance. Across time and space and God knows what else. He's been telling Robert that he comes from Qab. The world of Qab. For real!'

Penny was breathless with excitement. She was standing there wild-eyed under the street light.

And then I knew why she was telling me all this. We are bonded in our membership of the hard core of Qab. Whatever our subterfuges and investigations, both Penny and I are more than a little fascinated by the idea that this world somehow truly exists.

I didn't tell her that I already knew all of this. I didn't tell her that Marjorie let me into these secrets some days ago. I didn't let on that Marjorie thinks me trustworthy, and advanced.

Advanced in the ways of Qab.

I didn't say anything more to Penny.

The girl turned on her clumpy heels and without a further word hurried back towards the gaudy hotel where she works.

And I returned to my lonely house, to mull it all over once more.

New Year's Eve

Dear Kristoff,

It pops into my head.

Suddenly, without warning.

It's the early hours. I'm up, sleepless, trying to clear my mind of thoughts as I wander about the cluttered rooms. I'm looking at knick-knacks and gewgaws.

I've spent my whole life looking at knick-knacks and gewgaws. My life's been bound up in bric-a-brac. I was born into a house of antiques and brought up by old ladies. The first smells I remember are lavender, beeswax polish, toxic hairspray and mothballs.

I'm rifling through old drawers and gazing at my aunts' jewellery. My own tastes range into the theatrical, the clunky and the showily fake. My aunts, on the other hand, preferred the authentic, the classy, the real. Quite a small fortune is stashed away in these drawers.

I'm keeping them for best, I suppose. All this silver

and gold. These emeralds and rubies. And then I catch my breath. My best? When's that? Have I missed it already? Surely it's been and gone and I missed it all? And all this expensive tat was just here, going unworn.

Gloomy thoughts at six in the morning on New Year's Eve.

The windows are opaque with snow. It's going to be one of those stretched-out, blank New Year's Eves. My nerves are worn thin. I am exhausted, I realise.

Moving about outside, getting from place to place to do simple things every day, has been a struggle recently. An expedition.

My blood feels sluggish and coagulated in my veins. My own blood feels like it's flowing so slowly, it's turning back the other way, like a broken clock.

That's when the thought came to me: in the early hours of this morning.

Kristoff – I let them have your ashes.

I fainted on the spot on the night they murdered you, and they led me away from the scene of the crime in that swanky restaurant. They brought me here and I was unconscious and it was only the next morning that I could take everything in and realise you were gone.

I left your precious remains with them.

Cleavis is canny. He's no fool. He would have realised your ashes are potent still.

Because they are, my love, aren't they? In the right conditions, if there is enough of them left, they can be used, can't they? In a ritual? To bring you back?

Say it's true. Let me know.

I know it's true. I'm sure it is.

And your ring! That's how I was reminded, this morning. Looking into my aunts' drawerfuls of glinting treasure. The image of your silver and ruby ring popped into my head. I know how you jealously guarded it. How you'd had it for centuries. Somehow I knew that much of your ineffable power was bound up in your ring.

But where is it, eh? Where did it go?

They've got it. I know they have. Brenda and her fancy man.

I reel with the thought of it. How dare they add insult to injury like this? But what do they care? It's a job well done. They've cleared away the trash. Collected up the booty.

Well, I'm going round there. I'm having it out with them.

New Year's Day

Dear Kristoff,

I went round there yesterday lunchtime.

All bundled up in my heaviest sheepskin like it was

armour plating. Ready for a good scrap. I thought, maybe that was what I was needing. Get it all out of my system.

BANG BANG BANG on the side door.

Leena had been outside, setting out wonderful mangos and bananas and pomegranates in a display. They looked ravishingly bright in the hoar frost. She saw my look of determination, storming into the alley. She followed a little way. 'Erm, Effie . . . are you okay?'

'The ring. My beloved's ring. They took it.'

'Oh!' she said. She was still clutching a pineapple to her apron, looking confused.

BANG BANG BANG I knocked again, harder this time.

'You mean your gentleman friend? The one who . . . vanished.'

I scowled. 'He never vanished, Leena. They killed him. Them two upstairs.'

She looked suitably shocked at this. 'Brenda said he just went away! And that's why you were so mopey lately.'

'Mopey!' I launched a new attack on the B&B's side door. Then I stopped and looked at Leena. She was a member of the inner circle. I looked at her with new, searching eyes. We were in the same cult. We were committed to Qab together.

An unspoken communication flew between us. We both knew it.

I told Leena, 'Brenda is in league with a very wicked man. He has turned her head. She is completely under his thrall. Together they have reduced my beloved to a heap of ashes. And they have stolen his precious ring.'

'Oh!' said Leena again. She really isn't the brightest soul. But then her face cleared of confusion. 'How can I help?'

And there we have it, I thought. The unswerving loyalty of the cult of Qab. I was impressed, all of a sudden.

I felt stronger and even more resolute.

I am woman, Brenda. Hear me roar.

And I'm a proper woman, too. Not some chucked-together composite of left-over parts!

The door opened at last. Almost hesitantly, as if she knew that I was there with my heart brimming with bitterness.

She was standing in the gloomy hallway, looking harried and confused. 'Effie! What are you doing here?'

'I've come to have it out with you, lady.'

'I didn't think you were talking to me any more!'

'I'm not. Not properly. I've come to ask what you did with his remains. His ashes. And his ring. These are very important to me, Brenda.'

'His . . . ?' Brenda looked worried. She spied Leena over my shoulder and lowered her voice. 'Let's not have a barney about this in the street, lovey. We don't want the whole harbour seeing. Come inside.'

She left her guests to breakfast alone and led me up her side stairs, slamming the door on Leena. Leena's antennae were twitching, I just knew. She'd be keeping tabs on me. She'd report to the other ladies of Qab if I didn't come out of there again.

Did I really feel frightened, being alone with Brenda?

Entering her sitting room in the attic felt like coming back to somewhere I'd been exiled from.

She hovered round me. Great galumphing Brenda. She was nervous around me. Inspecting me.

She was astonished by my youth and my beauty. Yes, my beauty. I'd never been that before. But I was just then, I knew it.

I hoiked off my furry hat and my sheepskin gloves and tossed them on to her green armchair. I let her get a good look at me.

Lap it up, ducky, I thought. Take a look at me now.

'I can't stay long,' I told her. 'I merely want some answers.'

'Ooh, Effie love,' she warbled in a worrisome tone. 'I hate this. I hate this air of antagonism between us. I hated Christmas and not seeing you. It wasn't the same this year. It all rang a bit hollow.'

I arched an eyebrow in her direction. 'Did you expect me to celebrate the festive season with you? And today? I expect you think I've come round to wish you happy New Year!'

Brenda hung her head. 'I suppose not, no. I just wish—'

'I don't want to go over all of that now. You made your choice. You sided with Cleavis. You both thought Alucard should die.'

'I—'

'If you didn't, you'd have stopped him. Unless you are afraid of your own man friend. And that would be a very sad situation, wouldn't it?'

'Of course I'm not. It's just—'

'Just what? What, Brenda? How did you justify what Cleavis did?'

'Alucard was no good for you. He was leeching off you. Changing you. Making you think and do things that you didn't want to do. You said yourself – you admitted to me – you weren't at all sure about going away from Whitby and going abroad with him. And just look at you now! Look at you! You're so different . . .'

'I'm fabulous.' A shiver went through me as I said this. It was something I'd never dared think even inside my head. But the word was out before I knew it. And I *was* fabulous. I was gorgeous. I remember thinking: I'm worth ten of this shambling old moose before me.

'You've turned into something I don't recognise,' said Brenda.

'Good,' I told her. 'I'm glad. Now. To business. Kristoff's remains. His ashes. His ring. Where are they?'

'I don't know. We left everything there. In the restaurant. My main focus was you. You'd passed out. I wanted to get you home, to safety . . .'

'Don't give me that. You couldn't have been that concerned about me, lady. Come on. Tell me. Where's his ring? He'd worn that for centuries. Cleavis would have known how precious it is. Where have you put it?' I glared around her room.

Her safe. It'd be in there. Along with all her other rubbishy treasure and mementos of diabolical adventures past.

'I haven't got it!' Brenda protested. There were tears in her eyes. Tears of frustration. She was really upset.

What a shame.

'You'll find that ring for me,' I told her. '*Or* . . .'

'Or what?'

Ah. Listen.

Somebody had heard us. Our shrill raised voices.

We hadn't even realised we were shouting.

Here came Henry Cleavis at a run. In a shorty dressing gown somewhat on the feminine side, presumably not his.

'Brenda?' he barked. 'Are you all right?'

He came thundering into Brenda's sitting room. Direct from Brenda's boudoir.

'Henry,' she said. 'Go back to bed.'

He looked flustered. Newly roused from a deep sleep. The sleep of the just. I thought, fancy him sleeping while Brenda works like a drone.

He was staring at me. 'Good God,' he breathed. 'I've not seen you this close to. Not for days. Look at you, woman! Just look at you!'

Brenda's voice was hard. 'I've said it once, Henry. I'll deal with this.'

I laughed harshly. '*Deal with this?* Is that what I am? Another problem to be dealt with? An old bag of rubbish to dispose of?' I glared at Henry Cleavis. 'I didn't come on a social call, and I'm not here to cause problems either.'

'Well,' he said. 'Good.'

'I've come for Kristoff's ashes. And more particularly, his ring. I know you'll have collected them up. You wouldn't have left them behind. Not you.'

'Oh yes?'

'You've been after him for years. You and all your Smudgeling brethren. You wouldn't want a single speck of Alucard to remain in the world, out of your control.'

Brenda said, 'I've tried to tell her. We don't have what she wants.'

'I don't believe you, Brenda.'

She pulled a face. 'You'll have to. There's nothing here for you.' Her grim expression faltered. Real sorrow showing through. 'Oh, Effie. I hate this. We were such good friends . . .'

'That's all finished.'

'It can't be.'

I laughed in her face. 'How can you stand there and even imagine I'd ever forgive you?'

'You never loved him,' Cleavis said bluntly. 'And believe me, he never thought anything of you. He just wanted you as a slave. That's all he wanted from any of his women. There wasn't a shred of human feeling left inside that stinking cadaver. It was all put on. You fell foul of him, Effryggia.'

'You don't know anything about it,' I snapped. 'What do you know about love?'

He clamped his jaw shut and drew his dressing gown tighter across his woolly grey chest.

I jeered at them both. 'Neither of you know anything about love. How could you?'

160

'Effie,' said Brenda. She just wanted me to shut up, I know. These were uncomfortable truths.

'You! Jumping into bed with your professor! You old hussy!'

Brenda's eyes almost popped out. Shame flooded her face. She went a shade of puce. 'No!'

'What about Frank, eh? What about your poor old husband? You've betrayed him. You've betrayed him with this grizzled specimen . . . this ruthless killer!'

Brenda shook her head. 'But you could never abide Frank. You always said so.'

'So? You've still betrayed him. You don't half pick 'em, Brenda. These horrible men of yours.' I swung back to Cleavis. To the matter in hand. 'I didn't come here for a slanging match.' Though truth be told, I was almost enjoying letting rip and having my say. 'Give me what I came for. They'll be in Brenda's safe, I reckon. The revenants of my beloved.'

Brenda said, 'Effie, we haven't got them.' Her voice was full of pain. Like she was being torn apart, her whole body. I reflected that she must already know how that felt.

Yet I couldn't afford to feel compassion. I had to feel nothing.

Henry Cleavis drew closer to me. Lowering his voice till it was husky, intent. Studying me with a basilisk stare. An expert eye. 'I won't give you a thing. Nothing that belonged to him. It is too dangerous. Can't you feel it, Effie? Can't you tell? This thing inside you. This madness. This fever. It's gone too far. You have changed for ever. It's too late for you. You're spoiled. You're ruined. You've taken your whole life and given it to that monster. He has scrambled your brains. He has polluted your blood. It is over, Effie.'

'Henry, no!' Brenda cried. A real note of despair.

I suddenly saw how much danger I was in.

Cleavis was holding his crucifix up before him. In his other hand suddenly, slipping out of his shorty dressing gown sleeve – a freshly sharpened stake.

A cold wave of realisation hit me.

Oh no, surely not. How clichéd. How awful.

I lashed out with both hands. *Whhsssstt.*

My nails are like razors these days. They ran through the suede skin of his face.

I felt the flesh giving way and the dark blood welling. Ribbons of old skin and white beard fibres collected like scum under my perfect nails.

The old man howled. He launched himself at me, brandishing his stake. I screeched.

Over went the coffee table.

I could hear Brenda bellowing. Inhuman, cowlike, her cries rang in my ears as she barrelled into both of us.

I staggered backwards and fell, crumpled on the carpet.

My last thought as my head connected with the teak magazine rack: Which of us is Brenda trying to save?

I woke up still alive. So that was good.

She hadn't let him stake me on the spot.

It seemed that I was tied to a kitchen chair, still in her attic. They sloshed cold water in my face to wake me.

Henry Cleavis was sitting across from me. Grimacing and twitching.

For the first time it really hit me. This old coot was insane. He was completely crazy, after all these years of monster-hunting.

He didn't say anything to me as I came round. My head was pounding. He stared at me. Twitching. Gurning.

Brenda hurried in with a jar of some kind. 'I haven't got any fresh,' she said, passing Henry the jar.

I almost laughed. She'd brought out the Lazy Garlic. What were they going to do? Marinade me?

'You never let him kill me,' I said. 'Thanks, ducky.'

She sighed heavily. 'You know I wouldn't. Not just like that.'

'But the time might yet come, eh? When I have to be reduced to ashes. When you have to get the Dyson out to deal with your old friend. Just like Kristoff. Soon you'll decide it's time to put me out of the way.'

Brenda couldn't bring herself to answer. Cleavis did it for her. 'Quite,' he said coolly.

'You shouldn't have attacked Henry,' Brenda said. 'You confirmed all his fears.'

I struggled for a bit. She seemed to have lashed me to the chair with an old washing line. There were still a few faded plastic pegs clipped on.

'Listen to yourself, Brenda!' I shouted. 'You're no longer your own woman! You're his lackey! How could you? You used to be so proud of your independence. You always said that you'd never let any man tell you what to do.'

Cleavis chuckled darkly. 'Listen! How the wicked seductress works on you, Brenda. Oh, she's a charmer. Silver-tongued, just like her lover. He's passed on all of his gifts, hasn't he?'

'Oh, shut up, man,' I growled. 'I mean it, Brenda. You've let yourself down, dear. Are you really going to let some horrid old man decide the fate of your very best friend?'

Brenda clamped both pan-shovel hands over her ears. 'I can't stand it! I can't listen to it any more! It's Effie . . . but it's not her either. It's like . . . she's possessed!'

'Possessed!' I said hotly. 'I've never been more

myself, ducky! Listen to me. Look, I might have changed. I might have . . . vamped up a bit. But I'm still me! I'm still the Effie you always knew! I'm still your best pal!'

Cleavis snorted. 'She's getting hysterical.'

Brenda sobbed. 'Let's lock her up for a while. Till she calms down. I can't stand this, Henry. I can't stand to hear her raving on like this . . .'

It took the strength of both of them to drag me, kicking and screaming, spitting and howling, all the way to Brenda's en suite.

I wasn't as strong as I thought I was, though.

I was sapped of all vitality as I sat there in the tiny bathroom.

For a while I pounded on the door, but to no avail. They'd wedged it shut somehow.

What a way to spend New Year's Eve. I've had some rotten ones in my time. This had to be the worst.

I cursed and kicked and they took no notice. I heard them in hissed conference in Brenda's bedroom.

All I could do was sit on the toilet lid and wait. How long could they keep me here? How long before they decided what to do with me?

I was a fool to make myself vulnerable by going there.

This was something else I'd picked up from you, Kristoff my dear. Stepping in where angels fear to tread. Blithely assuming no harm could come to me.

Well, it could.

I wondered if that old fart Cleavis could convince Brenda I was better off dead.

I examined the tiny window. It was four floors up. I was svelte as anything, but there was no way I could make myself small enough to get out that way.

I sat helplessly, wishing I had learned from you all your other marvellous tricks: turning myself into a cloud of black smoke. A vampire bat.

I always thought the bat you turned into was rather jolly and cute. Did I ever tell you that? You were shaped a bit like a plump robin, only more evil-looking.

Time passed. The very fag end of the year was wasting away. I listened hard at the door, and with my newly heightened senses, I realised that Cleavis had left the building. He was away on some business of his own.

I heard mention of the police, of DCI Aickmann, and something about the Walkers at the Demeter. My heart went out to those boys of mine. It sounded like Cleavis was preparing to do something about them. Was I his hostage, then?

Brenda was alone in her flat.

I could hear her moving around, dusting and

hoovering. Her agitation was plain in every one of her movements. She was fretting, fretting. She was breaking ornaments, and bumping into things. I could almost hear her thinking, incredulously: I've got my best friend locked up in my en suite, at the behest of my elderly boyfriend. How did this terrible thing come to pass?

I could play upon her sympathies. I knew I could.

I let time slip by. I tried to be patient. I waited for her to come to her bedroom to make up the bed. I could hear the sheets crack and ruffle, and to my sensitive ears the sound was like thunder.

I knew that she was there, on the other side of the door.

'Brenda, ducky?' I called.

She stammered. She faltered. 'Effie, it's no use. I know you'll try to cajole me. You'll sweet-talk me and try to get round me.'

'Oh, rubbish, Brenda. Just let me out of here. Come on, this is a waste of both our time.'

'Henry said you'd be like this. But I know that I have to remember that you're no longer really you. You've been tainted. Taken over.'

'What? Who says I'm no longer really me? How do you make that out?'

'You're not the Effie I know.'

'But I am! I am! That's exactly who I am. I'm the new improved Effie. My priorities have shifted a little, that's all. But really, I'm happier like this. I really am.'

I was up against the door again. Listening hard for signs that she was going to relent and liberate me. Her voice was strained and weirdly distant. I think she must have put some heavy furniture in front of the door. That was what all the scraping and banging was about.

Damn Cleavis. Turning friend against friend. That's what dodgy old men and demon-hunters do.

'What about your victims, eh?' Brenda burst out. 'I can't believe that's what you're out doing every night, Effie. Attacking young men. Killing them.'

I sighed heavily. 'I've killed no one.'

'You have!'

'I've rendered a few of them undead. It's not the same thing. And I always ask which way they want to go. Whether they want the full conversion, or just to donate a little blood. You'd be surprised how many young people these days want to go the whole hog and become Walkers. Most of them are flattered to be picked out by me. Really. You'd be surprised . . .'

'That's disgusting! Have you heard yourself? You've created a colony . . . a hive . . . a nest of vampires here . . .'

'Most of that was Kristoff's work. But really, the

168

vamp population has been depleted for years in Whitby. We've merely been restoring the balance. This town was always a haven for our kind.'

'Oh, Effie.' Her voice was filled with sadness. 'He is going to put a stop to you, you know.' Her voice was so urgent, so small.

'I guessed that.' My heart started pounding. But I already knew, didn't I? I already knew that Cleavis was merciless. Once I was within his power, I was lost. 'You have to get me out of here. If you ever thought anything of me . . .'

She was silent for a moment.

I could hear her overheated mind seething with worry.

Then: 'I'll help you.'

Yes! Good old Brenda.

'Thank you, ducky! Now—'

'On the condition that . . . that you get away. Leave Whitby altogether while Henry is here. I'll say that you overpowered me and escaped. And . . . and I want you to go away somewhere, and use all your powers . . . to reverse this hideous thing that has happened to you.'

'That's impossible. There is no cure. You know that.'

'You're a witch, Effie. From a long line of witches. You have more magic under your command than anyone knows about. More than you've ever admitted

169

to. You just haven't learned to control it properly yet. All I'm saying is . . . go away for a while. Maybe abroad, like you were going to go with Alucard. Do something about your condition. Learn to control it. Deny your compulsions. Forget about drinking blood and—'

'Dear Brenda. You don't know anything about it. You don't know what it's like. You can't do, can you? These feelings, these compulsions as you call them. They are pure animal instinct. They come with colossal force. They're like . . . a dark undertow. Dragging me under. Down into my animal nature. Of course, you would never understand that. You have no nature. No spirit. No instincts.'

Her voice turned low and dangerous. I had annoyed her.

'We're not talking about *me*. We're talking about *you*. If I let you out, I'm taking a massive chance. I'm trusting you, for the sake of our friendship. If I let you out now, you must go. You've got to leave Whitby.'

'For ever?' I got a jolt of real feeling then. Something akin to panic. 'But this is my home.'

'I don't know for how long. You just have to get away.'

I could see that I had no choice.

But where? Where could I possibly go? And on New Year's Eve as well . . .

'All right,' I promised her.

I heard her start to move the heavy furniture away from the door. Grunting, straining and clumsy with sadness, Brenda laboured at setting me free.

And as she did so, I realised exactly where it was that I wanted to run away to.

The idea flared up inside me.

I started to shake with excitement, forgetting my fatigue and my fury.

I had an idea. A plan. An audacious scheme.

But could I make it work?

I had to.

The en suite door creaked open, and there stood Brenda. She looked unkempt and scared.

She eyed me warily. I couldn't bear it.

We fell into each other's arms for a goodbye hug. Neither of us had the heart to wish the other a Happy New Year.

Robert

Lately he'd been spending a lot of time hanging around The Spooky Finger. After a while he got used to the funny incense and the weird smoke. All that weirdo chanting music that Marjorie Staynes tended to play didn't get to him any more.

'Oh, you're back again then,' she would say, when he and Gila came in. They had to pass through the shop to get to Gila's room. Well, he called it a room. It felt like more of a cupboard to Robert.

Marjorie Staynes looked him up and down every time. Clearly unimpressed by what she saw. He didn't think much of her either, so that seemed fair enough.

'Look, if you'd rather I didn't come round, that's okay. Gila can come up to the Miramar. I'd rather that anyway.'

'No! It's fine. Fine. I don't mind. And I don't want him away from the shop. There's too much to do. Lots of work here. The Spooky Finger's only been in business a few weeks.

I need all hands to the decks. And this is a crucial time. Yes, a crucial time.'

He actually started to think that Marjorie Staynes was crackers.

He and Gila listened in to those meetings she held down in the shop. Twice a week now, her book group was. Robert knew all about her little cult. The cult of Qab. He sat on the top stairs landing round her place, on the gritty carpet. Amongst the boxes of books still waiting to be unpacked.

Gila would simply shrug. He had heard all of it before. The chanting. The strange philosophical stuff. He'd even seen Marjorie dressing up her cultists in those golden outfits before. The robes of the sisterhood. Their helmets with plumey wings. He took the outfits downstairs and helped the ladies into them, and Robert listened from above to their shuffling about and giggling with excitement.

The cult of Qab. Really!

Penny told him that it was all deadly serious.

'Oh, yeah. You can see it in Marjorie's eyes. She's full of it. Believes every word. Qab is for real, as far as she's concerned.'

And Gila too, as it happened. Robert had asked him about it. Time and time again. All right, so he knew Gila was not just a normal fella. He was obviously not from round there – or even anywhere else on this earth. But . . . something inside him was shying away from the way Gila would say it so blandly.

'Qab exists, Robert. It's real. And I know that because it's where I was born. Marjorie brought me here, to this land. I travelled here with her. I am her servant. All females have servants in Qab.'

Poor lad. Robert set about trying to get him away from Marjorie. She was no good for him. Crazy old bag like that. But it was hard.

Robert had started to think that he must really feel something for Gila. So quickly. All over again. Here he went: falling for another young bloke. Just because he was a bit mysterious and not from round there.

Brenda and Cleavis weren't sure at all about Gila. Robert had taken him round Brenda's on Christmas night when she had her soirée. They treated him with kid gloves. Brenda was friendly, of course. She'd always be nice to someone new, who Robert cared about. But she was wary.

Gila choked a bit on the snowball she gave him. Mixed very strong, this noxious yellow drink. He was a bit bewildered by the whole Christmas thing. He felt embarrassed because he hadn't brought anyone any presents. No one minded, though.

Robert was proud of him. Taking him to Brenda's. Leaving together when the evening was over. This man he'd hardly known for very long at all.

These were strange times. It felt like loyalties were shifting. Everything was turning on its head. How weird to be round

Brenda's and there was no sign of Effie.

In recent days Robert hadn't been able to have a good chat with Brenda. There had been no chance. Cleavis was there all the time. Robert wanted to ask about the things Effie had said the other night when they sat at his bar. He didn't know how much to believe. His head was still reeling with it all. The very fact that Cleavis had staked Alucard.

He wondered if it wasn't actually a good thing in the end. And he recognised, of course, that Effie was not right in herself somehow. She was like proper possessed, wasn't she? You could see that, with the way she was looking and moving about. She wasn't just posesssed, he thought: she was a proper vamp.

Everything was changing, turning on its head.

Maybe the old gang was finished. Maybe Effie had gone beyond the pale.

He was upstairs with Gila, who had brought them a tray of tea things. This funny herbal tea Gila liked.

They sat on the edge of the bed together. Robert told Gila he had to go soon. Work was calling out to him. He had been letting things slide. He had been relying too heavily on Penny to fill in for him.

'I too have work tonight,' said Gila. 'Extra duties. Marjorie has just told me. She wants my help with a special ritual this evening.'

Robert's ears pricked up at this, of course. 'Black magic?'

'Qab magic,' said Gila. 'I think I know what she's doing. She says Effie's coming round tonight, alone. She's going to try one of the advanced rituals.'

Immediately Robert was thinking it had something to do with bringing Alucard back from the dead. 'Effie should watch out for messing about with rituals and that. I've seen her possessed before. She's very susceptible.' He was wondering whether he should tell Brenda. Get her to nip in quick.

'Marjorie has done this before. When we were in Kendal, she had a few members who went this far. It's nothing really bad, Robert. Not really.'

He had such an earnest, sweet face. He was looking at Robert like he really wanted him to understand. But Gila couldn't tell him everything. Not yet.

'Just give me a clue or something,' Robert said. 'About what it is they're up to.'

Gila bit his pale lower lip. 'All right. Marjorie has a gateway into Qab. Obviously. It's how she brought me here. It's how she goes back and forth. It takes rituals to get it open again. It takes concentration and so on. The gateway hides away in secret until it is needed.'

His cool fingers were stroking Robert's hands. It was something he often did, without even thinking about it. He was very tactile. At first Robert shrank from that constant touch, not being used to it. He guessed Gila thought he was uptight. Now Robert was used to him pressing and punctuating his words with these little touches.

'She has sent people through, before. Back in Kendal. Some of the women elected to move to Qab. And off they went. But there was trouble. Husbands complained. Policemen were called. There was fuss. It was a disaster. It was hushed up. Marjorie had to move away.'

'She *sent* people there?'

'Only those who clearly wanted to go. Some of them begged her.'

'Oh my God! You think Effie has asked her? Effie wants to go there?'

Gila looked at him and nodded slowly.

'We have to stop her!'

'No!' Gila said urgently. 'We can't. We can't interfere.'

'Huh?'

'I can't go against Marjorie, if that's what she wants to do. She's my mistress. I am bonded. I must obey . . .'

Gila had let go of Robert's hands. Robert stared at him. 'But you've got a mind of your own!'

'In this matter, I have not. I cannot work against the ways of Qab. I cannot work against the sisterhood.' He stood up. 'Now. You had better leave.'

* * *

177

'So what does he mean by a gateway?' Robert asked Penny, about half an hour later. They were in his office below stairs at the Miramar.

'I think I know,' she said.

'It must be like when we went down to hell, to the other version of Whitby. Like the Bitch's Maw. Like a . . . what does Brenda call it? A rip in the Very Fabric of Time and Space.'

'Does she really call it that?'

'I'm sure I've heard her say it. Remember when the gateway opened at the abbey that night, when they were filming *Get Thee Inside Me, Satan?*'

She tutted. 'How could I forget? Me and you, shoving all the cameras and equipment and scripts through, out of harm's way. And then Karla dancing into the maelstrom . . .'

'Hmmm.' They were having KitKats and tea, just as they always did when holding a meeting about urgent hotel business together. Penny had a habit of dunking her chocolate fingers in her hot tea and sucking them till there was just soggy wafer left.

'We can't let Effie go,' Robert said resolutely. 'We just can't.'

'Of course not.' Penny nodded firmly. 'But if she's determined, can we stop her? And really, it's a bit dangerous for her here, isn't it, with Henry Cleavis and all.'

'But she can't go swanning off to . . . some other dimension. We can't let her. I've already watched my Auntie

Jessie and Sheila Manchu get lost in another world, in a different dimension sort of thing. I'm not prepared to see it happen to Effie as well. And besides, we don't know anything about this Qab place, do we?'

Penny shrugged. 'I do. I've read the books. I've been at the meetings. I know quite a bit.'

Of course! he thought glumly. Penny was one of the cult, wasn't she? Incognito. Gathering info. 'So . . . you could get in there tonight. For Marjorie's ritual. You could be there as a legitimate part of the endeavour.'

'I guess so . . .' She looked a bit wary then. Up till that moment it had been a bit of a laugh. Robert remembered this kind of hesitation of Penny's from their adventure up at the abbey on Hallowe'en. That was when the strange activities of Karla Sorenson opened up the gateway into hell. Penny seemed willing to go only so far and then she would start to lose her nerve. She caught his eye and saw the challenge there. 'Yes, you're right. I can get in there. I can be right on the spot. What do you want me to do? Stop Effie from going?'

'If you can, I suppose.' Now he felt at a bit of a loss. On an impulse he picked up the phone and rang Brenda.

'You've seen her?' Brenda burst out. 'Where? Where is she?' She sounded very anxious. 'I told the silly old fool to get away. Get out of town. On New Year's Eve, this was! She's meant to be away by now. I told her she should take a break in Scotland or somewhere.'

'She certainly seems to be making plans to leave,' Robert told her. Then he filled her in on what he'd learned from Gila.

Brenda gave an audible gasp on the crackly line. 'But that's ridiculous! So that Marjorie Staynes woman has really got Effie believing in this place? Just like it is in the books?'

'I think it's all true,' he told her. 'Some of the things Gila has told me.'

'You're very lucky to have that lad of yours,' Brenda said decisively. Her words were a bit muffled at this point. He could imagine her struggling to put on her heavy coat as she talked to him. She was ready to dash out of the house at once. 'I'm on my way. What time is this so-called ritual meant to start?'

'Midnight.' That was what Gila had told him.

'Another late night,' Brenda sighed. 'Well, I can slip out without Henry seeing. He's off about his work tonight.'

As she said this, Robert was wondering what kind of work this could be. A shiver passed through him.

'I'm on my way,' said Brenda. 'First I'm going to Effie's house. See if she's still there. Maybe she's packing. Can you take luggage through this portal thing?'

'I don't know.' It seemed absurd, him and her talking like this. Would Effie need a passport for this other dimension thing? Was she planning on ever coming back? Neither of them voiced any of these things, but they both had an idea of what the other was thinking.

'I blame myself for all of this,' Brenda sighed. 'Effie having to go on the run. I should never have listened to Henry. He scared me the other night, with all his threats and stuff. When he had her prisoner, tied to that chair, I was really and truly—'

'He had her tied to a chair?' Robert couldn't believe what he was hearing.

'I'll tell you the whole story later,' she said. 'But suffice to say, I've seen a different side to Henry Cleavis. The ruthless hunter came out in full force, and it gave me pause for thought.'

Then Brenda was gone and he put back the receiver. Well, he had always known what Henry was like. And so did Brenda, if she was honest with herself. Henry was a force of nature. He assumed always that he was on the side of the angels. He felt himself completely justified in using whatever means he could to rid the world of monsters.

'She's got herself all worked up,' Robert told Penny.

'Well, she would!'

'She's off looking for Effie. She reckons she told Effie she better get out of town for a bit. But not like this. Not through whatever awful thing Marjorie Staynes is planning. She just meant get on the train. Go to Scotland for a long break or something.'

'Effie always seems to overreact,' Penny mused.

'Come on then, lady,' said Robert. 'What time is it now?

It's getting late. I'd better check everything's all right upstairs. And then—'

The phone rang suddenly, shrilly. His private line.

'Darling Robert,' came a sickly-sweet voice, curdling in his ear.

He covered the mouthpiece, telling Penny, 'It's Mrs Claus.'

'Robert? Are you there? Are you listening? Listen, dearest. This is most important. You and I have had our . . . difficulties in the past. We have had our differences. But I think we must put these aside for the moment.'

'Oh yes?' he said cautiously. She was a wily old monster, this one. He still got goosebumps at the sound of that voice. It took him straight back to his days under her terrible thrall at the Christmas Hotel.

'I've had wind of something awful,' she went on. 'Some ghastly news. Whispers on the air. Something is stirring. Something's about to happen to a mutual . . . friend of ours. Someone whom we both care about, a great deal.'

He frowned. 'Who?' What was she playing at?

'I'm talking about Effryggia, of course,' purred Mrs Claus. Did he imagine it, or was there a touch of genuine concern in her bold vibrato? 'I happen to know that Effie has dug herself quite deeply into a vile situation, and that she is looking for a way out. Any way out. Desperate remedies. She should turn to her friends, to those who care. But instead she has made a woeful choice.'

Pause. 'I know,' Robert told her.

'You know, do you?'

'Yes. We think it's a bad idea too. Assuming it's real. Assuming it can be done. It's a very bad idea.'

'I'm glad we see eye to eye. What are we going to do about it?'

Now there was the question.

'We want to stop her,' he told Mrs Claus. 'The ritual is at midnight tonight, by all accounts.'

'And what are you going to do? Go dashing into The Spooky Finger? Causing a scene and a great big hullabaloo, hoping for the best as usual?'

Mrs Claus was right. That was about the extent of their usual kind of plan. 'Well, what do *you* suggest?' he asked her.

'I'm not doing it. I mean it, lovey. I'm not going round there,' Brenda said decisively. She drew herself up to her full height. 'Why do we need help from that old bag? When has she ever been on our side?'

They were by the reception desk at the Miramar. Brenda had winded herself dashing up the hill. She looked incredulous that Robert wanted to go straight to the Christmas Hotel. He said, 'I think she really wants to help. She cares about Effie.'

'My foot,' Brenda snapped. She was frustrated and teetering on the edge of an extremely bad mood. She had been banging on Effie's front door for ages. She had gone round the back and tried shinning up a drainpipe and knocked her elbow quite badly. There had been no sign of Effie at all. Her house and the shop below looked as if they had been shut up for months and no one was planning on coming back.

Robert knew that Brenda's mood was one of suppressed panic. She burst out: 'You know what I think? We should get straight round that bookshop and give Marjorie Staynes what for. She's encouraging Effie to believe in all sorts of nonsense. I could see it right from that first meeting I went to. That bookshop woman is involved in things she hardly comprehends.'

'That's as may be,' Robert told her. 'But we should take whatever help we can get to save Effie.'

'We don't need help from Mrs Claus.'

'I think we do.'

Brenda glowered at him. She knew he wouldn't back down, though. She had seen him like this before and knew that he would stick to his guns.

'I'm sorry, Robert,' she relented. 'I don't know where I am any more. Just the other night I was keeping Effie prisoner in my en suite. I hardly know where my loyalties are . . .'

'Yes you do,' he told her firmly. 'Your heart's always in the right place.'

She looked at him miserably and he wondered if he'd been

tactless, referring to her anatomy in such a direct way. But she smiled at him. 'Where's Penny gone?'

'She's already at The Spooky Finger. If there's a ritual on, like there is tonight, all the Qab cult members have to assemble.'

'If I'd have joined I could have got myself in there . . .' Brenda sighed. 'But I wanted nothing more to do with it. I told Henry, I'm backing off from the whole thing.'

I told Henry, Henry told me. Henry says this, Henry says that. Had Brenda really given up all her volition to that old man of hers?

Now they were out of the hotel and hastening down the back streets in the early evening gloom. The moonlight was harsh on the dirty, frozen slush. It was slippery going as they reached the elegant streets of the Royal Crescent.

'I don't understand how Mrs Claus thinks she can be of help,' Brenda said. 'Or why, even.'

'Effie's been going round there quite a bit recently,' Robert said. 'These little meetings with Mrs Claus.'

'I know.' Brenda shrugged heavily. 'I was sort of ignoring that. I didn't like it, but what can you say? I just thought it was all a part of Effie going to the bad.'

They stepped inside the hotel, where the Christmas festivities were still in full swing. For the rest of the world the New Year had already arrived and the decorations were feeling a bit old hat and faded. But not at the Christmas Hotel. There was a huge amount of noise coming from the dining rooms and the residents' bar. There was a cabaret going on in the ballroom. Some pensioners were playing blind man's buff in the foyer. In the buff.

The ancient concierge seemed to be expecting them. They were to be ushered straight into the inner sanctum. An elf appeared at their side to accompany them, but they brushed him off.

'This is a waste of time,' Brenda hissed. 'All this palaver.'

Robert whispered back, rather sharply, 'We always rush into things. That's where we go wrong. We go barrelling in too soon and cock things up.'

She looked at him, rather hurt, as they shuffled through twisting corridors, deep inside the Edwardian hotel. 'Cock things up?'

'We need to plan things out more. Have more of a strategy, kind of thing.' It sounded lame, even as he said it. Brenda looked highly sceptical.

'And you think Mrs Claus can help with that, eh?'

But he knew Mrs Claus was a shrewd old bird. She was cunning. She knew more than she would ever say. Robert understood that they would have to listen to her tonight. He glanced at his watch. It was only nine. They had time in hand.

'Look,' gasped Brenda.

They were passing one of the smaller bars in the Christmas Hotel. The Pine Lodge, it was called. It was always a favoured place when Robert worked there, for staff and guests both, being rather more select. Tonight there were a number of younger drinkers milling about. Not the usual old folk in their cocktail dresses and military blazers.

'Walkers,' Brenda said hollowly.

And she was right. They had massive rings around their eyes, those young blokes, like they hadn't slept in a week. They were very pale under the fairy lights. About a dozen of them. They had chased out the usual guests.

'Why's Mrs Claus inviting Walkers into her establishment?' Brenda mused. As they passed through, all the young men looked up as one to observe. It reminded Robert of once being at a zoo and going past a paddock full of wolves. They moved all of one accord, eyes narrowed, clocking his progress. It gave him the chills then, and it did now.

'Henry is right,' said Brenda. 'There's more of them than we thought. Alucard and Effie have been very busy . . .'

Robert still couldn't credit it. He couldn't believe that Effie would be doing such a thing. Seducing them. Biting them. Converting them. Helping Alucard build some kind of army of pale and languid young men.

But here was the evidence. Vamps out in the open. Propping up the bar, for God's sake, drinking pints of bitter and eating pork scratchings.

Maybe we were getting complacent, Robert thought. Thinking we could deal with anything. These past few days,

Whitby had seemed a whole lot less of a cosy place.

One of the young Walkers got up from his bar table and planted himself firmly in the way. He didn't look especially vampy, except for the pallor of his flesh. He was in a normal T-shirt and trackie bottoms. He was a vampire in Primark menswear casuals.

There was a blazing intensity in his eyes. A malign intelligence. He snapped at Robert and Brenda: 'You can stop interfering in her life, you know. She doesn't want you.'

Brenda gasped. She drew up her hard, shiny handbag, as if preparing to defend herself with its sharp corners. 'We don't have time to exchange pleasantries with the likes of you,' she said.

The Walker laughed and jeered at her. He glanced at his mates and they joined in. The ones playing pool stopped what they were doing and gathered around the newcomers.

'Just you let us through,' Robert said, and it was everything he could do to prevent himself from stammering. 'We're here on important business.'

'Yeah?'

It was bad, he knew, but he couldn't help thinking: what a common lot. What a rough lot. They're like lads that hang around by the arcades. Jobless druggies. Dropouts. Troublemakers. Rough trade. That was who Effie and Alucard have been preying on and recruiting. A shiver went through him. He had been with fellas like these. He had picked them up and, sometimes, let himself be picked up by them. When he looked around at them now, he felt they were fencing him in. They seemed so amused to see both him and Brenda squirming anxiously.

'Let us pass!' Brenda called out suddenly. 'Avaunt!' She had been taking lessons from Henry Cleavis, Robert thought. Sure enough, she reached into her bag and produced a silver crucifix big as an egg whisk, plus a plastic bottle of mineral water, though Robert guessed it had come from a font.

The Walkers simply laughed at her.

The one who'd got up first – their leader, he seemed like – took a step towards her and sneered. Robert hated himself for it, but he noticed how handsome this lead vamp was. That flattened, almost Roman nose. That thuggish brow. That whole rough lad look. Why, oh why, thought Robert, must we have *scally* vampires?

The leader wrenched the crucifix out of Brenda's hand. 'What gives you the right to wave stuff like this about?' he said. 'You're just as cursed as we are.'

Robert looked at her, and he knew straight away what she was going to do.

He yelled out, 'Brenda, no!' in the instant before she punched the Walker in the mouth.

He was straight back on his feet and all his fellows were diving in. It was the cue they had been waiting for.

Robert and Brenda were caught in a punch-up.

Sometimes Robert thought Brenda secretly enjoyed this kind of thing. When the words ran out. When exasperation got the better of her. When she was frightened and at her wits' end. She liked to roll up her sleeves and give her opponents a bloody good thrashing.

And she was good! Really, Robert was amazed every time. She seemed to rear up to twice her height. She set her jaw in this very fierce way. Usually that was enough to send most enemies packing. But these lads were feral. They weren't easily scared. And there were a dozen of them: surely too many for Brenda and Robert to deal with.

A few of them she sent sprawling in the first few moments. But sheer weight of numbers was her undoing. And Robert's. He got a few jabs and kicks in. But the Walkers didn't seem to feel a thing. They were laughing.

They grabbed hold of both Brenda and Robert, pulling them about. Pushing them from one to another. Toying with them. Waiting to get the signal to go for the kill.

We've done it now, Robert thought. We've really messed it up.

We're at their mercy.

Of course, he should have known that this kind of thing would not be tolerated for long at the Christmas Hotel. If there was any funny business, it was all at the command of Mrs Claus. Anything else was to be quashed immediately. She ran a very tight ship at the edge of the West Cliff.

It was the elf they'd brushed off who raised the alarm. Within seconds of their fracas in the Pine Lodge escalating into a full-scale brawl, the place was filled with elves in their figure-hugging felt outfits. They were stronger than they looked, flinging themselves at the Walkers and dragging Brenda and Robert out of danger.

There was a livid glint of excitement in Brenda's eye, Robert noticed. He would be all cuts and bruises tomorrow, but it looked like there was barely a mark on the old lady.

And here came another old lady entering the fray. The noise was such in this select bar that Robert didn't hear her motorised Bath chair until she was on top of them.

'What the buggery bollocks do you lot think you're doing?'

Her voice was fruity and shrill as iced limoncello. Her blazing eyes darted around the room accusingly. She was quite a formidable sight.

It had been a while since Robert had seen Mrs Claus livid as this. Her fury filled the room, and even the jukebox fell silent. The Walkers stood still. Naughty schoolboys shouted down by their headmistress.

'You lot! I let you come in here. Gawd knows why. I should never have let you anywhere near. You rabble. You scum. But I felt sorry for you, didn't I?' She curled her thickly glossed lips at them and her tinselled earrings jangled as she tossed her coiffed hair. 'Pity! On you! You scabby bunch.

How DARE you attack my friends!'

Brenda darted a sideways glance. Friends! she was thinking. She wanted none of this old dame's friendship. But she kept her counsel, wisely. She bit her tongue. She stowed her vamp-hunting paraphernalia back inside her handbag.

The head honcho of Mrs Claus's undead lads' club spoke up. 'We didn't know they weren't supposed to be here.' He nodded brusquely at Brenda. 'We thought it was a chance to nab her. While she's away from her fancy man. The killer. We thought we should scrag her while she was undefended.'

Huh! thought Robert. So my presence stands for nothing then, obviously. They never even thought of him as any obstacle. In fact, no one spared him a second glance during this whole face-off.

Mrs Claus ground her tiny pearly teeth together. 'I decide what goes on under my roof. Me and me alone. I'm not having you setting upon old ladies and trying to do them in. No matter how justified you think you are.'

'We are sworn to destroy her. And her old man,' the young man said. 'You might protect her while she's in this dump. But not outside. We'll get her. She has to pay.'

'Dump!' screeched Mrs Claus. 'Dump, indeed!'

'This was a mistake, coming here,' Brenda muttered, setting her beehive straight. 'Come on, Robert. Let's—'

'No!' shouted Mrs Claus. 'You're here for a good reason. These flaming louts need to understand that.'

'What?' jeered the leader of the louts.

'They're here to try to save Effie,' said Mrs Claus. 'That's why I've asked them here. You don't see, do you? Effie's Brenda's best friend. Even after everything. And she'll do anything to save her. That's why she's come here. For my help.'

The Walkers looked unconvinced.

'You want Effryggia to stay here, don't you?'

The ruffian said, 'Effryggia's going nowhere. She belongs to us.'

Brenda and Robert darted an alarmed glance at each other. How awful to hear Effie talked about like this.

'Effie's on her way out of here,' Mrs Claus said. 'She's leaving tonight. At midnight. She's making a most unorthodox exit to a place that you probably wouldn't be able to credit, even if you knew where it was.'

The vamps were stirring, miserably roused at her words. They were all a bit thick, Robert realised. Thicker than ever they were alive.

Their leader said, 'I don't know what you're on about. Where's she off to? The last Leeds train has gone by now, and the Middlesbrough one doesn't—'

'She's going somewhere by *magic*,' said Mrs Claus. 'You know she's a witch, don't you? Well, she's got another witch to help her. That Marjorie Staynes one. The one who runs The Spooky Finger bookshop on Silver Street.'

The Walkers nodded. They knew the place. 'She's leaving tonight? Midnight?'

'You can't let her leave town,' said Mrs Claus. She was smiling now. Licking her chops with pleasure. She was twisting these hooligans around her chubby little finger.

Brenda saw at once what she was doing. 'You mustn't send them round there!'

Mrs Claus rolled her eyes. 'We all want the same thing, don't we? We don't want Effie to leave town. We want this meeting – this arcane ritual – nipping in the bud, don't we?'

Already the lads were putting down their pints and yanking on their jackets. All twelve of them. Their leader was winding a scarf around his beautiful, scarred neck. 'We're going. We'll stop them. Effie's going nowhere.'

Brenda was looking at Robert in alarm. They were both frozen there.

All Robert could think was that Penny was in that shop. Incognito in the cult of Qab. And so was Gila. He was working there as usual. Being the loyal servant of Marjorie Staynes. The two of them were in there, along with Effie, and none of them would have any idea that the Walkers were abroad in the night.

And coming for them.

Robert and Brenda watched helplessly. Brenda stood in the doorway briefly before she got pushed aside.

'No! You can't! There'll be a massacre! There'll be murder!'

Mrs Claus spread her hands like she could do no more. She had wound these boys up and there was no stopping them now. 'We want Effie back, don't we? She's fallen into the clutches of the Staynes woman. Only this way can I bring her back.'

Deadlock. Brenda and Mrs Claus stared at each other as the last of the boys flitted from the room, cackling at the idea of the coming fun.

Robert was hunting in his jacket pockets for his mobile. He had to ring Penny. Warn her. Warn them all about what was coming.

'I should have known,' spat Brenda. 'I should have known what kind of help you would be. You're just making it worse. Like you always do.'

'Poppycock!' Mrs Claus shrieked. She gurgled with laughter and gestured to the elf behind the bar. 'Let's have a lovely drink and talk this over.'

'You delight in horror,' Brenda accused her. 'You're in your element, commanding those Walkers . . . those boys . . .'

'It's lucky they were here,' said Mrs Claus. 'We have a job needs doing and they're more than happy to do it.'

'You don't care about Effie,' Brenda flung at her. 'You just want to mix things up and cause a rumpus. You couldn't care less about Effie.'

Mrs Claus swung her creaking bath chair round and confronted Brenda full on. Now she was in deadly earnest as she said, 'That's where you're wrong. You know nothing. You never did. You can stop your gums flapping right there.'

'I'm Effie's friend,' Brenda shouted. 'Whatever's happened. I care what becomes of her. You don't. Why should you? Who are you to her anyway?'

And that was when the mistress of the Christmas Hotel floored both Brenda and Robert with just three words.

She said, quite simply: 'I'm her mother.'

Afterwards, Robert realised that he was prepared to stay there a bit longer and listen to Mrs Claus. Afterwards, he wished that they had. He wanted to hear what evidence she had. He wanted to know how on earth such a thing could be true. He had only a few brief seconds, standing in that bar before her bath chair, struggling to put it all together. The pieces were just about beginning to fit when Brenda whirled away with her hands over her ears.

'I'm not listening to this! It's just more rubbish! More of your evil lies to put us off our stroke!' She barged to the doorway, grabbing hold of Robert's sleeve. 'We're not staying for any more of it.'

'But it's all true!' Mrs Claus bellowed. Robert was struck by the lack of mockery in her tone. There wasn't a trace of her usual insincerity. She meant this. He could see it in her deeply lined face, which for a moment looked vulnerable. This was for real. She believed it.

'Brenda . . .' Robert tried to squirm out of her grasp. She was dragging him to the exit.

'Robert,' she warned. 'We're going. That old monster would say anything to distract us.'

'You'll believe me! You'll change your mind soon!' Mrs Claus raised her voice as they left the bar. They were heading back down the corridor with her voice warbling after them: 'You'll need my help pretty soon and then you'll come back! I've got something I think you're going to need!'

'What's she on about?' grunted Brenda, starting to run, taking them out of range of that awful voice. 'Why does she have to interfere with everything and make it all worse? We should never have come here, Robert.'

'I thought she wanted to help us!' Robert protested. But he guessed nothing good had come of this trip to the Christmas Hotel. As ever.

In the foyer and public rooms at the front, the residents were getting whipped up into a frenzy of festive hilarity. The main doors stood open in the scally vampires' wake.

Great buffeting winds came in with flurries of snow, but even that didn't affect the atmosphere of the Christmas Hotel. The place was always a madhouse.

'We've got to run,' said Brenda grimly. 'Those lads have a good start on us.'

And so began a heart-stopping dash through the elegant part of town. The going was tricky because of the accumulated snow and ice. As they struggled and skidded up Hudson Street, the wind tried to force them back down the hill. Their breath caught in their throats and their legs burned with fatigue, as if they were being held in check by some vast invisible force.

'Don't give up, Robert!' Brenda gasped. 'Those Walkers . . . we have to stop them . . . there's no telling what . . . they'll do . . .'

Robert had his phone redialling Penny, but hers must have been switched off as she took part in the cult's rituals.

Brenda was trying to ring Cleavis. She got him, and gasped into the phone as the wind whipped around them in a mini cyclone. Robert was standing next to her, and even he could hardly make out her words: 'Vamps . . . Spooky Finger . . . Effie . . . save them!'

And then she was putting her head down against the wind, tying her headscarf tightly under her chin and bracing her heavy shoulders as she barrelled forward. When they managed to reach Silver Street with its broad shop fronts, the going became a little easier. The elements had a harder time getting at them.

'Listen!' Brenda gasped.

All Robert could hear was the wind. His ears were scorched by the frozen air. He couldn't hear a thing, and then – suddenly – there was a great burst of sound. A crashing and tinkling of glass. Shrill screams. Shocked cries. Guttural laughter. They were just a few doors from the middle of Silver Street. That was where the noise was coming from.

They rounded the corner, and there was The Spooky Finger with its front window punched in. Smoky light came blazing on to the street. The shop's immaculate displays were wrecked, and books had been scooped into the street, flapping away on the wind like broken birds.

The noise from within was horrible.

Brenda and Robert were bracing themselves to plunge into that chaos of tumbling books and crashing shelves when the front door flew open and one of the vamp boys came staggering backwards into the street, like someone straight out of a Western barroom brawl. After him came Gila, Robert's Gila, looking furious and bloodied.

He was holding some kind of glittering golden sword. 'Robert! Hold him down!'

Robert dashed forward, but the boy in the hoodie with the crimson fangs was too strong for him.

Robert jumped backwards as Gila wielded that sword. It whirled about his head and the vampire snarled.

Brenda swore. 'This is what happens! I warned her! I bloody warned her!' Then she hurried past Robert and stepped into the shop.

Sssswwshht. Gila slashed at the vamp as another came out to join the fight. Robert dodged out of the way just in time.

Gila shouted at him: 'Robert, get inside there. Help them. Penny . . .'

He didn't need telling twice. He bolted towards the entrance, dodging his way through Gila's opponents. Gila could deal with them. But where had he got that sword, and what on earth was he wearing? Hardly anything. Some kind of golden loincloth thing.

Inside it was a scene of horrible chaos. Bookshelves had gone down like dominoes, scattering their precious cargo everywhere.

There was smoke in the air, and Robert didn't know whether a fire had broken out or if it was just incense.

There was yelling and screaming and the taunting cries of the scally vamps. The first person he recognised was Leena from the shop under Brenda's house, getting her neck bitten by some lascivious wretch.

Robert picked up a chair and smashed it on to the Walker's broad back, dislodging him from his gory snack. He could see that Leena's skin was broken. Livid blood was flowing down her neck, on to the golden priestess robes she was sporting. She clutched her punctured flesh and started screaming horribly.

Robert couldn't help her now. He could think only about the others. Penny. Where was Penny?

He waded into the shop and a few women pushed past him, fleeing into the night in their strange robes and headdresses. The vamps were letting them go, it seemed. Evidently none of these were the particular woman they were here for.

In the deepest recesses of the shop, Robert found Penny.

She'd been backed into the farthest corner by the leader of the vamps. He was spitting and snarling at her and yelling out questions. Penny was white-faced with shock. She couldn't say a word. She was mute with amazement.

'Where's Brenda?' Robert yelled, breaking into their scene.

The vamp leader whirled at the sound of Robert's voice, snapping the spell he had on Penny.

That was all Penny needed. She lifted up a weird heavy pot thing and brought it smashing down on the lad's head. He collapsed.

But they knew it wouldn't keep him down for long.

'Brenda!'

'I'm here. Wedged on the staircase.'

Dashing over with Penny at his heels, Robert had to lever himself round a fallen case of children's books and a tangle of ruined bonsai trees.

There on the familiar staircase was Brenda. She was holding Marjorie Staynes in a brutal headlock. The elderly bookshop owner was wearing a very elaborate set of golden robes.

'You can do what you want with me, you monster,' Marjorie spat. 'But Effie's getting away. You can't stop her. I'll exert every fibre of my being to prevent you from interfering further.'

If Robert's ears didn't deceive him, Brenda snarled at this. 'How are things downstairs?' she asked.

'Chaos,' he told her. 'But the women are getting away, I think. Mostly. The vamps are here for us and Effie . . .'

'How could you bring them here?' Marjorie moaned. 'What harm were we doing, really, in our cult? How could you set those fiends upon us?'

'We didn't,' said Brenda.

'But you did! You sent them ahead of you!'

Brenda tightened her grip on Marjorie's neck and Robert was starting to worry she would wrench her head off. 'You'll never believe me, but we really didn't. Now, you're going to get out of my way. Let me get to Effie.'

Behind Robert, Penny was calling out, 'There's something happening down here . . . !'

She was right. There was renewed noise. The battle in the bookshop had been rejoined.

Brenda knew at once who it was. 'Henry's here!' she said, as if that fact redoubled her strength. She forced Marjorie down the stairs and into Robert's waiting arms. 'Robert, keep her down there.'

'Where are you going?' he grunted with the effort of keeping Marjorie still. Her arms windmilled and thrashed about in the narrow stairwell.

'The lavvy,' said Brenda grimly.

'You interfering devils,' Marjorie snarled. Her nails reached out for Robert, tearing at his face. That was all the impetus he needed to shove her down the stairs. 'Penny, catch!' He'd had quite enough of this old horror. Her funny looks and nasty words every time he went round there. The way she treated poor Gila as her servant. Like something subhuman.

The noise in the bookshop was overwhelming by now. Crashing and smashing. Screams of terror. Weird explosions. Cries of triumph from Henry Cleavis. Robert recognised his bellowing voice. He was in his element. It was a massacre down there.

Robert left them to it.

He hurried up the stairs after Brenda, to the lavvy.

It was a confined space, that middle landing. Brenda wedged the whole space solid with her trembling bulk.

She was confronting her friend.

The bit of Effie Robert could see past Brenda seemed very unfamiliar to him. She was in robes, just as the other women in the cult were, but Effie's were even more elaborate. She had a headdress and a sceptre kind of thing, with which she was holding Brenda at bay.

'You're not taking me,' Effie said.

From her voice, Robert knew at once that she had gone crazy. Maybe it was the ritual, or some kind of drug Marjorie had been giving her. Robert didn't know. Maybe it was the vampire virus whizzing round her rejuvenated veins. But Effie was pop-eyed with hatred and determination.

Brenda managed to keep her own voice calm. 'Effie, this has to stop. I'm here to help you.'

'You?' Effie gasped. 'On New Year's Eve you were the one sending me away! You said I had to get out of town as quickly as I could. Well, that's what I'm doing. Good riddance, eh?'

'Not like this!' Brenda shouted. 'I said *Scotland*, didn't I?'

And then Robert could see more of the tiny bathroom where Effie was making her last stand. She was an incongruously magisterial figure by the toilet. But there was something else in there. Something weird. Something he had already heard Penny describe.

The Lakeland watercolour on the wall. It was morphing and shifting. A hole was opening up in the painting. A portal. A vortex through time and space, growing larger and larger as the two old friends confronted one another.

'I want to go to Qab,' Effie said. 'You can't stop me.'

'It isn't real,' said Brenda. 'That Marjorie Staynes woman has got you all confused. You're believing in things out of old books because your head's messed up. It's Alucard's fault, he—'

'Don't you criticise Kristoff! How dare you? Accomplice! Murderess!'

'Effie, don't . . . !'

Now the vortex was swirling purple and black, blanking out much of the wall on the right-hand side of the bathroom.

'What's this then, eh?' Effie shrilled, teetering on the brink. 'Where does this lead? This gap in the Very Fabric of Time and Space?'

'What is it, Brenda?' Robert asked her urgently. 'Is it another Maw? Another gateway into hell?'

'It's a Dreadful Flap!' Effie shouted triumphantly. 'And it's been opened up tonight by the combined willpower of the cult of Qab! By the women warriors of The Spooky Finger! Look what we have done! Isn't it marvellous?'

Brenda's voice sounded dry and small as she said, 'You mustn't do this, Effie.'

'Call yourself a friend.' Effie frowned. 'What do you do? Set my own vampire boys upon me and my cult! What were you playing at? Those boys are *mine*! How dare you try to twist and control them.'

'That was Mrs Claus,' Robert piped up. He wasn't going to have Brenda falsely accused. 'She sent them round here. She wanted to stop you opening up this . . . Dreadful Flap thing as much as we do.'

'She wouldn't interfere,' said Effie. 'She just wouldn't.'

Brenda's voice was even smaller. 'And why's that, Effie? Why wouldn't she?'

Effie's eyes lit up. It was clear that she had a strange and lovely secret to tell. 'She's my mother. Did I never mention that, Brenda?' She gurgled with horrible laughter and then turned to look with interest into the spiralling abyss on the lavvy wall. 'I've had enough of all this talking. It's time to go.'

They were interrupted then by a gruff male voice from the bottom of the stairs. 'Brenda! Brenda darling, I'm here! Is she there? Have you got her? Have you captured her again?'

Effie recognised Henry Cleavis, just as the others did. Her eyes narrowed. 'You've brought him after me. That killer. You've brought him here to murder me!'

Brenda shook her head. 'No, Effie, no. That's not . . .'

But Effie just scowled. She adjusted her headdress and straightened her shoulders, then without another glance at her former friends she stepped straight into the vortex.

And was instantly gone.

'Effie!' Brenda shrieked, jolting forward just as Henry came thundering up the stairs.

The Dreadful Flap gave a kind of satisfied shudder, as if it had ingested something delicious. Then, in a flash, it was gone. Leaving just that tatty watercolour on the wall.

'Have you got her?' Cleavis cried, reaching them at last, streaked with dust and vampire gore.

'She's gone,' Brenda said hollowly. 'Gone to Qab, she says.'

They stood looking at the empty bathroom.

Downstairs it had all gone a bit ominously quiet. Robert was hardly aware of Penny joining them on the landing and staring at the space that Effie had occupied scant moments before.

'But is there really such a place as Qab?' Robert asked aloud. 'It was just a silly game, wasn't it? Just that mad Marjorie Staynes having everyone on . . .'

Penny surprised him. 'I'm really not so sure, you know.'

Henry Cleavis put his arm around Brenda. She shrugged her lover off.

Brenda stayed very quiet.

Cleavis said, 'Erm. Well. Y'know. Actually. It does exist, you know. In actuality. Qab. It really does. I think. But I, erm, I have to check. I have to find out for sure.'

'And how do you do that?' asked Brenda wearily.

'There's a way,' said the old professor.

As Cleavis turned to lead them down the staircase, Robert's thoughts went to Gila, and he ran through the ruined shop to find his boyfriend out on the street.

Gila's enemies were slain or fled and Robert's lizard boy was standing in the icy road with his ornamental sword. He was looking crazy and very, very out of place.

Brenda in Bloomsbury

Sometimes my mistress would shout at me and I would dash out of the house to sit in Gordon Square till things died down.

She wasn't a nasty woman, my mistress, but she'd get herself all het up – especially when her work wasn't going so well. I'd sit on a bench, quietly, a few streets away, reminding myself what a grand spot I lived in. How lucky I was to have fetched up here, in Bloomsbury, and how fortunate it was that Mrs Mapp had been so good to me.

She had taken me in when I was on my last legs.

She had never been satisfied with her domestic help. Well, I have always been what they called then a good plain cook. And I can sweep up, mop and polish and do all the required household tasks. To me, all that came quite naturally, as if it had been built into me somehow, at my genesis. (Now there's a funny thought!)

I was only too glad to pitch in and work my fingers to the

bone for Mrs Beatrice Mapp of Tavistock Square. I'd sleep under the attic eaves of my very own room at the top of her house and I'd thank my lucky stars.

At that point in my very long life I hadn't had a room for many years. I'd recently come out of one of those periods that I spent wandering aimlessly, pillar to post, town to town. My brain was leaking sawdust and I retained hardly any memories or faces. When I staggered into Mrs Mapp's life the first time – bedraggled and starving – I was Brenda all alone in London, and it was as if I had no past at all. It seems to me now that my memories only stick when I'm somewhere I can be happy for a while. That's something I've learned. I didn't know it then – a hundred years ago – but I was already a century old. And yet I was still only just learning to be me.

I assumed that restlessness and unhappiness came with the territory and there was no other way for me to exist on the face of the planet. I never expected to put down any roots or retain any memories, fond or otherwise.

But pretty soon after starting my life in Tavistock Square, I grew fond of Mrs Mapp, though she could be harsh and shout at me when she wasn't happy with my work, her work, or in herself. She was plagued by her own demons, that poor girl. She had been widowed so very young. Her husband had been a banker, much older than her and dicky in the region of the heart. She had no one now, apart from me, though there were reminders all over that house of her gallant, danger-seeking brother, who was dead abroad and in a foreign grave. And reminders also of her uncle, who had left all his glass cases of stuffed beasties and insects for me to polish and dust. Some kind of naturist, he was meant to be, before he 'popped orf', as Mrs Mapp put it.

But it wasn't all the dead relatives and the sadness in her life that constituted Mrs Mapp's demons. No, that girl was plagued by the contents of her own imagination.

See how I call her a girl? Well, that's all she was, back then. Barely over thirty and the most beautiful complexion you've ever seen. Like softest whipped cream on your morning coffee. And yet she dressed in such drab colours. Plantpot hats and smart little shoes, that was Mrs Mapp. She wasn't one for painting herself up. She was rather scornful of women who made too much of themselves out of vanity. She dressed like a granny, but you could see she was someone special. She was something like a lily, I always thought. Slightly drooping and a tad melancholic in her ways. When she wasn't furious and stomping about, anyhow.

You know, I liked being her servant. I really did. That thought swims out of nowhere and it jolts me, the sheer truth of it. I relished that point in my life, that whole set-up. That time with Mrs Mapp writing her stories at all hours of the day and me looking after her. I can see her now, sitting in a muddle with her splotchy pens and messy papers, her ashtrays and those bone-china cups she liked to sip cold coffee from. She would write as and when the mood – or the muse – took her, in any corner of that five-storey house on Tavistock Square.

She would sink to the floor and go into a deep kind of trance. I'd rush to bring her writing things as her hands clenched spasmodically. Her eyes went wide and blank. Her long fingers scratched away at the pages, tearing them, spilling ink on the carpet. It frightened me at first, seeing her like that. I thought she was having some kind of funny do. A horrible fit. But she was just writing. That's all it was.

'I've gorn orf,' she would tell me. 'When you see me like that, Brenda, a-twitchin' and rollin' my eyes in my head, I've gorn orf to elsewhere.'

Oh, she did talk posh and funny.

'Ever since I was a gel,' she said, 'I've always gorn orf like that, elsewhere.'

I wasn't to be alarmed when she went off inside herself.

'This is the life of the mind, Brenda dear. Most likely, being low-born, you've never seen the likes of this before. But inside I am struggling with great forces. Primeval forces of creation. I am fusing together the fibres of the fragments of story that lie within this feeble female form. My imagination is making the world of my story come true. It takes such colossal effort, Brenda dear. I am like God, wrestlin' with vast chunks of matter – with molten mountains. With earth and wind and fire. It's quite a to-do. And that's what's happenin' when I've gorn orf.'

So, this was how she used to go on.

I would get rudely awakened in the night, whenever one of her creative fits took her over. I'd have to be ready with the papers and pens and the ready-rolled fags. And after a marathon session of composition was over and she emerged from her trance, she would demand sustenance. I'd be forced to come running with plates of kippers, bowls of hot broth and flasks of tea. She would consume this stuff mechanically, and all the while her inner eye would be focused on the faraway world she was intent on inventing.

Quite often she would deem these writing sessions a failure. She'd get up and storm about the house, slamming her frail form into the stately furniture that crowded her home. She'd smash up the crockery as she vented her temper. She spoiled some lovely pieces, did Mrs Mapp. I'd be the one picking up the smithereens, once her vexatious mood had passed.

Other times – less frequent – she might make a breakthrough. She'd write something that, when she read it back, she was actually pleased with. It was alive on the page. It was real. She'd read it to herself, lips moving rapidly, and break out in the most wonderful smile. Those were the happiest days in the house in Tavistock Square: when Mrs Mapp shocked herself by producing something *good enough*.

That was how she worked and how we lived. She wrote her world into existence slowly, obsessively, and I danced attendance around her. I dodged her moods and the flying crockery shards. I made eggy bread in the night and I patted her back when she sobbed because the writing wasn't working out and the world she was making was frittering away under her fingers.

Oh, it hurt her when it wasn't working.

'It isn't coming alive for me, Brenda,' she wailed and despaired. Those worst periods always seemed to be in the wee small hours. They were awful interludes, when Bloomsbury seemed very quiet and still all around us, as if we were the only two women alive in the world.

'I can't make it live. It is desolate, empty tonight . . . I can't bring the spark of life to my world. I can't reach it . . . I can't *get* to Qab . . .'

Well, sometimes the things she said left me utterly bewildered. I just got on with the most basic tasks. The everyday stuff.

I concentrated on my routines. The things I knew how to do. Things like eradicating the awful pong of cats in the back garden, or placing lavender in deep heavy bowls all around the house, hoping its lulling scent would soothe my mistress. I loved to wax the furniture she'd inherited from her parents. I would stroke those chairs and tables and cupboards, feeling them all over like I loved them so much I had to cover their every inch with my caresses. Bit by bit, every corner of that house became known to me, through the endless process of buffing and dusting. The house and its contents became as familiar to me as my own body.

On the other hand, Mrs Mapp seemed much less at home than I did, even in her own space. She minced about on those tiny feet. She floated and bobbed awkwardly about the place. She only seemed to relax when she went into one of her queer spells of composition.

'It's true, Brenda dear,' she once told me. 'I'm only really at peace when I've gorn orf elsewhere.'

I was dishing out the eggs and the devilled kidneys one morning in the breakfast room when Mrs Mapp found me and tackled me.

'Well, Brenda dear?'

I was making a big show of fussing with the silver salvers. 'Yes, madam?'

Then she was hovering over me. 'Tell me! Put me out of my misery! Tell me what you thought!'

I looked at her and bit my lip. 'You know, Mrs Mapp. Reading's not really my thing. I mean, only the paper, or a serial in my magazine, perhaps. I find it hard, concentrating on the high-flown stuff that you go in for. I don't know that I understand half of it, really . . .'

She put a hand to her forehead and I could see that she was marshalling her temper. She clenched her teeth and interrupted my idiotic flow. 'I happen to know that you sat up all night with it, Brenda dear. I sat on the stairs outside your door last night. I saw the light spilling on to the landing. I heard your bedsprings' ghostly rumbling. I could hear you turning the pages over. I know you read my manuscript last night, just as I begged you to.'

Begged! I thought, straightening up the crispy bacon rashers with the special tongs. Commanded, more like.

'So I know that you read my book from cover to cover, Brenda dear.' Her eyes flashed in triumph.

What cheek! I thought. The mistress spying on the maid like that. As if I had no right to privacy, or a decent night's unbroken rest. I looked at her and caught the desperate look in those watery blue eyes. I knew I had to answer her properly.

I had indeed sat up in my narrow bed all night long, giving my full attention to her bizarre story. I had been drawn along on that peculiar quest in the strange and savage land created by my mistress. In the story – as far as I could make out – a disparate group of characters travelled through all kinds of jungles and deserts and mountain ranges, making their way steadily towards a city. Not just any city. A city populated by warrior women, who all lived in their separate palaces, tended to by servile lizard men. All these warrior women believed themselves to be queen in their own homes. All of them vied for power and were ruthless, utterly ruthless, in the ways they went about gaining it. But all were ruled by the imperious Queen of Qab, who lived in the biggest palace of all, in the very centre of the city. Though they muttered and schemed, the warrior women could never get rid of this beautiful, wicked, blood-drinking queen. It was the Queen of Qab who welcomed the heroes of the book into her realm and the secret heart of her palace, and soon our heroes learned that they were at the mercy of *Her* who must always be obeyed. And that's when things turned very nasty indeed.

So that was Mrs Mapp's book. Just after dawn, when the birds were belting out their cheery songs over our rooftops, I came to the end of it. Maybe I didn't fully comprehend it. Maybe I had drifted off and dreamed some of the stranger bits. But now I felt muddled and somehow stirred up by what I had read. Mrs Mapp's book had disturbed me, and I didn't understand how or why.

I looked at her levelly. 'I wasn't quite sure what to make of it, to be honest, madam.' I watched my poor mistress flinch, like I'd turned round and slapped her. 'I'm sure it's very well written and all. But it isn't really intended for the likes of me, is it? I'm ignorant and I like down-to-earth things. I like a bit of crime and a nice detective mystery. All this talk of . . . of other lands and worlds. And that terrible queen who tortures them and plays with their minds like she does! Oh, I'd hate to meet someone like that. However did you dream her up? It leaves me feeling a bit creepy, really.'

Her expression had grown sour. 'Creepy?' she said, very quietly. 'I made you feel creepy, did I?'

'I'm sure it was all over my head. What you need is one of your friends to read it. Someone brainier than I am. Someone like . . . like Mr Rupert Von Thal, perhaps. Or his friend Professor Quandary. They'll be able to tell you. They'll be able to reassure you, I'm sure, that it's a marvellous piece of work. I'm sure it is. It's just . . . I'm just a servant, Mrs Mapp, and I don't know anything about other worlds and fancy books and what-have-you . . .'

She narrowed her eyes, studying me. 'Maybe that's not such a bad idea. Mr Von Thal is well travelled. He is what he would describe as a man of the world. I believe he has even written some articles of his own about his escapades with Professor Quandary in the further-flung reaches of the Empire. Hmmm. Yes, it's a very good thought, Brenda dear. Thank you. I will send a note round at once. I'll invite him to supper this evening and I will ask him to take away the manuscript.' She stopped musing and looked at me sharply. 'Where is it, by the way, Brenda dear? Did you put it tidily back into the folder? I hope you didn't cover it in tea stains and finger smudges and biscuit crumbs, hmmm?'

So the next thing was, I was dispatched to drop a note in person at the residence of Mr Rupert Von Thal – noted memoirist and brave explorer of the more savage and untamed tropical lands.

I had met him before, and taken his hat and cane, and served on him at dinner a number of times. I knew he cut a dashing figure. He wore one of those moustaches I'm rather keen on and was, on the whole, a fine specimen of a man. He was given to planting himself foursquare in front of the fire and congratulating me on my splendid chops. How I loved to hear him praise the sundry dainties I served up. It seemed I never failed to provoke that manly appetite of his. Secretly, I was rather glad to whiz round to his house near Regent's Park with madam's urgently scribbled supper invitation. It had been no accident that I had suggested his name. I liked a nice look at him, Mr Rupert.

It was a mild spring day. London was coming back alive. You have to remember, it wasn't so long since all the mess and disaster of the Martian invasion. There were still great big chunks of the capital missing and the rebuilding work was somewhat slow. That morning the city was alive with promise and I hardly felt my lack of sleep as I dashed through the narrow byways of Fitzrovia. Then I was bustling down the heavy thoroughfare of the Euston Road, dodging cabs and the new motorised vehicles.

I was just turning in to Baker Street when I was assailed by one of those weird moments of déjà vu that I'm prone to. I paused in the road as one of my fragmented memories came bubbling unwilled to the surface of my mind.

I had been here before. Not just in recent months, passing messages to and from Mr Rupert Von Thal. Several years ago . . . I had been here in Baker Street, hadn't I? I'd been up to my neck in some kind of adventure. I could just about remember being in an upstairs room in one of these narrow houses. There was a man . . . looking ever so crossly at me as I sat there on his settee. And another man was there, looking sternly at me also.

No use. It was gone. Whatever I had glimpsed was a part of some other life. It might as well be another Brenda. It was like I was fishing for memories sometimes. Like tickling for trout in a particularly murky stream. With a flash of brilliant scales the trout was gone, back into the depths.

I shook myself awake – just in time, as a milk van honked at me and I hastened to the kerb and took myself off to complete my mission as instructed.

Oh, these moments of reverie. How I wished they'd just leave me alone. Didn't I have enough in my life to look after? With Mrs Mapp and her tall house and her devotion to her art? Why did my obscure past try to reclaim me periodically? Really, what was so special about me?

I pushed these thoughts away. Thinking too hard never brought happiness to anyone, did it? Just look at Mrs Mapp and the way she cudgelled her delicate brains. And what for? Just to produce that strange book of hers.

It had made me feel downright peculiar. Even in the spring sunlight that sensation clung to me. I wondered what other people would make of it. People like the lovely and virile Rupert Von Thal.

Ah, here he was. Emerging on to the busy street bang in front of me. I had only just caught him in time, as he slammed shut his glossy front door. He took a deeply appreciative sniff of the London air. His momentous moustache looked to be waxed to a point at both ends.

I was about to step out in front of him when he turned to look me straight in the eye. Wonderful instincts he had. He always said his instincts were honed and very well seasoned by all the time he had spent in the bush.

Mr Rupert was amused by my flummoxing and stammering in his presence. Just as he was amused by Beatrice Mapp's curt missive:

'Mr Von Thal – you're needed. Supper tonight at Tavistock Square.'

That evening he appeared at our door with sheaves of pink lilies. Their scent greeted me in a rush as I led him into the hall. He was resplendent in a lounge suit of burgundy and cream. He looked rather like a summer pudding, and I felt myself go queasy as I relieved him of his unwieldy bouquet.

Naturally I overheard most of their supper conversation, these two old friends, as I waited on them. I was giving them my goulash – a rustic, peppery broth, the recipe for which I picked up somewhere, I can't even recall where. Mrs Mapp was gratified by this exotic savour, even as she fanned her mouth genteelly at the piquant spices. I hovered to see Mr Rupert's reaction to the meal I had carefully prepared that afternoon, and got a nod and a wink for my pains. He was far more intent on his conflab with the mistress of the house than he was on the stew before him.

Mrs Mapp had a touch of hauteur about her, I noticed. She liked to pretend to hold Mr Rupert at arm's length. I could always see through that. I knew that deep down she was mad about the boyish adventurer.

'Your mentor . . .' she began.

He frowned. 'He's not really my mentor.'

'Professor Quandary,' Mrs Mapp went on. 'The two of you together have experienced a number of strange exploits, have you not?'

Mr Rupert smiled, and I could see he was enjoying this latest jousting match. 'Indeed. But we go into these things, Mrs Mapp, as equals. The professor is not my mentor. We both have a great deal to learn from each other, and we complement each other with our separate gifts in these . . . adventures of ours.'

'Quandary,' Mrs Mapp tutted. 'What a ridiculous name. Made up, of course?'

'Only a very few know the true identity of the brilliant professor.'

'I should like to meet him again one day.'

'And he would like to see you too, Mrs Mapp. I believe you made a great impression on him, the day I introduced you, after his lecture on the affair of the wicked London Monster.'

Mrs Mapp seemed ever so pleased to be remembered by the famous professor. I hadn't met him as yet, but I'd read all about his many adventures in the *Illustrated Fitzrovian Spree,* several of them written up by Rupert Von Thal himself in his breathlessly enthusiastic prose. I'd even read the account of their besting that horrible London Monster, which Mr Rupert had just alluded to.

Anyhow, as I got on with clearing their supper things and topping up their goblets with tangy red wine, Mrs Mapp eventually worked her way round to the reason for the evening's peremptory summons.

'You've finished your book!' Mr Rupert's expression was alight with amusement, but also pleasure in Mrs Mapp's muted triumph.

'And it is an adventure story, Mr Von Thal. One I thought, perhaps, you may find of some slight interest.'

'I'm sure I will. An adventure! But Mrs Mapp – forgive me – what does a lady like you know about . . . ?'

'Adventures?' Her mouth quirked into a pretty little smile. She was an exquisite thing, really. The likes of Mr Rupert Von Thal stood nary a chance before her subtle charms. 'I know all I need to know about adventures. They are all up here, inside my mind. Here I have adventures all day and night long. Locked within my own seclusion . . . such outrageous happenings . . .'

His eyes were fixed on her. He gave a little cough before he said, 'May I read it? This book of yours?'

She nodded very slightly.

Oh, she was wily. Now he was gagging to read her opus. Mrs Mapp turned and gave me the prearranged signal that I was to bring in the manuscript, tied up in butcher's paper and hairy string. I put down the crockery I was manhandling on to the hostess trolley and ambled off to bring the book like it was another lovingly prepared course.

'Thank you, Brenda,' whispered Mr Rupert, taking the parcel from me with all due reverence. You'd think it was a missing gospel or some such holy tome, the way he held it before him and bore it off that night, exiting the house in Tavistock Square and hopping aboard his waiting hansom.

I watched his cab jangle away over the cobbles, the moonlight bright on the horse's flanks and painting the trees in the park a glossy jade. I pictured Mr Rupert sitting up in his bed, wearing some kind of nightgown. He'd be fingering his 'tache in the lamplight, turning those pages over one at a time, just as I had done the previous night. It even gave me a funny, giddy feeling, the thought of that book in my humble servant's bed and then it being taken to Mr Rupert's no doubt splendid, sumptuous place of repose at the top of his house on Baker Street.

Gaaaggghhh. I had to stop these daydreams about Rupert Von Thal. Servants shouldn't hanker after anything or anyone. Not even in the privacy of their own secret thoughts.

I wondered if Mrs Mapp's book would have the same disquieting effect on that beautiful man as it had had upon me.

What would Mr Rupert make of it all? I wondered, as I secured our house against the night. What would he think of Mrs Mapp's world of Qab?

Not a lot, it seemed.

Time passed, and poor Mrs Mapp grew crosser and crosser. Very vexed she was, because she had convinced herself that Mr Rupert had forgotten all about her book. He had eaten her food, drunk her drink and listened to her tale. She had tried to impress upon him, as best she could, how vitally important this matter was to her.

But to no avail.

Two weeks slithered by in Bloomsbury.

I started to feel very disappointed in Mr Rupert. It seemed he didn't care at all. Mrs Mapp was crushed. She was like those insect specimens of her great-uncle's in that cabinet I dropped, back when I first moved in. Oops-a-daisy, that time. Ah, poor Mrs Mapp. How she railed against the elegant adventurer.

'I suppose he must be laughin' at me. Silly, scribblin', sentimental fool. Thinking she has written something significant. Something worthy of a gentleman's attention . . .'

Those great dark woolly clouds were descending on Tavistock Square. She was working her way into a bad'un, I could tell. I remonstrated with her. 'Madam, I'm sure . . . Not Mr Rupert. I'm sure he really does care about your feelings . . .'

Though the fact was, he always was a bit cavalier. It was all too easy for me to imagine him tossing her manuscript on to the seat of the very cab he had taken home that night, and thoughtlessly leaving it behind as he alighted at his destination. Just the sort of thing he would do. Or he'd pop it on a shelf or console table at home in his rooms over Baker Street. It could have vanished from his mind in a flash, as some new urgent concern came rushing in. He was a man of action, Mr Rupert. He lived in the moment and was avid for thrills and novelty. He had never struck me as the kind to train his attention on novels, or any other sedentary occupation.

Mrs Mapp rounded on me, almost accusingly. 'You! You sat up all night! You kept on, awake, until you had finished readin' it till the very end. Loyal Brenda! Good Brenda! Brenda upon whom I can always rely.'

I blushed at this, and turned to continue going round her study with my feather duster. I was up on tiptoes, having a go at the topmost shelves, coughing heartily as I did so.

Mrs Mapp seethed as she coughed, too. 'I should have known that silly man would spare no effort. He'd rather be orf havin' important adventures abroad. He'd rather be orf dashin' about after that ridiculous professor of his, getting themselves into ghastly danger, having intrigues with Chinamen or fisticuffs with pygmies or whoever. I wouldn't be at all surprised if they weren't even in the country at the moment; if they hadn't travelled clear across the other side of the world on some ridiculous pretext. They'll be up to their necks in some silly escapade . . .'

I nodded. 'I can imagine that too, madam. Those gentlemen seem to go off gallivanting into adventures at the drop of a hat.'

And how my heart ached, all of a sudden, at the thought of joining them. Somehow. Anyhow. And I knew that Mrs Mapp felt exactly the same.

I knew it was all impossible, for me at least. What was I? A mere woman, and a servant to boot. And neither of those things authentically. Not really.

But I could dream. I could listen in. When people like Mr Rupert paid visits to my mistress, I could have vicarious excitements. Despite everything, I could still inhabit my imagination.

That was why I had stayed up all that night with Mrs Mapp's bundle of pages. Through it I had been transported and immersed into an adventure that was all my own. I had consorted with reptile men, beast men, winged lizards . . . and warrior queens.

Perhaps Mr Rupert wasn't impressed by the book simply because he took such things for granted. He was pretty blasé about the exotic, as anyone knew who had earwigged on just an evening's conversation with that gentleman.

'Damn him! Damn the awful man!'

Mrs Mapp's cries rang through the house. The heavy clouds tumbled round our rooftops and I prepared to weather my mistress's stormy mood.

But then, that night, there was a terrible banging at the front door.

It was teeming down with rain. Coming down in brutal, stiff curtains. At first I hardly recognised the wretched specimen standing on the doorstep. He was bedraggled, filthy, improperly dressed. But there was no mistaking him.

'Brenda?' shouted Mrs Mapp. 'There's a shockin' draught! Who is it? Tell them there's no one at home!'

Mrs Mapp was still in her awful vexed temper. She came tearing down the stairs to box my ears for letting out the house's heat.

She stopped in her tracks at the sight of the man in the front hallway. He had a month's growth of beard, at least. His clothes were expensive but hung in soaked tatters on his skinny frame. Under that lank, damp hair those eyes were eloquent with exhaustion and very familiar to both the women at whom they looked with such pleading.

His marvellous 'tache was in a shocking state.

'It's me,' he said.

'Rupert!' Mrs Mapp burst out. 'Mr Von Thal!' she corrected herself. Then she scooted around him, hastening me into action. 'Brenda, help him. He looks fit to drop. He looks like . . .' She glared at him sharply. 'Where on earth have you been, you silly man?'

His mouth worked without sound for a moment. It was as if even he could hardly believe what he was trying to tell us.

'I have been *there*,' he said hoarsely. 'I have been . . . been . . .'

'Where?' thundered Mrs Mapp. She hated signs of weakness and fallibility, especially in men. This performance was frightening her.

Somehow I knew what Rupert Von Thal was going to tell us.

Just before he collapsed on the hall floor tiles he said: '*I have been to the world of Qab . . .*'

She was trembling. She did her best to hide it but, as Mrs Mapp pitched in and helped me settle the poor man before the fire in her study, I saw that she had been profoundly shaken by his words. But he was babbling, wasn't he? He was feverish and gyppy. His mind was straying. He couldn't possibly know what he was raving about.

I banked up the glorious fire and helped him off with his wet outer things. He looked soaked to the skin, poor fellow. I brought him woolly rugs and blankets and held them out while he wriggled himself nude under their ticklish protection. Then he sat swaddled up by the flames.

I hurried off to heat brandy in milk and to see what else we could tempt him with. He looked as if he had lost half his body weight, wherever he had been. When I had taken that pile of sodden rags from him I had marked the appearance of his ribs before he hoiked up the blankets. He must be starving. I set a pan of soup bubbling on the hob, I sawed at a joint of ham and placed a hunk of cheese and bread on a tray with the rest. All the while Mrs Mapp was hovering.

'Did he really say what I thought I heard?' she asked me. Her voice was deadly serious. She looked white.

'Of course not, ma'am,' I shook my head. I was miffed at her lack of concern for Mr Rupert, truth be told. 'Do you think we should call the doctor? He doesn't look at all well.'

She blinked. 'Of course not. He's made of hardier stuff than that. And besides, I have to ask him . . . questions. I need to know.' She seemed to realise then that she was standing in her night things, including a rather demure dove-grey gown that swept the chilly stone floor of the kitchen. Her hair was up and her face smarmed with cold cream. She had been ready to settle in for the night. To place her head on her Egyptian cotton pillows and to dream about her strange land of Qab.

Instead she had this visitor. This man who was claiming to have brought the latest news from Qab itself.

Oh, these aristos and their funny ideas.

We gathered around the skinny and hairy Mr Rupert as he sipped his milk laced with brandy and slurped at his chicken broth.

'I haven't eaten anything decent in days and days,' he told us. 'For a while we subsisted on the strange roots and fruits we found in the forest. The professor fashioned a bow and arrow and shot a variety of swine, which we roasted. That's over three weeks ago, and it was the last hot meal I had. When we were in the palace, deep under the palace, and escaping through the catacombs, we were eating anything we could catch with our bare hands. Eating them raw. Insect things and pale grubs. It was . . . it was horrible . . .' His voice trailed away for a moment and he stared into the flames.

Mrs Mapp coughed discreetly. 'Mr Von Thal, I feel obliged to point out the discrepancy in what you are tellin' us. It is two weeks since you were here at my house. Two weeks to the day, in fact. Therefore, how can you talk about being . . . elsewhere for more than a month? How can that be true? Don't you see? I'm having some problems acceptin' the truth of what you are trying to tell us.'

He turned back to us both quickly, his shaggy head swinging round. A weird glint in his eye. Fury, was it? Frustration? I'd never seen him like that before. He was always so solicitous and kind. 'I tell you, I know where I've been, and for how long. Am I stupid? Am I mad?'

Mrs Mapp hesitated. 'No, of course not. But . . . in your condition, exhausted like this, perhaps you have become confused . . . about what has been happenin' to you.'

'No,' he growled, sounding as sure of himself as ever I had heard him. 'I know full well what has been happening to me. Time works differently there, Mrs Mapp. As you yourself know. If we cross over to that land, there is no guarantee that time will pass in equal measure there as it does here. The two planes of existence do not keep tally with each other. How could they? When we return here, who's to say how long will have passed by? You tell me it's only two weeks and I'm relieved to hear that. A hundred years might have passed. A thousand. I'm very glad . . . very glad indeed . . . to have made my way back to a time not so far from my point of departure. To be among friends again. I thought . . . I thought I might be lost for ever. As, I fear, Professor Quandary might be—'

'Professor Quandary. . . lost for ever?' Mrs Mapp broke in.

'He's still *there*,' said Mr Rupert. 'I couldn't help him. He's still in the clutches of . . . them. Of *Her*. I tried to save him. I thought I had. Yet I couldn't. No . . . he's still back there. In that dreadful, savage land.'

We both absorbed this. Professor Quandary! Lost!

My mistress's face was a study in perplexity. Questions flitted and buzzed in her mind. I could tell just by looking at her. She was gauging his ability to give us straight and honest answers. But his exhaustion was overcoming him. I could see that he was sinking.

I also thought he was still babbling. This talk of palaces and eating insects and Professor Quandary at the mercy of a mysterious *Her.* It was sounding extremely fishy to me. We were overhearing the fever dreams of a young man who'd picked up some nasty kind of bug, I thought.

'We should get him into bed,' I prompted. 'He needs to rest.'

'Yes, of course,' agreed Mrs Mapp, though I knew she was impatient. She was avid to learn more from our unexpected guest.

'Yes, yes . . . I need sleep,' said Mr Rupert, faltering as he stood, clutching the blankets around himself. 'Can I stay here? Have you room?'

'Mr Von Thal,' smiled my mistress, 'we have seven unused bedrooms here. There is only myself and Brenda. You are welcome.'

'Thank you,' he said gruffly, and looked to me to guide him to his room. I stepped forward to help him, and he suddenly swung round to say to Mrs Mapp: 'But how did you do it? How could you know about it? How on earth . . . did you possibly write about Qab?'

She stared back dumbly at him. 'I don't know. It . . . it came to me, that's all.'

He shut his eyes and took a long, shuddering breath. 'It

came to you. And I went to it.' He shook his head. 'There's some deep kind of magic going on here. Something . . . eldritch and perverse.'

I swear that Mrs Mapp's eyes lit up at this utterance of his.

'Come on, sir,' I told him, wedging my weight under his slight frame, helping him towards the hall. 'Time for rest.'

'Thank you, Brenda.' He smiled. 'But I must tell you. My clothes . . . those rags I was wearing. Where have you taken them?'

'Why, they're in the scullery. I just dumped them in the old sink. But I don't think they can be salvaged, Mr Von Thal. They were ruined. Rags, as you say.'

'Yes, but in the inner pocket of my blazer, there is a pair of scissors. Not scissors. Pinking shears. You must fetch them out. You must look after them. They must not be let out of your sight . . .'

Then his head was flopping about on my shoulder and he was just about passing out in my arms.

'You'd better get them, Brenda,' my mistress said. 'When you've put him to bed. The Blue Room, I think, would be best for him. Go to the scullery and find these shears. Make sure you look after them. They seem very important to him . . .'

She was rambling just as much as he was. I mean, pinking shears? What could he possibly want with pinking shears?

* * *

Both the mistress and myself were itchy with impatience the next morning. We carried on as if nothing was different – she nibbling at a portion of porridge, glutinous with lavender honey, and me bustling round at my myriad morning tasks. Neither of us were mentioning the novelty of there being a man about the house.

Come time for elevenses, and no sooner have I brought in the coffee than there's a creaking on the floorboards directly above us. That was the Blue Room up there. Mrs Mapp and I exchanged a sharp glance. So, he was up and about at last. I poured the coffee. Mrs Mapp returned to her scribbling, but I could tell her mind wasn't on it. Her attention was elsewhere.

We listened to the bath in the Blue Bathroom filling up, a lovely bass rumble. Mr Rupert kept us in horrible suspense as he shaved and scrubbed and made himself respectable again. As he made himself fit to face the civilised world.

As I lay in my bed the previous night I had stewed it all over. How could any of it be possible? These intrepid men's adventures often seemed a bit unlikely, verging on the impossible. But when Mr Rupert wrote them up in serial form in the pages of the *Fitzrovian Spree*, they always convinced me. I never doubted the veracity of his word. Those mummies they brought back from the pyramids of Peru were placed on public exhibition. As were the giant eggs they carried back from Africa. And the fragments of the last surviving Martian ship, inside of which they had had the most remarkable adventure, deep beneath the freezing North Sea . . . All of these things I – along with thousands of others – had accepted as true.

Why not Qab as well?

Because . . . if the warrior women and lizard men of Qab were real . . . then how did my mistress get wind of it all?

She believed that she had made it all up out of her head. Out of ingredients no more exotic than airy imagination, Indian ink and the effects of midnight snacks upon her delicate constitution.

Yet . . . I was used to having very queer dreams myself, wasn't I? I was prone to the oddest fancies and phantasmagoria. Sometimes I'd be hard pressed to tell what was real and what wasn't, the way my own mind and memories worked. And so I had a lot of sympathy with both Mr Rupert and Mrs Mapp, beset by the unreal as they seemed to be.

The coffee was finished with by the time Mr Rupert appeared. He was clad in a red silk dressing gown that had belonged to Mrs Mapp's late brother. She gasped at the sight of him, but quickly resumed possession of herself. 'Brenda, coffee for our visitor.'

I hurried out and back again with a fresh pot and sugar lumps and thick yellow cream and best china and I found Mr Rupert was already talking. The two of them were in armchairs by the long-dead fire. Coffee table. Conspiratorial tones. Rain clicking calmingly on the window that looked out on Tavistock Square. I poured coffee and my stomach roiled at its dark, heady tang.

'Brenda, please. Pull up a pouffe and listen,' said my mistress. 'Mr Von Thal's story involves you too.'

I did as I was bidden.

Mr Rupert favoured me with a special, very handsome, smile, and then he began.

'Those pinking shears, I hope you're looking after them. We will need them before long. They are very special. They are the most vitally important element in this whole strange saga.

'They belong to Professor Quandary. He wouldn't explain to me where he had procured them and nor would he explain how they worked. It seemed a bit of a rum do to me, when he first told me that those seemingly everyday implements could cut through . . . what did he call it? The Fabric of Time and Space. The *Very* Fabric, as he put it.

'What are pinking shears usually used for? Putting a nice edge on material, aren't they? A kind of jagged pattern. Yes, my mother was a keen seamstress, I remember. These were the Blithe Pinking Shears, the professor said, and they were possessed of incredible, mystical powers.

'They were not to be used willy-nilly, or for anything silly.

'He had been saving them up for an exploit as important as this Qab business.

'Because, you see, Mrs Mapp, and Brenda, as soon as I had read and digested *The World of Qab*, that very night I took it away with me from this place, I was hooked. I stayed awake until I had finished the whole story, and that night in my sitting room in Baker Street, I sat quite still, thrumming with excitement, until the sunlight was filtering in and the street noise was starting up. My housekeeper came in and shrieked at me for sitting there so quietly and giving her a shock. But I was in a kind of daze . . . This manuscript of yours, Mrs Mapp, it has a kind of hypnotic power to it.'

I gave a sidelong glance then, and as I expected, Mrs Mapp was looking very satisfied at this.

Mr Rupert continued: 'Professor Quandary came crashing into my rooms that very morning. All unexpected, as usual, and keen for some new kind of adventure. He often calls upon me like this when he's up in town. He's supposed to be at one of the museums researching, or giving a lecture at some hall or other, but he slopes off and comes to see what his old chum Von Thal is up to, knowing that it's bound to be some kind of adventure.

'That particular morning he found me vague and blinking in the morning light. My mind was filled with images of wonderful Qab. The professor thought I was back on my opium habit, or at the sherry again. He marched me out of my rooms, down the stairs and into the street to get my circulation going and fresh air into my lungs. He took us down the street and for a brisk walk around the fragrant borders of Regent's Park.

'As we stopped to watch the ducks, I started to tell him about your book and he was suddenly rigid with excitement when I mentioned its title. His great curly beard seemed to bristle and drops of perspiration stood out on the bald dome of his head. 'At last, at last someone has found it again,' he said, which was a very curious thing to say, and I told him so.

'"Found what?" I asked.

'He blinked owlishly. "The thread. The elusive thread. The thread that leads the way back to Qab . . ."

'I knew at once that he had heard of the place before. I explained that this could not be so. The book – though compelling, though vivid – was a fantasy. A very recent creation of a great friend of mine. A gentlewoman. "So you see, you can't possibly know about Qab! Nobody knows about Qab apart from Mrs Mapp and her servant and myself! It is a fiction, Professor! It's like . . . Lilliput or Wonderland or . . ."

'It was almost comical, the fashion in which Quandary went on shaking his head crossly. Now he was stomping away from me, leading the way back across the park. Even tramping over the grass and the flowerbeds in his eagerness.

'"No, no, no, Von Thal. You don't understand at all. Qab is more than an invention of some single individual or entity. And certainly not some female! The world of Qab, you see, insinuates itself into the psyche . . . finds a way to be born again . . . it makes its portals on this earth and draws souls towards itself . . . those who will trust and believe in it . . ."

'His words grew fainter as he gained a lead on me. I had to rush to catch up with him. He whirled around suddenly. "Where is the manuscript?"

'It was in my study, where I had last put it down, of course. "Look, Professor, are you saying that Mrs Mapp was somehow . . . led into writing this book? That she wrote it while under some kind of influence? And that the bally place is real?"

' "Exactly!" he cried. "And I've been looking for a way into that particular land for a very long time. A very long time indeed."

'Now this surprised me. "You already knew about Qab?"

' "As a whisper. As a rumour. As the kind of place that I might possibly, if I was very fortunate, one day receive an invitation to. I might have bestowed upon me the slightest chance of making the journey there . . . I have the means . . . I believe I know the ritual necessary to make the hop across the interstitial gap. We must open up what is known to the cognoscenti as a Dreadful Flap."

'The rest of that day passed in a strange blur. The professor insisted we return to my rooms. While I asked Mrs Brick, my housekeeper, to prepare for us a hearty breakfast – devilled kidneys and all, as I knew the professor relished – Quandary set about examining the manuscript. Every aspect of it fascinated him, from the string you used to tie it up, to the very warp and weft of the expensive paper you wrote it on.

' "You've read every word?" the professor asked me.

' "I stayed up all night," said I. "It is marvellous. I believe that my friend, Mrs Mapp, has a singular talent—"

' "It isn't her talent," the professor snapped. "This book was dictated to her through the ether, by forces unseen." He was on his feet and pacing. "I must read it at once. Will you allow me to take it with me?"

' "Where are you going?"

' "Back to Sussex, immediately. There is something I must fetch from home. I will return this evening, Von Thal. I will be bringing the pinking shears. You must be prepared."

' "W-what for?"

' "A very long journey."

'I tried to get him to pause long enough to explain what the pinking shears were for, and to eat the delicious breakfast that Mrs Brick was unloading from her hostess trolley, but the professor would be delayed no longer.

'Clamping the precious manuscript under his coat, he whirled out of my room and thundered down the stairs, pitching himself into the street and headlong into a cab that happened to be standing there. He had very good timing, did Quandary. He went around assuming that the world could be made to dance attendance on his every whim.

'Aha! How ghastly! Do you hear me referring to him in the past tense, as if he is dead? Or perhaps . . . perhaps I am using the past tense to describe his actions because the past tense is where he belongs. He is trapped there, you see. The dawn of time, I would say, is where Professor Quandary now languishes, as a result of the actions we took that very day. The dawn of time, or somewhere bally well like it . . .'

Mr Rupert didn't allow the mistress and myself much time to express our incredulity. I could see that Mrs Mapp was positively glowing with impatience to ask him a hundred questions at this point. There was also something prideful in her manner. She was very pleased that all of this palaver was due to her. These two adventurers in a tizzy and all because of her mysterious manuscript. The mistress was keen to hear Mr Von Thal continue with his narrative – as was I – so she squashed all her queries down inside herself and waited for him to drain his coffee cup in one huge gulp. He crunched up the grounds with relish (I always made coffee rather strong) and went on.

'As you may imagine, I spent the rest of the day in a perplexed fashion. Quandary had left with me a list of items he wished me to gather together. Some of his list included our usual equipment for adventures – pickaxes, ropes, hats, packed lunches, etc. – and so I sent my redoubtable Mrs Brick off to fill our knapsacks. She grumbled about it, as she always does. I, meanwhile toyed with the thought of nipping round here, to tell you about the professor's extraordinary reaction to your invention. But then I thought, no: better not, not yet, in case there is nothing in it.

'And at last, just before nightfall, Quandary returned, hotfoot from Victoria, lugging bags and equipment of his own. Upon arrival in my rooms he said barely two words to me, intent as he was about his business. He drew the heavy curtains and lit beeswax candles. He set some noxious incense burning, as if we were in some bally cathedral, and he explained that it was all in aid of getting us into the mood.

'He said that the two of us should kneel before my cheval mirror, and stare into our own eyes in the smoky dimness. Well, by now I wasn't at all sure he hadn't lost his marbles. "And we must chant, Von Thal. The words are immaterial. It's the state of mind that counts. Let me see . . ." He cast around the room, looking for some suitable printed matter. His eye lit upon the manuscript. He grabbed it. "Of course! What better?" And he made us chant together a passage plucked at random from your book.

'I needn't dwell for too long on the time we spent like this. It seemed to be the whole night that we were kneeling there, squinting at ourselves. My joints were aching and my eyes were streaming with soreness. The professor was undeterred. He has an iron will, of course. I was soon fatigued and quite ready to throw in the towel. But he made us go on. He had studied, of course, with yogis and shamen and all kinds of funny foreign fellows abroad. He knew all about the virtues of contemplation and meditation and so forth. He kept us at it, jabbing me with a finger whenever it seemed my focus was flagging.

'And do you know, it might have been exhaustion or suggestion, but at last, after quite some time, I really did feel a trance coming on. That huge, sonorous voice of the professor's worked its magic upon me. His vast bearlike arm clapped around my shoulder as we stared into the mirror kept me in its grip. My last cogent thought was that I hoped Mrs Brick wouldn't come bumbling in and catch us at this queer occupation, though as a rule she knows better than to come barging in. "Concentrate!" Quandary thundered. "You must muse on Qab! Consider Qab! Give yourself over to Qab! Let Qab infuse every fibre of your being . . . !"

'He said this as, with great ceremony, he stowed away your manuscript inside his coat and from the same deep pocket produced a pair of scissors. Not just any old scissors. The pinking shears, with their jagged teeth. And not just any pinking shears. This was the pair he had returned to Sussex expressly in order to fetch. I stopped chanting for a while to watch in amazement as he wielded these silver shears.

'He reached out thoughtfully towards the mirror and plucked at something. I blinked and then I saw it. It was a single strand of thread. A silvery end of thread, standing up, seemingly in thin air. The professor tugged at it. There was a ripping noise. A fraying, silken noise. Then he brought those shears up and insinuated one of the blades into the tiny hole he had made . . .

'*Sssshhzzztt ffssszzhhttt . . . rriiiiiiiiii-iiip . . .* He was slicing away with those pinking shears. Until a rippling slash had appeared in the very air between us and my tall mirror. The light within was queer and rippling. I couldn't quite focus on what lay beyond that Dreadful Flap . . .

'Then . . . and then . . . nothing for a while.'

By then the mistress and I were hanging on the very edge of our chairs. 'Nothing?'

'A vague swimming sensation. Immersion in a cool, unfamiliar element. It wasn't unpleasant. But I knew I was no longer in my beloved rooms above Baker Street. The professor was with me and we were elsewhere. Swimming together through some eerie kind of ether . . . And then: WHAM.

'The sun was bright upon my face. The heat was instant, cruel and wet. My clothes were sticking to me. I opened my eyes, startled and almost blinded by the sunlight.

'I was lying on some dense, fleshy vegetation and my ears were ringing with insect noise and the rushing, sealike cacophony of an immense forest. I was still clutching our bags, and beside me Quandary was hastening to his feet. For a few moments, neither of us could say anything.

'I looked up, and the sky above the hugely tall treetops was a rather outré shade of mauve. Just as you describe it in the third chapter of your book, Mrs Mapp. And then – even before I saw the lizard birds wheeling and screeching between the dense black clouds . . . I knew we had made it across. We were in your world, Mrs Mapp. We had made it over to Qab.'

Mrs Mapp sat back in her chair and exhaled noisily. 'I don't believe it!'

'But you must! Every word of it is true!' burst out Mr Rupert.

I almost cried out myself: 'You must, madam! Can't you see how sincere he is? How could he lie about something as vital as this? Something so weird and uncommon?'

'Brenda, bring us some sandwiches.' As if to demonstrate that avidity had made her hungry, Mrs Mapp's stomach gave a huge rumble at this point. I tore out of the room and threw together the fastest sandwiches of my whole career in service. By the time I had returned – with some very sorry-looking items ineptly stuffed with cold ham and hand-torn lettuce, I realised to my dismay that the tale had continued without me.

Mr Rupert was describing his and the professor's first days in the curious and alien world of Qab. They didn't know if they would ever be able to return home, or survive for very long, or how hostile this new environment might even be. They foraged for food, finding fruits and berries upon which to breakfast, and they rested under a crude tent made from massive, rubbery fallen leaves. It seems that it was all very exciting to them at first. Mr Von Thal even said that they were like two small boys, making up a camp and exploring their close environs with a mounting sense of wonder. Qab was stranger and more exotic than any place either of them had ever visited before . . .

Mr Rupert described the giant eggshells they discovered in the undergrowth, the offspring of monsters. They found one intact and roasted it on a fire and had their first decent meal. He described the shuffling and snorting and outraged cries of unseen beasts in the dark nights in that jungle. He described their fear, which the two men were careful not to disclose to each other. He described their first glimpse of the beasts of Qab, as the two of them decided to leave their place of arrival and set forth on a long hike to discover the lie of the land. And he described their first encounters with the intelligent humanoids, the natives of this place.

'Natives?' Mrs Mapp asked sharply.

'Oh yes,' said Mr Rupert. 'And never fear, Mrs Mapp. They were precisely how you described them in your book, the lizard men.'

Well, by now my hair was just about standing on end. The lizard men of Qab! It turns out they looked awful: gaunt and haggard, with eyes that stared coldly at you. They regarded humans with a kind of salivating contempt, Mr Rupert said. As if they were secretly keen to crunch on your bones and chomp on your warm flesh. The lizards had backed off in the face of Quandary's bluster, luckily. I came back into the room just as Mr Rupert was chuckling, telling how the reptiles were made to flee from the British explorers.

'I've brought the sandwiches,' I said, in a thick voice. 'Begging your pardon, sir, madam. You must eat. And . . . I'd like to go there, please! I want to go to the world of Qab!'

Mrs Mapp jumped like I had pinched her. 'Brenda! Stop it at once! What are you sayin'?'

I clamped a hand over my mouth. 'I-I'm sorry, madam.'

'Mr Von Thal, you have made my servant overexcited,' Mrs Mapp told him beadily.

I couldn't stop myself. 'But it's true! I want to go there! Just like the two gentlemen! And so do you, Mrs Mapp! Oh, you must do, surely?'

'Don't be ridiculous,' said my mistress frostily. 'I can't think of anythin' worse.'

But I could see she was lying. And so could Mr Rupert.

'It's your world, Bea,' he said softly, picking up one of my messy sandwiches. 'Down to every last detail, precisely as you described it in your book. The city of the lizard men. They took us there. As prisoners. Those great towers. We saw the palaces of the women warriors, though we weren't lucky enough to be shown inside. But that fact was more than made up for by our encounter with one single, special woman . . . the Queen who rules over them all . . .'

Mrs Mapp gasped. 'The Queen of Qab?'

'We met her,' said Rupert. '*Her.*'

I gasped too. 'You met *Her*!'

'On more than one occasion. We were led into her throne room by her servile lizard men and forced to make obeisances to Her Majesty.'

I had a very clear image in my mind of the Queen of Qab, gleaned from my night spent reading the book. These men had been face to face with *Her* herself!

Mrs Mapp still looked a little as if she suspected Mr Rupert of mockery. Was this all some cruel hoax? Was it a trick he was playing on her? 'I can't quite take this in . . .'

'I'm sorry,' he mumbled. 'And I wouldn't be blurting it all out like this if I didn't think the situation was . . .'

'Was what?'

'As serious as it is. Brenda is quite right, Bea. We must go there. At once. The three of us. Back to the world of Qab.'

Mrs Mapp licked her lips and gripped her chair arms very tightly. 'But why, for heaven's sake?'

'Because Professor Quandary is still there. He is still at the mercy of *Her*. I'm afraid I was forced to leave him there, in the palace.'

Both the mistress and I drew in our breath at this, wondering what it would be like to be left in Qab . . . left behind by your sole companion, who had taken with him the only possible means of escape from that world. What must Quandary be feeling, lost inside that alien domain?

'I don't know . . .' said Mrs Mapp. 'What can we do? We're women . . . feeble women, aren't we?' She looked at me and I knew that she was just casting around for excuses. She didn't believe for one second in our feebleness or inferiority to any man. But I think I half glimpsed her vertiginous horror at the idea of attempting to emulate the men's journey through the Dreadful Flap.

For Mrs Mapp it would surely be like travelling into the wellspring of her own imagination, with the intention of encountering the spectres that haunted her own inner life. It would feel like madness, surely? And I knew that what my mistress feared above all things was the madness that had afflicted her brother and both her parents. She rarely spoke or alluded to it, but the thought was always there . . . that one day she might wake up mad . . .

Now perhaps that day had come.

But she looked to me. I was always as sane and pragmatic as anyone. I was the most down-to-earth person she had ever met, and in many ways she relied on me to keep her grounded. But here was I, mad keen to travel with Mr Rupert to this other place. All I could think was, Oh, put me in that trance! Let me chant along with you! Let's give ourselves aching legs and smarting eyes and keep the candles and incense burning through the night! Let us meditate and cogitate on alien lands! And why don't you whip out those magical pinking shears, Mr Rupert Von Thal!

I could hardly contain myself, truth be told.

'Erm . . . Mrs Mapp,' he said. 'I wonder if you have a spare copy of your book? We'll need some pages for the chanting part of the ritual.'

She looked flustered for a moment. 'I believe I have some notes that we could use. But . . . but I do not have a whole copy of the entire thing.' All of a sudden she looked panicked. She went ashen.

So did Mr Rupert. 'Are you saying that you lent me the only copy of your book? The only copy in existence?'

'Yes,' she said, looking grave. 'Surely you haven't . . .'

'Left it there, yes.' He nodded, very ashamed. 'I thought it would be of more use to the professor than to myself, during his incarceration. As a sort of guide book. Never for one moment did I think that you would have given me the only copy . . .'

I stared at my mistress. I could hardly believe she would do something so foolish. She coloured with embarrassment, and I saw at that moment just how much she must trust Mr Rupert. And how much that was precious to her she longed to place in his care.

I watched as she struggled with these emotions and as a new clarity of expression, of determination, took over her whole visage. She stood up. 'We have no choice, it seems. We simply have to embark upon a second expedition. Immediately!'

Could I help it if I felt like cheering at her words?

It was down to yours truly, of course, to make all of the preparations. I was counselled by Mr Rupert not to pack too much, as the going was rough in Qab, and chances were we would have to cover great distances, as he and the professor had. He listed a few things that would have come in useful on his first visit: bandages, insect repellent, brandy, etc., and made sure I took note as I busied about the house, filling a vast carpet bag that had belonged to Mrs Mapp's grandmother. There was an excitement about both Mr Rupert and the mistress now. They were like children, dashing from room to room and making plans.

I went out to the area at the back of the house for a mug of tea and a few moments to myself. The daylight was fading early, I realised, squinting at the inscrutable backs of the houses that ringed our long, neglected garden. The trees were stirring in the wind and the leaves were starting to come down. The seasons were turning, it seemed. It was one of those strangely powerful changeover parts of the year, which played merry hell on my nerves and moods. I was rather glum, sitting there by myself, by the bins. Where on earth would I be by bedtime tonight? Was I ready to be whistled off to who-knew-where? Did the mistress even have the right to make me go with her?

I stumped off to get the whites off the line. Huge pristine bloomers and slips were buffeting and snapping like sails. I bundled them up in my arms. At least we'd have clean under-clothes on this adventure! This I was determined to make sure of. We wouldn't be like those grubby men.

Well, of course, all of these qualms and moods of mine – they were just worry turning itself inwards and making my stomach juices curdle. I was nervous, that's all. Of course I wanted to go to this other land! Of course I wanted adventure. Don't get me wrong, I loved my life in Tavistock Square, but the few shreds of memory I had remaining from my previous lives showed me all too plainly that I was used to a more hectic kind of pace.

So I packed a couple of bags, and kept it as spartan as I could. I even filled a flask with piping-hot tea. And then, as darkness came over the square, I lit the lamps and Mr Rupert was manhandling a tall mirror into the drawing room, in preparation for the ritual.

Fog was curling its way through Bloomsbury. Thick, twining yellow fronds of fog that came creeping round our house and rubbing themselves against the tall windows. I went to lock up the doors (who knew how long we'd leave our house empty?) and studied the suddenly impenetrable mist. We were leaving all of this behind. This smoky-smelling world, all damp at the edges and stewing in its own civilised melancholy. Time for a change. This had all become too familiar.

And then it was the ritual. Mr Rupert came thundering downstairs in clothes he had borrowed from the wardrobe of Mrs Mapp's poor dead brother. Quite dandified 1890s clothes they were, long out of fashion. But he filled them out quite nicely, I thought. Somehow their extravagance suited him – that cravat and the waistcoat, the velvet cloak. Mrs Mapp and I both admired him as he strode about, making preparations.

Mr Rupert asked us to draw back the heavy furniture and bade us kneel on the rug that the mistress's grandparents had brought back from Arabia. I was very familiar with its intricate arabesques from having swept it every morning since I had lived here. Now we were kneeling together as if pretending it was a magic carpet: one that could take our weight and bear us back to the magical land whence it came.

Mrs Mapp was very serious. Her face was pale and thin. She was intent now, as she produced the few scraps of her manuscript she had left. She gave us each a page to read aloud. I recognised my page as an early draft of one of the ritualistic songs from Qab, from a brutal, bloody sequence in which the Queen sacrificed the lives of a hundred young male slaves and drank their blood. I stumbled over a few of the more exotic made-up words, but I read along with the other two as they intoned their own verses. Oh, how Mrs Mapp's voice rang out. She was always a very good speaker. There was a tremble in her tones, though, as if she was almost overcome by the magnitude of what we were doing.

Lights down, incense smouldering, candles like pale beacons in the gloaming. We had to stare at ourselves in the tall mirror Mr Rupert had brought in from the hall and leaned against the chairs. That's when I almost started laughing – when the three of us could see ourselves, mumbling these nonsensical phrases and staring like loons. But soon the silly self-consciousness dropped away. The ritual went on and on and on and soon enough I had forgotten myself. This felt like magic. It also felt familiar.

I was starting to remember . . . I think . . . that I was no stranger to magic and queer rituals. The memories were seeping back. I felt tendrils of suggestion snaking through my mind . . . like that fog outside . . . creeping up on me . . .

But they were gone. The memories drew back to allow me to concentrate on the moment. A moment in which Mr Rupert took out his glinting pinking shears and brandished them proudly. He looked like St George before the dragon, wielding his lance. I blinked. I stared. I fixed my gaze on a flaw in the mirror's glass. It looked like a silver scratch on the sheeny surface. But in polishing that mirror I had never noticed a long white scratch before.

Mr Rupert reached out and took hold of that fault in the mirror. He plucked at it and suddenly it was secure between his fingers. It was a thread, just as he had said! Like before! The tiny end of a thread, fraying apart from material

254

existence. He tugged it. He pulled it harder. The fabric gave way with a satisfying ripping noise.

I heard my mistress sigh, short and sharply. She didn't move, though, and neither did I. We were frozen with delight as up came the pinking shears and . . .

Whiisszzztttt fsszzzhhhtttt!

Mr Rupert slashed accurately and with aplomb. He sliced beautifully through the rippling silky material.

'The Dreadful Flap,' my mistress said, inching forward to peer into the coruscating darkness beyond. It was a wonderful darkness. Like none I'd ever seen. It was the darkness of good, welcoming sleep. I inched forward too.

'Now,' said Mr Rupert. 'Do you feel drowsy? Do you feel safe? Do you trust me, ladies?'

'Oh, yes,' I answered for us both.

'Then we must go. We must slip away. Qab awaits us . . .'

'But how?' asked my mistress. That anxious tone was in her voice. 'How do we get there? Do we just step through? Do we . . . ?'

And that is all I remember, until we were waking up elsewhere.

Somewhere much brighter, much hotter than here. I thought I was having a funny turn, because the first thing I was aware of after the temperature was a tightness and a weight on my chest. Oh Gawd, not a stroke or a heart attack, I thought. Not in another, alien land. But it was just one of the carpet bags resting on top of me as I lay in the jungle undergrowth. That's all it was. So I sat up with some relief and glanced around at a wonderful scene.

It was a jungle out of prehistory. Everything was twice its natural size. It was humid and sticky and the colours were like something out of one of those Frenchmen's splashy paintings. I loved it all at first sight.

Mrs Mapp and Mr Rupert were already standing up and examining our new surroundings. When I cried out in triumph and clapped my hands, they whirled round to look at me and Mr Rupert grinned. 'What do you think, Brenda? Did you ever doubt me?'

Me? Doubt Mr Rupert? Never! Not even if we'd ended up down in Limehouse or Bexhill-on-Sea. I trusted him and believed him, and by golly I was glad he was right. Look at him in his dandyish clothes. What a gent!

'You were right about the sky,' said Mrs Mapp drily. 'It *is* an appalling shade of mauve.'

I don't think I've ever talked so much as I did that first day in the land of Qab. I went round exclaiming at everything. Millipedes as big as a mink stoles! Just look at that! Leafy canopies broad as the dome on the British Museum! I went about like some tourist, clapping and going 'Cor! Lumme!' while my superiors set to the actual practical tasks they felt were necessary upon arrival in a new world. They gathered wood for a fire, and fleshy leaves for a makeshift shelter. They were building a kind of camp at this, our point of arrival in Qab.

Ooh, that lovely humid warmth! I don't know if I've said, but I was an ungainly thing back in that time, too. A big-boned woman is how Mrs Mapp would put it, when she was of a mind to be generous. In northern climes, in wintry wet days in the capital, I would cut an unfortunate silhouette in my heavy astrakhan-collared coat and my lumpy hat. I felt achy and stiff most days, with the London damp in my joints and niggling at old scar tissue. I realised then, upon arrival in the moist heat of Qab, just what I had been missing. I was made for other climes. I was buoyed by the warmth. I felt like I was floating on the soggy air. Which was hard to explain to my two companions, who looked cross and red-faced by the time they had erected a strange sort of tent and set a small fire churning acrid smoke.

My companions! Yes, that was how I thought of them now. The delectable Mr Rupert, and Mrs Mapp over there, looking vexed as a cat. No longer my social superiors. Not here, in another world entirely. Here we were on a level playing field, you might say. The whole world was turned upside down. This whole creaking, shrieking, chirruping world was completely topsy-turvy.

'Brenda dear, do stop crashin' around in the underbrush,' Mrs Mapp sighed. 'You'll make every carnivore in the place alert to our presence. We'll have enough bother fendin' them off as it is . . .'

Ah, of course. Mrs Mapp knew this place better than anyone. She had invented it, after all. She knew the dangers that lurked in the velvety depths of this forest. With a smattering of natural history gleaned from day trips to the museum in Kensington and some weeks poring over the coloured plates in her grandfather's library books, Mrs Mapp had designed a flora and fauna for her world of exaggerated bestiality and extravagance. Right now she was having a few misgivings, it seemed, as she reminded us of innovations such as the flesh-eating lilies and the sabre-toothed tortoises with which her imagination had furnished the Qab landscape.

'Don't worry about it,' grinned Mr Rupert. 'You aren't to blame. I don't think you are really responsible for the horrors and delights we are bound to encounter here, Mrs Mapp.'

She looked deflated. 'Oh really?' Then she seemed defiant. 'But this *is* my world. Precisely as I imagined it. This is all familiar to me. The very breeze on my face. The reek of the fecund sod underfoot . . .'

She was getting a bit purple in her descriptions, which was always a good indicator of a dangerous mood. Mr Rupert was heedless, thrusting hand-made torches into the soil, in a ring around our camp.

'What I mean is, my dear, this place has insinuated itself into your dreams. It has murmured to you over from across the aeons and over vast distances, This world pre-existed you. You never invented it.'

'Oh,' she said, looking very cast down.

'It is still a remarkable achievement,' he said.

'But . . .' Mrs Mapp frowned. 'Your Professor Quandary. He knew about this place. He saw my book as a kind of reminder, a bridge to this place. . . He knew far more than he had any right to, as far as I can see.'

'Hmm, indeed,' said Mr Rupert, flinging himself down upon the little nest of verdant leaves they had made. 'There are many mysteries about the good professor that even I am not privy to. He knows about so many things.' Now Mr Rupert went off in an abstracted pause.

'I am sure he will be all right,' said Mrs Mapp. 'He can look after himself, from what I have learned. Your precious professor will have sweet-talked the wicked Queen of Qab. I wouldn't be surprised if he had wrapped her around his little finger. Why, I bet she has already made him her king.'

Mr Rupert chuckled at that thought. 'He's an old charmer, you're right.'

Mrs Mapp's expression hardened. 'I just hope he's looking after my manuscript.'

I broke in then, suggesting that we crack open the flasks I'd filled with piping-hot tea. I'd brought some vegetable soup, too. Even though it felt too hot to eat, we all knew that we should take what sustenance we could, and we were all glad we wouldn't have to go hunting after jungle prey or foraging for berries this first night.

Night came over the jungle treetops like someone pulling thick musty curtains against the skies. It was dark like dark falls in the tropics, with no qualms and great authority.

Straight away the jungle beasts set up their hullabaloo.

The three of us sat close together with our brass beakers of tea.

'It's like huddling in London Zoo after dark,' Mrs Mapp said, suppressing a shiver, despite the warmth.

'I live rather near the zoo,' said Mr Rupert. 'You're quite right. Those beasts can make the most unearthly, chilling brouhaha.' He jumped up to light the ring of torches to keep the night beasts at bay.

Camping out! My heart leapt up inside me with excitement. How far this was from our comfy, lumpy beds in Bloomsbury. All those sheets and pillowcases I scrubbed on Monday mornings, down in the scullery. How much more I preferred putting my head down here on fronds of gargantuan fern and slippery palm leaves, feeling the stink of leaf mulch and primordial decay tickling my sinuses . . .

I fell asleep quite happily, that first night in Qab, little suspecting the horrors that were just around the corner. Foolish Brenda. I seem to spend my whole like galumphing along heedlessly. And then everything suddenly goes to the bad.

* * *

It was such a difference to my usual routine, exploring this new world. I know that that seems like a ridiculous thing to say. But I had forgotten that I find change rejuvenating. I love a nice new set of horizons.

And so my heart was light as we went tramping around in the depths of the jungle. The light so dense and greenish blue it was like going about underwater, adrift in this soupy warmth. We advanced by clearing a path amid festoons of slippery vines and hacking through fibrous branches and monstrous stems. Suggestive flowers were bobbing and swaying, sticky with perfumed juices. Our eyes ached with glorious colour.

Mrs Mapp plunged headlong, brandishing her furled brolly like a sabre, cracking, thrashing . . . Our ears were filled with the slurping noise of uprooted shoots and fleshy fungi stamped on.

When Mrs Mapp looked back to make sure we were keeping up, her face was livid and gleaming with sweat. The sleeves of her print frock were dangling and she rolled them up with a businesslike air. She tucked the ends of her long skirts into her bloomers. She looked like a worker in the fields. There was a relish to the way she lashed out at the florid vegetation.

She cried out as she cut a swathe; she grunted with exertion. Grunted! I believe these were the most unladylike noises my mistress had ever emitted.

I was doing my bit. Bringing my much greater strength to bear upon our inhospitable environment.

According to all the rules of chivalry Mr Rupert should have been going first into this mysterious Eden. Yet he was content to bring up the rear. He was happy to concede his rightful place to Mrs Mapp and simply lug along a lion's share of luggage. He would pause now and then to take stock and direct us.

'I have a rather vague sense of the lie of the land. We need to make for higher ground, so that I may orient myself . . .'

Black mud sucked greedily at our feet. It was seeping into my sensible shoes, and Mrs Mapp's. What we could have done with were high boots like Mr Rupert's. We were quietly piqued at being inadequately shod.

I do think Mr Rupert might have warned us about the exploding mud. It was like attempting to walk on treacle toffee, as it comes up to the boil. Except that it stank like sour old bedpans . . .

Mr Rupert's hunch was that we were not too far from the spot where he had first arrived with Professor Quandary, what seemed like a lifetime ago. This was interesting in itself, he mused, as we paused for a breather in a less rancid and claustrophobic place. 'It is as if the fabric of the world itself is thinner here, and more permeable, in this particular region.'

I must say I was more interested in the fact that our drinking water was almost gone and I was becoming incredibly parched. The belting-hot sun in that mauve sky was pretty but it was merciless.

Around lunchtime, I suppose it was, my head was starting to spin as we set off again on our hike. I contented myself by remembering which household tasks I'd be up to were we still at home and that day was the same as any normal day. I'd be doing the silver, sitting at the dining table and rubbing away at the spoons. I'd be cleaning out the grates. I'd be giving the stair carpets some gyp with my old dustpan and brush.

I had spent too long in service. I had spent too long about those old routine tasks in the house on Tavistock Square.

How long had I been there? I couldn't even remember.

I found I was no longer blindly grateful to my mistress. Yes, she had taken me in. She had given me a new life. But hadn't I paid her back by now? Couldn't I stop being beholden to her?

I watched her skinny body advancing ahead of me, dodging round trunks and ducking under vines. Her wispy hair was one big frizz, coming loose from her bun. That straw hat of hers was battered to shreds. I began to feel something closely akin to panic. How long had I been a servant to this woman? When did I sign my whole body and soul over to her? And what had become of me in my previous life? How come I was destitute anyway?

The details were erased. They had run out of my head like

sand from an egg timer. There were just grains left. I could feel my past ebbing away from me. As we hacked and hacked and hacked our way forward in the primordial forest, under the noonday sun, I felt my whole life shrinking around me, till its days were as close-packed and indistinguishable as the trees that surrounded us.

Mercifully we found a pool where the water was ice cold and good to drink. Delicious, in fact.

We didn't stand on ceremony. Like the good bohemian she hoped she was, Mrs Mapp threw off the limp rag of her dress and waded in her slip into the cool bronze of the water. Quite daring, I thought.

Normally I would have been far more proper – especially in the presence of a gentleman – but we were in a different world now. I needn't feel ashamed of anything, for once. That's how it seemed in that mad moment. Everything was changed about and besides, I could feel my dusty skin calling out for that water. When I sloshed my way in, disturbing the sheeny mirror of the surface, it felt like my pores were drinking it in. The cold pebbles felt wonderful under my feet, slimily insecure as I minced along, wincing at the cold. I felt light as a prima ballerina as I sank under the surface, hoping the other two hadn't taken any notice of my raggy underwear. Underwear that in those days, mercifully, covered rather more flesh than later underwear did. My scars weren't on display. My oddity wasn't so obvious to my companions. Though really, I don't think either of them were that bothered about looking at me.

I turned coyly back to the bank, mostly submerged like a curious hippo – just in time to watch Mr Rupert strip himself completely bare. Goodness, but he had no scruples – nor anything to be ashamed of. He was all pink and gold and glorying in the afternoon. He came dashing into the water shrieking with joy and splashing us ladies. What a noise we set up in reply, splashing him back as he turned cartwheels and dive-bombed all about the place. Mrs Mapp was howling in quite an unfamiliar way.

For a moment I lay back and floated across the span of the jungle pool. Pausing only briefly to check that my wig was holding fast. I pondered what we had become in this place. Transported here we were like beasts. Like primitive people. We were strangers to ourselves. Capering about and forgetting ourselves.

Oh. And then I went too far and got stuck in the quicksand.

I almost died.

I tried to stand up and I couldn't. Something strong had caught hold of me. The ground had turned hungry and I panicked. I screamed to gain the others' attention.

I felt such a fool.

There I was, flailing about in the mud and coughing up my guts. This awful sinking feeling was my only reward for a life of drudgery, and this was my imminent and ignominious end. Here, in this Qab jungle, I would return to clay; to the muck that had spawned me.

Funny how you can go a bit philosophical as you're getting sucked under.

I was also fighting for every breath.

By now, Mrs Mapp and Mr Rupert had come straggling to my rescue. They were wading carefully, very carefully, lest they got caught themselves in the same rotten flux. I reached out desperately and then I was clinging to my friends. Depending upon them.

The strength in my fingers was surprising to them, I think. Panic augmented my already considerable strength. I was bringing up red welts on Mr Rupert's forearms as I gripped. He'd feel the bruises, I was thinking, as the mud started to give way with a long, obscene sucking noise . . .

I tried not to feel a fool. As they both said afterwards, it could have happened to anyone.

I lay about in our camp trying not to remember what it was like, thrashing about in that quagmire.

Mr Rupert went off jauntily with his hunting knife, promising us wild pig for supper, and the mistress and I sat complacently by our fire.

My underwear was steaming on the clothes horse we'd built out of branches and I was wrapped in a tartan picnic blanket. As we sat talking quietly, it felt for the first time as if we were equals.

But who was I kidding? However long we were in the place, and no matter how many adventures we shared, when it came time for returning to civilisation, we'd be back in our old roles, surely.

That was *if* we ever got returned.

I was questioning now whether I even wanted such a thing.

'You're lookin' very contemplative, Brenda.' She'd never seen me be anything but busy.

'I reckon I am,' I said, a little stiffly. I suppose I was still embarrassed about needing to be rescued. I'd done a fair bit of swearing and cursing, too, while I was struggling against the rising mud.

'We've been here only a day or so, but everything feels so different. Do you feel that, Brenda? We've been castin' off the shackles of respectability . . .'

She shivered. I put myself in her shoes for a moment. She was inside her own invented land. She must feel liberated. Excited.

'What do you think of Mr Von Thal?' she asked me suddenly. A strange hesitation in her voice. I hardly knew what to say. I thought my admiration was all too plain whenever he was near or his name came up. I felt my ears burn bright with blood when he talked to me. I was full of blushes for that man. Had she never noticed?

'I've always thought of him as just a boy, really,' Mrs Mapp went on. She didn't wait for my thoughts on the matter. 'But recently he has started to remind me of my older brother, Duncan. In lots of ways he really does. And then to see him swaggerin' about in Duncan's old clothes like that . . .'

'He's a very romantic figure,' I put in. 'Glamorous. Adventurous. He looks like a hero now.' I was picturing the base of his neck and the little hollow where it met his chest. And the broadness of that chest, especially when he flung off his ruffled shirt.

'Yes,' she agreed. 'Now that he is in my world. I've changed the boy into a man . . .'

She fell to musing for a while. And I was thinking: she loves him! She really does! And I knew it all along. I had seen it all earlier, hadn't I? Before Mrs Mapp even knew about it herself.

Then I thought: what chance do I stand now of him ever looking at me in any way other than as a servant?

But what chance did I ever stand? I was being ridiculous. Look how old I was, and look at him. And our backgrounds . . . and everything else. The sun and the damp were getting to me. The humidity was making my mind reel with ludicrous fantasies. I should be happy to hear that my mistress was at last coming to her senses. I should be delighted that she was responding to Mr Rupert's courting ways. Because, of course, that was what was going on. He'd been beating a path to her door for a long time now, and only here and now in Qab was she starting to bend to his insistent pressure.

I could have wept. Sitting there under that blanket. Damp to my bones and still hacking up algae. Fingering black mud out of my clogged ears.

And then the screaming started.

'Mr Von Thal!' Mrs Mapp cried, and was on her feet in a flash.

He was under attack! Some way into the jungle there was all this clattering and shrieking. Then there was an unearthly wailing and crying, coming from an unknown creature.

I struggled to my feet, still swaddled in tartan and ungainly as I lumbered after Mrs Mapp on my bare feet. What use was I going to be in a fight? Mrs Mapp plucked up her brolly and sallied fearlessly forth into the trees.

And there we found Mr Von Thal face to face with a hideous insect-type creature standing about seven feet tall. It was like a mantis, or one of the ghastly specimens standing about in glass cases all over the house in Tavistock Square. Bloated to incredible size. Mandibles a-twitching and lithe acid-green legs darting about. Its eyes were the worst thing. They were like silvery metal, agleam with hateful intelligence.

The thing was fighting Mr Rupert for the dead piglet he had brought from his hunting trip.

'Ladies, keep back! I have it! I can . . . I can deal with the beast . . .'

He lashed out with his gory knife, liberating a stream of nasty green blood from the creature's muscular arms. But the arms were closing around our hero and pressing his body to that hideous thorax. What would it do to him? Those serrated limbs could slice him apart in seconds ... and was it poisonous? Could it paralyse him and turn his flesh to mush? And drink him up right there in front of us?

Mrs Mapp went wading in, smashing at the brittle hide of the animal with her umbrella. She was using some language I would never have expected from her.

'I can do this! Just keep back!' Mr Rupert insisted.

'Mr Von Thal!' my mistress shouted imperiously. 'One thing is called for here, in order to disable this brute. You must' – and here she raised the point of her brolly high about her head – 'stab the thing in the eye!' Which she did, with a hefty and well-aimed poke of her ferrule.

The mantis screeched the most hideous protest and its arms flew up to its damaged, swivelling eye. A gout of black ichor showered down on the three of us and Mr Rupert took immediate advantage of the thing's distraction. He scooped up Mrs Mapp and took hold of my arm and he barrelled us backwards, away from the jerking limbs of the swaying mantis.

'STAB IT!' Mrs Mapp was howling. 'Don't run away yet! Make sure it's dead! Stab it in the other eye! Hoik its brains out! KILL THE BLOODY THING!'

She was ranting like a madwoman. But Mr Rupert knew better than not to obey. As the mantis pitched forward on to the grass, still screaming about its eye, Mr Rupert fell upon it with his knife and made short work of it.

I actually felt a bit ashamed of us then. Bringing disaster and death into this innocent, primitive place.

We returned to our poolside camp in rather subdued fashion. We were lathered in horrid black and green fluids.

'You have made a dangerous world for us to explore,' Mr Rupert told her.

'I thought you said that this place was not my responsibility?'

He shrugged and looked rather grim. We sat by the fire and I kept stoking it up, and making sure that our torches continued glowing bright. The jungle beasts chattered and gibbered all night and I don't think I slept a wink.

All day was spent wending our way deeper and deeper into the woods while Mr Rupert related more of what he knew about the esteemed Professor Quandary.

'I believe I have known the professor longer than I have known you, Mrs Mapp. It's hard to recall the exact sequence of things. You and I met that summer at Lyme Regis, didn't we? I was just down from Oxford and you were there with your uncle. Specimens, yes, of course. Well, by then I knew Quandary. I believe I showed off to you, rather, when we first met, about some of the pickles I had been in already, so early in my career. Remember my telling you . . . ? Well, Quandary was involved in all of those.'

The lustrous mud of the forests was giving way to rockier terrain. The plants were stringier and hardier here and the going was tougher. We weren't allowed to take many rest stops, though.

'Quandary was in Oxford for a while, lecturing . . . he wasn't attached to any college . . . he just sort of turned up one day. He appeared in a flash. Everyone spoke about him in awed whispers. There was a lot of mystery about him. Everyone had heard something about him . . . some little whisper of the legend.

'That was the year he invented a special kind of paint, which, when used, somehow read the minds of the room's inhabitants and projected them on the walls, which was marvellous for parties. And we were involved in the search for the Antarctic Phoenix, and so on . . .

'It isn't really worth enumerating all of our adventures now. I believe Brenda here is already an aficionado of our published accounts anyhow. She knows the kinds of things we get up to, hmm?'

I nodded and smiled and found I was too breathless to say very much. The air was definitely becoming thinner as we tackled these ever-steeper slopes.

'Anyhow, as to the question of Quandary's provenance,

Mrs Mapp, I simply don't know. It's been such a bally rush and a hoo-ha, every time I'm in the professor's presence – I've never had any chance to ask about his background or his past. So the truth is, I really don't know where he comes from originally, so to speak. I don't know what his secret is, for I am sure he must have one.

'I do have some suspicions. Some very strange suspicions. He will let something slip now and then, some reference to – I don't know – politics or some super kind of motor car or an unfamiliar monarchy, and it won't be quite right. It is like the professor is trying to remind himself all the time of relevant details about our society. He is brilliant about most things, but hesitates and stammers over details with which even a child brought up in this country would have no trouble.

'I thought he might be a foreign spy at one point. A German, perhaps. With his bluff manner and very precise ways. Or perhaps a Russian – that big bushy beard of his. But I don't know. There are other things . . . his watch, for example. It's like no device I have ever seen before. Incredibly advanced . . . it emits the strangest noises. And his knowledge of scientific matters . . . sometimes it seems impossible, the breadth and depth of his knowledge. But again, he appears to be holding some things back – as if the sum total of his knowledge is something he has to hide and prevent pouring forth; like that whole thickset body of his was a kind of dam.'

We were dragging ourselves past rocks and boulders now. They were curiously gemlike under the blazing sun. Ahead of us was a ridge like a jawful of broken teeth. It was as if Mr Rupert was trying to distract us from the harshness of our environment by bombarding us with words.

'I don't know, though. I'm not sure what I'm saying even . . .' he mused, pausing and wiping the sweat from his face with his handkerchief. He stared into the far distance, his mind still focused on his mysterious friend. 'He is like a demon in human form, with his tempers and rages and brilliant inspirations. But you see, Brenda, Mrs Mapp, though I have been his loyal companion on escapades all over our world, under and above it – and now in a different world altogether – I hardly know the professor any better than you do, through your chance encounters with him or reading about him in the *Fitzrovian Spree*.'

Now followed the final assault on the most perilously steep part of our ascent. We could still stand upright, but only just. It wasn't very comfortable, staggering and reeling after my two companions, sending flurries of sand and shale down the rock face behind me.

Mr Rupert still talked, though by now his words were punctuated by some rather heavy breathing. 'One thing, however. One recent thing. To do with his present incarceration. One thing that disturbed me because it demonstrated a side to the professor I hadn't encountered before. Something strangely disquieting. When we were here first, a few weeks ago, and we were taken to the city . . .'

Ah! And here we were, all of a sudden.

Mr Rupert fell silent as we came to the top and drank in the scene before us.

It was as if, as we surmounted that craggy spine, we didn't quite know what to expect. The vista before us was astonishing. It quite stopped my breath, even though my lungs were bursting and crying out for air. Beside me Mrs Mapp was in quite the same stupefied state: staring at the lush valley below, nestled and cradled by multi-hued and misty mountains. Yet in Mrs Mapp's reaction, there was also a sense of satisfaction, I think.

She looked like a woman who had – in some sense – come home at last.

Before us, far below, lay the splendid city of Qab.

To me it looked like a marvellous mishmash of all kinds of architectural styles, from all over the world. I saw towers, minarets, onion domes and spires. I saw things that wouldn't have looked out of place in Venice or Florence, and other buildings, crammed hugger-mugger, that seemed to come from our Far East or Arabia. I saw humble stone dwellings planted in rows and spirals, radiating out from serried ranks of palaces, glimmering gold in the sun. One vast building dominated all, however. It was a lumpen castle, shaped a bit like something gigantic termites might build. Its towers leaned eccentrically, peering out all over the city. Its windows were luminous slits.

What was most striking, apart from the chaotic sprawl of styles and types of building, was the sheer profusion of life that was in evidence, all over Qab. We could see narrow streets and they were teeming. Strange beasts hauled carts and servants bore their mistresses along on sedan chairs. Crowds gathered in market spaces and along commercial streets. The endless, restless tussle of the day's business was going on in this fabulous place, just as it did in every other great city. To those down there, all of this might even have seemed mundane.

My mistress and I were speechless. Mr Rupert was not.

'Sublime, is it not? Oh, look at this land, Mrs Mapp. Your land. Qab. Is it everything you dreamed it would be?'

'Hmm? Oh yes,' she gasped. 'Oh yes, indeed.'

Now I was watching the birds wheeling and dipping around the chimneypots and towers. Huge birds, they were, screeching and cawing and returning to their nests in the city's highest roosts.

It struck me: we were going down there. Into Qab. Just as in the book. We would be among the many citizens, and part of all that life.

Mrs Mapp managed to wrench her attention away from studying this glittering, sun-baked mirage of a metropolis. She urged Mr Rupert to continue with his tale. This was vital stuff: his description of his and his friend's reception within the grey walls of that ominous palace down there.

'So what was it, then?' she asked Mr Rupert. 'What was this strangely disturbing thing about Professor Quandary? When at last you were faced by the woman who had ensnared you and brought you to her throne room?'

'Blow me, but if he didn't recognise *Her*! And she recognised him!'

'What?' gasped Mrs Mapp, at this plainly impossible fact.

'You could have knocked me down with a feather,' said Mr Rupert. 'There we were, in all this splendour – beaten copper panelling and polished stone . . . a tall throne on an impressive dais, and all her guards around her. Those lizard men . . . they give me the creeps, they do. Ah, look . . . you can see them now, moving about in the thoroughfares down there. I believe they'll be setting out on their hunting expeditions. We shall have to beware . . .

'Well, to go back to my story . . . I'm looking about, all impressed, and there's the queen of the whole world standing before us in her robes. Magnificent she is, if a bit pale. Beautiful. Lovely to look at. But frightening as well. I mean, I wouldn't want to get too close. And I was right, as well, in my intuition, to keep my distance, as I found out a bit later on . . .

'Suddenly she's growling and spitting at us! Like she can't bear the sight of us!

'Next to me, the good professor's gone likewise. His beard's bristling with irritation. His face is red with fury as the two of them start hurling insults at each other.

'Obviously, what I wanted to know . . . how on earth could the two of them be such old enemies? How on earth could they have met before?

'We were on Qab. This was *Her*. The embodiment of female power in the land of Qab. You know *Her*, Mrs Mapp. How could the queen in your book know my professor so well? Know him at all?

'All I knew was that neither of them bothered to fill me in. My presence was an irrelevance. They had eyes only for each other, those two.

'"You followed me," she said to him. "Why? What do you want from me? How dare you come after me like this?"

'"Believe me," he rejoinered. "I wouldn't if I didn't have to . . . erm, I wouldn't *choose* to place myself in your ineffable effing power!"

'"You had no choice!" She ejaculated crossly. "My people captured you! Brought you here!"

'"I allowed us to be captured," said he, in more measured fashion. "I wanted to come here. I wanted to see you. We have many things to discuss."

'"There's nothing I want to discuss with you," she snapped. "This is my new life here. My new world. I am happy here."

'"I'm sure you are. Surrounded by servants. Everyone at your beck and call. Fed and pampered like the queen in her hive . . ."

'"How dare you? How can you criticise me for finding something new? It was you who *ruined* my previous life . . ."

'"You're a very sick woman," he told *Her*, and the queen responded as if he had leapt on to that dais and slapped her. She screamed for her guards and they came running with daggers held aloft. They grabbed hold of Professor Quandary. And that was the last I saw of him, I'm afraid.

'As they pulled him away I shouted out, "Professor!" in this madly futile kind of way.

'"Keep back, Rupert," he told me. "The Source. You've got to get back to London. Somehow. You need to bring . . . the Source . . . bring it here . . ."

'The Source? What could he have meant by that?

'I had no idea what he was on about. Some of his mystical mumbo-jumbo, no doubt. At first I thought he meant a sauce like, you know, tartare sauce or gravy or whatnot. But later, as I lay in a filthy cell deep beneath the palace, in the catacombs, I realised he meant *Source* . . .

'And that can only mean you, Mrs Mapp, can't it? The source of all this? The source of Qab itself?'

Mrs Mapp looked surprised.

'You brought us here, to Qab . . . to this city we see before us . . . because Professor Quandary told you to?'

'Quite so.' He nodded sadly.

'But we came here to save him! We are here on a rescue mission!'

In the past Mr Rupert had been a big-game hunter, trolling about the veldt for beasties. And now Mrs Mapp was his prey. She felt stung, I could tell just by looking at her face.

She went on, 'You told me that the professor said that Qab had somehow got inside my head . . . It inveigled its way into my mind, and forced me to write it into existence. You said that the professor thought that this place – this grand, glorious, all-too-real world – actually pre-existed my writing about it. That's what you said, back in my drawing room.'

'And that is what we thought,' said Rupert grimly. 'But I don't know any more. I simply don't know. Professor Quandary called you the Source. You are the source of all of this. Everything around us.' He stood on the brow of that hill, with all of the valley and the strange city behind him.

I was dumbstruck as Mr Von Thal went a bit philosophical at this point. 'Who knows where other worlds come from? Who's to say who creates them? Could this place exist without your imagination? Did your dreams cause it to be?'

We both looked at his face. It was twisted up with thought, almost feverish-looking. Mr Rupert was a man of action, quite unused to this kind of intellectual wrangling. I could see that it wasn't doing him any good at all.

It was me who took the decision to direct everyone's attention back to palpable things and the matter in hand.

I focused on the lizard men in the valley below. Beyond the borders of the extravagantly eclectic city they were moving in packs through the tall jungle grass. I studied them for some time. Horrible-looking things. Like men, really, only paler, and faintly green. Their faces were much more lizardy, with rictus grins filled with jagged teeth, and those funny, untrustworthy eyes – though I never saw those, of course, until we had carried ourselves down into the valley and came face to face with the brutes. Take me to your leader and all that business, which we felt we had to do, of course. Easiest way of getting yourself inside the place: just march up to the guards and announce your presence.

'We have to watch out,' Mr Rupert counselled. 'We have to be very careful. They are savage and, I think, merciless. See those whips they carry?'

Indeed we did. They lashed out with them indiscriminately, using the nasty things to clear away the rushes and vines. The snapping and slashing could be heard from miles away.

'They take those whips from some tree that grows here. They emit a kind of sting on contact, a kind of poison. And the lizard men use those whips to capture their slaves.'

Mrs Mapp nodded. 'This really is my world, down to every last detail, isn't it?'

In her book, the lizard men went abroad to enslave the local human beings. A shabby, underdeveloped lot. Reading her novel, I felt a bit cross at these bits, as if I was privy to how Mrs Mapp and those of her ilk saw the ordinary people, the working people. Shambling, inarticulate brutes in musty flea-ridden rags, who had to be whipped and told precisely what to do. Was that how the mistress saw me? I remember thinking, as I sat up in my bed. But then the story had moved on and I had buried the thought. It would never have done to ask her about it.

The human slaves were not the only kind in Qab. As a keening, screeching noise filled the air, I realised that we were about to see the other sort, too. My heart gave an excited bounce at this, for we were going to see the bird people.

Sure enough, as we started to make our way down a sharp declivity of volcanic rock, we saw a party below with their bird people wheeling and dipping through the magenta cloud cover. They had hugely long chains that clanked and jingled, tethering them to the ground and holding them steady.

'They're hunting the blood beasts?' Mrs Mapp said, though she knew the answer already. We all did.

The going was hard on this ashy, uneven ground. We clutched hold of each other and advanced as carefully as we could down into the valley.

Every now and then we would see one of the bird men circling, far in the distance. Amazing creatures with huge spans, diving and screeching, full of the joy of the hunt. They looked rather like those hulking brutes, the vultures I had observed in London Zoo. Reeking of carrion and with their unkempt feathers matted and slick with old blood. The bird men's bills were even crueller-looking than any bird I had seen and their claws were more horribly dextrous. We saw one take a blood beast mid-flight. Mr Rupert pointed it out to us. The bat creature must have been roosting in the highest part of the forest's canopy. One of the birds had spotted it a mile off and homed in on silent wings. Its talons flashed and slashed and took hold of the dozing beast. No contest. The bat was sated and fat, clinging to those upper branches, with no idea what had hit it. The bird man soared, cawing with triumph, holding the bat close to his chest in an unlockable embrace. It was almost as big as he was.

'The thing is full of blood, after a night's hunting,' Mr Rupert said. 'They'll take it straight to *Her*. They'll squeeze every drop of blood into one of her silver churns. She needs gallons of blood every day simply in order to survive. She'll take it from anywhere. From whatever the blood beast has been feasting on.'

I recalled all of this from Mrs Mapp's book. I looked at her and wondered why she couldn't have invented somewhere a bit more pleasant. Or perhaps she had no choice and Professor Quandary had been right in the first place: this land had come looking for her and seeped foully into her imagination. She herself was looking somewhat queasy. A vampire queen? Lizards who enslaved those bird men to hunt giant blood-filled bats? What was she thinking of? Was it all that Welsh rarebit she used to demand that I bring her in the middle of the night? Was melted Cheddar behind all of this?

And then, as we reached the forest once more and the ground underfoot became less rocky and steep, we were spotted. A great cry went up from a passing squad of lizard men. Oh, my calves were aching from that descent into the valley. Mr Rupert had led us at quite a trot. He was no respecter of this shambling, middle-aged body.

'Aha!' he cried now. 'I see they recognise me. Hmmm. I was the one who gave them the slip a little while ago. They won't be very pleased with me, I don't suppose.'

'Chin up, laddie,' Mrs Mapp said, sounding very staunch and proper all of a sudden. She drew herself up to her full height as if she were about to meet someone from a far-off land, someone whose customs she felt were savage but who must, for the sake of good manners, be treated as an equal. 'Good morning,' she called out to the advancing lizard men, waving her wrecked straw hat about.

Quite an impressive sight they were, close to. It was now that I took note of those scaly, brawny chests. That tinge of green about their gills. The crest of scarlet flesh atop their bony skulls, which would ripple in accordance with their mood. Those teeth, those eyes. We were truly in the presence of utterly alien creatures, and the very thought thrilled me in ways I never would have expected it to.

'We are new to your world,' Mrs Mapp went on breezily, sounding as if she was making conversation at a garden party. 'We come from very far orf indeed. I wonder if you people would mind very much takin' us to your queen?'

The lizards hissed and mumbled amongst themselves for a while.

Mrs Mapp looked at Mr Rupert sharply. 'They do speak English, don't they?'

'As in your book, yes, they do. Though I don't know who but you ever taught them it.'

She nodded with satisfaction. 'Curious, looking at the brutes. I feel as if I know what is runnin' through their heads. Their single-mindedness of purpose. The tiny preoccupations they have. All they care for is the hunt and serving their queen. And their bird men, which they think of as their kites. And the blood banks too, of course, which they tend to. That's all the life I gave them. That's all they have to their characters, I'm afraid.'

The lizard men were finished with their conflab, evidently having come to some sort of resolution. They rounded on us roughly and we were corralled and led into the trees.

'They're doing it,' Mr Rupert said. 'Well done, Mrs Mapp. They're taking us to the palace. You actually made them listen to you!'

She shrugged modestly, as if to say, what are lizard men for but to do your bidding?

I had the sense of moving into the midst of a society and a civilisation quite unlike any I was used to. Mr Rupert seemed less overawed, but then he had been here before, and besides, he was an adventurer and a man of the world, taking simply everything in his stride. Mrs Mapp was filled with keen interest, peering at the wattle-and-daub dwellings of the lizard people. Observing them about their everyday business with the eye of a proprietress. I felt a bit glum and tired by now. It was strangeness heaped upon strangeness. I had thought I could cope with it all, but now I felt I just wanted a touch of the familiar for a little while.

We progressed to a wide thoroughfare, lined with tall palms. A crowd had come out to see us. Lizard people and some of the human slaves, who were very definitely a lower class. How pale and hollow-eyed they looked. Like some of the walking cadavers I'd seen in Whitechapel and Limehouse. Had they been worked and flogged to a state near death? A sense of outrage filled me at the sight of these pathetic human creatures. I could see that Mrs Mapp was similarly disturbed.

'They have been bled as well, then,' she mused. 'Paying tribute to their queen.'

I remembered how, in her manuscript, the great queen – *Her* herself – had demanded blood tribute from her human populace. A horrible feeling went through me. All of sudden I wanted to be out of this primitive city and away from this world. I wished we had never come here, and yet there seemed to be no chance of turning back.

We were at the great doors of the palace before we even knew it. The building was huge, and even stepping back to crane our necks, we couldn't see its many turrets. They stretched into the boiling clouds above. The doors themselves were three storeys high, taking at least six of the lizardy lackeys to screech them open to admit us.

Within, it smelled of dark and tangy blood. The lighting was smoky and dim and I wasn't at all happy about accompanying my companions inside.

'Oh, do come on, Brenda,' hissed Mrs Mapp. 'There's nothin' to fear.'

I couldn't take her word for that. Her face was gleaming. She was in a rapture, just like she was when she wrote. She had, in her own parlance, *gorn orf*.

There was no one to rely upon, I suddenly felt. Mr Rupert was conferring with our lizard guards. He was thick with them. Murmuring, explaining. I felt a stab of guilt for suspecting him. But the thought remained: he had brought us here for a purpose. He was under instructions. This was all part of somebody's plan.

As if he knew I was thinking about him, he turned to me with a tight, awkward smile. 'Buck up, Brenda old thing. You wanted to see the palace, didn't you? You wanted to see the queen?'

'I'm not so sure.' As we shuffled down the smoothly polished rock of the dark chambers, I was taunted by the memory of seeing real royalty. Our royalty, all dressed up. I recalled happy days of being dripped on by the piddling rain outside Buckingham Palace. Standing patriotically with the steaming, soaking crowds for parades and whatnot. I wished I was back in London now, where everything was common-place and dull.

More spectacle! More ritualistic rigmarole! More spectacular antechambers and vaulting ceilings! Ooh, and lovely stained glass all midnight blue, just like the chapel of St Chapelle in Paris. Instantly I was back there, in all that blue on the Ile de la Cité . . . though when was I ever in Paris? I couldn't remember. Some point in my murky past.

This wasn't Paris. This was the throne room of *Her*, just as I had pictured it in Mrs Mapp's book. And then I set to wondering how on earth that worked: that it was *my* version of the place that we saw. Surely Mrs Mapp and Mr Rupert had pictured creatures, places, things, buildings differently to how I had? Why was it my version that held sway?

I was thinking too much. It was the heady scent of the billowing purple incense and the roar of the furnace that was sending me into a drowsy state of contemplation. Those lilac and green flames licked merrily in a huge pit between us and the golden throne upon which the queen must sit.

And above the pit a cage was suspended. Too high up to burn the sole occupant to a crisp, but close enough to the lapping flames to bring him out in a nasty sweat.

'Professor!' Mr Rupert was shouting. 'Professor, it's me! Rupert! I'm back! I've been home and back again!'

He sounded much too cheery and pleased with himself, that one.

My eyes were smarting with the smoke and heat, but as I gazed upwards, along with Mrs Mapp, I saw who it was Mr Rupert was calling to. The lumpy, disconsolate figure of Professor Quandary.

Now, I had only ever caught glimpses of Quandary. He had never been for dinner at Tavistock Square, but a sherry once, when Mrs Mapp held an evening salon. I once saw him dashing into a lecture hall where he was due to make some brilliant speech about his latest findings at the equator. I milled with many other admirers of his amazing adventures, just for a glimpse of the great man. And I had seen the drawings and an occasional photograph of him in the papers in which appeared accounts of his escapades. He always cut a very impressive figure. Rotund, barrel-chested, resolutely fierce of mien. That heroic beard thrust out arrogantly. A safari hat cocked at a jaunty angle.

This figure in the swaying cage seemed like a broken man in comparison. One of the reptile men jabbed him awake by thrusting a spearhead none too gently through the bars.

'Professor Quandary,' gasped Mrs Mapp. 'How dare they treat you like this? We must make them get you down at once. Unfortunately we have had some difficulties communicatin' with the brutes, but this situation cannot be allowed to go on!'

Professor Quandary was getting shakily to his feet, clinging to the bars and making his cell rock back and forth. 'Beatrice Mapp? Is it really you?'

'Yes, indeed,' said my mistress, very proudly. 'We have come a long way to see you, sir.'

'My dear girl! You came all the way to Qab!'

'Isn't she marvellous?' said Mr Rupert, and his voice was bursting with pride.

'This is your world, my dear,' the professor said. 'The world that you have worked to bring back into being. Everything is just as it is in your book. It is amazing, Beatrice. What you have done is simply—'

'Yes, yes,' she said brusquely. 'But where is the manuscript? Mr Rupert tells me that you have my only copy still about your person.'

Professor Quandary looked alarmed at this. 'The only copy?'

I suddenly saw how shabby he was, as a burst of flame leapt higher than the others and illumined us all brightly for a few moments. He cut an even more ragged and filthy figure than had Mr Rupert, when he turned up that night in Tavistock Square. The professor had been beaten soundly and drubbed in muck, it was plain to see. He had suffered terribly through his incarceration.

'Where is the book?' hissed Mrs Mapp, in a voice tinged with anxiety. Far more anxiety than she had shown throughout any of our misadventures thus far, I noted.

'I don't have it,' said Quandary, in a strained voice. 'She has it. I mean, *Her*. *Her* has it.'

None of us needed to ask who he meant.

Now it was Quandary's turn to ask an urgent question. This time, of Mr Rupert. 'And you, Rupert? Did you bring what I asked you? What she commanded me? Our part of the bargain. Our freedom to return home safely . . .'

Mr Rupert nodded. Shiftily, I thought. 'The Source, she said. Yes, Professor. I have made sure that we brought the Source. To *Her*. For *Her* to do with what she will.'

I stared at them. What source? Whatever were they talking about? Mrs Mapp?

But then one of the lizards was bashing an old brass gong. A huge booming drowned out our furtive chit-chat with the captive. We were chivvied with swords and spears and daggers and led around the pit of emerald flames to stand before the throne.

It was obvious who was next on the bill. We three glanced at each other. My throat was jammed silent with terror. The other two didn't look much better off as we faced front and were forced to our knees by the scaly henchmen.

Oh, Brenda, I told myself. When – or if – you get back to Blighty, you're going to swear off adventures of all kinds, all right? Never again. No more excitements for you, my dear.

Just at that moment a figure emerged from the darkest recesses of the royal chamber. She moved with great purpose and finesse on to her stage like an opera singer making her entrance for the grand finale.

She was wearing gorgeous black robes. Goodness knows where she did her shopping in a wilderness like this. Maybe she ran them up herself.

I was babbling to myself, I knew.

She – *Her* – was a beautiful creature. A youngish woman. Perhaps approaching middle age. Very pale and well preserved. Like a white lily shrouded in black foliage. That small, wry expression looking out at us.

When she spoke, I don't know what I was expecting.

Certainly not a broad Yorkshire accent.

'So. You're back, then. Very good. I like a man who keeps his word. I shall consider keeping mine as a result. Do you have the pinking shears? I think I'd better look after them, don't you? And this is Mrs Mapp, is it? I've got your manuscript, ducky, don't worry. What a remarkable thing that was. Fancy you being able to write it. Really, really amazing. Quite spooky, in fact.'

I looked at Mrs Mapp and she was staring dumbstruck at the queen of the world she had apparently invented. I don't think *Her* was quite how she had imagined *Her*, either.

And then *Her* looked straight at me.

Her livid eyes seemed to bore right into me. Deep into my secret heart.

'And here *you* are, Brenda. Brenda, my dear. Here you are in my new home. They brought you! They brought you here for me!'

'H-how do you know me?'

'Ah, but you're so young, ducky. So very young.'

I felt myself blushing. I stammered, 'I'm not so very young! You'd be surprised! You don't know what you're talking about!'

'I know what you're going to say. You're going to tell me you're already over a hundred years old.'

I gasped. 'What?'

Mrs Mapp gasped as well. 'Whatever does she mean?'

'Am I?'

'Oh yes, I know all sorts of things about you, lovey,' said the Warrior Queen of Qab. *Her*, in all her glory. 'But the important thing is, you came here to help me. Like friends always should.'

'Did I?' I asked. 'Is that why I'm here? I don't know who you are! Outside of the mistress's story, I've never encountered you before in my life . . .'

'But you will, ducky. You certainly will! You see, Brenda, you're going to save me. You're the Source, you are. The source of my deliverance. My salvation. You're going to save the life of your best friend! Even if you don't even know her yet! You haven't even properly met her yet!'

'But . . . who are you?'

'Here, as you know, I am *Her*. *Her* who must be worshipped. But you know me by the much more ordinary name of Effryggia Jacobs. Effie for short.' She raised her glittering black sleeves into the air and commanded her guards thus: 'Take my guests to somewhere they can rest and recuperate from the rigours of their journey! At once!'

They dragged us apart then, and it came as a dreadful wrench. The lizard men were upon us before we knew it, and they were taking Mrs Mapp and Mr Rupert away, somewhere deep inside this palace. I cried out, but the servants had me locked in a terrible grip and there was nothing I could do. It flashed through my mind in an instant that the mistress and I had never been parted from each other for a very significant portion of time, and certainly never forcibly, like this. Mrs Mapp did a certain amount of kicking and protesting, but it was no good. She was taken away, her cries still ringing in my ears. I suddenly felt bereft, standing there, with this queen who called herself Effryggia.

'Effie for short,' she had added, Her affable tone at odds

with the regal gown and haughty mien. 'And I wouldn't be too cut up about being separated from them two, Brenda. I really wouldn't.'

I snorted back my tears and said rudely, 'What would you know about it?' And the guard holding my arms gave a sibilantly menacing hiss. I must remember that I was talking to *Her*, and she must be respected and obeyed.

'Oh, look,' she was saying now, 'we can't stand about all day in this throne room. It's a bit clammy in here. And it's a bit ghoulish with that old fella up there in his cage.' She cast a disparaging glance at Quandary, now unconscious above the licking flames from the pit. 'Why don't we go and sit in my parlour, Brenda, eh? We can have a proper talk there . . .'

I almost spat back at her: what do we two have to talk about? What did the likes of *Her* have in common with me? But I bit my tongue and nodded dumbly. 'Y-you won't hurt Mrs Mapp, will you?'

Her tutted. 'Why should you care? She has exploited you for years, Brenda. This is your chance to liberate yourself, ducky. Have you never read Marx? Have you never thought that she was taking more than she was giving?'

I followed the woman known as Effie through a honeycombed warren of dark passages. I felt puzzled and quite alienated by now, and rather passive, as if all my energy had flowed out of me. I had no idea what was to become of me, for it was clear that there had been machinations and wheels turning behind my back. Things I hadn't been aware of . . .

'They betrayed you, Brenda,' said the queen. 'Can't you see that? They engineered all of this. They brought you here as an offering to me. They want to swap you for their musty old professor and for Beatrice Mapp's manuscript. And trusting as you are, you just wandered in. Good-hearted, daft as a brush. Too honest for your own good.'

'No!' I burst out. 'Mr Mapp would never . . . She'd never betray me like that . . . for whatever price!'

Now we were sitting in the somewhat more homely room that Effie described as *Her* private living quarters. I was surprised to find it decorated bizarrely, as if for Christmas. Blackened pine trees stood in a ring around us, covered with rudimentary carved Christmas decorations. I was given a tankard of some strange sticky liquor – brewed from jungle creepers, she told me brusquely, 'Drink it down, it'll do you good. No, don't sip. You don't want to taste it.'

I thought about the moment that the lizard men had seized hold of Mr Rupert and my mistress in order to separate us. At the time the severance had seemed the worst and cruellest thing. Now I looked at Queen Effryggia in the flattering glow of the prehistoric Christmas lights. 'They offered me as a . . . sacrifice, you say. But why? Why on earth would you want me?'

Her smiled. 'You don't know how important you are, do

you? Hm? Especially at this stage in your very long life. The times have been cruel to you, Brenda. They have made you into a servant. Made you a drone. You have been crushed underfoot so thoroughly that you have forgotten what a singular and important creature you are.'

I felt the irksomeness rise in my breast. 'I am not a creature.'

'Nor are you fully human.'

I flinched at this. However, I knew intuitively that she was not intending to insult or upset me.

'I wish I could take the time to remind you of all your past, of who you are and where you came from. But that will have to wait. We must proceed with my plan. I have so very little time.'

'Why?' I said harshly. 'What's the matter with you?'

She paused and licked her lips. 'I'm not a well woman, Brenda.'

It was true, I thought. This close to, sitting in her parlour and getting a good look at her, you could see that she wasn't right in herself. That complexion wasn't just for glamorous effect. She looked deathly pale. She looked emaciated.

'As your employer might have told you, my appetites are very unnatural. I feed off . . . well, off blood. I was infected with a rare condition some time ago, and ever since, I have been trying to sustain myself with the blood of living beings.'

'A vampire!' I gasped. 'So it's true. I read Mrs Mapp's book and I know everything. Everything she wrote is true, isn't it?'

'We can still make up our own destiny,' said *Her* darkly. 'We are not bound up in the inventions of that dreadful Bloomsbury bint. We are free to change our scripts for ourselves. Why, your coming here has even changed the ending Mrs Mapp was proposing for her story.'

I stared at the woman. So calm, she was: telling me that she was a true vampire. Well, naturally I knew such things existed. I had met them before, hadn't I? Ah, there was a frayed end of a faded ribbon of memory tickling at me. Yes, indeed, I had encountered her hellish type before. Somewhere, some time in the previous century . . .

But there was no time to tease out that strand right now, for suddenly I could feel terror sneaking up on me. This was surely no mere fireside chat. I was in the most dreadful danger.

'You would think I would have endless supplies here, wouldn't you?' said Effie. 'Being queen, I have the pick. I can take the cream of the crop. And it's true, my boys work very hard for me. Harvesting the primitive human beings. Offering their own – rather thin and chilly – blood for my delectation. It's rather like sipping cold coffee, though. And they hunt those hideous bloated bat things that go swooping about the quagmires of this benighted land . . .

'Oh, but it's a dreary diet, Brenda. I can feel myself ailing, weakening . . . turning lackadaisical and wan. This isn't my world, really. This place cannot sustain me.

'I came here looking for escape. I thought it would be all I would need. I was fleeing an awful man whose sights were set on destroying me, like he does with all my kind. But he is out of the picture now. I have fettled him. Though I don't suppose you'll be glad to hear that, if you knew yet who he was. Ah, but that's all in your future, isn't it? I must try harder to keep the timelines from tangling, otherwise things become too complicated . . .'

She was raving, I was certain. This was nonsense she was talking. She was iller than she seemed. Her mind was addled.

'Do you know, when I first came to this queer land I felt this huge sense of relief?' she told me. 'For the first time in my entire life I wasn't haunted. It's hard to believe. All my life I have heard the voices of my aunts in my head. All of them witches, generations going back and back. All of them knowing more than me, knowing better than me. Until I came here, to be queen over all of Qab, I had never really known a day of perfect peace and quiet, without their ghostly intervention. They wanted me to reach my full potential as a witch and become a fitting successor to them all . . .'

Oh help, I was thinking. Now it's witches as well!

'I relished that quiet for the first few weeks and months in my new world. I never missed them one bit. Them with their mithering and chuntering inside my head. Time went by . . . and I had a few misgivings. It was hard work being queen. There were decisions to be made. Quandaries to be . . . shall we say solved. Sometimes I actively wanted my aunts to come back to me. I wanted their counsel.

'I was lucky. I should have known I couldn't fully escape. I should have known I could rely upon them. And so it was my favourite who came to me one sleepless, hot and sticky night. My Aunt Maud materialised in my queenly bedroom, looking spectral, mannish, and piqued.

'"It's taken all our collective psychic energy to project me through the ether to talk to you, Effryggia," she glowered. "We had better be quick."

'Sitting up in my sumptuous bed, I could have wept at the sight of my dear old aunt.

'"Ach, don't get sentimental, girl. Who was it left us behind? Who ruined everything by letting that cadaver bite her in the first place? Who delighted in becoming a creature of the night? Who schemed to get herself into a new world, far away from her phantom relatives and those who were close to her and cared for her?"

'I hung my head. "Me. All of that was me."

'"I told your other aunts. You've got more of your bloody mother in you than any of us had reckoned on. Headstrong and selfish. And fond of being treated like a queen. Anyway. As I say, I haven't much time. I won't spend it all admonishing you. You want our help, don't you?"

'"Yes." No use denying it. Aunt Maud always knew what I was thinking.

' "The bloodlust is wearing a bit thin, is it?" she taunted. Not cruelly. She was never cruel. She simply looked like the person who always knows better than you do. The person who expects to be proved right in the end. "Sick of bloodsucking are you? Cheesed off with eternal youth, eh?"

' "I-I don't feel right," I told her. "I feel dreadful, actually. Thinned out. Sickly."

' "They don't call it being undead for nothing, you know. After the initial bloom and excitement, I've heard tell it's meant to be a bit of a miserable existence. Your chum Alucard never told you that, did he?"

' "I would give anything to go back," I burst out, all of a sudden. "To return to my normal state. To return home. To my house. Our house. By the sea. In my own time and place. And to be old again. And normal. Tell me, Aunt Maud . . . please! Tell me! Is it possible?"

' "A cure?" My aunt mused and stroked her bristly chin. "A cure . . . Well, you must know that such a thing is difficult. It's well nigh impossible."

' "Oh, please! I'm tired of it here. The climate is so awful, and all I've got to talk to are lizards . . ."

'That was when she told me that I might soon have human company. That Rupert Von Thal and his mysterious mentor Professor Quandary were about to arrive in my world. Most intriguing, I thought.

'Then my Aunt Maud confided in me that her powers

were failing. She was flagging and so were her sisters. She would return home to Whitby along the astral plane and I was to rest assured: my spooky aunts would put all their efforts into finding me a cure. They would discover a way to bring me back home, to where I belonged.'

I was agog, listening to Effie. 'And did they? Did she come back? Did she have a cure for you?'

Effie smiled grimly at how involved I was in her tale. 'I should have known that my witchy aunts would not let me down. I was a fool for trying to leave them behind. I felt rather ashamed of that.'

'Sometimes it is necessary to move on in life . . .' I said.

'Not me. I know where I truly belong. And I would do anything, and sacrifice anything, in order to get back there, Brenda.'

I shivered at these words, I don't know why.

'It was thirteen nights later,' Effie resumed, in her story-telling voice, 'and I had started to suspect that my aunts had forgotten me. Or they had elected to let me stew in my own juices and to take my punishment in this dreadful land that time has ostensibly forgotten. I was tossing and moaning miserably in bed one night when my Aunt Maud came shimmering evanescently on to my veranda and called me awake, none too gently.

'"Effryggia, you must listen. Help is at hand. Your aunties have worked long and hard. We have consulted the old books of magic in our house. We have even delved into the forbidden volumes of the Books of Mayhem for the knowledge you require. We have spoken to creatures and spirits we would normally think twice about consorting with. All of this we have done for you, Effryggia, last daughter of our house . . ."

'"Th-thank you, Aunt Maud," said I shakily.

'"Don't thank me yet," said the spectre gruffly. 'You might not like what you're about to hear. In fact, I am sure that you will baulk at what we have learned. For we have uncovered a secret lost in time. A valuable, incredible secret."

'"Oh, please," I urged. "Get on with it."

'Aunt Maud gazed at me levelly. Her black eyes seemed to contain all the dark places in the universe. As if she had looked into them all, prying after arcane secrets.

'"You must drink the blood of a human being who has no soul," my auntie said. "A truly rare being. An almost impossible being. But a few such beings do exist. This soulless creature is your salvation, Effryggia. She is the source of the substance that will bring you back to humanity. You must find her and drink her life blood and it will become yours. It will neutralise the filth that the vampire's bite put into your veins. It will quell that endless thirst . . ."

'"A soulless person . . ." I gasped. I knew at once who and what my Aunt Maud meant.'

Queen Effie looked at me then. *Her* who must be

worshipped was staring straight at me. Rather forlornly.

I burst out: '*Me!* It's me! That's why I'm here! That's why you made Professor Quandary send Mr Rupert to fetch Mrs Mapp and me and bring us here! It was *all* for me! You know . . . somehow you know . . . that I have no soul. I am a hollow woman with nothing inside me. Just organs and blood. Precious blood.'

'It was the only way, Brenda. I'm sorry . . .'

She was looking at me with infinite regret. But . . . if it was true . . . if her awful condition could be cured for ever, as her aunt said, by just a pint or two . . .

'How much?' I asked her. 'How much of my blood will you need to take? In order to save yourself?'

Now Effie looked stricken. 'I . . . I'm afraid . . .'

'Tell me!' I cried. But by then I feared I already knew the answer.

'All of it,' she said. 'Every single last drop. In order to save myself, Brenda, I have to drain you completely dry.'

Two Brides

Robert disliked the early, dreary days of January anyway, so it was no bother for him to put his head down and lose himself in work for a while. New Year came and went without much fuss, and business became a bit slacker at the Hotel Miramar. He focused his energies on cleaning and restocking and preparing for the year ahead, and making a number of adjustments necessary to accommodate Gila more fully into his life. Gila had moved into his tiny flat at the top of the Miramar.

'It's okay,' he had to keep telling the young lizard man. 'You're welcome here. Course you are. She can't get at you here. That Marjorie Staynes. She doesn't own you really, you know.'

But Gila's eyes looked haunted and doubtful.

Marjorie Staynes had been quiet ever since their tumultuous night at The Spooky Finger, when Effie had vanished into that vortex in the ladies' room.

She hadn't pressed charges. She hadn't even sent a nasty

note or come round in person to cause a fuss. Penny said there had been a round robin sent by email, telling the members of the book group and the rather more select Qab cult that all meetings for the next month or so were being postponed. Marjorie was pleading nervous exhaustion. The way the story got bruited about, her bookshop had been attacked that night by a brutal gang. *The Willing Spirit* never reported as much, but everyone in Whitby knew that it had been a mob of vampire lads that had descended upon The Spooky Finger that night. People spoke in whispers and in tones of escalating fear about the gangs of undead scallies roaming town in the night and filling the dowdy pubs by the harbour in the daytime. Something would have to be done about them.

Another reason for Robert to lie low. He didn't want to be facing off against vamps again any time soon. He'd had his fill. Gila felt much the same. The night of Effie's disappearance had shocked him so much that he could hardly talk about it. He had fought that night and that was something that had never come naturally to him, even back in the savage land of Qab.

'Is he all right?' Penny asked Robert, more than once. She was concerned that Gila didn't really seem to leave Robert's quarters.

'I'm worried he might be having a breakdown,' Robert told her. 'He's severed ties with Marjorie Staynes and with everything he's ever known. He's just got me now. That's got to be hard. He doesn't even belong here, does he?'

Gila had chosen just that moment to turn the corner and appear behind them. He overheard this last utterance of Robert's, and Penny saw his face fall dramatically.

'Gila! He didn't mean that!'

But Gila hurried off, and out of main reception, into the street. He pulled up his hoodie against the freezing wind, covering his strangely scaled head so that no one out there would take notice.

'Poor lad,' Penny sighed. 'I like him. You should try harder with him, Robert. Make a go of it, you know?'

Robert pulled a face at her. 'Oh Penny . . . it's not . . . it wasn't meant to *be* that serious. At least, it wasn't going to be. But now it's like I've got no choice.'

He decided that Brenda was the person he wanted to talk to about it. Or maybe she could distract him by talking about something completely different.

When he rang her, she suggested that she come up to the Miramar.

She told him, 'I'm going stir crazy in this place of mine. Henry's out somewhere, up to goodness knows what. I'm just dusting for the sake of it. Why don't I fling on my hat and coat and you can treat me to lunch in that fancy restaurant of yours?'

The restaurant at the Miramar had been really fancy in the heyday of Sheila Manchu, but now it was looking slightly dowdy. Robert was fond of the old look, and hadn't done anything about tarting it up or changing it as yet. He had a particular favourite table in an alcove, from which he could see the whole room and the staff busying about, and also the ex-beer garden through the tall windows. As he sat there waiting for Brenda, nursing a G&T, he was wondering whether he ought to get that garden sorted out this spring. Reopen it as a beer garden again, and maybe even rename it in tribute to Sheila? Or to Effie – a much more recent loss.

Had she really gone for ever? Robert couldn't . . . he wouldn't believe it. Effie was a fixture here. Brenda and Effie. They were inseparable in his head. The mardy old cow couldn't just have tootled off into the ether like that, never to return. It just wasn't feasible.

Then Brenda roused him from his reverie, standing beside their table and letting the waiter take her good woollen coat and her shapeless hat.

Green Thai curry with chips. Proper comfort food, as Brenda said.

'That chill has gone right through me,' she told him. 'I hate this time of year. My boiler's on the blink, I think. Probably need a new one.'

They filled up a half-hour with chit-chat like this.

Then Brenda said, 'Henry's on a mission. He's going to destroy each and every one of the vampires Effie and Alucard created.'

'He doesn't stand a chance. They're just toying with him. Keeping him chasing after them. They like a good fight. And meanwhile, they'll just proliferate. Maybe if he left them in peace they'd settle down. Can't he see that?'

Brenda frowned. 'But he can't just let them run amok, Robert. That'd be no good, would it?'

Robert shrugged. 'I've lived here longer than you, Brenda. And my Aunt Jessie lived here years before that, remember. She would talk about some of the vamp infestations they've had here over past years. If you let them go in peace, there's less fuss all round. We've just got used to them being more thin on the ground in recent years. And besides, they can be useful.'

She looked sceptical. 'That rabble? How?'

'By helping with some of the minor-league monsters. Some of the demons and such that come out of the gateway. The vamps keep some of those creatures at bay. They could make your job as guardian a bit easier, you know. It's a bit like keeping a cat to control the rat population, or spiders to gobble up flies. We've not heard a squeak out of the Limbosine or Hans Macabre or any number of other minor menaces lately, have we?'

'Henry doesn't see it like that,' she said, and called to the waiter for extra green Thai sauce, which came in a dainty milk jug. She emptied it and absent-mindedly popped the jug into her handbag. She's losing her marbles, Robert thought.

'Henry *wouldn't* see it like that,' he said. 'Henry just wants to destroy all monsters, doesn't he?'

Brenda was biting her lip. She lowered her eyes to her dinner plate, which was now swimming in a surfeit of gloopy curry sauce.

Robert knew at once that something was wrong. 'Tell me,' he prompted.

'It's about Henry.'

'What's he done now?' Robert was instantly on the alert.

'It's not so much what he's done. . . well, yes, it is, actually. He's hypnotised me again. Several times. For several hours at a time. Most notably over New Year's Eve.'

'So that's why you were so quiet! You weren't answering your phone or anything. You went out of circulation. I thought you were doing what I was doing, licking your wounds and—'

'Not quite,' Brenda said. She glanced side to side to make sure no one in the half-empty restaurant was earwigging. 'He put me under. It was like an orgy of mesmerism round mine over New Year's. I've been in one of Henry's deepest and most powerful trances. Oh, I hate it, Robert. I don't know why I let him. But he kept on and on at me. Badgering me and battering at my defences. Until at last I gave in. And . . .'

'And?'

'I went very deep. It worked. I went back into the past. I . . . recovered a whole heap of lost and forgotten memories.'

'What for? Why? Why did he want you to do that?'

'Because they're pertinent to what's happening now. Really, really pertinent. More than even Henry had bargained for . . .'

Brenda wasn't going to go into it over lunch. Robert felt a bit left out. 'You've got to tell me! What have you found out?'

But his friend was resolute, finishing the last of her chips and dabbing her lips with her napkin. 'No. There's no time. I've a heap of work to do at home. The last of my guests are leaving and I want to make my place shipshape. And you've got a job to do this afternoon, Robert.'

'Have I?'

'Your young friend Gila. We need his help. He's completely invaluable for what I'm planning. Where is he?'

'Erm, he went out earlier.'

'You two haven't fallen out? He hasn't run off?'

'No, nothing like that. But it's hard . . . hard for him to adjust to another world.'

She nodded. 'Of course it is. Poor lad. Well, you just find him this afternoon and tell him that he's got a very particular job to do for us in the next little while. You're coming out tonight, aren't you?'

'Where?' said Robert blankly. Suddenly Brenda was full of gumption and he felt like he was struggling in her wake.

'We've unfinished business at the Christmas Hotel, I think. What with Mrs Claus's bizarre revelations and claims . . . and besides, she rang me this morning. Says she is in possession of something she thinks I might need.'

Robert's heart sank. He hated going to the Christmas Hotel. But he knew he had to be brave. 'And you want me to bring Gila too?'

'Spot of dinner. Bit of a chat with the evil old ratbag. Maybe even a twirl around the dance floor. Come on, Robert, don't let me down!'

He studied her expression. 'At least give me a clue about what you remembered in your hypnotised state.'

She was getting up to go, shouldering her heavy bag. 'Like I say, it was very pertinent. To do with . . . Qab and Beatrice Mapp.'

'Really?'

She took a deep breath. 'I *knew* her, Robert. I had my suspicions, I've had them for a while . . . and I was right. I knew Beatrice Mapp a long time ago, in another life . . .' She checked her watch. 'Look, I'll see you and Gila later. The table's booked for eight p.m.'

He wished he hadn't had such a big lunch now. His green Thai curry lay a little heavy on him for the rest of the afternoon.

He found Gila on the other side of town, high on the stormy headland as the day faded. His hood was still up and he was shivering on a bench in the graveyard at the clifftop.

He didn't even have to look to see that it was Robert who had joined him. By now Robert was used to those weird heightened senses of his.

'We don't have the sea, like this, at home,' Gila said. 'When I arrived here, it was the first time I'd seen anything like it.'

Robert stared at the greyish-brown bands of the endless North Sea. It all seemed very commonplace to him.

'I think this must be my favourite place in all of Whitby, even despite the cold.'

'*This* is your favourite place?'

Gila shot him a look. 'What did you think I'd say, Robert? That my favourite place was with you? In your room? Right beside you?' He laughed. 'Believe it or not, I really do have a life and ideas outside of you. I'm not that needy. I'm not utterly slavish in my devotions.'

Robert sat down heavily and blushed. 'I'm sorry. I think I've been carrying on awful. Treating you like you're daft—'

'Look,' Gila interrupted. 'You don't have to look after me. Really. Just because I'm new to this world. I know that you're not . . . serious about me. I get that. I certainly don't want you to feel like you're lumbered with me . . . now that I'm stuck here, and seemingly cut off from Qab for ever . . .'

There was a new seriousness to him. A sheen in his eyes that wasn't just the reflection of the silvered sea. He knew he had burnt his boats with Marjorie Staynes by going off with Robert. He was being pragmatic about his chances of ever returning home. Suddenly Robert believed him. Believed that Gila was quite capable of surviving and making a life for himself here. He didn't intend to rely upon Robert for anything. All of a sudden that was clear and Robert was ashamed for assuming otherwise. He really had imagined that he'd be lumbered with Gila.

'I *am* into you,' he protested. 'You know I am.'

'Maybe,' said Gila. 'And maybe it's enough. We'll just have to see how it goes, won't we?'

Robert nodded ruefully and looked away, hoping that was the end of their talk. What's wrong with me? he wondered fiercely. What would be so bad about someone relying on me? How come I don't want to be needed?

He looked sideways at the pale, coarsened skin of the lizard boy's face. It was tilted upwards, taking in the stars as they came out.

Robert changed the subject decisively. 'My Auntie Jessie once lived in a cave at the bottom of these cliffs,' he said. 'Don't look at me like I'm making it up! It's true! When she was transformed, that time, into a primitive being from the dawn of time. I won't go into the whole sorry tale now. But she went berserk for a while, poor Aunt Jessie. She was completely out of control. So I ended up helping her hide away down there, deep inside a cave. I'd bring her food stolen from the kitchens at the Christmas Hotel, twice a day . . . kippers and sausage links . . .'

'I'm sure you did your best for her,' Gila said. Robert didn't know how to read his expression.

'Only Brenda and Effie knew that she was hiding away down there. They came out to see her. They were really concerned for her.'

'They're good friends to have,' said Gila. 'Well, Brenda is. I haven't managed to see much of Effie's good side, have I? And now it looks like I've missed my chance.'

'She'll be back,' said Robert. 'She has to come back. She just has to. She can't stay in some other world. Some strange other place where none of us have ever been.'

'I have,' Gila reminded him. 'That strange other place is the most familiar place in the world to me.'

'Of course.'

'I must admit, though, I'm not sure how Effie will be fitting in there. To me she seemed just like any other nondescript old lady from Earth.'

'Oh, she's much more than that,' said Robert. He stood and zipped his jacket up. 'Come on. If I'm frozen solid, you must be twice as cold. We've got just enough time to go home and get warmed through and then we need to get ready. We have to go out again tonight.'

'Do we?' Gila looked disappointed. He had wanted to stay indoors tonight, basking in the warmth of the Miramar.

'We've got a night out planned by Brenda. We're going to

dinner at the Christmas Hotel. Mrs Claus has something special in store. Something she wants to give us . . .'

Brenda tapped lightly on Henry's door.

There was the sound of his gentle snoring emanating from the scarlet bedroom. He had been up all night, out in the town, and now he was catching up, poor love.

She inched round the doorway and surveyed the rumpled chaos of his room. Clothes and papers, maps and various weapons were strewn all over the place. Henry lay in the middle of it all, arms flung out in abandon.

Oh Henry, she thought. If only he wasn't so bloodthirsty. In many ways they were so right for each other. He made her laugh. He made her feel like he was looking out for her, in a way that didn't feel patronising to her. He respected the fact that she had ambled along in her own way, looking after herself, for a very long time indeed. But if only he didn't feel the need to be so gung-ho about his monster-slaying.

Perhaps if she could persuade him to lighten his workload a little. She could gently suggest he get back to his research and his academic work. She could pack him off to the fjords of Norway for a while, perhaps. Though even there, instead of tinkering with translations and legends, he would probably end up finding frost monsters or abominable gentlemen to do battle with.

Certain things he had let slip in recent days led Brenda to

believe that his old colleagues in the Smudgelings had distanced themselves from his activities. The successors of his old colleagues in that secret Satanist-routing outfit had become rather alarmed by Henry's dedication of late. He was seeing monsters everywhere. He had been over-conscientious in recent years.

Brenda was ashamed, but she had peeked at some of his private correspondence and she had discovered that she was certainly not the only one fretting about Henry's devotion to killing . . .

Now she was looking at his stakes and axes, propped up by the console table and the dressing table she'd installed only recently. He'd banged something against the dressing table and taken a nick out of the woodwork, clumsy man. And there was flaky brown blood on all the blades and the stakes. He'd got some on the carpet and on the armchair she'd only recently had re-upholstered. Vamp blood was blotched everywhere, now that she looked carefully. It was dark under his fingernails and splattered on the front of his velvet jacket, which he'd fallen asleep in.

Oh, she couldn't put up with this much longer. Lying awake at night, along with half her guests, waiting for the slamming of the side door. Imagining him out there half the night, hunting and slaying.

His eyes were open, watching her.

'Don't go down to the shop.'

'What?' She blinked at his non sequitur.

'Use the supermarket. Go to the big shop. Don't go downstairs.'

'To Leena and Raf's? Why? I've used their shop for ages . . .'

'She's been bitten. Probably that night at the bookshop.'

'Oh no . . .'

'We should have checked the cult members more thoroughly at the time.' He sat up against the satin headboard. 'Why are you all dressed up? Where are you off to?'

She frowned at his tone. Who did he think he was, quizzing her about her comings and goings?

'Poor Leena.'

'I found her with her head in their fridge. Eating raw liver. Poor dear doesn't know what she's doing any more. Her husband's been covering up for her. Offering her his blood to keep her in at night. I don't want you to go anywhere near them, Brenda.'

'It's times like these, Henry, when people need their friends. And they can't hurt me. You know that.'

'I don't want you getting into danger.'

She tutted. 'Don't you stake her. I'm warning you. If I come back tonight and find that you've been down there . . .'

He clicked on the bedside lamp. The light was harsh and sudden, making them both realise that outside, dusk had come down quickly. His eyes were red and sore-looking. There was even more dried blood on him than she'd realised. 'I don't think you, erm, quite get it, Brenda. The bigger picture. You're too busy fretting about that friend of yours. She's gone. You have to accept it. And Effie was just one, erm, old woman. This is a whole townful of people. You've got an infestation. You've got a big problem here. Why is it only me who's taking that fact seriously and doing something about it?'

'We're all trying to do something about it, Henry.'

'Oh? And where is it you're off to tonight? Are you coming out with me, hunting and slaying?'

'No, I won't. You know I don't believe in slaying anyone. There has to be another way.'

'There is no other way.' He clambered off the bed, stiff with exhaustion. 'You won't help me, then?'

'I've got things to do,' she said hurriedly, and left him alone. She scuttled up the stairs to her attic to fetch her coat and bag. What if he followed her tonight? she wondered. What if he tried to stop what she was up to? What would she do then? If she and Henry were at complete loggerheads?

Oh, but poor Leena downstairs. There had to be a way to sort this business out. There had to be a way to reverse all of this horror. A peaceful way. Surely?

* * *

Robert could tell she was hiding her feelings as they tramped through the side streets towards the Western Cliffs. They passed through the chintzy holiday lets with their maritime liveries, dodging the huge seagulls that roosted here on the low roofs. As they walked in the early evening gloom they were mostly quiet, and Robert knew that Brenda was thinking about all the many times she'd come this way to the Christmas Hotel accompanied by Effie, the two of them on the brink of yet another implausible adventure. Effie had never felt further away than she did tonight.

Robert was wondering what Effie was doing right at this moment. Or whether that was even the right way of thinking about what might have become of her. Did that other world run in parallel with this one? Or was it as if Effie had ceased to exist on this plane of existence, and was translated somewhere else, in some slightly altered form?

'When we went to hell, a little while ago, in order to rescue you,' he began, looking thoughtfully at Brenda, 'although it was a tricky business all round, it was quite feasible . . . the business of moving between worlds.'

Brenda looked at him sharply. 'Hmmm.' She fiddled needlessly with the knot in her headscarf.

'What I mean is . . . people seem to move back and forth . . . between these places. Once you're there, it's not as if there's no going back . . .'

The words were sticking in his throat. They felt like dried-out Christmas cake left too long in the tin. It was as if nothing he could say would do any good. He couldn't allay anybody's fears. At his side, Gila was mostly quiet. Gila was dressed up ready for a night out. Clothes were one thing he particularly enjoyed about being on earth. There wasn't much variety when it came to the loincloths of Qab.

As they came within sight of the glowing edifice that was the Christmas Hotel, Robert sidled closer to Brenda and said, 'I wish you'd tell me more about what was revealed when Henry hypnotised you . . .'

'All in good time,' she muttered. He could see she was intent and pressed for time. He knew that set to her jaw, that look in her eye. 'I'll tell you it all before long, I promise.'

All she'd let slip were a few alarming facts. Headlines, Robert called them. She had told him: 'I knew Beatrice Mapp personally. We went to Qab. Years ago. I have been to Qab.'

He asked her again now: 'And you remember it all? You remember what it was like?'

Her face clouded over. 'Some of it.'

He expected to be ushered into Mrs Claus's private quarters, so that she could conduct this meeting with them away from the glare of public scrutiny. But it turned out it was pie-and-peas supper night at the Christmas Hotel, and Mrs Claus hadn't missed a single one of these in twenty-five years of owning the place.

She was sitting at what Robert recognised as high table, from which she could survey the whole host of mumbling pensioner hordes, their party-hatted heads ruminating over their steak and kidney pies. There was the occasional muted bang of a cracker above the Christmas muzak.

Mrs Claus cried out in delight as they approached. She took particular care to fuss over Gila. His pale skin glowed with chameleon colours at her attention. 'Oh, darling. This is your boyfriend from the land before time, isn't it? Oh, isn't he handsome? But oh, so skinny. You're very welcome here, dearie. Making an honest man of our poor old Robert. Making him settle down a little bit, eh? That's very good, because we'd like to see Robert a bit more settled . . . emotionally, I think. You need to feed this lizard boy up, Robert! So skinny!' She was patting Gila's hand. He had no choice but to sit right by her. 'I've taken the liberty of ordering dinner for you all.' She eyed Brenda, and the two women seemed wary of each other, extending cool greetings. Mrs Claus went on, 'I've heard all the details of your terrifying night at The Spooky Finger, with all those nasty vampire boys. It all came to naught, didn't it, eh? Effie still managed to slip away through the interstitial gap into that other world, the silly girl. But I did hear how brave you all were and how you tried to save her from herself. Especially you, Gila, dearie. Waving your sacrificial sword about and fending off those awful boys. I'm very grateful to all of you for your efforts.'

Robert saw that Brenda was scowling. She was thinking that the whole job would have been a whole lot easier, and perhaps more successful, without the interference of Mrs Claus.

Brenda harrumphed as the elvish waiting staff brought out champagne. 'I don't see why you're suddenly so concerned about Effie and me and everyone. After all those times you tried to defeat us and have us killed!'

Mrs Claus almost choked on her first sip of bubbly. She did a very good job of looking scandalised. 'I never did! I always had your best interests at heart! Truly, Brenda, if you think back – to all the things I ever did – I was always simply trying to save her. My wonderful daughter. I was trying to keep her away from danger. It was your meddlesome ways, Brenda, your stirring up the hornets' nest of evil that surrounds this town . . . it was you who were putting her in danger each time. You were always drawing Effryggia deeper and deeper into horrible, mysterious entanglements. She was gaining a thirst for danger. A fascination with thrills. Eventually she became enamoured of the arcane and the undead . . .'

Brenda looked furious as the hostess trolley came towards them and out came the pies and peas and steaming-hot gravy. She was horrified at the skilful way Mrs Claus could always turn the tables. Now she was making out that it was *Brenda* who had always been a danger to Effie. It was only in order to protect her daughter that Mrs Claus had interfered so much. Brenda sat upright in shocked realisation.

'That's why you called up Frank, isn't it? It's why you lured my poor ex to Whitby. That's why you were determined to see us get back together again. You wanted me out of the way. Away from your Effie. Marrying me off was the best way you could find to break up our friendship.'

Mrs Claus cracked open the crust of her pie with her silver fork and savoured its aroma. 'You've been a good friend to my daughter. I can see that. You tried so hard to give your friendship. But you're bad for her. Can't you appreciate that fact? You're cursed, Brenda. Everyone and everything you touch turns to the bad in the end.'

Brenda gasped. Her two friends either side of her looked appalled by what their hostess was saying.

Mrs Claus shrugged, simpering and looking as if this pained her to impart it. 'It's because you have no mortal soul. You make human things wither and die, just through being close to them. You're rotten inside, Brenda. Cankered and hopeless.'

Brenda felt tears prickling up. No. She wouldn't give in. This evil old mare was baiting her, as usual. She wouldn't let her lies upset her. Not now. Now there were things she had to get done. Personal attacks by this blowsy hag were the least of her worries.

'You can say what you want about me,' Brenda snapped.

'Yeah,' Robert put in. 'Alucard was Effie's big mistake, not Brenda. It's that old vampire who shafted everything for Effie.'

Mrs Claus smiled. 'Yes, Robert. Very elegantly put, dearie. But who drove Effie into his arms, eh? I believe if it wasn't for Brenda, then my daughter would never have been so keen to run to the embrace of that dandified cadaver.'

'That's not true,' snapped Robert. 'Brenda was always dead against their relationship.'

'She encouraged Effie to think that emotional and romantic relationships could work between the living and the dead; between natural human beings and monsters. Effie came to believe they could actually work out! Well, she was wrong. They can't. Sorry, boys. But it's hopeless. Now. We must all put our heads together and try to undo this awful situation that has been wrought by Brenda, Alucard and the irresponsible Marjorie Staynes. We must bring Effie back home.'

Brenda nodded. 'Yes. That's the important thing. Not all this flim-flam of yours. You can think what you like. Now, you said you had a way . . . a means . . . a special something you wanted to give me . . .'

Mrs Claus was fidgeting in her motorised bath chair. 'Oh, yes. Of course. Now . . . where is that box . . . ?' She snapped her fingers and one of her most trusted elves came dashing. He brought an elaborately wrapped present to the table. It was done up with bows. He went on one knee and offered it to his mistress.

Immediately Brenda, Robert and Gila were aware that this was no ordinary present. A strange sort of power was emanating from the box. They couldn't say what it was exactly. Something weird. Something . . . unearthly.

Mrs Claus snatched up the box and tossed it carelessly across the table to Brenda.

'Here you are, dearie. A belated Christmas gift. This is how you get between the worlds. Use the contents of this box wisely. I have had them a very long time. I've hardly ever dared use them. But now is the time. Yours is the risk to take, Brenda. To make amends for the bad things you have brought about. You must do your very best. And bring my Effie home. Bring her home to her town and her mummy . . .'

Then, abruptly, as Brenda clumsily hugged the box to her chest, Mrs Claus reversed her chair and left their table. Suppertime was over, with none of them having eaten a morsel.

'Penny . . . ? Look, I can't stay on long. We're doing it tonight. We're going right away. If we can manage it . . . if it actually works.'

'What? Robert? What are you saying?'

'Oh, my battery's low. I'm sorry, pet. I don't have time to explain it all now.'

Robert was lagging behind as Brenda and Gila led the way

through the zig-zagging streets of Whitby. A yellowish mist was curling up from the harbour, like malign tendrils snagging at them as they bustled along. Penny's voice squawked tinnily in his ear.

'What do you mean, you're doing it tonight? Doing what?'

He took a deep breath. 'Going to Qab. If we can. Brenda thinks we can manage it, because of Mrs Claus.'

Penny was shrieking at the other end of the line. He hoped she wasn't at the reception desk doing that. 'You can't! You can't go there tonight and just leave me here! I'm on duty!'

'I know, and I'm sorry, pet. Ordinarily you'd be first on the list to come with us. But I need you there, in charge of the hotel . . .'

'I don't want to be in charge of your crummy hotel! I want to be coming to Qab! You don't understand, Robert. I've waited my whole life for this . . . an opportunity like this . . .'

Errk, he thought. Of course. She's been a member of the cult of Marjorie Staynes. Friend she might be, but she's still been got at by the otherworldly rhetoric. Now he'd made her furious. 'Look, Penny. I'm really sorry. Thing is, we've got an important task to follow through. I don't know how long we'll be, and we've every reason to believe that time gets all buggered up in Qab anyway. I need you to stand in for me at work.'

Silence. Had she put the phone down on him? No. The buzz of background noise was still there.

'I can't believe this,' she said at last.

Robert realised that he was quite some distance behind his friends now. They had hurried on to Silver Street and were leaving him behind as he wrangled with Penny.

'This is just typical of my life,' she was saying. 'I always miss out. Every time. Why can't you stay behind? You don't care about going to Qab.'

He could have told her: no, I don't. And I'd rather be doing anything else tonight than . . . whatever it was they were going to have to do with those weird implements Mrs Claus had put into Brenda's custody.

'I'm going now,' he told her flatly. 'Be good, Penny. Look after the hotel. And keep away from Marjorie Staynes and The Spooky Finger.'

He snapped his phone shut. Penny would hate him. Perhaps she'd never forgive him. But she'd look after the Miramar like he asked her. Until they got back from tonight's destination.

If they ever got back.

There was a very nasty surprise awaiting them outside Brenda's B&B.

Lights were on in the shop downstairs, which wasn't unusual, as Leena and Raf prided themselves on being open almost twenty-four hours a day. As the small party approached, though, they could see something was very wrong. The boxes of vegetables had been overturned outside, their contents sent rolling down the hill. The glass panels of the door had been broken, as if someone had kicked them in, or slammed the door too hard on leaving. And inside, as Brenda warily eased herself through the door, it was silent. No Bollywood-style music. No constant chatter.

'Got you!'

Strong arms went around her neck. She wriggled and cursed and called out to Robert and Gila to help her. She was pinioned in a strong grasp.

'I've got you, you . . . you . . . !' The struggle slowed as her assailant recognised her. 'It's you, Brenda. I thought it was . . . it was . . .'

She had been grabbed by Rafiq. His arms dropped away to his sides and he set her free. She turned to see him looking battered and very defeated. Instantly she went into a flap of concern, helping the shopkeeper to a wooden chair. He had a cut on his forehead and he was shaking, she realised.

'What's happened here?' Robert asked urgently. 'Where's Leena?'

Raf looked at them all. 'She's gone. She's fled the coop. My beautiful Leena.' His eyes flashed. 'This is her home! We've been here for years! He has no right . . . no one has any right . . . to drive her away . . . to scare her like that . . .'

Brenda had a dreadful feeling that she knew what was coming. 'What's happened here tonight?'

Raf fixed his teary eyes on her. 'You don't know anything about it, do you? Please . . . tell me, Brenda . . . if you'd known what he was going to do . . . you'd have stopped him. Or warned us . . .'

She gasped, realising. 'Henry! Henry's been here tonight!'

Raf nodded. 'He came in all cheerily, pretending he was just after pipe tobacco and wine gums. Next thing I know he's grabbed hold of her. Dragged her half over the counter, where she was marking up magazines for delivery. She was shrieking like a banshee, Brenda. I've never heard her like that. Terrified. Mortally afraid. I came running out . . . and he – your fella – he had this sharpened stake pressed right against her chest. He had hold of her by the throat . . .' Raf sobbed as the images came back to him. 'There was a horrible scene. I had my heavy stapling gun with me. I lobbed it at the bastard and that got him off her for a second or two. And then we were at each other's throats . . .'

'I'm sorry, Raf. I didn't think he'd do that. He knew she'd been infected, but I never thought he'd be so . . . brutal.' Brenda bit her lip, realising that she had known no such thing. She knew that Cleavis was capable of anything. His quest to destroy all monsters knew no bounds. Of course a couple of shopkeepers wouldn't give him pause for thought. 'I should have been here,' she said. 'I could have stopped him.'

'He's like a man possessed,' Raf said. 'He fought me like a demon.'

'What happened? Where's Leena now? He didn't . . . ?'

'No, thank God,' Raf gasped. 'She saw what was going on. She saw that Cleavis would kill me too, the way he leapt at me and was throwing me about. Look at the state of this place! Our little palace! Our treasure trove! I only built this place up for Leena. It was all for her, Brenda. Without her . . . it means nothing.'

'We'll get her back,' Robert said firmly.

'He's right,' Brenda told him. 'Where did she go?'

'She saw that Cleavis wouldn't be deterred. She did the only thing she could, to stop him attacking me. She knew that I would stand in his way before he could get to her. And she saved me. Even . . . changed as she is . . . there's still enough of the old Leena in her to know that she wanted to save me. And so she fled. She took off into the night.

'She smashed through those doors and screamed at Cleavis that he had to follow her. Chase her. If he wanted her, he'd have to come running . . .' Raf started to break down again. 'I'll never forget her, standing there in her ripped pinny, just before she turned and fled. Her hair hanging down all over the place, her throat scratched where he'd grabbed her. Then Cleavis let out this huge roar and threw me down against the chilled cabinets. She led him out into the night and that was the last I saw of the two of them . . .'

'How long ago was this?'

'It's been an hour. I . . . I dread to think what's happened . . .' He clutched at Brenda's sleeve. 'You'll go after them, won't you? You'll help her?'

Robert and Brenda exchanged a glance. Both knew they had more pressing concerns that evening.

'Of course,' said Gila, surprising them all. 'We'll help you. She'll have gone straight to the nest, though, you know. That's what she'll be doing. Seeking strength in numbers . . . finding the other infected ones . . . She'll be leading Cleavis there . . .'

Brenda drew herself up to her full height and determinedly took charge. 'We'll sort all of this out. Rafiq, you make this place secure and get yourself to bed. Hot tea with lots of sugar. Spicy tea. You're in shock. Let us deal with this.'

Once they were upstairs in her attic she told the two boys that no, they weren't going straight after Leena and the vamps. 'We'll have to see to that afterwards, when we come back.'

If we come back, Robert thought. She was writing Leena off, he realised. It was already too late for her.

Brenda looked at him. 'We can't go chasing vamps through the night, Robert. We'd be hopelessly outnumbered. Henry Cleavis knows what he's doing. We just have to hope both parties don't do each other too much harm.'

She got Gila to pack a bag with some essential supplies. He was filling an old flask with hot tea and popping a sponge cake and some ginger biscuits into Tupperware. It felt to

Robert that they were treating it like some kind of day trip. He couldn't get his head round the idea that they were going to another place . . . immeasurably far away . . . this very night . . .

Then came the moment when Brenda set down Mrs Claus's beribboned parcel on her dining table. She took a deep breath and stripped away the layers of paper.

'I wonder how long she's had these. And I wonder how she got hold of them in the first place,' she said, lowering her voice to a hush as she took the lid off the box.

Inside: a pair of scissors, almost as big as garden shears. They were encrusted in a kind of glittery substance. It was hard to tell what colour those shears were as Brenda took them up with both hands and held them reverently before her.

'The Blithe Pinking Shears,' she said. 'Only one pair in existence. I've seen them before. Many years ago. No one knows where they came from. No one knows how they were made. These are legendary, these things.'

Gila had a very strange look on his face. 'Our legends tell of them too.'

Robert said nervously, 'What do we do?'

Suddenly Brenda was full of purpose. The whole rigmarole of what to do was very clear to her from her memories recovered under hypnosis. She instructed the boys to bring her largest mirror in from the downstairs hallway and to prop it up in her attic sitting room. When they came wrestling it in, they found she had lowered the lights.

'I thought about lighting candles,' she mused, 'but I don't want to leave them burning when we go off to another dimension. The whole place could catch fire.'

She had found her copy of her Qab book and located the particular passage that had been so effective during the first expedition to Qab. It was a passage that appeared in every Qab novel: a poetic invocation.

'We have to repeat this verse again and again, all three of us, staring into the mirror. Now, don't worry, boys. It won't hurt. It's just a little bit disorienting at first . . .'

'I've been through the Dreadful Flap that Marjorie Staynes made,' said Gila. 'It wasn't so bad.'

'Ah, of course you have, lovey,' said Brenda. 'See, Robert? You're with two old hands here.'

He tried to smile. 'You still haven't said much about what it's like and what happened to you when you were there.'

'There isn't time,' she said brusquely. 'Besides, we're not going to see the sights, are we? We're going there to grab Effie and bring her back. Only she can stop these vampires running amok in Whitby.'

He nodded. Of course. Brenda was capable of much better focus than he was sometimes.

So they crouched in front of the mirror, chanting and intoning the verses about Qab. Robert thought they were awful doggerel, but he had to admit there was something strange about the stupor they seemed to inflict . . . the sonorous buzzing in his ears . . . the sudden drowsiness . . . though really, that could be the effect of another late night and a certain amount of high tension and . . .

There was smoke inside the mirror. Weird-tasting lilac smoke that came rushing out of the silvery depths to meet them.

'Brace yourselves, boys,' Brenda whispered. 'Don't let your concentration lapse. Ahh, here we are.'

Robert thought there was a crack in the mirror. But it was a white thread sticking out of the glass that Brenda, with great confidence, took hold of. She pulled it hard.

'What are you doing?' he gasped.

Gila touched his arm. 'No, it's okay, Robert. She knows what she's doing. She's found the beginnings of a Dreadful Flap.'

Like a badly stitched seam, the Very Fabric of Time and Space began to fall apart at Brenda's insistent tugging. Beyond, there was a shimmering miasma that Robert felt drawn to, though he could barely look straight into it.

This is it, he thought. Another threshold into another world. Somehow it was so much more frightening than looking into hell.

'Come on,' Gila urged him, and they clambered up off their knees.

'Let's hold hands,' Brenda suggested, with an oddly shy smile. 'All right, fellas? Shall we go?'

So saying, she led them through the magical fissure between the worlds.

He didn't remember much about the actual journey. To him it felt a little like it had scurrying through the warren-like Whitby streets, with Gila and Brenda outpacing him and him trying to get through to Penny on the phone. Only a little more swimmy, somehow. He still felt like he was lagging behind and preoccupied.

Then it was all over and he was waking up on a floor that felt disgustingly springy and moist. There was a curious smell. Compost, he realised. Like they had been magically transported to the bottom of Brenda's well-tended back garden.

But no. When he opened his eyes they ached with vibrant colour. The forest floor around him was a riot of purples and blues. Even the foliage didn't look very natural. It was twisty and vine-like.

All the noises were wrong too. Forests in England were creaking, crackling, hooty places. The occasional snuffling, burrowing, tweeting noise perhaps. The noises here were monstrous and absurd. It was like being inside the gurgling, shrieking intestines of somebody not very well at all.

He looked at his companions. He cursed them for looking

blasé. Brenda was brushing herself down. She'd even taken off her woolly hat, it was so warm. Warm! He was lathered in sweat already. His tank top was sticking to his shirt, which was sticking to his back. He was dressed all wrong. He was dressed for January on the north-east coast. And here he was in . . .

'Welcome to Qab.' Gila grinned at him, helping him to his feet. He held him in a quick embrace. 'Welcome to my home, Robert.'

'Err, thanks,' Robert said. Once again he sighed and tried to keep his expression neutral. But he was wondering why he could never find a boyfriend with just a nice, normal background.

'Robert's still acclimatising,' Brenda pointed out. 'I remember. I was completely gobsmacked when I first came here. One hundred years ago, it was.' She looked around breezily, staring into the canopy of scarlet creepers above. She looked bizarrely content, Robert thought.

'Is it just how it was?' he asked.

'Oh, yes, exactly. I can't believe I ever forgot about coming here. But you know me and my memory.'

'Can you remember where we have to go?'

'The palace of *Her* is deep inside the jungle. I think, if we can find a hilltop, we'll be able to suss out the lie of the land. That's how Mr Rupert did it.'

'Mr Rupert?'

'I'll have to tell you the story as we go along, I think.' She smiled. 'The story of my first visit to this world. When I came here with my mistress and her friend, the adventurer Mr Rupert Von Thal. I was a servant then, Robert, working in Bloomsbury for the esteemed novelist Mrs Beatrice Mapp . . .'

As she spoke, she gathered up their few supplies and belongings, and led them through the trees into the jungle. She made it seem as if she was chatting to them on any ordinary day, and the three of them were strolling along Church Street simply window-shopping.

Sometimes Brenda still amazed Robert.

The journey was further than she was expecting. A long time had passed since Brenda was last here and she hadn't reckoned on the sheer size of this land. Gila had to gently remind her that it wasn't a simple case of popping down the valley to the palace. Their journey might take them some considerable time. The lizard boy shinned up a strange-looking tree to sniff the evening air and came down looking pleased.

'Actually it's not too bad. I'd say we were about a day's walk away from the city of *Her*.'

They set up camp for that night in a clearing, and Robert brought all of his boy scout skills to bear on building them a shelter and a camp fire. It reminded him a little of a TV show at home, in which celebrities had to survive in the jungle.

Gila returned from a trip into the undergrowth with a dead animal. It looked like a cross between a rabbit and a badger and Robert wasn't at all keen to roast it over his tidy fireplace, but his stomach made up his mind for him.

That evening Brenda was rather quiet and glum. It was as if she had talked herself out during the course of that day, describing what she could now recall of her first visit to Qab.

'We don't know how much time might have passed in this world,' she said, chewing delicately on a piece of meat. It actually tasted all right, the three of them had decided. ('What do you call this beast?' Robert asked Gila. 'Err, it's a rat.')

'You mean,' said Robert, 'that time moves differently here to home . . . so we've no idea how long it's been since you were here with Mrs Mapp and Rupert. It could be a hundred years, like it is on earth . . . or . . .'

'It could be no time at all, as well. Rather than a hundred years, it might be mere decades or months or even days,' said Brenda. 'I think you're right: our worlds don't seem to keep pace with each other. I think you could leave our own era and go further back in Qab's history than someone from centuries in our past. Or vice versa. I think Qab somehow brings you to the place and time you need to be when you travel here. Does that make sense? It's a very inexact science, all this world-hopping, from what I remember.'

'Those pinking shears . . . Where did they come from?'

She shrugged. 'All I know is that Professor Quandary was in possession of them back then, and Mrs Claus has them in our time. But wouldn't you know she'd be wrapped up in it somehow?' Brenda took the glittering shears out of her bag and waved them in the air so that they caught the firelight. You could tell just at one glance that there was something weird and magical about them. The air seemed to ripple about them, as if the fabric of reality itself was longing to be sliced into by those enchanted blades.

'They're sort of legendary,' Brenda said. 'I've heard whispers of them, over the years. They seem to get passed hand from hand. Very, very sought after in some quarters, as you can imagine. They are capable of opening up holes throughout the multiverse.'

'The multiverse!' Robert said, suddenly amazed at the way Brenda was speaking. Like she knew a thing or two about this whole spacey business.

'At home we've got the Bitch's Maw, haven't we? And we know what kind of bother that can cause. Well, imagine having the power to create gaps in reality wherever and whenever you liked. That's what these shears give you. That's why they're so sought after and so dangerous. With them, you could turn all of existence into a great big . . . doily.'

Robert burst out laughing. 'A doily? Is that the best analogy you can come up with?'

She frowned. 'It'd sound better if I said a piece of antique lace, wouldn't it? Or something clever and mathematical.'

'A doily! Typical!'

They ate in companionable silence for a while. Then Gila said, 'I think you are very brave, Brenda. I am starting to appreciate how very many adventures you have had. How many decades you have spent getting caught up in things like this . . .'

'Hmm,' she said, yawning and stretching. 'I'm getting on. I feel like I should be slowing down somewhat.' She grinned at both boys, but they could see that she actually seemed less tired and worn than she had of late. She looked invigorated by her arrival in this land.

'I am in awe of you,' Gila said, with his usual embarrassing directness. 'When you came to our savage land before, you faced dangers . . . and now you return, to face them again, in order to bring home your friend.'

'I'm sure Effie would do the same for me,' she said. Though thinking about it, she wasn't at all sure that was right. Effie could be downright selfish when she wanted to be. She was easily put off, at any rate, especially by physical danger. 'I like to think we're a team. All of us. And we'd always be there for each other. You too, Gila,' she added generously. 'You're part of our gang now.' She smiled benignly and pulled on her cardy, since the cold was creeping in with the encroaching gloom.

Gila thanked her graciously. It was true, he had never felt so included before. His cool heart glowed at her words. Then he spoiled it. 'Still, it must bring back awful memories, this place. The way that your friends Mrs Mapp and Mr Rupert betrayed you . . .'

Robert shot his fella a glance. The same thought had struck him, as Brenda was telling her story that afternoon. The fact that Brenda had only been brought here the first time as part of a hidden agenda. Effie had told Professor Quandary that she needed Brenda's blood. Rupert had been set free to return to Bloomsbury to fetch it. Even Mrs Mapp was in on that ghoulish mission. Or at least that was the way it looked to both Brenda and the Queen of Qab.

'I was indeed betrayed by them.' Brenda nodded sadly. 'Or so I thought. By Mr Rupert, certainly. I don't think Mrs Mapp knew what was happening, not really. She couldn't have been in on it. I was more than a servant to her. And besides, when would Mr Rupert have had a chance to appraise her of such an awful plan? I was always there, by my mistress's side.'

The boys nodded. She had convinced herself that Mrs Mapp was innocent. And for all they knew, perhaps she was.

'At any rate,' Brenda contined, 'as far as Mr Rupert – who I had idolised! – was concerned, they had brought me here as a bargaining chip. A mere belonging. A big bag of blood.'

Robert said, 'I'm sure there was more to it than that.'

She smiled at him. 'I hope so, lovey. Remembering that bit left a nasty taste in my mouth, I don't mind telling you. When I came here with Mr Rupert and Mrs Mapp, I really felt that we were suddenly equals. Away from home and the restrictions of polite society, it was like we were on a level playing field. We could see each other for who we really were, unbound by convention. I loved that. For the first time I was free. Free in the world of Qab. That must be one of the attractions of this savage world. That's how it hooks all those readers and cultists.'

'But what happened?' Robert said. 'Did they take your blood? When they brought you to the palace of *Her*?'

'I don't know. That was as much as Henry could learn through hypnosis. I couldn't go any further in the story. It was like some thick veil came down.' She sighed and tossed the gnawed remains of her supper on to the fire. 'Typical, isn't it? My recovered memories are so melodramatic that they come complete with blummin' cliffhangers.'

'Well,' said Robert cheerily. 'At least we know that they can't have killed you. You can't be dead, back there in your past.'

'Can't I?' said Brenda.

'Because you're here with us! We know you survived!'

Brenda didn't look at all convinced. All she would say to him – very darkly and mysteriously – was that time was a funny old thing. Absolutely nothing could be taken for granted. And what was more, time travel was an absolute bugger.

They settled down for the night shortly after that, making up pallets of some kind of rushy grass to sleep on. They were going to take turns to sit up, tending the fire and making sure that none of the increasingly noisy jungle beasts came into their camp.

Gila came to lie down near Robert, some distance away from where Brenda kept watch.

'We can't fool around,' Robert warned him, shocked at even the suggestion. 'Don't be daft. I'm not doing anything . . . rude. Not with Brenda just over there.'

Gila rolled his lizard-like eyes at his primness. They looked more alien than ever in the firelight.

'Anyway, I'd feel weird . . . messing around like that in an alien land . . .' Robert wasn't sure why, however, and what he'd just said struck him immediately as a particularly dopey comment. He rolled over, away from Gila, and tried his best to fall asleep.

The next morning saw the small party in a subdued mood. In the misty, mulchy dawn, after a night in which no one had managed to get a good rest, everything seemed a bit bleak. The reality of their predicament was starting to settle in. As they struggled to brew some tea on the revived camp fire

(Brenda had stuffed her handbag with spicy tea bags), they were all very quiet. Mumbling, achy and stiff.

Robert was thinking about how there weren't any guarantees at all. There was absolutely no guarantee that they were going to find their bearings in this bizarre place. And even if they got to the palace, who was to say it wasn't all going to go wrong? They could be in the wrong time altogether. There was no guarantee whatsoever that they could ever go back home.

He sat back with his tea feeling very gloomy indeed.

He couldn't let despair come over him, though. He needed to buck himself up. We've been in worse places, haven't we? Things looked pretty bad and pretty inescapable, that time we went down into hell. And just a couple of months ago, just last Hallowe'en, Brenda and Effie wound up in a very strange place. They fell into the DVD extras of a movie that shouldn't even exist! So really this place should be a doddle. Just think of it as a quick jaunt. A trip to see Gila's folks.

'Hey, I've not asked,' he said. 'Have you got family here? Will I meet them?'

Gila's smile as he turned to look at Robert rapidly faded. 'No, Robert. I've never told you the whole story. I was taken away from my homeland, deep in the swamps, when I was just a child. Slavers took me away, as they do with all the lizardkind. Bringing them here, to serve the Warrior Women of Qab. I've got no one here.'

'Ah.' Robert wished he hadn't asked. So much for bucking himself and everyone else up.

'Come on, let's pack up our camp,' Brenda said, though there wasn't much to take. Just some empty Tupperware. They'd eaten all the biscuits and sponge cake for breakfast.

We're caught in a prehistoric land with nothing but Tupperware to defend us, Robert thought. That's just typical of us.

Nothing much was said for the rest of that morning as they set about trekking in earnest. The going was hard. Every few yards they had to do battle with the thick foliage. Their hands were cut to pieces and sticky with lurid green sap. Their faces ran with sweat as the sun rose higher above the canopy. The weird cries of alien birds rang out above them. They caught sight of brilliant, flaming plumage in amongst the boughs and they saw stranger creatures lurking and slipping past. Gila went first, plunging into the jungle, quite at home and moving lightly between the trees.

Some time in the middle of the day they found a shadier spot and paused to eat some peculiar fruits that Gila had picked for them. He said they were safe, but they tasted horrible. Like feet, Robert said. Again he felt like he was on that daft celebrity jungle show. But at least on that, people were watching at home to make all the tribulations worthwhile somehow. At least on that, people could suddenly say they'd had enough and be taken home.

They set off again. That afternoon they were more talkative, settling into the rhythm of their march. The going seemed easier. The ground was less rough, the trees less thickset. There was a gentle incline, but nothing too exhausting. Their spirits lifted because Gila reminded them that it was higher ground they were looking for. From a hill they could see where they were going.

Brenda spoke a little more about her recovered memories. She described the days she'd spent in Edwardian London, tending to the novelist Beatrice Mapp.

'Imagine what the ladies at The Spooky Finger would say!' Robert said. 'If they knew you had known her personally . . .'

'But you'd best never say, Robert,' Brenda puffed, pausing for breath. 'I've had to warn you about this before. You must never spread word about my . . . previous lives and anything you ever find out about me. You must never make that kind of thing public. I don't want any more attention drawing to me.'

He nodded. He should have remembered that Brenda could be touchy about her secret longevity and her amazing connections.

'I'm just saying that it's extraordinary. There you were in Bloomsbury in those days. You must have met them all. All the famous writers and thinkers and stars.'

'I suppose I did,' said Brenda. 'But you know, I was mostly below stairs. Waiting on. Tending to them all.' She sighed deeply. Robert could tell she was still distressed by the thought that her mistress had betrayed her, all that time ago. Mrs Mapp had hoodwinked her into coming to Qab so she could barter with her servant's blood.

They plodded and plodded as the mossy ground grew sandier and rockier and the vegetation more sparse. The sky was a lurid purple in the late afternoon. There was no doubting it now that they were on the side of a hill. They could see a crest ahead of them.

'The valley's on the other side,' Gila burst out, with great certainty. He put on a sudden spurt of speed, legging it up the hill, and his enthusiasm proved infectious to the others. They clambered and heaved themselves up the last two hundred yards, steeper and steeper, until at last they teetered at the very top.

Gila was right.

A vast crater welled open before them. A darker, deeper, even more verdant jungle spread out below. There were buildings, taller than the trees. Smudges of lilac smoke. Signs of life. Their hearts lifted on seeing these things.

'We're almost there!' Gila grinned at them. 'This is it! This is the city! This is Qab as I know it! We're here!'

They had covered most of the distance down the slope on the other side when they made their stunning discovery.

They were yomping down the hill, ploughing through

crimson sand and stumbling in their haste to reach the cooler shade of the trees. It was just as they entered the forest that Robert tripped on some kind of rock.

'I've twisted my flaming ankle,' he cursed, sitting there and feeling a fool. The others fussed around him. 'Typical. Why don't you just abandon me here? I'll only hold you up. I knew I was bound to do something bloody clumsy sooner or later . . .'

'Calm down,' Gila told him. 'Where does it hurt?'

Brenda had moved away and was studying the rock that Robert had fallen against. Except it wasn't a rock. It was a brick. A whole pile of bricks, covered in sticky blue moss. And as she hacked her way through the bushes, she found more bricks and the remains of some kind of wall. 'Oh!' she gasped. 'Look at this!'

Both boys caught the note of shock in her voice. 'What is it?' Robert got Gila to hoist him up and prop him against his shoulder.

They heard Brenda swear very loudly and fluently, which was quite unlike her.

'Brenda, what is it?'

She had vanished inside the undergrowth now. They followed awkwardly and the light was soupy. 'Brenda?'

'I've . . . err, found something, boys. It's a building. Or it was a building. A long, long time ago.'

Gila nodded. 'That's not that unusual. Qab is an ancient

place. Settlements come and go. Buildings are abandoned. The fertile jungle claims their remains and gradually reduces them to rubble.'

'Hm,' said Brenda. 'I'm sure that's quite true. But I think you had better come and see this. Robert especially.'

Now they could see her. She was standing in front of a whole heap of bricks and rubble, mostly overgrown. Robert tried to put as little of his weight as possible on his painful ankle and Gila helped him manoeuvre his way across the messy glade until they were standing right beside Brenda.

She stood up, dusting her hands. She had a hanky in her hands, and she had been scraping the accumulated muck away from what seemed to be a very wide plank of wood.

'Look,' she told them.

They looked.

It wasn't just a plank of wood she had been dabbing at with her hanky. 'It's a sign,' Robert gasped.

'A sign?' Gila said. 'Like a portent, you mean?'

'No,' said Brenda. 'A *sign*.'

And suddenly all three could make out what it said.

Cod Almighty.

They were quiet for quite some time, absorbing the shock.

Robert said, 'But . . . but . . .' But that was all.

They backed away from the undeniable sign and emerged

350

back into daylight. Robert was hobbling still, but the pain was nothing compared to the pounding in his head. Was it possible to get a migraine from being perplexed?

The three of them moved away from the rubble and bricks and sat down heavily. They looked at each other.

'This can't be right,' Gila said at last.

'But we all saw it!' Robert said, suddenly irritated by his helpless tone. 'It's Cod Almighty. That's Cod Almighty back there. That's the remains of a fish shop! Our fish restaurant! It even had the bloody phone number on the sign still!'

Brenda was trying to puzzle it through. 'What if . . . somehow . . . the whole restaurant fell through a Dreadful Flap in time and space and was transported to Qab?'

Robert seized that idea. 'Is that possible?'

'I don't know. Gila?'

The lizard boy shrugged. 'I've never heard of whole buildings coming through the gaps.'

Brenda shook her head savagely. 'No. Our first thought was correct, I think. Our instincts were telling us something else, weren't they? That fish restaurant has been there a very, very long time. Thousands of years, even. Mouldering away. It hasn't moved anywhere. It's where it's always been. Right here.'

Robert stared at her. 'But . . . that means . . . You're saying that . . .'

'I am.' She nodded grimly.

'You're saying that this is Whitby! Qab is Whitby! Far in the future!'

Gila hissed, 'Whaat?'

Robert stood up quickly, crying out at the pain in his ankle. He staggered about excitedly. 'But it has to be, doesn't it? Can't you see, Gila? We've been propelled into the far future and this place . . . your world . . . is what will eventually become of our world. But how will it happen? How will everything end up like this? And how far forward are we?'

'I can't accept this,' said Gila woefully. 'Qab is its own world. It's in a different dimension. Clear across the cosmos from your earth. The connections are very tenuous . . . we're a world in our own right . . .'

'I don't think you are, lovey,' Brenda said, patting him gently on his back.

'So that's it!' Robert burst out. 'That's the truth at the heart of Qab!'

They all fell quiet then, as their minds raced to catch up. They were wondering what it all meant.

'But . . . where's the sea?' Brenda said. 'Whitby's a harbour town. Cod Almighty is right on the water front. Where has the North Sea gone?'

Robert whistled. 'Gone! All of it gone! We must be a long, long time into the future. Gila, you told me that you had never seen the sea before. You hardly knew what it was. There must have been great seismic shifts here . . . or some ecological disaster . . .'

Brenda said, 'And all the tea shops and cobbled streets and locals of Whitby have been replaced by jungles and lizardkind and warrior women . . .'

They didn't get any more time to think just then.

Their raised voices had attracted attention of a very unwelcome sort. If Gila had been less astonished and more in his right senses, he would have warned them of the dangers of this part of the jungle. He was reminded rudely by a hideous, keening cry that cut through the swampy air.

'Oh no,' he said.

The other two were instantly on the alert. 'What is it?'

'Blood beasts,' he gasped. 'Quick. Grab something, anything, to defend yourself with. Get wood, see if we can make torches. They can't stand anything bright. . .'

Robert was just about to yell at his boyfriend when he saw his first blood beast swooping out of the trees towards them. He fell back with an agonised shriek.

The thing was six feet tall and looked like the fattest bat he had ever seen. Its wings were ragged and satiny. It was almost impossible to believe they could support the weight of so corpulent a creature. The thing screeched, dive-bombing the small party. It was joined by more of its kind, all of them just as fat and equipped with fangs that were hissing and dripping like steam irons.

Brenda had produced a *Whitby Gazette* and a *People's Friend* and was rolling them frantically and setting light to one end. Robert even heard her shouting, 'Back, foul fiend!'

It was suddenly darker, as if a great cloud had passed in front of the Qab sun. Robert looked up to see that the light was being blocked by a pulsating mass of leathery wings. 'There's dozens of them!' he realised. 'We'll never fight them off!'

'We mustn't,' Gila said. 'If we fight them now they'll slaughter us. I've seen this before. Our only chance is to give ourselves up to them. They won't hurt us, not at this stage. They'd prefer to take us back to their lair quietly and with minimum fuss.'

'All right,' said Robert, who hadn't relished the idea of a fight to the death. 'Brenda, did you hear? We have to give in.'

She was lashing out with her smouldering torch and her collapsible brolly, which was now little more than a flapping remnant. 'What? What did you say?' she grunted.

'Gila says it's best if we give ourselves up. Go with them.'

'Go with them where?' Brenda shouted. Her hair was hanging down in tatters. She looked appalled at the filthy beasts that were now dropping out of the sky, parachuting gently to join them on the jungle floor.

Gila said, 'They'll take us back to their larder. They'd really rather not damage their food supplies. That's why we're relatively safe from harm. For now, that is.'

* * *

It wasn't a very comfortable journey, what with Robert shambling along on his damaged ankle and, somewhere along the way, Brenda managing to cut her hand with her wrecked brolly.

'So that's it,' Robert said, sounding rather sulky. 'We get eaten by these terrible things and that's the end of it?'

'We'll get away,' Gila said. 'We have to. We've come so far.'

Brenda added, 'That brolly was a gift from Effie. Christmas 2006. It was ever such a nice one.'

Soon enough they were approaching a dripping cavern deep inside the forest. This was the larder of the blood beasts, Gila explained, which cheered no one, especially when they encountered the rank smell and the scattered body parts and bones in the grassy dell outside the murky place.

The blood beasts were lumbering, oafish beings. They grunted and hissed at their prisoners, urging them along.

'All right,' snapped Brenda. 'We're hurrying as much as we can.' She waved her hands in the face of the creature nearest her.

Her bloody hand scattered a few dark drops, which landed on the creature's golem-like face. Its eyes widened and turned a strange colour. Brenda's blood on its purple flesh hissed. Then the bat creature gibbered and drew back in fear.

'What have you done to it?' gasped Robert. 'What's the matter with it?'

Brenda stared at her bleeding hand. Other blood beasts were pulling back now, gurning and gurgling at her.

'It doesn't like my blood, for some reason,' she mused. 'I wonder if that means they'll let us go?'

No such luck.

The blood beasts regathered their nerve and shoved their prisoners inside the dark larder.

They sat there in the gloom, quiet for some moments.

'This place stinks,' Robert said.

'I wonder how long we've got,' Gila said. 'Before they get hungry.'

Robert groaned. 'Shurrup.'

'They'll put on some kind of ceremony,' Gila said. 'With chanting and dancing and blazing braziers. And then they'll drag us out and hang us upside down—'

'Enough!' Robert shouted at him. 'Why do you have to live in such a bloody awful brutal world? Why couldn't you have come from somewhere nice?'

'Where's *nice*?' Gila muttered. 'Every world is full of monsters, isn't it?'

Brenda wasn't paying the boys much attention. 'I wonder what it is about my blood. They certainly seemed spooked out by it. I wonder . . . I wonder if what Cleavis and Effie and her Aunt Maud thought was true. . .'

'What was that, Brenda?'

'Oh, just things that were said at the very end of my

recovered memories about this place. Things that they were saying about me . . . about the reason they brought me here in the first place . . .'

Robert frowned. 'They said you had no soul, and so your blood was quite different.'

'Exactly.'

'Why don't you have a soul?' Gila asked. 'Even the humblest creature, we are told, has a soul. Even lizards. Why don't you, Brenda?'

'There isn't time to go into that now, lovey,' she said kindly. 'But rest assured, it's true. I'm a unique creature on the face of this earth. Well, apart from our Frank, of course, though goodness knows where he's beggared off to.'

She sat quietly for a while, thinking furiously.

'I still can't believe this place is Whitby in the future,' said Robert dismally. 'They've let it go to rack and ruin.'

Brenda said, 'I once knew a fella with a time machine. Friend of Mrs Mapp's. He'd built this thing and it just looked like a pile of chairs really, on top of an old brass bedstead. He kept nipping into the far future and oh, he said it was horrible. Just a few mollusc-like creatures flopping about on a radioactive beach. He didn't have much good to say about it.'

Robert was staring at her, open-mouthed. 'Brenda! Your memories!'

'What?'

'You're remembering more than ever! Listen to yourself, woman!'

She boggled at him. 'You're right!' She brought both hands up to cover her face. 'I'm remembering things about the early part of the last century, and Mrs Mapp . . . all without the aid of hypnotism and Henry! This is . . . this is so strange!'

'Must be something in the air,' Gila said.

'Something besides the reek of carnage,' added Robert. 'What else? What else do you remember? Think! You might come up with something useful!'

She looked confused. 'I don't know. Something strange is going on . . . it's like my head's filling up . . . like something or someone has opened up the floodgates. Ooh, I'll have to sit down . . .' She did so, and the boys gathered round her. 'The Martians! I remember the Martians! The actual Martians from Mars. And . . . and . . .'

Robert rubbed her back. 'Keep calm, Brenda. Now's not the time to go freaking out.'

'I need a pen and paper . . . I need to . . .' She stopped. 'I wonder if this is an effect of going through the Dreadful Flap and travelling through time? Do you think it could be? It's made me . . . more complete . . . unearthed some of my past for me at last.'

Robert wasn't about to point out that, nice as that may be, it wouldn't be much use to any of them for very long. Outside in the clearing some kind of fluting, hissing chanting had begun. Some of the bats were banging drums. The ceremonials were about to start.

'Dr Watson!' Brenda burst out. 'How could I forget him?'

'Brenda.' Robert shook her shoulder gently. 'We have to do something about saving our necks. The bloody bats are starting up their rituals out there.'

'Hm, lovey?' She blinked at him. It was as if it took a lot of effort to drag her thoughts back to the present moment. 'You'll never guess what I was up to the day the Martians invaded! And who I was with!'

Robert hated being short with her. 'We have to think of something fast, Brenda.'

'Oh . . . Oh! You're right.'

But she was having a funny turn.

The rough doorway's festoon of jungle vines was yanked back and one of the more burly of the blood beasts was silhouetted there all of a sudden. Looking very menacing indeed.

'They've come for us,' Gila said.

'They're not messing around, are they?' said Robert. 'They must be thirsty.'

Brenda surprised them all by bursting out laughing. They turned to see that she was still absorbed in her own precious theatre of the mind. 'Oh my goodness! The sixties! Of course! So that's what I was doing! Ooh!' Robert distinctly heard her add, 'MIAOW.'

'Brenda!' he hissed. 'Snap out of it!'

'What was that, lovey?' She shook herself and saw the creatures that had come for them.

From Brenda's journal.

To be placed inside my safe, with all my other souvenirs of mad adventures past. (Just in case anyone ever needs to know what went on in Qab.)

I could be resentful. I could be cross. I'd have every reason to be. I mean, just think about it. Look at the curious state I was in, right then and there. My memories were coming back to me! After all that time! My mind was unscrambling and proper pictures were forming. It was like some TV repair man of the mind had come round, taken my back off, and had a proper poke around with my dusty insides. Everything was suddenly clearer and the pictures were back in colour. All the interference was gone.

But there we were with those blood beast things. We were helpless in the face of their strength and overwhelming numbers. They strapped us to stakes with leather thongs and danced around us, doing all this chanting. And spitting. The boys were looking alarmed, as if this was absolutely the finish, and there was no way out of it. They don't really have the experience with adventures that I've got of course. But I was pretty doolally by then, concentrating on my swirling thoughts.

And then the bird men attacked. Just in the nick of time, I suppose, so from one point of view we should have been very grateful. The first we knew of it was the note of terrible alarm in the chanting of the blood beasts. Then the swishing sound of razor-like claws cutting through leathery hide and bat wings. An awful fight was breaking out in that clearing, as the bird men swept in.

Robert and Gila looked pretty shocked. The blood beasts moaned with fright and dismay. Robbed of their sacrificial victims at the very last moment!

With the bird men – what beaks! What golden eyes! – here came the lizardkind. Storming into the jungle glade and cracking whips all over the shop. The blood beasts were battered and cowed. They whimpered and shrieked at the onslaught. They were led away and their wings were tied so that none could escape.

We were untethered and gibbered at by our new captors. They stared at Gila and jeered at him. He looked terrified, poor lamb. He was back in their clutches now.

And so the lizard men brought us down into the valley. They brought us through their city. And finally, to the palace of *Her*! Your palace, Effie!

Of course, by then I could remember almost every detail of my first visit. The rudimentary buildings and the dusty roads were the same. The snarling faces of the guards were terribly familiar.

I remembered being dragged before you, Effie, all of a hundred years ago. Being told that you were going to drain me of all my blood. My soulless blood would cure you of what you now realised was the curse of Alucard.

You know me, I'd do anything to help. Especially for a friend. But what you were asking back then. It was too much. If I drained every drop of blood . . . I'd be dead, wouldn't I? Even I couldn't withstand that. Did you know in your heart of hearts what you were asking for? Queen Effie could demand anything, of course. She was *Her* who must be worshipped. *Her* who must be obeyed.

But I was here again, wasn't I? I was here again, in another form.

I was led into the vast black edifice of your castle. It was lit inside by weird glowing torches, their flames a lurid purple. The boys with me were quiet and awed. Gila had never actually seen inside the palace before. He was far too lowly a citizen of Qab. So was Marjorie Staynes, as it turned out. No one had ever heard of her. And yet she had puffed herself up, hadn't she? As such an authority on the place. Such an integral part. But she was nothing. Just a woman in thrall to the mysterious land. A woman driven crazy by a dream of a different kind of world.

And then, at last . . . we were brought before you, Effie. Here you were. Looking rather marvellous, of course. Looking more magnificent in your midnight robes and your glowing flesh than I had ever seen you before. But at what cost, eh, lovey?

The lizard men fell to their knees. Supplication. Cries for mercy. They knew you could lash out and have them punished and killed for the least little thing.

As we stood there before you – oh, Queen Effryggia – I was aware of that pit of green fire and the cage suspended above it. I was aware of the figures held captive within. I couldn't make out their features, but I could see that they were human. And they were vaguely familiar.

Robert spoke up first. 'Effie! What are you playing at? Look at all the bloody fuss you've caused!'

He was clubbed to the ground by a lizard man for his lack of respect. Gila helped him to his feet, 'You've got to talk to her properly. Don't look directly at her. Address her in tones of respect. Otherwise the lizardkind will kill you, Robert. They will not allow *Her* to be insulted.'

Robert swore and rubbed his aching limbs. I could see the poor lad was at the end of his tether.

I stepped forward. I straightened up my wig, shrugged my cardigan straight and looked you dead in the eye. Queen or no queen. You were still my best friend. We were equals and I wasn't about to be cowed by a load of reptiles.

'Queen Effryggia,' I said. 'We've come all this way to see you.'

'So I see. Welcome back, Brenda. Welcome back to my world of Qab.'

'I came here before, a hundred years ago, in my lifetime.'

'That's right.' You nodded, and you did, I must admit, look quite regal. You'd got all of that down pat, during the time you'd spent in this place. 'A hundred years ago in your years, but a matter of hours and days in mine.'

'What?' I gasped. 'Only hours and days? Then . . . ?'

'You and your companions from a hundred years ago are still here,' you said, raising your voice oh-so-grandly. And then you said, 'Behold!' in this very impressive way, holding out your sceptre thing and pointing it at the cage suspended above the pit of flames.

Oh my goodness. There we all were. In the cage. From back then. It was like *This is Your Life* but with time travel involved and human sacrifice thrown in.

'B-Brenda?' called Mrs Mapp's quavering voice. Oh, I remembered it so well.

'Can it really be her?' came Mr Rupert's manly tones. 'Can she really be here in two aspects?'

I gave them a helpless sort of wave. What could I say?

I couldn't very well start shouting accusations at Mr Rupert, could I? About using me. Giving me up as a sacrifice to you. It hardly seemed the time to go accusing, what with them being so helpless above that pit of fire.

Robert and Gila were staring in shock at the cage's occupants. I couldn't quite make out me, though I knew I must have been up there with them. Ditto Professor Quandary. Was that him sitting on the cage floor, looking disconsolate, with his head in his hands?

'Please,' I turned to you, 'let them down from there. It doesn't look all that comfortable. It's got to be a bit hot for them.' I beseeched you. I held out my hands. I was hoping to play upon your sympathies and penetrate the layers of oddness and queenliness you had acquired for yourself here in the future . . .

The future!

Of course!

I wondered if you even knew. Perhaps you, like all the others, were quite unaware of the secret of Qab.

I would break it to you very gently.

I jumped up on to the raised dais where you were sitting, impressively, on your throne of polished jet.

'Effie! You'll never guess. You'll be so shocked when I tell you. Me and those boys over there. We've unearthed the most tremendous secret . . .'

That caught your attention. You looked a bit surprised – and then miffed – that someone was up on your raised dais with you. But you were listening, weren't you? I saw a flash of the old Effie in those green eyes of yours.

Then your voice came out sounding more like your own everyday voice. 'Oh, Brenda. I'm so sorry about all of this. You were quite right. About Alucard, and everything. I've been a foolish old woman, thinking his kiss was a blessing—'

'Never mind that now,' I told you. 'We've come all this way to sort things out and rescue you.'

'I thought I could brave it all out. I thought I could make a good stab at being queen here. But it's an awful place, Brenda. I just want to go home.'

'Well I can see why,' I said. 'I've trekked through that jungle twice now and it's not got much to recommend it. But listen! I have to tell you! I must tell you what me and the boys found there in the jungle wastes . . .'

I was aware of everyone else in that throne room craning their necks to overhear our conference on that raised dais. But we had our heads bent together, sharing confidences. The others would just have to wait.

'Honestly, Brenda. If I could turn back time, I'd never let Alucard have his way with me. I could have averted all of this, I know—'

'It's even worse than you think it is!' I interrupted you, realising that I was talking with a certain ghoulish satisfaction. 'We found some rubble, some ancient abandoned ruins in the depths of the jungle. And we found a sign that read . . . "Cod Almighty".'

Effie, you looked thunderstruck. Was it my imagination, or had you started to age? Were you looking a bit more like your everyday hag-like self? Were you re-acquiring all those wrinkles and dewlaps of the Effie of old? I know that shock can do terrible things like that.

I elucidated further. 'Cod Almighty, Effie. The name of our favourite fish restaurant in Whitby. Remember? I always have whitebait. We both like the crème de menthe knickerbocker glories. It's one of the places we go to as a treat, and to talk over the finer points of our latest cases. And it's here. All decayed and tumbled down. Centuries have passed, but it's here. We are in the future, Effie. We are here in some ghastly future Whitby.'

Your claw-like hands scrabbled for the armrests of your jet throne. Claw-like hands! Couldn't you see? Couldn't you tell that you were reverting?

But your mind was still on the shock of my revelation about the fish and chip shop. I could tell that my news had knocked you sick. Evidently you had no idea of the true nature of Qab. 'But how? How could the sea have boiled away? How could the sky be purple and the land covered in jungle? How could there be lizards and vampire bats everywhere?'

'I don't know exactly. I think we're talking thousands of years after our own time. But those blood beasts that captured us . . . I think they are the vamps you created, Effie. You and Alucard. They are the evolved remains of those vampire boys.'

'No!' You looked scandalised.

'This is the world you created, Effie,' I told you, being rather harsh, I know. But I had to make you see sense, you old bag. 'You and Alucard together did this to our world and now you're queen of the whole horrible place. Well done!'

You gasped at me. Your mouth opened and closed like you didn't know what to say. 'What shall we do?' You reached out to grab hold of one of my hands. 'Brenda, you have to help me. You'll know what to do. How do I stop this? Turn things back? How do I make amends?'

I patted your hands reassuringly. 'I'm glad you asked me that. It's what I've been brought here to do. I was sent for. From the past.'

I wasn't looking forward to this at all, though. I was going to have to go through something hideous in order to help you, Effie. I just hope you appreciate it all in the end.

My hand was still bleeding where I had cut it on my busted umbrella. You winced and at first I thought I was gripping you too hard. But it was my blood. My blood from that small cut was stinging you. Burning you. Just like it had the blood beasts. My blood was inimical to your vampire nature.

'Just like Aunt Maud said! When her ghost came here . . . to tell me . . .'

'I think my blood will kill you or cure you,' I told you. 'But you can't have it all. You can't take every drop and wring me dry.'

'I wouldn't have done that. You know I never would . . .'

'That's why I'm here now. It's why I have come here twice, Effie. You can take half the blood you need from me, and half . . . from her.'

We both turned to look back at the cage suspended above the weird green and purple flames. And I saw my own face staring back at me from between the bars. Full of trust and puzzlement. My heart went out to my own self then.

Robert and Gila tried to talk me out of it.

'Half your blood? That'll kill you!' Gila gasped.

'No it won't. It'll just make me weak and a bit helpless for a while. Same with the other Brenda. We'll both have to depend on our friends to get us back to our respective homes safely.'

Robert said, 'But this place is hardly sanitary. You can't go doing blood transfusions in a place like this.'

'We have to,' I said. 'It's the only way to help Effie. To drain her of all her vampish, infected blood and replace it with a cocktail obtained from both me and my younger self.'

Robert's eyes widened. 'This is hellish! I know these affairs are always a bit dangerous, but this is horrible, Brenda.'

'Effie's Aunt Maud is going to manifest herself as a ghost. She's going to help out with the medical stuff. She was a proper healer, you know. She'll know what to do.'

'She was a witch!' Robert burst out.

I shrugged helplessly. 'What else can we do? We have to save Effie, don't we?'

'Do we?' he hissed. 'She's made her prehistoric bed, she can lie in it. I think we should just use those magic pinking shears of yours and take ourselves home, right now.'

But I wouldn't hear of it. Robert had just got himself wound up. He would do anything for you really, you know, Effie.

And then, just as we were hissing at each other in this fashion, I was aware of another figure shuffling towards us. We were tucked away in a corner of Queen Effie's throne room, having our little conference. Then there was this lumbering, hesitant woman breaking in on us. I turned and looked at her. Her hangdog expression and her dowdy frock. Suddenly I remembered, most powerfully, being that poor woman.

'Erm, hello?' she said.

I smiled at her to put her at ease. 'Brenda,' I said warmly. 'Now listen, I know this must be very confusing for you . . .' I was patronising my own self! My memory wasn't so good that I could remember my own reaction to meeting myself, but her face squinched up with irritation then.

'I'm not daft,' she told us. 'I know this is obviously some time-travel kind of thing. Professor Quandary said it was the best solution, and the best way of saving my life and of curing Queen Effryggia over there. By bringing you from the future. Laying plans and clues and bringing you here. I am amazed it's worked. And I'm amazed to see you here. From . . . when? A hundred years in my future?' The younger

Brenda shook her head and whistled. I was still marvelling at how clipped I sounded. I spoke quite differently then, I realised.

There was so much for me and this younger me to say to each other. I wanted to tell her that everything was going to be all right in the end, even though her life seemed so ramshackle now. Even if sometimes it seemed like hard work and felt a bit lonely and loveless. Eventually it would settle down. She would feel less of an outcast. She would have a home. She'd have friends. She'd have a purpose . . .

Right now she looked scared and mystified as to why she'd want to sacrifice anything at all for the queen of this world. What did she really owe anyone?

She'd come to see, I thought, eventually.

Robert came over to tell us, 'Brendas . . . err, Effie's Aunt Maud has manifested herself in an antechamber.'

My younger self looked up at me. 'What does that mean?' Her face was full of trust.

'They're ready to . . . take from us what our friend Effie needs to lift her curse. It won't hurt. We won't be harmed.'

'All right,' she said.

I led the way across the throne room to the antechamber indicated. On our way we were met by the rest of the party from 1909. They had come to wish their best.

Mrs Mapp was sobbing. 'I would never have simply given you up, Brenda. I wouldn't have let them take you and sacrifice you.' I noticed she was hugging her recovered manuscript to her chest.

'Good luck, old girl,' Rupert told us.

They both looked rather strangely at me. They couldn't understand how I got to live for so long.

'Where's Professor Quandary?' my younger self asked. 'This was all his idea. He's saved our life, in a way. By suggesting bringing an older Brenda here. He knew how to save us. We should thank him . . .'

Ah. There he was. The bearded adventurer himself. Hanging back in the shadows. Professor Quandary. Legend and man. He shuffled forward. 'Hello, my dears,' he said. 'Erm, good luck.'

He kissed my younger self's hand. Then he looked up at me.

Professor Quandary my eye.

It was Henry Cleavis.

I was gobsmacked. My face went numb. My eyes bugged right out of my head. I had no idea. I really had no idea. My mouth flapped open like I was a dead fish on a slab.

I just couldn't see it. I couldn't work it out.

'How. . . how can it be you?' I asked at last.

He smiled at me. He had the nerve to smile at me. Him there in his great frock coat and tattered dress shirt. Now that I looked, I saw that he was a little different to the Henry I

372

knew. He was more grizzled. More fleshy, perhaps. Deeper lines, more life behind him. But how could that be, as well? He should be younger, not older, if he came from 1909.

'Brenda, Brenda, Brenda,' he sighed. He clapped his great meaty paws on my shoulders. 'It's been so long. I'm so sorry. About all of this. We're not so much star-crossed as time-crossed lovers, you and I.'

'Oh, sod off,' I snapped. 'Don't go all misty-eyed and mystical on me. What are you up to? You should be back in Whitby! We left you behind, did me and the boys. You should be back there, on your killing spree. Seeing to the vampires . . .'

'Hmmm,' he growled.

'Brenda,' Mrs Mapp put in. 'It's me, my dear. Hello. I'm so sorry. We have dragged you here twice now. I'm sorry to put you all through this. But I gather you . . . are acquainted with the queen here. And you can help her.'

'That's right.' I was staring at Bea. All those years later. I was staring at the ratty manuscript she was clutching. 'That manuscript,' I told her. 'You publish it, you know. And then you go on to write many more books about Qab. Many, many more.'

'Do I?' She blinked at me. A delighted smile played about her lips. She wasn't sure she should look so pleased with herself, with all this other stuff going on.

'Oh, yes. You become a cult. A cult novelist. Women seek

out your works. They join together in little groups. They come to believe that Qab is real and they try to come here, by fair means or foul.'

'Goodness,' said Beatrice. 'I always knew there was magic in it. When I was orf in my trances. Didn't I always say? It felt too real, too weird.'

'A self-fulfilling prophecy,' gasped Henry Cleavis – or, as they knew him, Professor Quandary. 'Mrs Mapp writes the book, which somehow manages to survive through time and create this world, which in turn calls out to her and makes her write the book in the first place . . ..'

I shot him a glance. 'Don't you start off on your mind-benders again. I'll talk to you later about all that. I assume you'll be coming back to the twenty-first century with me, hm?'

'Doesn't it sound grand?' grinned Rupert Von Thal, who had been standing quietly by, looking most perplexed. I looked at him and found him just as impressive as I did when I was a girl a mere century old. Oh, those clingy breeches he sported. 'The twenty-first century! And that's where you belong, Brenda! You're there in the future! Having more adventures than I've ever dreamed of!'

'We're all in the future now,' I told him, feeling a bit rueful. 'Now. We've got to get this business cleared up. We've got Effie's life to save, and then we all go home, right? You lot must look after that poor, bewildered younger me. She'll need

374

taking good care of, with half her life's blood missing. And my friends will return me to 2009. Agreed?'

Professor Quandary – my Henry – produced his pinking shears. 'I take it you have your own pair, my dear?' he asked me.

I nodded. I didn't dare push the point and ask him again which century he would be returning to. To his friends, he belonged with them. But he knew me too. He must be the Cleavis I know, I thought. He has to be. But how can he belong to both times like this?

But that was only a minor mystery. I'd had enough fretting and wrangling my brains around in the cause of Henry Cleavis.

Right then I had to think about you, Effie. Saving your life. Bringing you back to normal. Bringing you home.

I let the lizard men lead me away.

There was an antechamber. Or rather, an auntie chamber. It was where the shade of Aunt Maud had brought herself into being.

The room was dimly lit. There were three makeshift pallets. Effie was supine on one, looking like a corpse, bless her. My younger self was clambering awkwardly into her own little bed.

I'd never seen Effie's Aunt Maud before. Even though the ghost had lived next door to me, as long as I'd lived in my B&B, and even though I'd heard all about her opinions on any number of subjects, I'd never seen the wraithlike old woman in the flesh, so to speak.

Well, here she was. Rather faint, rather grey. Good stout shoes and a prim little hat. A mannish old woman with a severe expression.

'You know this is the future, don't you?' she snapped at me. 'You know this is the world that Whitby will become?'

I nodded at her.

'Speak up!' she barked. 'I can't stand nodders and mumblers! Yes, well, this is why you and Effie have to keep up the good work. Guarding the Bitch's Maw and so on. Because if and when hell breaks out, you see, this is how it will be. Like Qab. Ghastly bloody place. The future isn't fixed.'

'Isn't it?' I was staring rather worriedly at the tubes and glass tanks and whatnot that the lizard men were fiddling with. They seemed rather expert in this blood transfusion business. This must be how they fed their queen every day. Wheeling in vast supplies of blood for *Her*. The thought gave me the willies. Then I realised what brusque Aunt Maud had just said. 'Isn't it fixed? Are you saying the world doesn't have to wind up like this?'

'Of course not,' she snapped. 'The pinking shears bring you to different worlds, different possibilities and dimensions. This can all be averted.'

Now they were taking hold of me, those chilly lizard men. They were lying me down on the black silk of the bed. I wished I'd managed to say goodbye to Robert properly. What if it all went wrong and I never woke up? I should have handed him the pinking shears for safe-keeping. Oww. That was something jabbing in my arm. Oww oww. Something else. There was a swirling sensation, not unpleasant. And a dragging feeling, like I was being pulled along, stumbling into shallow waters . . . I could feel the deeper ones beckoning . . .

'How do we avert this future?' I asked Aunt Maud. She had all the answers, Effie, you always said. Aunt Maud always knew what to do. She was smoothing your furrowed brow as you lay there. You were hooked up to a huge glass vessel. It was filling up gradually with your dark, dark blood. Strange how dark your blood was. It made a ringing noise as it drummed against the inside of the glass. It rang with energy and malice, your blood. They were taking all your bad blood away. But oh, you looked so pale. Like paper, Effie. Like a cut-out doll of the Queen of Qab. Hurry, hurry. We must hurry with our blood to fill you up. Half each. Half of both Brendas to keep you alive.

Aunt Maud said, 'Just make sure that Beatrice Mapp never publishes her book. She must be stopped. If her book disappears, then Qab will never come to be. You will see. I have told that old boyfriend of yours. Quandary or Cleavis or whatever it is he's calling himself now. He has to go back with her to 1909 and put a spoke in her wheels. That's the only way. Only then can everything come out right.'

I was feeling very strange indeed by then. The blood was flowing. I was shrinking down to nothing. I was gliding about on the ceiling. I was wafting down to the floor like autumn leaves. I felt like there was nothing left inside of me. I was doing all of this for you, Effie . . . both of us . . . both Brendas . . . we were doing all of this for you . . .

And we were relying on our friends to get us home again. To the right times and places.

Home again, home again . . .

And that was when I stopped talking to your rather mannish old auntie and it all went dark.

That was the last I remember of being in the world of Qab.

Return from Qab

What was she doing here? After everything? What on earth did Penny think she was up to, coming back to The Spooky Finger?

But here she was. In the headdress and everything. Dressing up in the fake battle armour of a woman warrior of Qab. And pretty uncomfortable it was too. Something was digging in, somewhere under her rib cage, some kind of buckle. And she felt such a fool, sitting there in the back parlour of The Spooky Finger with fifteen other women.

Fifteen other women! Numbers were up. How strange.

Since that terrible night when Marjorie Staynes's shop was attacked by the vampire lads, it seemed that whispers of Qab had only increased. The mystical place had somehow gained in allure. Add to that the mysterious disappearance of Brenda and Effie, Robert and Leena . . . People were becoming aware that something truly weird and quite real was centred about this bookshop.

And so, when it reopened and the book group started up again, it was only natural that the cult began meeting again. And its members began donning their golden armour once more.

Penny was coming along only to learn what had happened to her friends. Marjorie Staynes was inscrutable. She welcomed Penny, but she was evasive. She wouldn't answer any of her questions.

Chanting, chanting, incense and dressing up. And somewhere across the universe, her friends were in peril. Penny felt pretty hopeless. She stared at Marjorie Staynes, all got up as a high priestess and waving her chubby arms about sinuously. You caused all of this. You brought this trouble to our doorstep.

Oh yes, Penny had carried out further research on the internet, digging deeper into the bottomless archive of Qab fan discussion. She had confirmed her suspicion that Marjorie Staynes had, in fact, belonged to the chapter of the Qab cult that had caused such trouble in Kendal. The group that had had to be forcibly closed down. Marjorie Staynes appeared to be the only surviving member. The rest had gone to ground or vanished completely.

Now the same thing was happening here.

Henry Cleavis wanted to put a stop to it all immediately.

'I could get them cleaned up,' he had told Penny. 'My superiors in MIAOW won't let this Staynes women operate a

Dreadful Flap for long, not if I tell them. Sounds to me like my people were behind the Kendal closure. They operate a, erm, scorched earth policy, where dimensional transgressions are concerned.'

Penny stared at him. This was last night. They were having dinner in a new bistro on LeFanu Close. Sipping Merlot in the window, Penny agog at Cleavis's terse words. This was the man whose otherworldly books she had adored as a kid. And he was so blasé about all this business. His monster-hunting activities. He was telling her all about them.

She supposed that was because he had no one else to talk to, what with Brenda gone. It was Penny who was hearing about his routing of the scally vamps. His slayings and his pursuit of Leena. Except he hadn't found her, had he? The vampires were toying with him, he was starting to suspect. Their numbers were increasing. It was looking hopeless. He might have to call in the bigger guns . . .

'And we don't really want that,' he grumped. 'The big guns can make a mess of a little place like this. A quaint little town like this.'

Penny gulped, and then their main courses had arrived. That was when she told him about going back undercover at The Spooky Finger.

He tutted and whistled. 'That Staynes woman has no idea what she's meddling with.'

Penny looked into his eyes then. She could see how

worried he was for Brenda. It was over a week now, and there had been no word.

Cleavis had been round to the Christmas Hotel. He had quizzed the inscrutable Mrs Claus. Eventually she had told him about the pinking shears.

'The shears!' he had gasped. 'The actual shears. But. . . how did you come to have them?'

On this point Mrs Claus had ground to a halt. She looked quite shifty. 'I've had them for years,' was all she'd say. 'I've hardly ever used them. They draw attention. Magic like that. It can get you in hot water.'

He gazed at her steadily in her Christmassy boudoir. 'Yes. Um, you're quite right. It can get you into a lot of trouble. MIAOW have been after those pinking shears for a long time.'

Mrs Claus shrugged. 'They've been quite safely put away. Until recently. Now Brenda's got them.'

A greedy look was on Cleavis's face at this point. To Mrs Claus it was quite unmistakable. 'I want them,' he said.

'I thought you were looking for Brenda,' she taunted him. 'Your beloved Brenda.'

'Of course,' he snapped. 'And your daughter, too. The silly bitch who caused this whole, erm, fandango in the first place.'

Mrs Claus had reacted as if he'd slapped her. 'Silly bitch!'

She called for her elves and had him dragged away. Dumped on the pavement outside the Christmas Hotel. This gave the old woman some slight, small satisfaction. But still she was unwell with worry. A week now and no word from Qab. They might be away for years. They might never come back at all.

Sometimes Mrs Claus was disparaging about the efforts of Brenda and Effie to protect Whitby from the creatures of the night. Sometimes she even stood in the way of that task. But she realised that the place would be worse off without them.

'Oh, Effie, dearie. Come back. Throw off this curse or whatever it is. Come back to your senses. Come back to Whitby . . .'

When Mrs Claus heard that the Qab cult was meeting again, she urged Penny to rejoin.

'You must! Maybe they'll send you through the Dreadful Flap as well! Maybe . . . maybe you can go after them!'

This was on the phone. Penny quailed at the suggestion of following her friends into the unknown. But she knew Mrs Claus was right. It might all fall to her. She was the next one who had to step up to the plate.

Everyone else was gone, weren't they?

Now the chanting had reached a fever pitch. As the clouds of sweet-smelling incense just about obscured the features of the worshippers across the room from her, Penny came back to her senses.

Here she was. At The Spooky Finger again. Listening to Marjorie Staynes spouting off about the sainted Beatrice Mapp and her magical connection with the world they all knew was real.

Penny had lost her enthusiasm for Qab. Now that it was seemingly more than fiction, she felt peculiar peering into those stale yellow paperbacks. It was as if she expected to find her missing friends translated on to those pages.

The chanting finished abruptly with a high, keening note from Marjorie Staynes.

There was a heavy, smoky pause.

Then Marjorie said, 'Well, ladies. Let's break there, shall we? I'll put a brew on and we can mingle for a while.'

Everyone seemed relieved to have time out.

Penny nipped up to the bathroom. She made sure she did it while Marjorie was busy with the tea urn and biscuits. She wouldn't want Penny upstairs. Not when she knew of her connection to those who had caused the kerfuffle here.

Penny locked herself in and stilled her breathing. Calmed herself down.

Then she looked at the framed watercolour of the lake. It was unharmed. Even the thin glass was unbroken. There was nothing to show that it was anything out of the ordinary.

She looked closer. Perhaps it was a stormier landscape than she remembered. The clouds were darker, more purple. The waters of the wide lake were nearly black. They were so cleverly painted. She hadn't really noticed that before. It was as if they were rippling, shifting . . .

Penny gasped. Unconsciously she lifted a hand to touch the glass.

It was soft. Like warm melted toffee. Just like before.

Something was stirring in the Dreadful Flap.

Tea break was over. Marjorie clapped her hands to draw her ladies together once more. She sighed at the mess, all the cups and saucers and plates of cake crumbs. Gila would have whisked away the detritus in a flash. But now she was having to do without her servant boy.

She believed she would never see him again. In her own way, Marjorie Staynes had been rather fond of Gila. She dreaded to think what had become of him.

Enough. She must push these troublesome thoughts aside. She had to thank her lucky stars that she was back on her feet. The cult was thriving. The Spooky Finger was back in business. On that terrible night Effie had vanished in the upstairs toilet, it had seemed that it was all over for good. The number was up – again.

Oh, Marjorie had had to live with failure before. The lesson of the Kendal chapter had hit her hard. Best to keep dabblings with other worlds quiet and discreet. Don't let too many people know . . .

The thing was, people *did* know about her connection

with Qab. People like Henry Cleavis. But he hadn't bothered her since that dreadful night. And so she thanked her lucky stars.

'Ladies,' she said loudly, shaking herself out of her reverie. 'Perhaps we should proceed to the more formal part of the meeting, hmm?' This was where she'd pass the bucket round. Sting these keen old girls for hard cash.

Then Marjorie glanced at the stool where Penny had been sitting. It was empty. Had she slipped out unnoticed? Marjorie frowned. She had let the girl join back in with the group's activities, even against her better instincts, which were warning her that Penny had strong connections with Brenda and her gang. But Penny's interest, even fervour, in the subject of Qab intrigued the old woman. The group needed younger blood, and so she had allowed her to stay.

But where was she now? Poking her nose in somewhere, maybe. Somewhere she shouldn't be. Marjorie asked the group if anyone had noticed where Penny was. The ladies of Qab looked puzzled and took a moment to hunt around the small maze of bookcases.

Then came the weird noises from the bathroom on the first landing.

There was a loud crashing sound, and a series of muffled thumps. They came all in a rush, so there was a stunned pause among the women downstairs, who weren't sure what they were hearing at first. It sounded very much as if a team of inexpert removal men were manoeuvring something bulky and heavy rather clumsily within a small space.

Marjorie cried out and, hoiking up her golden robes, bustled to the side stairs, pushing past her cult members. As she reached the stairs, the noises were louder. There was smashing glass, splintering wood. Loud cries and indistinct words.

All she could think was: it's all going wrong again! They're making a mess of everything for me all over again! Just when everything was tidied up and sorted out!

But she didn't have very much longer to think along those lines. Her attention was consumed by what was going on above her.

First of all there was Penny backing slowly away down the stairs.

'Penny! What is it?' Marjorie Staynes shouted over the noise. 'What's happening, girl?'

There was a muffled series of shouts and crashes then, and Penny took no notice of Marjorie.

The bathroom door was off its hinges and had crashed on to the hallway carpet. The console table and Marjorie's aspidistra were underneath it somewhere. And just then, as Marjorie drew level with Penny, she saw that figures were emerging from the small bathroom.

Backlit by the eerie swirling purple lights beyond the Dreadful Flap, a number of figures were staggering out into the world they called home. They were disoriented and ragged, stumbling about in the tiny space of the toilet.

Marjorie started backing away again.

Here came Robert, supporting the shambling form of Brenda. She looked pale and terrible. Dead on her feet. Her eyes were half closed and she was walking like an automaton. Gila was there, supporting her from behind. Gila! He was back! But his attention was on helping Brenda, not on his erstwhile mistress, now shouting out his name from the staircase.

Penny was dashing forward again, to help them with Brenda. 'What's the matter with her? What's wrong with her?'

'We can lie her down,' Gila was saying. 'My room, look. The jump through the gap has weakened her . . . she needs to lie down . . .'

There was another figure emerging from behind them. A calmer figure. Walking very carefully. Stepping over the rubble of the hand basin, which had been somehow wrecked.

It was Effie. Moving steadily in her robes of black and gold. She looked regal and abstract, as if her thoughts were miles away. She looked older. Lined. More like her original self, perhaps. But also, marked by a terrible knowledge. But she was back! Back home again and dressed like a true Queen of Qab.

She stood blinking on the hallway landing.

Marjorie fell to her knees. Her home-made robes crinkled

and rustled as she perched awkwardly on the middle of the stairs. How cheap and nasty they seemed, how horribly fake they were compared to the real thing. There was a dense, heavy, alien smell that accompanied the new arrivals. It was the very atmosphere of the other world. They had brought a whiff of it with them, like an ancient breeze at their backs. Now it was dissipating, of course, and Marjorie Staynes breathed hard, trying to suck that oxygen into her lungs.

'Your Majesty,' she addressed Effie.

Effie looked at her sharply.

At that moment, the swirling lights of the vortex in the bathroom abruptly shut off. The Dreadful Flap had closed behind them, shutting off the link with Qab.

The light was dreary now. It shone fitfully on the broken door and basin, and on the chunks of plaster that had been knocked from the wall.

Effie was watching as the others dragged Brenda away down the hall, to find somewhere to lay her down. Effie looked bewildered, as if she hardly knew what was happening.

'Majesty, you call me?' she asked Marjorie.

'You are the Queen of Qab, aren't you?'

'Queen?' Effie smiled sadly. 'I think I might have been. I think . . . oh, a long time ago. Perhaps.' She glanced around at the dingy hallway. 'What is this place? Where have they brought me?' She swayed on the spot and Marjorie hurried forward. 'Oh, I don't feel so good . . .'

'Majesty!' cried Marjorie, darting forward to catch her as she fell. 'Highness!'

Effie toppled over in a dead faint, as if the weight of her robes had dragged her down.

Hurriedly Gila ushered them into the bedroom he'd thought he would never see again. Nothing had changed, he noted, as he clicked on the light. Vaguely he wondered how long had passed since he and his friends had left, but there was no time to work that out now.

They were hoisting Brenda on to the bed. She was a dead weight. She had stopped muttering and thrashing about now. She was unconscious, he thought. She felt very cool and looked terribly white. The other Brenda had been the same. Robert and Gila had been alarmed to see the results of the operation the twin Brendas had willingly submitted themselves to.

'They've gone too far,' Robert had said. 'They've weakened themselves too much. What if both of them die? What then?' Now he wasn't saying anything. He simply stared at Brenda, and Gila knew he was wondering what they should do next to help her and make her comfortable.

'What's happened to her?' Penny was asking, frantic now that they had their friend safely on the bed.

'She gave half her blood to Effie,' Gila said. 'Half of her life force she donated to save her friend's life. But it might have been too much.'

'Oh my God . . .' breathed Penny. She turned back into the hall. 'Effie!' she shouted, seeing Effie toppling to the carpet and Marjorie trying to help her.

'We're back,' Robert was saying. 'We're actually back . . .'

It took some little while for that fact to sink in.

Brenda's friends gathered around her bed and wondered what they ought to do now. They knew from past experience that it was useless calling a doctor out, or taking her to A&E. She would never thank them for exposing her body and its rather strange nature to the medical profession. Brenda had intimated at various points that she had spent rather a long time keeping her curious form out of just such clutches.

But what to do with her? They weren't even sure they could carry her out of this room, down the stairs and across town. It was almost as if that now she had relaxed into this deep, coma-like state, she had become even heavier and denser.

'She's recuperating, I just know it,' Robert said. 'We have to wait and let her rest.'

Penny had hugged him and Gila hard. They stared at her in her fake Qab finery.

'I'm going downstairs to send all the cultists home,' she said. 'We don't need them fussing around.'

Downstairs she found Marjorie Staynes doing just that. The women looked worried and submissive. Marjorie would brook no argument. She had the Queen of Qab upstairs and she wasn't prepared to share *Her* with anyone.

'Where's Effie?' Penny asked her, once the last of the Qab women were gone.

'My room,' said Marjorie. 'She needs her rest, like Brenda. What have they done to her? Why is she so drawn-looking? She looks decades older.'

'I don't know.' Penny frowned. 'Something about blood, they said. Brenda's donated a lot of blood to Effie. To cure her, they were saying . . .'

Marjorie nodded, though she was clearly out of her depth.

'I'm phoning Henry Cleavis,' Penny decided. 'He can help with this.'

Marjorie yelped and clutched her mohair cardigan tighter over her chest. 'Not that man! Don't bring that man here! Not after what he did last time!'

'I have to,' Penny said. She fetched out her mobile. 'He needs to know they're okay.'

'Please,' Marjorie said. 'Don't let him stake anyone else.'

As Penny keyed in the number for Brenda's B&B, she secretly agreed with the bookshop owner. It was Henry's staking people that had caused all this fuss in the first place.

'WHAAAT?' he bellowed at her, from the sanctuary of the Red Room, where he was polishing up the tools of his trade. 'I'll come at once. And you're sure she's all right? She's alive?'

'Brenda's . . . unconscious. But we think she'll be all right.

And Effie is . . . they say that Effie is . . . cured.'

He made a noise at the other end of the phone line. To Penny it sounded like the verbal equivalent of a scowl. 'There is no cure, Penny. Not for what she is.'

'But there is! There is! Brenda's blood is the cure. That was one of the secrets of Qab. You'll see, Henry! You'll see!'

'Brenda's blood?' he said wonderingly. 'Yes, yes . . . I knew it! So . . . the legends were true.' Then he added, 'I'm coming at once.'

Penny blinked as he disconnected the line. 'He's on his way,' she told Marjorie, who cringed at the thought.

Penny went upstairs to tell the others.

Robert took her aside. 'So . . . you told him Effie was cured?'

She nodded. 'Yeah, we don't want him coming round and shoving a stake in her, do we?'

He frowned. 'But did you tell him *how* she was cured?'

'With Brenda's blood. Erm, yeah, I think I did . . . erm . . .'

Robert sat down heavily. 'Ah. That might cause problems . . . if he knows.'

'Why? If he knows that Brenda's blood is somehow, magically, able to change vampires back into human beings, and save their souls and prevent them from biting anyone else . . .'

Robert looked at her bleakly. 'What's he going to do with

that knowledge, Penny? What do you think?'

Her breath caught in her throat.

They both turned to look at Brenda, still as could be on Gila's bed. Gila was mopping her brow and hovering anxiously at her side.

'He wouldn't,' said Penny. 'He couldn't . . .'

Robert said, 'It all depends what means more to him, doesn't it? Whether Brenda means more to him. Or whether Henry's more concerned about his lifelong battle with the forces of darkness.'

'Oh God,' said Penny, sitting down hard on an armchair piled with unironed clothes.

'He could rid the whole town of vampires. Maybe more. But what would he have to do, eh? What would he have to sacrifice?'

They sat staring at Brenda as she lay there breathing shallowly. She was quite oblivious to everything that was going on around her.

Their quiet, tense expectancy lasted for some time.

Long enough for Henry to go dashing out of Brenda's side door at the B&B. He went haring past the boarded-up front windows of the shop downstairs. He clattered up the cobbled lanes, dragging his bag of clanking work tools with him. His wispy hair streamed behind him, along with the tails of his long coat. His mind was whirling with images and ideas. What to do . . . what to do . . .

She was back. His lady love was back. She was more precious than ever. Infinitely more precious.

He tore along LeFanu Close. A dark, chilly evening. Frost setting hard on the pavements. The sky was inky and sheeny with lilac cloud. Few souls about. Fewer than ever during these vamp-infested days.

Henry yomped along Silver Street. His breath was ragged, white clouds of exertion all around him, like a locomotive coming to its destination. Nearly there. The bookshop was lit up brilliantly.

She was in there. As were the others. They had come back to Whitby. Come back to him. They had brought with them secrets from another land.

Despite everything, Henry Cleavis found himself grinning at that thought.

Now it was Beatrice Mapp who was traipsing up and down the many stairs of her house, bringing the tea tray with nourishing meals and pots of tea. Porridge and honey, chicken broth and hearty stews. She was working in the kitchen every day for Brenda. The roles were reversed. But Beatrice didn't mind. She wanted to help her erstwhile servant. She had to. She felt like she had to make amends.

She had led Brenda into that savage land. Although she hadn't known what Rupert Von Thal's plans were beforehand, Mrs Mapp still felt terribly responsible. She felt that she had been led along into a situation in which they ended up with no choice but to exploit poor Brenda. They had robbed the servant of the chance to make up her own mind, and that was wrong of them. Beatrice Mapp felt as awful about it as if she had, in fact, been in on the plot. Ignorance was no defence. Where had her common sense been? She had been so caught up in her dreams of Qab, in her excitement that the land was real. She had failed to protect Brenda through her negligence and intoxication with Qab. She had, in short, gorn orf. To an almost deadly degree.

Beatrice Mapp still felt bewildered by the whole journey and their return home. Even two weeks later she was having to remind herself that she was home again. Boring old London. Safe old Blighty. Tavistock Square, blustery and grey.

Today the patient was looking much better. Perky, even. Colour in her cheeks. Beatrice let herself into the bedroom – the best spare bedroom, overlooking the square (there was no way Beatrice was tending to Brenda in her usual place, at the very top of the house). And there was Brenda looking better than she had for ages, in a pretty knitted bedjacket, sitting up and writing in a cheap notebook.

'I'm trying to get some of my thoughts down.' She smiled. 'My memories are a bit . . . scrambled. I'm trying to put them in order. Each day I wake up, there's less there, less to remember . . .'

Beatrice put on a sympathetic expression. 'Don't worry

about it, dear. You're still recovering from your tribulations. Your mind will heal itself. You will remember everything you need to.'

Brenda screwed her eyes up tight. 'I know we went somewhere together. Somewhere . . . hot. Very hot and . . . exotic. And there was something weird about it . . . and those men were there.'

'It was just a trip, Brenda,' Mrs Mapp said sternly, setting down the tray. 'Now look, here are some eggs. And toast.'

'You're very good to me.'

'I need my Brenda, don't I? I can't have her wasting away.'

'So . . . did I get ill on our holiday then?' Suddenly Brenda looked alarmed. 'Did I spoil it? Did you have to come back early?'

'It doesn't matter now. It really doesn't.'

'I must have picked up a nasty foreign germ, perhaps. Something in the water, do you think? Maybe I was bitten by something?'

Beatrice urged her to eat. 'Brenda, don't go thinking about that. You're fine now. You're better. We're safe at home in London. Everything is all right.'

Brenda nodded, almost submissively. She pulled the tray towards her and examined the badly poached eggs. They were watery and unappetising. 'It's just that I remember . . . hardly anything at all, ma'am. Before our return to Tavistock Square. Everything before that . . . everything in my life . . . it's fading into the distance.' She held up her notebook, which was half filled with mostly illegible scribbles. 'What has happened to me, Mrs Mapp? Why am I like this?' She fought back a sob. It would be wrong to cry in front of her mistress, who was being so good to her.

'There, there, Brenda dear.'

'Who am I, Mrs Mapp?'

'You're Brenda,' said Beatrice Mapp. 'You needed my help. You came here unannounced and I took you in. I don't know who you are or where you came from. But we can start again, can't we? A clean slate? What more do you need to know, hm? You have a job here. A life here. Come on, Brenda. Don't worry yourself about it.'

Brenda nodded and poked a fork into the eggs. 'Yes, ma'am.'

Beatrice Mapp left her to her supper.

She went downstairs to her study.

The house was chilly throughout, and dark. She was quite used to the silence. Just the odd creaking of the old wood. The gurgle of the ancient pipes. She hardly even noticed the regular chimes of the clock in the hallway. Tonight, though, she did. She counted eleven. It was later than she had thought.

Today she had frittered away the hours between Brenda's meals, thinking about Qab.

Unlike Brenda, Beatrice Mapp remembered everything.

She was making her own notes.

Since their return she had been writing again, and making plans. She had been going over her ragged and stained manuscript and comparing its contents with her own experience.

How did I do it? How did I know about that place?

She didn't know.

I used to be rational. I used to believe in real things. The evidence of my senses. And now I'm not so sure.

When she reached her study, she paused at the half-open door. Some sixth sense was warning her.

Her hackles went up. There was someone in there.

Someone was waiting for her.

Beatrice took a deep breath.

'Professor Quandary,' she said. 'You might have knocked at the front door. I would have let you in.'

'Would you, my dear?' He was at her desk. He had her papers out. He was rooting through them. Filling a briefcase. Now he was staring at her over his glasses. Not a very kindly look. An expression of regret, perhaps. And how old he looked, suddenly.

'If you aren't Professor Quandary . . . if that is, in fact, an assumed identity and a made-up name . . . then who are you?'

'Do you really want to know?' He shrugged and picked up her manuscript. Her Qab book. He was reclaiming the single copy. He dropped it into his case. 'Does it really matter? I'll be gone soon. Gone for ever out of your life.'

'Really?' she asked. 'Does Rupert know? Does he know you're leaving London?'

'I'm leaving London and this era, I'm afraid,' sighed Quandary. 'None of you will ever see me again.'

'Mr Von Thal will be most upset to hear it.'

'Rupert will get over it. He'll find somebody else to have adventures with. Perhaps he will have them with you, Mrs Mapp.'

She frowned at him, as if at some note of impropriety. 'And so you are returning to the future? Where you belong?'

He nodded and grinned at her canniness. 'Clever girl.' He took the pinking shears out of his coat pocket and waved them at her. 'With these I can go anywhere. Anywhere my superiors need me to be.' His round glasses seemed to twinkle at her. 'MIAOW,' he added, as if this explained everything.

'And you're taking my work with you. My book.'

'Ah, yes. You see, you won't be allowed to publish this. I'm afraid I'm here in your era in order to stop this. The decision has been taken. Time and history are being changed. The world of Qab is being contained. Sealed away.'

Beatrice stiffened. 'I see.'

'Forty years I've lived here in the past,' Quandary told her. 'Forty long years on a mission that ends tonight.'

'W-will you kill me?' she asked.

'What?' For a moment he looked shocked. 'My dear, we aren't complete brutes in MIAOW, you know. Though sometimes our . . . erm, methods must be cruel. Justifiably cruel. But, no. You will live. You will live until 1969, in fact, as I happen to know. But obscurely. Eking out a living. Writing novels the, erm, whole world will elect to ignore. I'm sorry. And you will never return to Qab. Your imagination will never bring to life anything quite so vivid again.'

She didn't know what to say to that. She watched him click his briefcase shut and march towards the door.

Just as the ungainly professor was about to pass her, he turned, as if suddenly remembering something of vital importance. 'Oh yes. Another thing. Something else I must take off your hands.'

Her voice quavered, betraying her. She was scared of this man and he knew it. 'Y-yes?'

'Your housemaid. Your servant. She's well enough to travel?'

'What?'

'Brenda.'

'No! She's still recuperating . . . and besides, she's my friend. I'm looking after her. She is my responsibility, Professor Quandary, or whoever you are.'

'No,' he said. 'I'm afraid not. I am taking her away with me. Tonight. We're leaving right now.'

'No! You can't!'

But the professor was already in the hall, marching across the parquet floor towards the staircase. 'You don't have any choice in this, Mrs Mapp,' he told her. 'I'm relieving you of your responsibilities. Brenda is coming with me.'

'But . . . w-where? Where to?'

He turned smartly on the staircase and gazed down at her. 'Oh, wouldn't you like to know? But I'm afraid you can't. Your part in this tale ends this evening. But Brenda's continues. Without you. Elsewhere.'

Many, many years later and much further north . . .

Brenda met Effie once more at their usual spot for coffee and walnut cake on a weekday morning.

'The Walrus and the Carpenter.' Brenda smiled, breathing in the alluring scent of charred toast and frothy mocha. 'I never thought I'd see this place again.'

Effie blinked and stared around owlishly from her place at the corner table. It was their favourite banquette, where they could perch and see everyone coming and going. 'Hmm.' She nodded. 'Yes, indeed.'

Brenda cast a quick glance at her friend. She still seemed a bit peaky and unsure. Perhaps she wasn't yet fully recovered from her bizarre ordeals. Perhaps it was too early to take her yomping around the town.

'I'm all right, Brenda,' Effie sighed. 'Don't you worry about me. I can see you watching over me like a great big mother hen. Why don't you worry about your own problems instead?'

'Like getting my boiler fixed,' Brenda agreed. 'The place was perishing this morning. February mornings are the worst, I think. It's the coldest, deadest part of the year.'

'This year I don't mind February,' said Effie, with a shadow of a smile. 'I'm just glad to be back to normal. To be well again. And not . . . not . . .'

They let the words go unspoken. But they both knew what she meant. And somehow it would seem a bit funny, Effie saying out loud in a little café like this that she was relieved not to be vampire queen of another savage land any more. Best keep a lid on that kind of thing.

'How's your memory doing?' Effie asked Brenda sharply.

'Fading again,' said Brenda glumly. 'Everything that was starting to come back. I think it was the shock. Maybe the blood loss. I don't know. I'm having trouble piecing together the details of the things that happened in Qab, too.'

Effie shuddered. 'Don't even say the name. I can't stand it.'

'All right. We won't mention it any more.'

They chewed on their walnut cake thoughtfully.

'No word from your Henry Cleavis?' Effie asked.

'You know what he's like. When a job's over. Off he pops. No warning.'

'Is it over, though?' said Effie. 'The whole town's still swarming with vampires.'

Brenda pursed her lips. 'Well. He's gone, at any rate. Again. Just like before. You know, I don't think he really can have any feelings for me. I was duped once again by him. Taken in completely.'

'Never mind, ducky. Eat up. Shall we go mad and order some more coffee? Another slice of cake?'

Brenda nodded. 'He went, and you know what else he took?'

'The towels?' Effie smirked. 'The duvet?'

But she could see that Brenda was serious. 'No, he took the pinking shears. The ones your m— Mrs Claus gave us, in order to rescue you.'

Effie set her cup down with a sharp click. 'He took them? You let that man take the pinking shears?'

Brenda was startled by her reaction. 'He nabbed them while I was recuperating! I had no idea . . . until after he was gone. After he'd taken himself off . . .'

'Then he could have gone anywhere,' said Effie. 'Those things . . . they can open a gap into anywhere at all.'

'He could be gone for good,' said Brenda.

'Like Kristoff,' Effie said, looking down at the crumbs on her plate. 'Oh dear. We're being rather mawkish, aren't we?'

'A bit.'

'Who needs them, eh? Those two men. They really messed us about, didn't they?'

'I'll say,' said Brenda.

'I reckon we're better off without them.' Effie started waving energetically at the waitress. 'Come on! More coffee!

In fact, let's have a sweet sherry. Warm us through. We could both do with a tonic.'

'A sherry! At eleven in the morning!' Brenda laughed.

'And we can toast my fantastic idea,' said Effie.

Brenda had to wait till they both had a drink before Effie would tell her what the idea was.

'Remember Alucard's plans for me? The travelling we were going to do? Well . . . I don't know about you, ducky, but I still like the sound of seeing Paris and Venice. Even if it's just for a holiday.'

'Ooh, yes,' said Brenda.

'What do you say? There's nothing stopping us! We could go right away if we wanted. We could be two merry widows abroad!'

Love Paul Magrs' books?

Then look out for something even more spookily
mysterious, coming in Autumn 2011:

666 Charing Cross Road

Read on for a sneak preview . . .

Prologue

Where was Shelley?

Somehow, Daniel had forgotten her. She hadn't come home that night, which was just as well, of course. He'd other things to concentrate on. Other fish to fry.

The apartment was in a godawful state. Candles had dripped on to the carpets. There was blood on the shagpile and sofa. There was the acrid reek of smoke damage. There'd been a little fire some hours before: he'd doused it out with tonic water. He'd been drinking all night and now – in the early hours – Daniel couldn't quite be sure what was real and what wasn't.

He sat up gradually and saw it was still dark outside. The clock said five o'clock. An evil hour on a December morning.

Something was very, very wrong. No Shelley. Shelley was gone. She hadn't even been home. And he felt so strange. Like he'd been on a long run. He was exhausted. He looked down at himself. He was naked and covered in blood and for a few minutes he was terrified. What had he done to himself?

And Ricardo? Had that Ricardo been round? That sexy Latino? Daniel shook his head confusedly. Surely not. He wouldn't have been so stupid as to invite him. He couldn't have smuggled him in. But how did . . .

And then the memories started leaking back.

He moved to the blinds and peered out at the night. Snow was falling. Gently, remorselessly, unexpectedly. He looked down into the street and saw that it was lying. Everything down there looked so smooth already.

He found the *Gallimaufry* on the sofa. It lay unassumingly on the black leather. Battered and a bit bloody, just like Daniel himself. It was open, quite casually, at a frankly terrifying etching of a demon from hell.

Oh no.

Something stirred. Something murmured and shifted in its sleep inside Daniel's mind. Like a cat dreaming of shredding its prey, the thing in Daniel's head flexed its claws. It snickered at Daniel as he became aware of its presence.

What have I let in? he thought. Madly, furiously. He hardly knew what he was thinking.

Then: the ritual. I did the ritual. I tried it out. I invited him . . . I . . .

And then he started choking and coughing. Great wheezing gasps doubled him over. It was like he had

410

something caught. Something stuck in his throat. He cried out, retching. His throat was parched. He was thirsty. Yes, thirsty, of course. He'd never been so thirsty in all his life. He'd never known anything like this.

In the kitchen alcove he ransacked the cupboards and fridge. He drank milk straight from the carton. Then tonic that had lost its fizz. There was some soda Shelley had left and he gagged on its saccharine taste. No. This wasn't what he needed.

The creature in his head was stirring awake. It was languid and amused. It knew where it was. It stretched and gloried in its liberation. It spoke to Daniel. It told him why he was thirsty. It explained everything. In a voice that was little more than a purr; a voluptuous murmur, it laid down the law to Daniel. It told him how things were going to be.

Daniel bowed his head and listened.

For a few moments he balked at the things the creature was saying. His still-human self rebelled against the chocolatey voice in his head. Those deep, gorgeous tones telling him what he must do to survive ... he could ignore them, couldn't he? He could pretend they weren't there. He was strong willed. He didn't mind being thirsty. It surely didn't have to be that way.

Oh, but it does. The voice gave an oily chuckle.

Daniel had opened the book. He had read aloud the correct words. He had understood the invocation. He had known what it was meant to accomplish. And this was a fate he had brought upon himself.

He should be pleased. He should be astonished. This was promotion, wasn't it? He was going to be king of the city. He'd be the first of his kind. Prince of New York.

And tonight was when it would all begin.

Come along, Daniel, the voice commanded. It curled around his limbs. It tingled through his nerves. It played about his every fibre so suggestively. So in control of his every move. Come along, Daniel. Let us go together, you and I.

While the snow falls and pacifies the city that never sleeps.

Let us glide across the newly formed drifts. Our feet need hardly touch the ground. You have powers now, Daniel. Powers you don't yet even know about or understand. But I can show you. I can be your mentor. I can tell you everything you need to know. But first . . . first we must slake this thirst. We share this intense hunger tonight and it must be appeased. You are newly formed and you must be blooded. I am very old and I have not feasted for more than a hundred years. Can you imagine what that must feel like?

So tonight . . . right now . . . we have hours before the weak December sun comes up over Manhattan island . . .

All right . . . All right . . . thought Daniel, addressing the creature inside his mind. We can go. We can go outside. Just . . . tell me what to do . . . direct me.

I know there is no escape from you.

Good, very good, said the being. You're correct. You invited me in. There's no going back now. Now that I'm free. And at last I can see this fabled city. Somewhere that, in life, I often dreamed about visiting . . . a city of the future, and a great concentration of throbbing life . . . Tell me, is it really the twenty-first century?

Oh yes, answered Daniel. How long have you slept?

Since eighteen ninety-six, said the creature. So you can imagine my plight. My thirst. My desperation. Thank you, my dear, for hosting me. So very kind.

Daniel gasped as he felt the creature writhe with pleasure inside him. He shuddered and gave himself no time to think. He suppressed his thoughts. The creature would hear him. He had, instead, to throw on some warm clothes. He had to brave the early hours outside. Eighth Avenue, Hell's Kitchen, the meatpacking district. They would find what they were looking for. They were bound to.

Time to go hunting, Daniel, said his mentor. Time for us wolves to go running in the snow.

One

Making an Exhibition of Herself

Daniel stared up at her handiwork and shuddered. It wasn't the reaction that Shelley had been hoping for.

'My God. What a horrible old thing. Where did you dig *that* up?'

Despite herself Shelley grew flustered in the face of his cool disapproval. 'Apparently it's been in storage for years. Down in the basement.'

Her boss sniffed. The sharp noise echoed in the gloomy exhibition hall. 'Best place for it. Hideous thing. What's it doing out now?'

Shelley coughed. It had been her idea. It had seemed such a great one at the time. Putting this larger-than-life effigy at the centre of her exhibit.

'I thought it would work brilliantly, as part of the "Women

and Madness" show . . .' Her voice trailed off as she watched Daniel peer even more closely at the tall, witchlike woman. What was it made out of? Shelley didn't even know. Bones and leather, wool and papier-mâché. The stringy hair was like dried grasses. Her ancient garments were grimy tatters. All Shelley knew was that, when she had found the thing, hidden away in a trunk deep beneath the New York Museum of Outsider Art . . . she had to rescue it. She had to put it on display.

Not *it*.

Her.

The feeling had been very strong. It was starting to wither slightly now, as Daniel pulled faces. 'It smells awful as well,' he said. 'What it? Mould? Formaldehyde?'

Shelley found that she was in awe of this effigy, this gigantic doll, no matter what Daniel said. From the very first she had had a keen sensation that this was a very old creation. It had travelled a long way, and the fact it was still intact was a miracle. To Shelley's – admittedly inexpert – eye, this object needed to be prominently shown in the museum where she worked. 'Women and Madness' month seemed to be the perfect slot.

Shelley hadn't worked for very long here, at the Museum of Outsider Art, tucked away between offices on Lincoln Square. She had been dating her boss, Daniel for an even shorter time. Well, only a few dates yet. Early days.

Technically he was her line manager, which made Shelley feel strangely awkward. Especially at moments like this.

'I wonder where the dreadful artefact came from in the first place,' he mused. 'Was there any paperwork with it?'

'Scotland, according to the records. One of the islands. She's some kind of effigy. Probably built to be sanctified, like a—'

'Guy Fawkes dummy?'

Daniel was English. Shelley loved his accent. She loved his whole manner, apart from when he was being stiff and slightly pompous, like right now.

'I think it's more . . . pagan than that,' she whispered.

'God help us,' he sighed.

To Shelley there was something very human about the effigy. The more she studied it, the more anguished its expression seemed. The tattered, faded dress, could it even be a wedding dress? Something about the giant doll made Shelley conjure up terrible images. Burning and sacrifice. When was it from? When had the remote tribes given up their strange festivals and rites?

The yellowed teeth were too real-looking, set inside that twisted mouth, giving the withered turnip skull a slightly mocking, dangerous look.

'Well, I'd never have dragged it out of cold storage,' Daniel said. 'But I guess it'll make a striking centrepiece for your, um . . . Crazy Ladies display.'

He turned neatly on his heel and clipped away down the corridor, leaving a faint scent of lemon and tea tree aftershave. Funny how offhand he was with her at work, when he could be quite different in their time off. It was as if he was trying especially hard to maintain a professional distance. She'd not figured him out totally yet. He had a certain mystique. But maybe that was just his being English.

Just then Shelley was joined by Ruthie from the gift shop. Ruthie was so covered in junk jewellery you could hear her coming from a mile away. She wasn't the usual kind of person you might see working in a midtown gallery, but the Outsider Art Museum was a curious sort of place. It was dedicated to the preservation of work by untrained and unheard of artists from all over the world. Ruthie was similarly inclusive in outlook: warm and loud. She made people feel welcome. She boasted that she had worked in gift shops of every possible kind, the length and breadth of Manhattan Island. This job was her favourite so far, she claimed, because it was the quietest. She thought some of the academic-looking men about the place – especially Daniel – were *hot*.

Now she was staring at the Scottish Bride, as Shelley was starting to think of the effigy. 'Jeez. Would you look at her! Are you sure about this, Shelley?'

Earlier this morning it had been quite exciting. When they brought the packing crate into the exhibition space it had been unnerving, but tinged with pleasurable anticipation. With Ruthie helping her, Shelley had felt a bit like Howard Carter at the opening of the tomb of King Tut. She saw at once, as they hoisted and lifted, that her instincts had been right last week, during stocktaking. She knew in her gut that this monstrous woman would be a fine centrepiece for the display.

My first exhibit, she reminded herself. With her straw-like hair standing up every which way and her gown hanging in faded tatters over her twiggy limbs. She was holding out a cobwebby bouquet of some kind.

'No one's gonna forget seeing her,' Ruthie said. She was more used to the tamer exhibitions of dumb paintings, needlepoint and weird pottery they showed here. Usually Ruthie was politely mystified by the stuff they put on the walls, so reverentially. Shelley's mystery lady was different. It spoke to her somehow . . .

'That poor dame,' she said now. 'She looks like she's been through a tough life.'

Shelley found herself agreeing, and thinking about what Ruthie had said, later on, that lunch break. She picked up some soup and a sandwich from a crowded deli and wandered into the park, finding a favourite spot on a bench by the pond. It was chillier, certainly. She was glad she'd brought sweet and sour soup, which she blew on and sipped carefully, watching the ducks. Daniel had been so dismissive of her female effigy. Almost disparaging. Could she really see a man romantically, who was inclined to put her work down like that?

Her phone went and she had to juggle her lunch bags as she reached into her jacket pocket. 'Aunt Liza?'

She wondered if her aunt was in the park this lunchtime. But she tended to walk Rufus later in the afternoon, when the crowds were thinner.

'I'm downtown, shopping,' said her aunt. That deep, scratchy voice of hers burst loudly into Shelley's ear. 'I'll pick up anything I think you might like. How's work?'

Shelley put on a tight, bright voice. 'The exhibition's almost done. I can't wait for you to see it.'

'Yeah, yeah, sure,' said her aunt. 'I'm looking forward to it, honey. Listen, I just wanted to check that you and your new friend are OK for tomorrow night, and my little gathering.'

Shelley cursed herself. She hadn't reminded Daniel. Somehow she just knew he wasn't going to be pleased if she badgered him about this. But she wanted him to meet her aunt, and one of these gatherings at her aunt's tiny apartment was the best possible way. There he would see Liza at her best and most relaxed. Shelley wanted almost more than anything for him to like her aunt. That was the ultimate test of a boyfriend, she thought. If they didn't get on with Aunt Liza, then they could forget it.

'Sure, we'll be there,' she assured her.

'We can't miss a Hallowe'en together,' fretted Aunt Liza. 'We never have and we never will, right?'

Shelley allayed the old woman's fears, talking and sipping spicy soup at the same time.

'OK, listen, I'm meeting a young man for lunch. My young friend from the bookshop, Jack. I gotta go.'

Shelley put her phone away, shaking her head ruefully. Here she was, about to go back to work for the long slog of the afternoon. Her desk was aswarm with paperwork – to counteract the fun of unpacking the Scottish effigy. And there was her aunt, skipping about merrily in Greenwich Village and having lunch with young men. Shelley sighed.

At least she had Daniel.

PAUL MAGRS

Conjugal Rites

No matter what she tries to do, trouble has a way of finding Brenda and when her old adversary Mr Danby starts filling the airwaves with his late-night phone-in show it can only mean one thing.

But fate has an even bigger surprise in store. Romance is in the air for Brenda and, do what she will, she cannot deny that she and her man were made for each other – literally.

As usual, Brenda and Effie face up to whatever dangers come their way with fortitude and grace: even if that means journeying to places beyond their wildest dreams.

Praise for *Something Borrowed*:

'Gloriously, zanily ludicrous . . . unique, idiosyncratic and unclassifiable . . . a cliffhanger that promises much in store. It can't come soon enough' *Guardian*

'This is ideal holiday entertainment' *Independent*

978 0 7553 4643 1

headline
review

PAUL MAGRS

Hell's Belles

Discover the secret world of Whitby: mystery, mayhem and delicious black comedy.

Brenda never meant to tell anyone the truth. She's got used to keeping secrets over the years. But in Whitby, people have a habit of working it out. Especially best friends like Effie, who sniff out the unusual, and expect the unexpected. And Brenda needs friends. She can't keep us safe all by herself. Not any more.

Praise for Brenda:

'The combined talents of Alan Bennett, Angela Carter and *The League of Gentlemen*' *Independent on Sunday*

'A brilliant extravaganza, gripping, ingeniously plotted, and tragically funny, with unforgettable characters' Shena Mackay

'Utterly original. I was totally charmed by Brenda's valiant attempts to create a little ordinary happiness and comfort out of the madness around her' *The Times*

978 0 7553 4646 2

headline
review

You can buy any of these other bestselling
books by **Paul Magrs** from your bookshop
or *direct from his publisher*.

FREE P&P AND UK DELIVERY
(Overseas and Ireland £3.50 per book)

Never the Bride	£7.99
Something Borrowed	£7.99
Conjugal Rites	£7.99
Hell's Belles	£7.99
The Bride that Time Forgot	£7.99

TO ORDER SIMPLY CALL THIS NUMBER

01235 400 414

or visit our website: www.headline.co.uk

Prices and availability subject to change without notice.